THE PLATINUM COLLECTION:
CLAIMING HIS INNOCENT

THE PLATINUM COLLECTION

January 2018

February 2018

March 2018

April 2018

May 2018

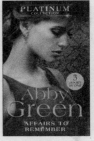

June 2018

THE PLATINUM COLLECTION: CLAIMING HIS INNOCENT

LYNNE
GRAHAM

Published in Great Britain 2017
By Mills & Boon, an imprint of HarperCollins*Publishers*
1 London Bridge Street, London, SE1 9GF

THE PLATINUM COLLECTION: CLAIMING HIS INNOCENT ©
2017 Harlequin Books S.A.

Jess's Promise © 2011 Lynne Graham
A Rich Man's Whim © 2013 Lynne Graham
The Billionaire's Bridal Bargain © 2015 Lynne Graham

ISBN: 978-0-263-93188-4

09-0118

MIX
Paper from
responsible sources
FSC
www.fsc.org   **FSC™ C007454**

JESS'S PROMISE

Lynne Graham was born in Northern Ireland and has been a keen romance reader since her teens. She is very happily married to an understanding husband who has learned to cook since she started to write! Her five children keep her on her toes. She has a very large dog who knocks everything over, a very small terrier who barks a lot and two cats. When time allows, Lynne is a keen gardener.

CHAPTER ONE

CESARIO DI SILVESTRI could not sleep.

Events in recent months had brought him to a personal crossroads, at which he had acted with innate decisiveness: he had stripped the chaff from his life in order to focus his energy on what *really* mattered, only to appreciate that, while he had worked tirelessly to become an extraordinarily wealthy tycoon, he had put next to no work at all into his private life. The only close friend he fully trusted still was Stefano, the cousin he had grown up with. He'd had many women in his bed, but only one whom he'd loved—and he had treated her so carelessly that she had fallen in love with someone else. He was thirty-three years old and he had never even come close to marrying. What did that say about him?

Was he a natural loner or simply a commitment-phobe? He groaned out loud, exasperated by the constant flow of philosophical thoughts that had recently dogged him, because all his life, to date, he had been a doer rather than a thinker: a great sportsman, a dynamic and cold-blooded businessman. Giving up on sleep, Cesario pulled on some shorts and strode through his magnificent Moroccan villa, impervious to the opulent trappings of the billionaire's lifestyle that had lately come to mean so little to him. He filled a tumbler with ice cold water and drank it down thirstily.

As he had admitted to Stefano, by this age he would have liked to have had a child, only not with the kind of woman who cared more about money than anything else. For such a woman would only raise her child with the same shallow self-seeking values.

'But it's not too late for you to start a family,' Stefano had declared with conviction. 'Nothing is set in stone, Cesario. Do what you *want*, not as you think you should.'

Hearing the shrill of his cell phone, Cesario headed back upstairs, wondering which of his staff thought it necessary to call him in the middle of the night. But there was nothing frivolous about that call from Rigo Castello, his security chief. Rigo was phoning to tell him that he'd just been robbed: a painting, a recent acquisition worth a cool half-million pounds, had been stolen from Halston Hall, his English country home, and apparently the theft had been an inside job. Cold outrage swept Cesario at that concluding fact. He didn't get mad, he got even. He paid his employees handsomely and treated them well and in return he expected loyalty. When the guilty party was finally identified, Cesario would ensure that the full weight of the law was brought to bear on him...

But, within a few minutes, his outrage and annoyance subsided to a bearable level and a grim smile began to tug at his handsome mouth as he contemplated his now inevitable visit to his beautiful Elizabethan home in England. There he would undoubtedly run into his very beautiful Madonna of the stable yard again, as his horses required her regular attention. And unlike the many women he had known and deemed to be almost interchangeable, his English Madonna did rejoice in one unique quality: she was the only woman who had ever said no to Cesario di Silvestri…and utterly infuriated and frustrated him. One dinner date and he'd been history, rejected out of hand by a woman for the first time in his life and he still had no idea why. For Cesario, who was by nature fiercely competitive, she would always be a mystery and a challenge…

A small, slightly built brunette with her long dark curly hair caught up in a practical ponytail, Jess kept up a constant stream of soothing chatter while she wielded the shears over the cowering dog's matted coat.

The job had to be done. As the sheepdog's painfully emaciated body was revealed Jess's soft full mouth hardened; the suffering of animals always upset her and she had trained as a veterinary surgeon in an effort to do what she could to help in the way of welfare.

Her volunteer helper at weekends, a pretty blonde schoolgirl, helped to keep the dog steady. 'How is he?' Kylie asked with concern.

Jess sent the teenager a wry look. 'Not bad for his age. He's an old dog. He'll be fine once I've seen to his sores and fed him up a bit.'

'But the older ones are very hard to rehome.' Kylie sighed.

'You never know,' Jess said with determined optimism, though actually she did know very well. The little tribe of dogs she had personally rescued in recent years were a motley group, each of which was either older, maimed or suffering from behavioural problems. Few people were willing to take a chance on such dogs.

When Jess had embarked on her first job in the village of Charlbury St Helens, she had lived above the vet's surgery where she worked. But she'd had to find other accommodation when the practice's senior partner had decided to expand the business and turned the small flat into an office suite instead. Jess had been lucky enough to find a run-down cottage with a collection of old sheds to rent just outside the village. Although her home was not much to look at and offered only basic comforts, it came with two fields and the landlord had agreed to her opening a small animal sanctuary there. Even though she earned a good salary she was always broke, because every penny she could spare went towards animal feed and medical supplies. Even so, in doing what she loved, she was happier than she had ever been in her life. But then she would be the first to admit that she had long preferred animals to people. Shy, socially awkward and uneasy with men after a traumatic experience at university that had left her with both physical and mental scars, Jess struggled to fit in with human beings but was totally at home with four-legged beasts.

The sound of a car pulling up outside sent Kylie to the door of the shed. 'It's your dad, Jess.'

Jess glanced up in surprise; Robert Martin rarely called in on her at weekends. Recently, in fact, she had seen less than usual of her father and, when she had, he had seemed abnormally preoccupied with work. As a rule, though, he was a regular visitor, who often helped out by repairing the animal housing and the fences. A quiet man in his fifties, he was a good husband and an even better dad, for, while other family members had believed that Jess had been aiming too high in dreaming of becoming a veterinary surgeon, Robert had encouraged his daughter's dream every step of the way. His love and support meant all the more to Jess when she reflected that while Robert was the only father she had ever known he had had nothing whatsoever to do with her conception. That, however, was a secret known to few outside the family circle.

'I'll get on with the feeding,' Kylie proffered, as the stocky grey-haired older man nodded to her and entered the shed.

'I'll be with you in a minute, Dad,' Jess promised, bending over the prone dog to attend to his wounds with antiseptic ointment. 'It's not like you to call in on a Sunday morning...'

'I need to talk to you. You'll be at church later and you're often on duty in the evening at weekends,' he said gruffly, and something odd in his voice made her lift her head, her unusually light grey eyes questioning.

She frowned because the older man looked pale and strained and every year of his age and more. 'What's happened?' she prompted in dismay. She had not seen him look that frightened since her mother's diagnosis of cancer the previous year.

'Finish up with your patient first.'

With difficulty Jess mastered the spasm of fear that had immediately rippled through her. Goodness, had her mother's cancer returned? That was her first panicky thought and her hands shook slightly as she finished her task. As far as she was aware, though, her mother had not had a check-up scheduled and she told herself off for being so quick to expect bad news. 'Go into the house and wait for me. I won't be long,' she told him briskly, suppressing her apprehension.

She put the dog into a pen where food was already waiting for him and briefly watched the animal tuck into what was obviously his first proper meal in weeks. After pausing in the bathroom to scrub her hands clean, she hurried on into the house and then the kitchen where Robert Martin had already seated himself at the worn pine table.

'What's wrong?' she prompted tautly, too anxious where her mother was concerned even to put her fear into words.

Her father looked up, his brown eyes full of guilt and anxiety. 'I've done something stupid, really *really* stupid. I'm sorry to bring it to your doorstep but I can't face telling your mother yet,' he confided tightly. 'She's been through so much lately but I'm afraid that this business will break her...'

'Just spit it out...tell me what's happened,' Jess pressed gently, sitting down opposite him, convinced he had to be innocently exaggerating his predicament because she just could not imagine him doing anything seriously wrong. He was a plain-spoken man of moderate habits, well liked and respected in the neighbourhood. 'What did you do that was so stupid?'

Robert Martin shook his greying head heavily. 'Well, to start with, I borrowed a lot of money and from the wrong people...'

His daughter's eyes opened very wide, for his explanation had taken her aback. 'Money is the problem? You've got into debt?'

The older man gave a weary sigh. 'That was only the beginning. Do you remember that holiday I took your mother on after her treatment?'

Jess nodded slowly. Her father had swept her mother off on a cruise that had been the holiday of a lifetime for a couple who had never earned enough to take such breaks away from home before. 'I *was* surprised that you could afford it, but you said that the money came from your savings.'

Shamed by that reminder, Robert shook his head dully 'I lied. There were never any savings. I never managed to put any money aside in the way I'd hoped when I was younger. Things have always been tight for us as a family.'

'So you must have borrowed the money for that cruise—who did you borrow from?'

'Your mother's brother, Sam Welch,' Robert admitted reluctantly, watching his daughter's face tighten in consternation.

'But Sam's a *loan shark*—you know he is! Mum's family are a bad lot and I've even heard you warn other people not to get mixed up with them,' Jess reminded him feelingly. 'Knowing what you do about Sam, how on earth could you have borrowed from him?'

'The bank turned me down flat when I approached them. Your uncle Sam was my only option and, because he was sorry your mother had been ill, he said he'd wait for the loan to be repaid. He was very nice, very reasonable. But now his sons have taken over his business, and Jason and Mark have a very different attitude to the people who owe them money.'

Jess groaned out loud and she was already wondering frantically how she could possibly help when she had no savings of her own. That realisation made her feel very guilty, since she earned more than either her parents or her two younger brothers, yet she was still not in a position to offer assistance. But, perhaps, she thought frantically, *she* might be able to take out a loan.

'The original amount I borrowed has grown and grown with the interest charges. And Jason and Mark have been at me almost every day for months now,' the older man told her heavily. 'Coming after me in the car when I was out working, phoning me at all times of the day and night, constantly reminding me how much I owe them. It's been a nightmare keeping this wretched business from your mother. Jason and Mark wore me down—I was desperate to get them off my back! I had no hope of paying that money back any time soon, so when they offered me a deal—'

Jess gave him a bewildered look and cut in, 'A deal? What kind of a deal?'

'I was a bloody fool, but they said they'd write off what I owed if I helped them out.'

The look of overwhelming fear and regret in her father's face was making Jess so tense that she felt nauseous. 'What on earth did you help them to do?'

'They told me they wanted to take pictures of the inside of Halston Hall and sell them to one of those celebrity magazines…you know, the sort of thing your mother reads,' Robert extended with all the vagueness of a man who had never even bothered to look through

Jess was thinking sickly about Cesario di Silvestri, the billionaire Italian industrialist, the theft of whose painting her father would ultimately be held responsible for. Not a man to take such a crime lying down, not the forgiving sort either. How many people would even credit her father's version of events? Or that he had not willingly conspired with his wife's cousins? The fact that he had worked for almost forty years for the Halston estate would cut no ice, any more than his current lack of a criminal record and his good reputation. The bottom line was that a very serious offence had been committed.

As the older man took his leave and urged her not to mention the matter to her mother yet Jess frowned in disagreement. 'You need to tell Mum about this and quickly,' she objected. 'It'll be a much bigger shock for her if the police turn up and she doesn't know.'

'Stress could make her ill again,' Robert argued worriedly.

'You don't know that. Whatever happens, there are no guarantees,' Jess reminded her father of the oncologist's wise words following her mother's treatment programme the previous year. 'We just have to pray and hope for the best.'

'I've let her down...' Robert shook his head slowly, his dark eyes filmed with tears. 'She doesn't deserve this.'

Jess said nothing, as she had no words of comfort to offer; the future did indeed look bleak. Should she approach Cesario di Silvestri and speak up on her father's behalf? Unfortunately, when she thought about the background to her own distinctly awkward relationship with Cesario di Silvestri, that did not seem quite such a bright idea. She had gone out to dinner with Cesario once. When he had invited her, she'd had no choice but to accept out of courtesy, because of her father's employment with him, and also because he was their most important client at the practice. Her face still burned though whenever she thought back to that disastrous evening when everything that could have gone wrong had done so. Now, she hated visiting the Halston Hall stud while Cesario was in residence. He always made her feel horribly self-conscious and her professional confidence took a nosedive around him.

Not that he was rude to her; in fact, she had never met anyone with more polished manners. She could not accuse the smoothly spoken Italian of harassment either, because he had never made the smallest attempt to ask her out again since. But there was always an ironic edge to his attitude that made her feel uncomfortable, as though she was a figure of fun in his eyes. She had never understood why he'd invited her out in the first place. After all, she bore no resemblance to the extremely decorative and flirtatious party girls, socialites and starlets who usually entertained him.

Cesario di Silvestri had a downright notorious reputation with the female sex, and Jess was very well aware of the fact. After all, her parents lived next door to his former housekeeper, Dot Smithers. The stories Dot had told of wild house parties and loose women flown in for the benefit of the rich male guests were the staples of village legend and had provided the fodder for several sleazy tabloid spreads in the years since the Italian billionaire had bought the Halston Hall estate. More than once Jess had personally seen Cesario di Silvestri with two or more women vying for his attention and she had no reason to doubt the rumour that he did, on occasion, enjoy more than one woman at a time in his bed.

So, in the light of that information, there had never been any question of Jess wanting an invitation to dine out or in with Cesario. Even without all the attendant scandal of his raunchy lifestyle, she remained convinced that he was way out of her league, both in looks and status, and she very firmly believed that nothing good could develop from a relationship based on such obvious inequality. In her opinion, people from different walks of life should respect the boundaries that kept them separate. Her own mother, after all, had paid a high price when she'd chosen to flout those boundaries as a teenager.

And Jess's belief in that social division had only been underlined by that catastrophic dinner date. Cesario had taken her to an exclusive little restaurant and she had quickly realised she was seriously underdressed in comparison with the other female diners. He'd had to translate the stupid pretentious menu written in a foreign language for her benefit. During the meal she had struggled in sinking mortification to understand which pieces of cutlery went with which course and was still covered in blushes at the recollection that she had eaten her dessert with a spoon rather than the fork Cesario had used.

But the highlight of the evening had to have been his invitation for her to spend the night with him after just one kiss. Cesario di Silvestri wasn't just fast with women, he was supersonic. But his move on her had outraged her pride and hurt her self-image. Had she struck him as being so cheap and easy that she would fall into bed with a man she barely knew?

All right, so the kiss had been spectacular. But the dizzy sexuality he had engulfed her in with his practised technique had unnerved her and had only made her all the more determined not to repeat such a dangerous experience. She had far too much self-respect and common sense to plunge into an affair with an impossibly wealthy womaniser. Such an imbalanced relationship could lead to nothing but grief, the results of which she had already seen within her own family circle. In all likelihood, if she had slept with Cesario that night he would have ticked some obnoxious male mental scoresheet and never have asked her out again.

In any case, in recent years Jess had pretty much given up dating in favour of a quiet uncomplicated existence. Her sole regret on that issue was that she adored children and, from her teenage years, had dreamt of one day becoming a mother and having a child of her own. Now, with her thirty-first birthday only months away, she was afraid that she might never have a baby and she made the most of enjoying her brother's two young children. She also recognised that in many ways her pets took the place of offspring in her affections. Once or twice she had considered the option of conceiving and raising a child alone, only to shrink from the stressful challenge of becoming a single parent who already worked long unsocial hours. Children were also supposed to do best with a father figure in their lives and in such a scenario she would not be able to offer that possibility; she did not think it would be fair to burden her own father with such an expectation.

The following morning, after a disturbed night of sleep, Jess went into the surgery, where she checked on the sole resident patient, a cat with liver disease. After carrying out routine tasks, she took care of the emergency clinic, which encompassed everything from a goldfish in a bowl that was as dead as a doornail, to a dog she had to muzzle to treat and a moulting but healthy parrot.

That night she lay awake worrying about her father until almost dawn. Her mother, Sharon, had not phoned, which she knew meant that Robert had not yet summoned up the courage to tell his wife that he was in trouble. Jess's heart bled at the prospect of her mother's pain and anxiety once she understood the situation. Mother and daughter had always been very close.

Jess had little hope that a personal appeal to Cesario di Silvestri would help her father's cause. After all, why would anything *she* had to say carry any influence with him? On the other hand, if there was even the smallest chance that she *could* make a difference she knew she owed it to her family to at least *try*. Already painfully aware that Cesario had arrived the previous evening in the UK, she accepted that she needed to make her approach to him as soon as possible.

On Tuesday she was scheduled to make a regular check on the brood mares at the Halston stud and she planned to make her move then. With her travelled half of her little tribe of dogs, for she routinely divided them into two groups and took one out with her on alternate days. Today there was Johnson, a collie with three legs and one eye after a nasty accident with farm machinery, Dozy, a former racing greyhound who suffered from narcolepsy and fell sleep everywhere she went, and Hugs, a giant wolfhound, who became excessively anxious when Jess vanished from his view.

Cesario knew Jessica Martin was on his land the instant he saw the three scruffy dogs outside the archway that led into the big stable yard. He smiled at the familiar sight, while idly wondering why she burdened herself with other people's rejects; a less appealing collection of misfits would have been hard to find. The tatty hound was whining and fussing like an overgrown, fractious toddler, the greyhound was fast asleep in a puddle, while the collie was plastered fearfully against the wall, shrinking in terror from the noise of a car that was nowhere near him.

As his head groom, Perkins, hurried to greet him, Cesario glanced straight past the middle aged man to rest his dark, deep-set gaze intently on the slight figure of the woman engaged in rifling her veterinary bag for a vaccination shot. A glimpse of the sheer classic purity of Jessica Martin's profile gave Cesario as much pleasure as the image of a Madonna in a fine Renaissance painting. Blessed with skin as rich and fine in texture as whipped cream, she had delicate but strong features and a luscious Cupid's-bow mouth worthy of a starring role in any red-blooded male's fantasies. And the footnote to that list of attributes was amazing eyes that were a luminous pale grey, as bright as silver in certain lights, and a foaming torrent of long black curly hair that she always kept tied back. She never used cosmetics or indeed wore anything the slightest bit feminine if she could help it, yet no matter how she dressed her diminutive height, beautiful bone structure and slender and subtle curves gave her an exceptionally arresting appearance.

Clad in faded riding breeches, workmanlike boots and a waxed jacket that should have been thrown out years ago, she was the living, breathing antithesis of Cesario's usual taste in women. Cesario had always been a perfectionist and great wealth and success had only increased that natural inclination. He liked his women sophisticated, exquisitely groomed and clothed. Every time he saw Jess Martin he reminded himself of those facts and questioned the depth of her apparent appeal for him. Was it simply because she had once said no and sentenced him to a cold shower rather than the pleasure of slaking their mutual attraction? For, although she denied it and did what she could to hide the fact, the attraction *was* mutual. He had known it when she looked at him over the dinner table and, since then, every time she went out of her way to avoid his eyes or keep him at arm's length. Either some man had done a very good job of souring her attitude to his sex or she had a problem with intimacy.

But his suspicions about her had not the smallest cooling effect on him while those breeches clung to every line of her slender toned thighs and the gloriously pert swell of her behind. Strip off the clothes and she would be pure perfection. As the familiar stirring heaviness at his groin afflicted him, Cesario's perfect white teeth gritted behind his firmly modelled mouth. *Per l'amor di Dio!* He went from enjoying the view to exasperation because he had never been a guy happy to look without the right to touch. Lust from afar was not his style. She was not at all his type, he reminded himself brutally, recalling the dinner engagement from hell when she had turned up wearing a black tent dress and had barely talked. She didn't even know how to speak to him. Look at her now, pretending that she hadn't yet noticed him to put off the moment of having to acknowledge him for as long as she possibly could!

Jess felt almost paralysed by the awareness that Cesario di Silvestri was nearby. Prior to his arrival she had noted the frantic activities of the stable staff, keen to ensure that everything looked good for the boss's visit, and she could scarcely have missed the throaty roar of his Ferrari, for, while other men might have chosen a four-wheel drive to negotiate the rough estate roads, Cesario travelled everywhere in a jaw-droppingly expensive sports car. Slowly she turned her head and looked at him while he spoke to Donald Perkins and, in that split second of freedom, she took in her fill and more.

Cesario was so gorgeous that, even after a couple of years' exposure to him, his charismatic good looks still exercised a weird kind of fascination over Jess. With the exception of a tiny scar on his temple he was without flaw, an acknowledgement that only reminded her of her own physical scars, and which chilled her. Cesario stood comfortably over six feet tall and enjoyed the long, lean, powerful build of an athlete. Even in country casuals he looked as elegant as though he had just stepped off a fashion catwalk, as his garments were tailored to a perfect fit, enhancing his broad shoulders, narrow hips and long muscular thighs. He wore his black hair short and cropped and his skin carried the golden hue of the Mediterranean sun. His narrow-bridged arrogant nose, sleek, proud cheekbones and sardonic, sensual mouth were arranged in such a way that you looked at him and then immediately had to look back again. Turning back to her task, she wondered frantically what she was going to say to him about her father. The fact that Robert was still walking around free meant that the older man's role in the robbery had yet to be identified.

'Jessica...' Cesario murmured smoothly, refusing to accept being ignored.

Flustered, her cheeks warming with colour, for he was the only person alive who ignored the diminutive by which she was known and continually employed her baptismal name, Jess twisted back to him. 'Mr di Silvestri...'

Cesario was reluctantly impressed that she had finally pronounced his name correctly without stumbling over the syllables like a drunk. She'd simply ignored repeated invitations to call him by his first name, keeping him at a distance with her cool reserve. Then Perkins asked her advice about a stallion with a tendon injury that was not responding well to ice packs and bandaging and she accompanied him into the stables to examine the horse. Soldier was a valuable animal and the head groom should have called her in sooner to administer anti-inflammatory drugs, but Jess could not bring herself to criticise his decision to hold fire in front of his employer.

'Jessica should have been consulted the day the injury occurred,' Cesario commented, picking up on the oversight with ease.

Jess finished her tasks and moved slowly towards the arch that led out of the courtyard. Sadly when, for once, she would have welcomed an attempt, Cesario made no move to keep her longer by striking up a conversation. Finally steeling herself, with her backbone rigid, she turned back and said without any expression at all and a tightness in the foot of her throat that gave her voice a husky edge, 'I'd appreciate a word with you, Cesario...'

Cesario settled brilliant dark eyes on her, making no attempt to hide his surprise at her use of his first name. Colour crept into her cheeks again as she gripped her bag between clenched fingers, fiercely uncomfortable below his intent scrutiny. Of course he was staring, one satiric ebony brow slightly quirked like a question mark because he could not imagine what she wanted. After all, she rarely spoke to him if she could help it.

'I'll be with you in a moment,' he responded in his rich, dark, accented drawl.

And no moment had ever stretched longer for Jess as she hovered with her dogs beyond the archway waiting for him. Worst of all she still had no idea at all of what she was planning to say to him...

CHAPTER TWO

'Perhaps we could conduct this dialogue over dinner this evening,' Cesario suggested with rich satisfaction.

The suggestion that she might be fishing for the chance to go out with him again inflamed Jess and stung her pride. She flipped round to face him, light grey eyes bright as silver with antagonism. 'No, I'm sorry, that wouldn't be appropriate. I need to talk to you about something relating to my family.'

'Your...*family*?' Lean dark features stamped with a bemused frown, Cesario dealt her an enquiring glance, contriving without effort to look so breathtakingly handsome that he momentarily made it virtually impossible for her to concentrate.

A prickling shimmy of sensation pinched her nipples to tautness and made her spine stiffen defensively, for she recognised that physical response for what it was and loathed it. He was a devastatingly handsome man and she was convinced that no healthy woman with hormones could be fully indifferent to that level of masculine magnetism. Her body was literally programmed to react in what she had long since mentally labelled a 'knee-jerk response' to Cesario's chemical appeal. It was

Mother Nature, whose sexual conditioning she could not totally suppress, having the last laugh on her.

Her colour fluctuating in response to her rattled composure, Jess sent her eyes in a meaningful sweep in the direction of the stable staff still within hearing. 'I'd prefer not to discuss the matter out here.'

His attention locked onto her taut facial muscles and the nervous pulse flickering in a hollow at the base of her slender throat, Cesario was even more curious to find out what she could possibly be so wired up about. He was also noting in a haze of innate sensuality that her skin was so fine that he could see the faint blue tracery of her veins beneath it. That fast he wanted to see her naked, all that creamy skin bare and unadorned for his benefit. Naked and *willing*, he thought hungrily. 'Follow me up to the house, then,' he instructed, irritably shaking free of the sexual spell she could cast to swing into his low-slung sports car.

In the driving mirror he watched her coax the sleeping greyhound from the puddle up into her arms, without worrying about the mess the bedraggled animal would make of her clothes. As she settled the dog into the rear of the old Land Rover she drove her other pets fawned on her as if she had been absent a day rather than an hour. Aware she took in the local homeless animals, he had always been grudgingly impressed by her compassionate nature, even if he could not approve of her indifference to her appearance. Although she was beautiful she did not behave as if she was, and that could only intrigue a man accustomed to finding women superficial and predictable. Somewhere along the line something had happened to Jess Martin that had prevented her from developing the narcissistic outlook of a beauty and the expectation that she should always be the centre of attention.

Jess parked beside the Ferrari at the front of the magnificent rambling Elizabethan house. Built of mellow brick and ornamented by tall elaborate chimneys and rows of symmetrical mullioned windows that reflected the sunshine, Halston Hall had considerable charm and antiquity. Although Dot Smithers had on one memorable occasion entertained Jess and her mother in the kitchen quarters there, Jess had never set foot in the main house. The Dunn-Montgomery family, who had owned the hall for several centuries, and whose male heirs had been often prominent in government, had not held open days at their ancestral home. Dwindling cash resources had forced the family to sell up six years earlier. To the great relief of the staff, who had feared that the property would be broken up and that they would lose their jobs, Cesario di Silvestri had bought the estate in its entirety. He had renovated the house, rescued the failing land with modern farming methods and set up a very successful stud farm.

Dot's male replacement, following her early retirement, a middle-aged and rotund Italian known as Tommaso, ushered Jess indoors. The splendid hall was dominated by a massive Tudor chimney piece with a seventeenth-century date swirled in the plaster above it. Her nervous tension at an all-time high in the face of such grandeur, Jess defied the urge to satisfy her curiosity and gape at her surroundings. She was shown into a room fitted out like a modern office, in surrealistic contrast to the linen fold panelling on the walls and the picturesque view of an ornate box-bush-edged knot garden beyond the windows.

'Your family?' Cesario prompted with a slight warning hint of impatience. Propped up against the edge of what appeared to be his desk in an attitude of relaxation, he was the very epitome of English country-casual style with a twist of elegant designer Italian in his tailored open-necked shirt and beautifully cut trousers.

'They're tenants of yours in the village, and my father and my brothers work for you here on the estate,' Jess volunteered.

'I was aware of those facts,' Cesario countered with a wry smile. 'My estate manager made the connection for me the first time I met you.'

Jess lifted her chin and straightened her slight shoulders, wondering if that information had originally been given to emphasise that she hailed from working-class country stock, rather than the snobbish county set. If so, the news of her humble beginnings and lower social standing must have failed to dim his initial interest, for the dinner invitation had followed soon afterwards. Stubbornly refusing to meet those gorgeous dark eyes in a head-on collision and blocking her awareness to him as she had learnt to do to maintain her composure and show of indifference, she breathed in deep. 'I have something to tell you and it relates to the robbery here…'

With a sudden flashing frown, Cesario leant forward, any hint of relaxation instantly banished by her opening words. 'The theft of my painting?'

Beneath that daunting stare, the colour in her cheeks steadily drained away. 'I'm afraid so.'

'If you have information relating to the robbery, why haven't you gone to the police with it?'

Jess could feel her ever-rising tension turning her skin clammy with nervous perspiration. Suddenly aware that she was way too warm, she shrugged free of the heavy jacket she wore over her shirt and draped it clumsily over the seat of the chair beside her. 'Because my father's involved and I was keen to get the chance to speak to you first.'

Cesario was not slow to grasp essential facts and his keen gaze glimmered as he instantly added two and two. As the estate handyman, who also acted as caretaker when the hall was unoccupied, Robert Martin had long been entrusted with the right to enter the hall at any time to perform maintenance checks and carry out repairs. 'If your father helped the thieves, you're wasting your time looking to me for sympathy—'

'Let me explain what happened first. I only found out about this matter yesterday. Last year my mother was diagnosed with breast cancer and it was a very stressful time for my family,' Jess told him tightly.

'While I am naturally sympathetic to anyone in your mother's situation, I fail to see what her ill health has to do with me or the loss of my painting,' Cesario asserted drily.

'If you listen, I'll tell you—'

'No. I think I am much more inclined in this scenario to call in the police and leave them to ask the questions. It's their job, not mine,' Cesario cut across her to declare with derision, his lean, darkly handsome features forbidding as he straightened and began to reach for the phone with a lean, shapely hand. 'I am not comfortable with this conversation.'

'Please don't phone the police yet!' Jess exclaimed, grey eyes wide with urgency as she moved forward suddenly, appearing as if she was trying to physically impose her slight body between him and the telephone. 'Please give me the chance to explain things first.'

'Get on with the explanation, then,' Cesario advised curtly, leaving the phone untouched, while surveying her with dark eyes flaming bronze with suspicion and anger. Even so, on a primitive masculine level he was already starting to get a kick out of her pleading with him. The tables had been turned with a vengeance, he savoured with satisfaction. She was no longer treating him to frozen silence or looking down that superior little nose of hers at him.

'Dad was worried sick about Mum and he wanted to take her away for a holiday after she finished her treatment, but he had to borrow the money to do so. Unfortunately he borrowed it from my uncle at an extortionate rate of interest.' Stumbling in her eagerness to tell the whole story, Jess outlined her father's efforts to deal with being pressed for his debt, followed by the approach and the offer made by her cousins.

'This is your *family* you're talking about,' Cesario reminded her dulcetly, marvelling at what she was willing to tell him about her less than scrupulous relations. For the first time it genuinely struck him that, for all her educational achievements, she truly was, unlike him, from the other side of the tracks.

'My mother's brother was in and out of prison for much of his life. He doesn't much care how he makes his money as long as he makes it. But his sons have never been in serious trouble with the police.' Her cheeks burned red with embarrassment as she filled in the disagreeable facts. 'My father believed what he was told—that Jason and Mark only wanted to get into this house to take photos which they could sell.'

Cesario dealt her a withering appraisal. 'This property is full of valuable antiques and art works. Are you seriously expecting me to believe that any man could be that stupid?'

'I don't think my father's stupid, I think he was simply desperate to do what they asked and be free of that debt. He was frantically trying to protect Mum from the distress of finding out how foolish he had been,' Jess confided ruefully. 'I don't believe he thought beyond that and what he did was very wrong. I'm not trying to excuse his behaviour. He's had access to this house for many years because he was a trusted employee and in acting as he did he betrayed your trust, but I'm convinced that my cousins intentionally targeted him.'

His handsome mouth taut with angry constraint, Cesario studied her grimly. 'It is immaterial to me whether your father was deliberately set-up or otherwise. Your mother's illness, the debt that ensued...those are not my concerns. My sole interest is in the loss of my painting and unless you have information to offer about how it might be recovered and from whom...'

'I'm afraid that I don't know anything about that and nor, unfortunately, does my father. His only function that evening was handing over his key card and the codes for the alarm.'

'Which makes him as guilty as any man who conspires with thieves and provides them with the means of entry to private property,' Cesario pronounced without hesitation.

'He honestly didn't know that anything was going to be stolen! He's an honest man, not a thief.'

'An honest man would not have allowed the men you described into my home to do as they liked,' Cesario derided. 'Why did you make this approach to me? What response did you expect from me?'

'I hoped that you would accept that Dad was entirely innocent of the knowledge that a crime was being planned.'

His sardonic mouth curled. 'I have only your word for that. After all, there was a robbery and it would not have happened had your father proved worthy of the responsibility he'd been given.'

'Look, please listen to me,' she urged with passionate vehemence, her pale grey eyes insistent. 'He's not a bad man, he's not dishonest either, and he's devastated by the loss that his foolishness caused you—'

'Foolishness is far too kind a description of what I regard as a gross betrayal of trust,' Cesario interrupted in flat dismissal of her argument and the terms she used. 'I ask you again: what did you hope to achieve by coming to see me like this?'

Jess settled deeply troubled eyes on him. 'I wanted to be sure you heard the full facts of the case as they happened.'

Regarding her with hard cynical eyes, Cesario loosed a harsh laugh. 'And exactly what were you hoping to gain from this meeting? A full pardon for your father just because I find you attractive? Is that what this encounter is all about?'

Her oval face flamed as though he had slapped her, colour running like a live flame below her skin as he made that statement. It had not even crossed her mind that, with the very many options he had, he might still find her attractive. 'Of course, it's not—'

Cesario's handsome mouth curled with scornful disbelief at that claim. '*Maiala della miseria…*at least tell it like it is! While I may lust after your shapely little body, I don't do it to the extent that I would forgive a crime against me or write off a painting worth more than half a million pounds. You would need to be offering me a great deal more in reparation.'

Jess was gazing back at him in shock, her soft pink lower lip protruding. 'What sort of a man are you? I wasn't offering you sex!' She gasped in horror as she grasped the portent of his words. 'Of course, I wasn't!'

'That's good, because in spite of the scurrilous rumours the British tabloids like to print about me I don't pay for sexual favours or associate with the kind of woman who puts a price on her body,' Cesario declared with an outrageous cool that mocked her seething embarrassment.

'I really *wasn't* offering you sex,' Jess muttered in repeated rebuttal, shattered by that demeaning suggestion.

A well-shaped ebony brow lifted above heavily lashed dark-as-night eyes that remained resolutely unimpressed. 'So, I was just supposed to let your father off the hook for nothing? Does that strike you as a likely deal in such a serious situation?'

'Deal? What *deal*? You're talking like my cousins now. You have a sordid mind,' Jess condemned chokily, her mortification extreme as she snatched up her jacket and began to fight her way into its all-concealing folds. The remainder of her speech emerged in breathless spurts of smarting pride and resentment. 'For your information, I don't sleep around and sex isn't something I would treat like a currency or...or a takeaway meal. *In fact...*'

Unexpectedly amused by her bristling, blushing fury and the discovery that she was much more of a prude than he had had previous cause to suspect, Cesario was striving not to picture her creamy, curvy little body writhing in ecstasy on his silk sheets because he was well aware that that was most probably a fantasy designed to go unfulfilled. 'I'm delighted to hear it.'

'I'm a virgin!' That admission just leapt off Jess's heated tongue and she froze, appalled that she had let that little-known fact slip. 'Not that that has any relevance when I wasn't offering you sex anyway,' she continued, striving to bury her too intimate confession in a concealing flood of words. 'But I admit that I would have offered you virtually anything else to get my father off the hook. I am *desperate...*'

She lifted her dark head to find Cesario staring back at her with raw incredulity. 'A virgin—you can't be at your age!'

Jess dug hands clenched into fists deep into her pockets and tilted up her chin in defiance of his disbelieving scrutiny. 'I'm not ashamed of it. Why would I be? I didn't meet the right person, it just never happened, and I can live with that.'

But Cesario was not sure he *could* live with the new and tantalising knowledge that she had given him. Suddenly he believed he had finally discovered the source of her discomfort in his radius. Naturally he had assumed she was much more experienced with men and he had treated her accordingly that one evening they had shared. He had probably come on too strong, frightened her off...or very probably his notorious reputation with her sex had done it for him, he reflected in sudden exasperation. Jessica Martin was untouched and, although he had never had a virgin in his bed before, he knew there and then that he would still very much like to be the male who introduced her to that essential missing element in her life. Feeling the taut, charged heaviness of sexual response at his groin in answer to that beckoning tide of erotic imagery, he suppressed a curse and straightened, willing his too enthusiastic body back under firm control again.

'Look, there must be something I can say to you... something I can do to change your mind about Dad's role in this horrible business,' Jess reasoned frantically, literally feeling him disengage from her in the remote set of his shielded eyes and the harsh lines of his lean bronzed features. She was on the edge of panicking. He had asked her what she expected from him and she honestly didn't know. He had not responded with the understanding that she had hoped to ignite with her explanation about her mother's illness and her father's deeply troubled state of mind. He had not responded in the slightest: it had been like crashing into a stone wall at a hundred miles an hour. She had crashed and burned, her persuasive abilities clearly not up to so steep a challenge.

Tears had pooled in her eyes and turned them to liquid silver. Cesario was not a man who responded to tears, but he was unprepared for that feminine softness in her. He had always viewed her as a tough little cookie, assured as she was working in what was so often a man's field, confidently handling his most temperamental stallions while freezing out his every attempt to get closer to her. Yet seeing those tears he still bit back cutting words.

'Promise you'll think over what I've told you,' she urged him in desperation. 'My father is a decent man and he's made a really appalling mistake that you have suffered for. I'm not trying to minimise the loss and distress that you have undergone, but please don't wreck his life over it.'

'I don't let wrongdoers go unpunished. I'm much more in the eye-for-an-eye, tooth-for-a-tooth category,' Cesario delivered, wondering why she was persisting when he had given her so little encouragement. Had she gone on his reputation alone, she would have been expecting him to build a gallows for her father out on the front lawn to stage a public execution. A hard-hitting businessman, he had never had a name for compassion.

'*Please…*' Jess repeated doggedly, standing by the door as he stopped her advance with one assured hand and reached in front of her to open the door for her with the easy display of effortless courtesy that came so naturally to him. Of course, such smooth civility was totally unfamiliar to her. Her brothers would have broken their necks to get through the door ahead of her and her father had never been taught any such refinements.

'I'm not going to change my mind, but I won't call in the police to tell them what you've told me until tomorrow morning,' Cesario intoned, questioning why he was even willing to cede that breathing space.

From the front hall he watched her drive off in her noisy ancient four-wheel drive. *There must be…something I can do to change your mind…I'm desperate…I would have offered you virtually anything else to get my father off the hook.* And finally he thought about the only thing he really wanted that he couldn't buy and he wondered if he was crazy to even consider her in that light. Was there even enough time left in which he might fulfil that ambition?

He could have her and… *Infierno*, in spite of the other women he had sought out to take the edge off his frustration he *still* wanted Jessica Martin! Given some luck he might also be able to gain what he longed for most from her and on the most fair of terms. In a life that was fast threatening to become shadowed by a bitterness he despised, Cesario was in dire need of a distraction. A woman, the very thought of whom could keep him awake at night with sexual frustration, struck him as the perfect solution.

Of course, it wasn't just desire that motivated him, he reasoned with native shrewdness. She had traits he admired, traits that set her indisputably above most of the women he had known in the past. She was a hard worker who was extremely loyal to her family and she had just willingly sacrificed her pride on their behalf.

She devoted all her free time and cash to taking care of animals other people didn't want. Even his wealth, such a magnetic draw to others of her sex, had failed to tempt her into his bed. She was not, by any stretch of the imagination, a gold-digger. Indeed she had good strong standards and he liked that about her. But would those same standards come between her and her family's salvation? A ruthless calculating smile starting to play around the corners of his hard mouth, Cesario decided to go for the challenge and give her one last chance.

Jess was on duty until nine that evening and she was very tired and low in spirits by the time she drove home with her dogs fast asleep in a huddle in the back of her car. She kept on expecting her mobile phone to ring and for her to hear her distraught mother tell her that her father had been arrested. Cesario di Silvestri had promised to wait until the next day but she didn't believe she could afford to have faith in that proviso because, when she thought about their fruitless exchange, she reluctantly appreciated that she had been guilty of asking him for the impossible.

Even if he didn't personally report her father to the police, Jason and Mark certainly would if they were questioned and implicated in the crime. Her cousins would be eager to spread the blame. The painting had been stolen and there was little hope of retrieving it without the whole sorry tale of its theft being told in detail. There would also be the matter of the insurance claim that would surely be made. Wouldn't the insurers demand assurance that every possible step had been taken to apprehend the perpetrators? So how could

Cesario protect her father from being held responsible for his actions?

Letting her other, waiting three dogs out of their fenced run, Jess headed indoors. The cottage was cold and untidy. The old coal-fired kitchen stove had gone out and she sighed, hurrying off to change into clean clothes. She would grab something quick to eat and go out and tend to the animals' needs first. Magic, her deaf Scottish black terrier, bounced round the room as though he were on springs, full of pent-up energy. In between getting changed and washed she repeatedly threw his ball down the hall for him to retrieve. Weed, a skinny grey lurcher, hovered ingratiatingly by the door. Years of loving care had failed to persuade Weed that he could afford to take his happy home for granted. Harley, a diabetic Labrador with a greying muzzle, lay quietly on the floor by the bed, just content to be with her again.

Standing by the kitchen window, Jess ate a sandwich and drank a glass of milk before heading out into the fading light of a late spring evening to take care of the usual evening routine of cleaning, feeding and watering her charges. When she finished and went back indoors, she still had to relight the stove, which always took more than one attempt. Gritting her teeth, she got on with the task.

The phone call came when she was getting ready for bed and so bone-weary that she had all the animation of a zombie.

'It's Cesario…' He reeled off his name in that dark deep rich drawl of his as naturally as if he were in the habit of phoning her, when in actuality it was the very first time he had made a personal call to her.

'Yes?' she queried, cautious in tone as she swallowed back an instinctive urge to ask him angrily who had given him her mobile number.

'Can you come back up to the house at nine tomorrow morning? I have a proposition to put to you.'

'A proposition?' Jess repeated, intense curiosity leaping high inside her to release a tide of speculative thoughts. 'What kind of a proposition?'

'Not the sort that can be discussed over the phone,' he murmured crushingly. 'May I expect you?'

'Yes, tomorrow's my day off.'

Jess came off the phone, her face pale and still, and then she let out an explosive whoop that startled her pets and jumped up and down on the spot in a helpless release of the tension that had held her fast all day. Evidently, Cesario di Silvestri *had* listened to her! That phone call had to mean that he had listened to her and mulled over what she had told him. Now, in response, he had come up with a 'proposition', which was really just another label for that other word 'deal', which she abhorred.

Acknowledging that truth, her ready sense of optimism and relief began swiftly to recede in the face of less comforting thoughts. After all, an eye-for-an-eye guy would be very unlikely to pardon her imprudent father in return for nothing. Hadn't he said so himself? What would be in it for him? Was sex likely to be involved? With his reputation and the interest he had previously shown in her, it was difficult to believe it would not be. She winced in the cosy cocoon of her sensible pyjamas, thinking of the scars on her abdomen and back, shivering. It was little wonder that she had never been keen to strip to reveal those blemishes to a man or relive the horror of explaining what had caused them. Sex was out of the question. In any case, bearing in mind what she had read in the sleazier newspapers' 'kiss 'n' tell' accounts made by his former lovers, she would never be able to measure up to Cesario's exotic and adventurous habits in the bedroom...

CHAPTER THREE

CESARIO had a clear view of Jess climbing out of her old Land Rover with several dogs leaping out in her wake.

She had said it was her day off and he had naturally assumed she would dress up for the occasion. Smarten up for their meeting even a little? Surely that was a normal expectation? But she was wearing jeans and a T-shirt roomy enough to fit him below a tweedy woollen cardigan that would not have shamed a scarecrow. Nothing she wore fitted or flattered. He clenched his even white teeth, acknowledging that if, against all the odds, they contrived to reach an agreement, there was definitely going to have to be a lot of compromise on both sides of the fence. She might not do couture, but he definitely *didn't* do dog hairs.

Tommaso beamed at Jess as if they were old friends and showed her into an imposingly large reception room decked out with almost rock-star glamour in dramatic shades of black and purple. Sumptuous velvet sofas, glass tables and defiantly modern art set the tone. A few minutes later, the older man reappeared with a tray of coffee and biscuits and assured her that his employer would be with her very shortly.

'Business...always business,' he lamented, mimicking a phone to his ear with one hand and rolling his eyes with speaking disapproval.

So jumpy that she couldn't sit still, Jess lifted her cup of coffee and wandered over to examine a colourful painting, struggling to work out if what looked vaguely like a weird face really was meant to be a face. Her taste in art was strictly traditional and very much confined to country landscapes and animal portraits. She would not have given houseroom to Cesario's valuable collection of contemporary art. Her mobile phone trilled and she dug it out one-handed, hastening over to a side table to set down her coffee once she realised that it was her mother, Sharon, calling.

Sharon was in floods of tears, which made it hard to distinguish what she was saying, but Jess soon picked up the gist. Her father had bared his soul over breakfast and had then beat a very fast masculine retreat from the questions and reproaches hurled at him in the aftermath of his confession. Her mother was in emotional bits, convinced her husband was on the brink of being dragged off to prison for his part in the robbery at the hall.

'That stupid holiday...all this over that stupid holiday I could very well have done without!' Sharon sobbed heartbrokenly. 'And we'll lose the house into the bargain...'

Jess's brows pleated. 'What are you talking about?'

'Well, Mr sodding di Silvestri is not going to let us stay in one of his properties after what your father's done to him, is he?' Sharon wailed. 'I've lived here since I was eighteen and I couldn't bear to lose my home too. And what about your brothers' jobs on the estate? Mark my words, Martin faces won't fit at Halston Hall any more and some way will be found to get rid of us all!'

Jess said what she could to calm her down but Sharon was an emotional woman and a natural pessimist. In Sharon's mind the worst that could happen had happened, and she and her family were already homeless, jobless and broke. Having promised that she would call in later that morning, Jess finally got off the phone and found Cesario watching her from the doorway.

For a split second, she just stared, totally unnerved to find herself the target of that silent scrutiny. Formally clad in a dark business suit and vibrant silk tie, Cesario was effortlessly elegant and intimidating, only the shadow of dark stubble around his strong jaw line making it clear that his morning had commenced at a much earlier hour. She had always thought he was very good-looking but at that moment he looked stunningly handsome, his need for a shave adding a sexy rough edge to his usual immaculate appearance.

'My mother...my father finally worked up the courage to tell her what he had done,' Jess explained awkwardly as she put away her phone, her cheeks pink from her thoughts. 'She's very upset.'

'I'm sure she must be.' Cesario noted the level of stress etched in the tightness of her delicate features. It was an immediate source of satisfaction to him that it was within his power to banish that anxiety from her life. He had lain awake half of the night working out exactly what he wanted and what would work best: a simple straightforward arrangement free of demanding emotions and unrealistic hopes. In the most essential way they would each retain their independence.

'You mentioned a proposition...' she muttered nervously, digging her hands into her pockets, unable to conceal her tension from him

'Hear me out before you give me an answer,' he advised her quietly, registering that, in spite of her unprepossessing clothing, when she looked directly at him she looked so amazingly young and lovely that it was an effort for him to recall what he had planned to say to her. 'And remember that by the time our agreement would come to an end you would be in a most advantageous position.'

She was mystified by that assurance and reference to an agreement, her smooth brow indented, her confusion palpable. But, keen to hear what he had to say, she nodded slowly.

Cesario viewed her with hooded eyes. 'At its most basic, I have come up with a way in which you could help me and in return I would not prosecute your father.'

Eyes wide and hopeful, Jess snatched in an audible breath. 'All right, tell me. How could I help you?'

'I would like to have a child but not in the conventional way,' Cesario explained wryly, his lean aquiline profile taut as she gazed back at him, fine brows rising in surprise. 'I've never been convinced that I can meet one woman and spend the rest of my life with her. On the other hand I believe I could handle a marriage that had a more practical foundation.'

Jess was now frowning more than ever as she struggled to follow what he was telling her and divine how

on earth such a topic could relate to her father's predicament. 'How can a marriage be practical?' she asked
him uncertainly, convinced that in some way she had
misunderstood, because she found it hard to believe that
he could possibly be discussing the subject of marriage
with her.

'When it's a straightforward contract freed from
flowery ideals and expectations like love, romance
and permanence,' Cesario outlined with unconcealed
enthusiasm. 'If you will agree to have a child with me
I will marry you, give you your freedom back within a
couple of years and ensure that you need never worry
about money again.'

In the grip of astonishment at that sweeping suggestion and his clear conviction that he was making her a
generous offer, Jess looked away from him momentarily before turning her head back sharply to stare at
him. 'You can't be serious—for goodness' sake, you're
young, handsome and rich,' she pointed out. 'There must
be any number of women who would be eager to marry
you and give you a family.'

'But I don't want a hedonistic gold-digger for a
wife or, for that matter, as an unsuitable mother for my
child. I want an intelligent, independent woman who
will accept my terms and know to expect nothing more
lasting from me.'

Not unpleased to be styled both intelligent and independent, Jess stood a little taller. 'But if you're not
prepared to commit to a long-term relationship with a
woman, why on earth do you want a child?'

'The two are not mutually exclusive. I would commit
to my relationship with the child,' Cesario declared with

conviction, willing her to see the sound sense behind his arguments. 'I'm not being selfish.'

Jess shook her dark head slowly, her disapproval patent. 'Are you so keen to have a child that you can't wait until you meet the right woman to marry?'

'I would like to say yes and impress you with my credentials as a child-loving male. I do very much want a child of my own,' Cesario proclaimed, his strong sensual mouth compressing with a level of gravity that she had not previously seen in him. 'But that isn't the whole story...'

Unsurprised, Jess nodded acceptance of that admission. 'I thought not.'

'I am the descendant of a long unbroken line of di Silvestris,' Cesario recounted, his brilliant dark eyes narrowing and focusing on a distant point beyond the windows, his attitude one of detachment while his crisp drawl became oddly flat in its delivery. 'My grandfather was immensely proud of that fact. He was obsessed with blood ties and he devoted his life to researching our family tree. Unfortunately he tied his Tuscan estate up in such a way that I cannot legally inherit from my late father unless I have an heir. Male or female, it doesn't matter, but I must have an heir to retain ownership of the family home.'

'My goodness, that was very short-sighted and controlling of him!' Jess commented helplessly. 'I mean, you might have been gay or not remotely interested in having a child.'

'But I'm not gay,' Cesario pointed out drily. 'And I am now choosing to look on this as a project that can be completed.'

'A project…having a baby is a *project*?' Jess repeated in consternation, her thoughts in turmoil.

She thought that it was deeply ironic that he should cherish a desire for something that lay so close to her own heart when they had absolutely nothing else in common. He wanted a child for mainly practical reasons, while she simply wanted a child to love and share her life with. 'I think it would be very wrong for you to bring a child into the world just so that you can inherit some family property.'

'That's one angle, but there are others. I would love my child, who would enjoy a fine education, a supportive family, and who would ultimately inherit everything that I possess,' Cesario responded levelly. 'Any child of mine would enjoy a good life.'

'Why don't you just hire a surrogate mother?' Jess asked bluntly. 'Surely that would make more sense?'

'That wouldn't meet my requirements at all. I come from a conservative background and I prefer that my child be born within what would appear to be a normal marriage for its duration. I also want my son or daughter to have a mother's love and care. I grew up without a mother,' he admitted with an expressive twist of his sensual mouth. 'That's not at all what I want for my own child.'

'I assumed that, in the circumstances you mentioned, you would be seeking full custody of any child that you had,' Jess remarked.

'No. I would not seek more than shared custody and visiting rights. I firmly believe that a child needs a mother to flourish.'

'And a father,' she added abstractedly, thinking of her

own childhood when she had adored having her father's attention.

'Of course,' Cesario di Silvestri conceded, but the clipped edge of his voice and the austerity of his expression drew her gaze and she could only wonder what unhappy memory she had contrived to awaken as his lean dark features had shadowed with an expression of regret.

Jess breathed in slow and deep, her brain racing over the outrageous proposition he had outlined, lingering on the pitfalls she saw in the concept and almost immediately rejecting it in full. What he was asking was not only impossible, but insane. She, personally, could not marry a man she did not even like, get into a bed with him and conceive his child. Even thinking about taking part in such a shocking scheme made her tummy somersault and her face burn with the heat of embarrassment.

'You're asking me, but I couldn't possibly marry you,' she declared in a feverish rush.

Cesario dealt her a long measuring look as cool as iced water, for while she might be flustered by the tone of the conversation, he was most definitely not. He also knew that if she rejected his offer he would very much regret having made it. 'You must accept that this is the only option you have and the only offer I have to make you.'

'But it's scarcely a reasonable offer,' Jess complained, her chin coming up in an open challenge.

'I disagree.' His dark eyes gleamed gold below the thick dark screen of his lashes, his lean, strong face implacable. 'In return, I would be making a considerable sacrifice in letting your father and his partners in crime go unpunished. I would also be accepting the permanent loss of my painting without financial compensation as, in this situation, I could not approach the police or make an insurance claim.'

Sobered by that view of the consequences of any agreement being reached, Jess swallowed hard. He had not been joking when he'd talked about offering her a deal. He wanted something in return for the loss of his valuable painting and why not? She thought it unlikely that Cesario di Silvestri was accustomed to being on the losing side of any exchange. And the only thing he seemed to want right now was to become a father without agreeing to the level of commitment or the expectations that would accompany a conventional marriage.

Bearing in mind what she knew about Cesario di Silvestri, that made very good sense to Jess. No woman had ever held his interest for long and it was a challenge to picture him settling down with one woman to start a family in the usual way. On the other hand, choosing a wife and future mother for his child on the basis of cold, hard practicality would sentence him to fewer restrictive ties. A wife who was only pretending to be a proper wife would not require much time or attention either. Yes, as she considered his proposition she could certainly see the advantages from *his* point of view.

And from this practical wife's point of view? A cold contract with a pregnancy and an eventual divorce already organised and agreed upfront? Jess studied her tightly linked hands. Was his proposition really any more distasteful than the conception by artificial means that she had once considered? Much as she longed for a baby, she had not been attracted to the possibility of visiting a sperm bank to be inseminated so that she could conceive a baby by a man she would know next to nothing about. But at least actual intimacy would not have featured in that arrangement.

'If I wasn't so attracted to you I wouldn't even be giving you this option,' Cesario murmured under his breath, the husky timbre of his voice rasping down her taut spinal cord like a physical caress.

Jess glanced up from below her lashes, grey eyes wide and troubled. She felt like someone needing to take cover from a hail of bullets when there was no hiding place available. Her brain was telling her firmly and repeatedly that she could not accept his offer and that some things, not least conception, were sacred and could not be bought. But at the same time when there was no other alternative and her father was in so much trouble...

'If we have not reached an agreement by the time that you leave, I will be calling in the police,' Cesario spelt out with a quietness that was all the more chilling for its lack of volume. 'I now have the proof I need to have charges laid against your father.'

'For goodness' sake, you can't expect any woman to just agree to have a baby with you when there's no existing relationship in place!' Jess exclaimed, shattered by the speed with which he had turned up the pressure on her.

'Why not? Women get married and have children with men they don't love every day of the week. Marriage is a legal contract for good reasons. Many women marry

for money, security or status,' Cesario contended. 'You
are not being asked to make a huge sacrifice.'

Jess bit down on her impetuous tongue and viewed
him from behind furiously resentful silvery eyes for
demanding the one thing she could not face agreeing
to give him. In her opinion his outrageous offer was
just typical of his arrogant, insensitive personality.
Giving him a child wasn't a sane doable proposition
for a woman like her. She was a very private person
and solitary in her outlook. His very lifestyle, habits
and tastes were anathema to her and she knew that for a
fact before she even tried to add in the horrors of going
to bed with a stranger. 'Is that so?'

'Yes, that is so. As far as I'm aware there is no boyfriend in your life to complicate matters and I too am
free of any ties. I assure you that if you were to become
my wife I would treat you with respect and generosity.
This house would be your home. I would not expect
you to make a permanent move to Italy on my behalf.
In many aspects your life would continue as it always
has.'

Jess tried to imagine him in her bed with life continuing as it always had, and almost loosed an overwrought
giggle in blunt and incredulous disagreement. But native
caution was already beginning to restrain her from a
too hasty response.

'Perhaps it is the thought of having to get pregnant
that you find most off-putting—'

'No,' she cut in abruptly, surprising herself as much as
him. 'I'm at an age when I would very much like a baby,
even if it did mean ending up on my own as a single

parent. But have you really thought about this idea? You could marry me and I might fail to conceive.'

'That would be fate. I would be disappointed but I would accept it with good grace,' Cesario declared.

The sunshine coming through the window drenched his tall powerful figure in shades of bronze and gold and turned his dark deep-set eyes to gleaming topaz brilliance. As she stared her colour fluctuated and her antipathy to him was only heightened by the quickening of her heartbeat. If she said no, it would be because she did not know how she could possibly hope to fulfil the terms of giving him a positive answer. But she did not feel that she had a choice, or at least she had no choice when faced by the likelihood of her father being imprisoned and the family she adored being torn apart by the fallout from Robert Martin's folly.

Almost thirty years earlier, Robert had promised to bring up Jess as his own child. He had stood faithfully by that promise, even when he'd been censured for not marrying Sharon until her daughter had been almost a year old because everybody had simply assumed that her child was his. In those days, having a child out of wedlock had still been a big deal in a country village and Jess's mother had had a tough time during her months as an unmarried mother. Robert Martin had taken a big gamble when he'd married the woman he loved who, at the time, had willingly admitted that she did not love him. Sometimes, Jess reckoned, in a state of painful anxiety and uncertainty, the only way to move forward was to close your eyes and take a leap in the dark.

'All right...I'll do it!' she breathed with an abruptness that shocked even her as she suppressed her teeming flood of misgivings and tendered agreement without allowing herself to think too hard about what she was doing.

And Cesario di Silvestri actually smiled, but not with the usual curl of his handsome mouth that had on previous occasions left her unimpressed. He gave her a dazzling smile powered by enough charisma to float a battleship, his lean, darkly handsome features energised by that expression on his wide, sensual mouth.

'You won't regret this,' he asserted with confidence, reaching for her hand to mark their accord. Just before he released her fingers he noticed the line of paler scar tissue along the back of her hand and asked abruptly, 'What happened here?'

Jess froze and paled, her heart suddenly beating frantically fast. 'Oh, an accident…a long time ago,' she heard herself say, only just resisting the temptation to yank her hand free again.

'It was a nasty one,' Cesario remarked, releasing her fingers.

He had picked an unfortunate moment in which to notice that scar and rouse bad memories. Indeed Jess had barely agreed to marry him before she fell into the turmoil of doubt and regret, but she rammed back those feelings and simply nodded, focusing her thoughts on the future rather than on that distressing episode from her past. The end would justify the means, she told herself urgently. Cesario would get what he wanted but so would *she*. Her child would still be her child to keep and he or she would benefit from a father. She would not think about the bedroom end of things, she absolutely would not think about that aspect until she was forced to do so.

'I'll get my staff to make a start on the wedding arrangements,' Cesario informed her.

Jess studied him in dismay. 'You *are* in a hurry.'

'Naturally…I wouldn't want you to change your mind, *piccola mia*,' Cesario sent her a winging appraisal, his beautiful mouth taking on that sardonic curl she had always disliked. 'And we have no reason to waste time before we embark on our project, have we?'

'I suppose not,' she mumbled as she bent to lift her jacket.

Cesario extended his hand and, when she failed to grasp his intention, simply and coolly removed the jacket from her grasp before shaking it open for her to put on. Colouring as she finally realised what he was doing, she turned to slide her arms into the sleeves, tensing beneath the familiarity when he tugged her hair out from below the collar where it was caught.

'I'll look forward to seeing your hair loose,' he told her with husky anticipation.

And something in his dark voice and the intensity of his appraisal as she turned her head spooked her so that she backed off a hasty step. No man had ever had the power to make her so conscious of her own body, and around him she always felt clumsy and naïve.

Cesario ignored the arms she had crossed in front of her like a defensive barrier and touched her cheek with a reproving brown forefinger. 'You're going to be my wife. You will have to get used to being touched by me.'

'And how am I supposed to do that?' Jess questioned,

infuriated by the fact that at such speed and with even less effort he had reduced her to a state of almost adolescent awkwardness in his presence.

Ignoring the distrustful vibrations that she was putting out, Cesario closed his hand over one of hers and tugged her inexorably closer. 'Try relaxing first...'

Her teeth momentarily chattered together behind her closed lips as if she had been plunged suddenly into an icy bath.

'I'm only going to kiss you,' he imparted silkily.

Jess froze, her silvery eyes flickering with dismay at even that prospect. 'No—'

'We have to start somewhere, *piccola mia.*'

But he surprised her by releasing her hand and she snatched it back and was about to retreat further until it occurred to her that she could no longer afford to follow her own inclinations where he was concerned. If she couldn't even allow him to kiss her, he would naturally assume that she couldn't handle their agreement and he would withdraw his proposal. She froze like a bird confronted by a hungry stalking cat.

Cesario laughed softly in triumph and colour ran like a fire up over her cheekbones. She gazed up at him, properly aware for almost the first time of how much taller and heavier he was, six feet plus inches of lean, power-packed muscle. Her colour drained away, silvery eyes veiling as she reminded herself that she had no reason to fear him, but her body wasn't listening to her brain, for it was angling backwards without her volition, almost tipping her off balance. Her heart was positively thundering in her ears.

'There are some things I'm very good at,' Cesario

delivered with innate assurance. 'And this is one of them, *piccola mia*.'

And his mouth slid across her sealed-shut lips as lightly as a dandelion seed borne by the breeze. She had expected passion, but he defied her expectations and her heart set up an even louder thump behind her breastbone, the pace speeding up as he brushed his knowing mouth back over hers and the extent of her tension made her rigid. The tip of his tongue scored that seam of denial and her body came alive when she was least prepared for it, a jerky quiver of feminine response slivering through her with almost painful effect as she parted her lips to let him kiss her properly. It was slow and hot and very thorough and it shook her up because her nipples pinched into hard little buds and her breasts swelled so that her bra felt as if it was constricting her ability to breathe. As his tongue delved with erotic skill into the sensitive interior of her mouth, moist heat surged between her thighs and she trembled.

'That's enough,' she said shakily, her hands rising against his broad shoulders to push him back from her. Feverishly flushed, she found it hard to accept that once again she had enjoyed the feel of his mouth on hers. She had thought it was a fluke the last time he had kissed her and she had been intimidated by the pent-up passion she could feel in him.

'No, it's only the beginning,' Cesario husked, smouldering golden eyes fringed by dense black lashes roving boldly over her averted face so that when she glanced up, she flinched at that visual connection and hurriedly looked away.

'This wedding you mentioned,' Jess remarked hurriedly, keen to move on to a less controversial subject because she was taken aback by the way he was looking at her. She stifled an urge to shiver because she felt cornered. She was not so naïve that she didn't recognise the force of his desire for her and she could hardly afford to knock the source of her apparent appeal when it was probably the main reason he was offering her a wedding ring and her father's freedom. 'When would it take place?'

'As soon as it can be arranged—it *will* be a proper wedding,' Cesario decreed without hesitation. 'With the dress, the big guest list, the whole bridal show.'

'Is that really necessary?' Jess pressed uneasily, wincing at the prospect of having to play the blushing bride for an audience of posh strangers.

'It won't look like a normal marriage otherwise,' he pointed out.

'Oh, my goodness, what am I going to tell my family?' she suddenly gasped in an appalled undertone.

'Not the truth, for that is only for you and I to know,' Cesario spelt out in a tone of warning.

He had just given her an impossible embargo, but Jess was already reaching the conclusion that it was better not to blurt out unwary comments around Cesario. She knew even then that she would tell her mother the truth, but that she would present it in an edited version to satisfy her father's curiosity without making the older man feel responsible for her predicament. She breathed in deep and slow, reminding herself firmly of the positive aspects to her situation and repeating them over and over to herself in a soothing mantra. Her father would not pay the price for his stupidity and her family circle would stay intact. She would hopefully end up with the baby she had long dreamt of having and she would even have that all important wedding ring on her finger first, since her mother set great store on a woman being married in advance of the arrival of children.

So what if it was a project rather than a wedding? She could cope with that. She was very realistic and, if he was as good at everything else as he was at kissing, given time she would surely come to terms with the more intimate aspects of their relationship. Women didn't always marry just for love, she reminded herself doggedly, and neither did men, as Cesario was about to prove. If such a marriage was good enough for him when she was convinced that he could have so many more exciting options, it should be good enough for her as well.

'Why did you choose me for this?' she heard herself ask without warning.

His dense lashes swooped low over his brilliant dark gaze. 'Ask me on our wedding night,' he advised, a piece of advice that not unnaturally silenced her...

CHAPTER FOUR

'I LIKE the dress with the full skirt best,' Jess repeated doggedly, ignoring the raised brows of Melanie, the hip fashion stylist Cesario had hired to work with her in what bore all the hallmarks of a tip-to-toe makeover.

Jess, however, was determined to at least choose her own wedding gown. 'It suits me,' she added.

'It's very, very pretty,' Sharon Martin agreed with unconcealed delight at her daughter's choice.

'Well, if you like bling,' Melanie said drily, encouraging the saleswoman to display the dress so that the pearl-beaded bodice and the scattered crystals on the skirt sparkled in the light, her lack of enthusiasm palpable. 'It has certainly got buckets of bling.'

Jess had surprised herself with her choice. Although her taste generally ran to the plain, she had fallen head over heels in love with the unashamedly romantic wedding gown. Melanie's efforts to persuade her client to pick a restrained satin column style instead had fallen on stony ground.

On that score, though, it had to be admitted that Jess had enjoyed a rare victory. She had already had to accept an entire trousseau of new garments for her up-and-coming role as the wife of an international tycoon and her preferences had often been politely ignored. Cesario was a perfectionist who dotted every i and crossed every t, while Jess was someone who never ever sweated the small stuff if she could help it. And arguing on the phone about something as unimportant as clothes with a male as single-minded and accustomed to getting his own way as Cesario was, she had learned, exhausting and ultimately pointless.

It was a fact that Jess had taken virtually no interest in clothes and cosmetics since that traumatic episode in her late teens when she had decided that it was safer and much more comfortable not to dress to attract male attention. Now willing to admit that she was out of date with regard to fashion and the art of self-presentation, she had agreed to accept advice and grooming. As a result, her uncontrollable black waterfall of curls had been shaped and tamed and her brows plucked. While she could see that her appearance had improved and her hair was much more manageable, she was appalled that the time she had already had to spend in the beauty salon was now being extended into the territories of waxing, facials, manicure and pedicure sessions. Was there no end to the vanity sessions she was expected to endure? Her colleagues at the veterinary practice had pulled her leg unmercifully as the ugly duckling—as she saw herself as—was ruthlessly repackaged into a would-be swan.

Although only three weeks had passed since Jess had agreed to marry Cesario di Silvestri, the comfortable groove of her life was fast being erased. The wedding was set for a date only ten days away and Cesario had been abroad on business almost from the day they had agreed to marry. A giant diamond cluster, delivered by special courier, now adorned her ring finger and an announcement about their engagement had appeared in an upscale broadsheet newspaper that nobody Jess knew read. In response to that first public reference to her new position, a photographer had just the day before popped up from behind a hedge to take a ghastly picture of her returning to the surgery after a difficult calving, bedraggled and dirty with her hair like a bird's nest. The subsequent picture, comically entitled *Jet-Set Bride?*, had appeared that very morning in a downmarket tabloid. Jess had merely pulled a face when a colleague showed it to her, because getting messed up in her field of work was an occupational hazard. Cesario, however, had requested that she meet him for lunch to discuss the matter.

'Don't go falling in love with Cesario,' Sharon advised her daughter as she was being driven home, shooting Jess a troubled glance. 'It worries me that you will and then you'll get hurt…'

'As it won't be a real marriage I'm not going to fall for him,' Jess fielded with a sound of dismissive amusement, wondering if she had made a mistake in telling her mother the truth about Cesario's proposal of marriage.

'Don't you fool yourself. If you have a baby with the man, it'll be just as real as any other marriage,' her mother forecast ruefully. 'And I know you. You have a softer heart than you like to show.'

'I'm also almost thirty-one years old and I've never been in love in my life,' her daughter reminded her crisply.

'Only because you let that creep at university put you off men!' Sharon Martin retorted with an expressive grimace that recognised her daughter's sudden pallor and tension. 'Cesario is a very handsome guy and I think it would be easier for you than you think to lose your head over him. You'll be living together, sharing your lives, for goodness' sake!'

'But we won't be sharing anything but a desire to have a child,' Jess pronounced flatly, her cheekbones colouring as she made that point. She had told her mother everything and sworn her to silence for her father's sake. Robert Martin had swallowed the contrived story that Jess had been seeing Cesario on the quiet without telling anyone and he saw no reason why even a billionaire should not be bowled over by his beautiful daughter. 'Cesario made that quite clear, Mum. He likes his own space. He wants a child but that's the extent of it. He certainly doesn't want a wife who might get too comfortable in the role.'

'I know…it's a marriage of convenience, just like your dad and I made…'

'Not at all like you and Dad,' Jess protested firmly. 'Dad was in love with you, even if you didn't feel the same way at the time. That made a big difference. Cesario and I have already agreed to a divorce before we even get married.'

'It's not as easy to keep emotions out of things as you think it will be,' Sharon retorted, unconvinced by her daughter's arguments.

Jess watched her mother walk into her terraced house in the centre of the village before reversing her old Land Rover to drive over to Halston Hall and meet Cesario for lunch. Once Sharon Martin had adjusted to the shock of her daughter's confidences, which Jess had presented in a very positive way, she had gotten excited by the prospect of the wedding and the very fact that her beloved daughter was about to marry a very wealthy and influential man.

Jess drove past the public entrance to the extensive parkland that Cesario had thrown open to the public. It contained a lake, a playground he had had built at great expense, wooded walks and picnic spots. His tenants, employees and neighbours were free to stage events with permission in the grounds as well. It was ironic that a foreigner like Cesario di Silvestri had already done more for the community than the Dunn-Montgomery family had done in several centuries of having owned the great house. The man she was about to marry for the most practical of reasons had an admirably public-spirited side to his nature, she acknowledged reluctantly.

Aware that her heart was thumping so fast it left her breathless, Jess climbed out of her car and headed for the arched front doors of the hall. She was already running through a mental checklist. The engagement ring was in place, her hair tidy and she was dressed in an elegant pair of trousers teamed with a lace-edged grey cashmere twinset. All she lacked was a set of ladylike pearls and the thought made her grin. That morning she had barely recognised her reflection in the mirror. Being married to Cesario was going to be like taking on a new and taxing job with different rules from those she was accustomed to following.

Tommaso greeted her with his usual enthusiasm

and swept her through to a reception room a little less opulent than the drawing room.

'Jessica...' Cesario strolled towards her with the pure predatory grace that always contrived to draw her attention to the lean, well-balanced flow of his powerful body.

The instant her gaze found his lean, darkly handsome features she remembered the heat and taste of that wide sensual mouth on hers and hot pink warmed her cheekbones. He was too good-looking, way too good-looking, she thought in vexation, meeting dark deep-set golden eyes fringed by ebony lashes longer than her own. She felt as if a stream of liquid fire were slowly travelling from the tautening tips of her breasts down into her pelvis to create a pool of wicked waiting warmth there. It was an unnerving sensation and it overpowered her earlier sense of being in control.

Cesario ran his intent scrutiny over her petite figure, now enhanced by garments that actually fitted her delicate proportions; he was entranced by the beauty of her fine-boned face and the lush heaviness of the ebony curls now falling round her cheekbones. 'You look amazing...'

'I think that's a major exaggeration,' Jess told him awkwardly, hugely uncomfortable with the compliment.

'Not when you compare it to this,' Cesario remarked drily, lifting the newspaper lying on the coffee table to display the photo of her in muddy bespattered clothing and wellington boots. 'How can you let yourself be seen out and about looking like that?'

That question hit Jess like a slap in the face and she bridled, tipping her head back to stare at him. 'I had just spent three hours at a calving. The calf was dead but the mother just survived. I was filthy and exhausted—that's what my working day is like sometimes.'

'In your role as my future wife I will expect you to consider your image,' Cesario drawled as smoothly as though she had not spoken up in her own defence.

Jess's chin took on a defiant angle. 'I can't help it if a photographer lies in wait to catch me looking my worst. I couldn't care less about that sort of silly stuff.'

'We do not need to discuss this. The bottom line is that I will not accept you appearing in public looking like a tramp,' Cesario informed her in a tone of cold finality.

'Then we've got a big problem,' Jess countered, refusing to yield an inch of ground in the face of his unjust censure. 'My job is often dirty and I often have to work outdoors. I have no intention of giving my job up just so that I can always look like a perfect doll for your benefit.'

'I'm not asking you to look like a doll,' Cesario fielded in exasperation, marvelling that she could be so indifferent to appearing in print in such a state.

'Then how is it that after only three weeks of being engaged to you, I already feel like a dress-up doll? You seem to think I have nothing better to do with my time than shop or sit in a beauty salon enduring endless time-wasting treatments,' Jess condemned thinly, her grey eyes darkening with anger to the colour of steel, because she felt he was being most unfair when she had already obediently jumped through so many hoops to smarten up.

'Until I intervened you made no effort with your

appearance at all. A woman with healthy self-esteem wants to look her best,' Cesario contended grimly. 'What's wrong with yours?'

'The level of my self-esteem is none of your business!' Jess fielded flatly, her temper rising, as she was annoyed that he had noticed that she did not like her looks to attract attention. 'I'm just an ordinary working woman.'

'You work so many hours that you haven't got time to be a woman,' Cesario delivered, dark eyes gleaming gold with displeasure because she was refusing to accept his point of view. 'I had no idea how long a day you worked until I began phoning you. You're hardly ever at home and when you are you're chasing after those animals you keep. It's ridiculous.'

A flush of indignant disbelief slowly washing up over her face at that summary criticism, Jess shot him a furious look of resentment. 'You said you wanted an intelligent, independent woman but obviously you lied. My career is the most important thing in my life.'

'I thought your family was.'

The reminder sobered her but it also felt as though he were cracking a whip over her head to remind her of the terms of their agreement. Aggravated, she compressed her soft full lips. 'If you try to interfere with my job, this arrangement isn't going to work for either of us,' she warned him tautly. 'For goodness' sake, you said you'd want a divorce in a couple of years, so why should you try to hinder my career?'

'I also want a wife I see occasionally and you are rarely available in the evening or at weekends.'

'Do you know what the *real* problem here is? You

want a little wifey-slave who focuses only on her appearance and on you, a domestic goddess with nothing better to do with her time.'

'A boudoir goddess would be more my style, *piccola mia*,' Cesario derided with a sardonic smile. 'You're not being practical. At the very least, you'll have to reduce your hours of employment to a more acceptable level.'

'That's out of the question!'

'Perhaps while you remain a comparatively junior employee, but if you were to buy into the veterinary practice as a partner, you would have more control over the hours you work.'

At that unexpected suggestion, Jess rested stunned eyes on him. 'What on earth are you talking about?'

'I will buy you a partnership.'

'No...*no*, you will not!' Jess decreed in a shaking voice, so angry she barely trusted herself to speak. 'Stay away from the surgery and don't you dare meddle. My goodness, you're unbelievable! If you can't immediately have what you want you try to buy it!'

'When I see a problem I come up with a solution,' Cesario contradicted in a tone of ice-cased steel. 'And, right now, it is obvious that you have three options.'

'Three...*options*?' Jess parroted with wrathful emphasis.

'You allow me to purchase you a partnership, or you ask to work part-time hours *or* you quit altogether,' Cesario enumerated, watching her flinch in disbelief with an impassive countenance. 'Something has to give in your current schedule. At present there isn't room in it for a marriage, a husband and the conception of a child.'

'I agreed to marry you, not let you take over my entire life!' Jess snapped back at him in raw rampant incredulity. 'Or tell me what to do and what not to do!'

'*Madre di Dio*...take a deep breath, calm down and think about what I'm saying,' Cesario urged, stunned by the force of her fury. 'You will have to make changes.'

'No, I'm not about to listen to another bloody word of this nonsense!' Jess lashed back at him, more angry than she had ever been in her life and unable to tolerate his evident conviction that he now had the right to mess about with her career. Swivelling on her heel, she headed back to the door, prompted by some sixth-sense caution that warned her to get out before she lost her temper entirely.

'If you walk out in a tantrum, you needn't bother coming back,' Cesario pronounced with a chilling hauteur that hurt and stung as much as an ice burn. 'My cousin, Stefano, and his wife are waiting in the next room to meet you at lunch.'

Jess froze and gritted her teeth like a feral cat ready to hiss and snarl in attack. He had a knack no other man had ever equalled—he filled her to overflowing with pure rage. She knotted her hands into fists by her side, shocked by the tempest of fury gripping her and barely able to credit that she had been the most laid-back of personalities.

'I like to deal with potential pitfalls in advance,' Cesario asserted in soft and low continuance.

Just at that moment Jess imagined pushing him off the edge of a cliff and had the funniest suspicion that if he went over he would take her with him. She wondered in genuine horror how on earth she would ever live with him. Her narrow spine still turned to him, she breathed in slow and deep, praying for calm and composure while she reminded herself doggedly of all she stood to lose. And, embarrassingly, it was not her father's plight that came first to mind, it was the baby she had been trying to picture at dawn that morning. A little boy, a little girl; she didn't care as long as her baby was healthy. Her breathing began slowing in speed.

'Obviously I've taken you by surprise with this.'

Grey eyes still openly alight with hostility, Jess spun back to him. 'I live alone, I do as I like. I'm not used to anyone trying to limit me.'

A drumbeat of tension and reluctant arousal assailing him like an erotic pulse, Cesario studied her vivid and mutinous little face and marvelled that even those spiky defences of hers and the mud had contrived to keep her single and unattached for so long. For a few moments there, he had genuinely thought she would stalk out like a tigress breaking free of her cage. Her temperament was much more emotional and passionate than he had appreciated. It was a discovery that should have worried him but in reality it turned him on. Cesario was already beginning to learn the hard lesson that what he needed was not always what he wanted.

'But you will consider those options and make a decision,' he breathed huskily, unable to resist the suspicion that having got her metaphorically back into the cage again he was now deliberately provoking her.

The dark melting timbre of his accented drawl shimmied over Jess like a sudden disarming caress, awakening the awareness that she was accustomed to suppressing whenever he was in her radius. In severe discomfiture she shifted off one foot onto the other, but she still recognised the fullness of her breasts and the pinch as her nipples tightened followed by the dragging ache of longing between her legs. It was lust, just good old-fashioned lust, a natural and normal human prompting and not worth getting upset about, she told herself urgently. But that reassuring thought did not have quite the soothing effect she hoped it would because Cesario di Silvestri was the *only* man who had ever affected her that way. One look the first time she met him and she had burned, and the knowledge still infuriated her and intimidated her in his presence.

In a desperate effort to throw off the effect he was having on her Jess struggled to continue the conversation without giving ground. 'I'll think over what you've said.'

'And make a decision…'

'And you really want that decision right now, don't you?' Jess blasted back at him before she could stamp down her temper again. 'You're so ridiculously impatient!'

Cesario looked levelly back at her, his eyes very dark and uninformative below the shade of his lush lashes. 'We have a great deal to accomplish in a short space of time. I need your co-operation to do this.'

Mortified by her imperfect grip on her anger when he was as much in control as he had ever been, Jess nodded stiffly.

'You will obviously move your animal rescue operation to Halston as well.'

As Jess parted her lips in shock at that supposition,

which she had not even considered, Cesario dealt her a silencing appraisal. 'Nothing else would make sense. I assumed you would wish to retain that interest and I have already spoken to my estate manager.'

'Have you indeed?' Jess cut in before she could swallow back the hot, hasty words.

'Naturally. You could scarcely continue your work at a property several miles away and why should you want so inconvenient an arrangement? Land here will be put at your disposal and you may of course order custom-made buildings to house your charges. Naturally I will cover all the costs. I would also suggest the hire of at least one full-time employee.'

A choky little sound of incredulity escaped Jess and she viewed him with enraged silvery eyes. 'Anything else?'

'We will be staying in Italy for around six weeks after the wedding. You will need a trustworthy staff member to take care of your animals.'

Jess folded her arms with a defensive jerk because it was preferable to throwing something or walking out in what he had earlier clearly seen as a childish tantrum. He thought of everything. No corner of her life was to be safe from his interference and he was laying that on the line. He was in the driver's seat now, not her.

Cesario searched her taut face. The vibrations in the atmosphere were explosive. He wanted to skim his fingers through that wonderful hair, run a soothing hand across those rigid little shoulders and tell her that if she pleased him the sky was the limit, because there was virtually nothing he would not do for her, nothing he would not give. But that was not possible in the circumstances and might well have given her dangerous ideas. His inherent caution kept those spontaneous urges under control.

'Come and meet Stefano and his wife, Alice. They're my oldest friends,' Cesario murmured, a light hand at her spine guiding her across the hall towards the drawing room.

For an instant he paused and she looked questioningly up at his lean dark face, sexual awareness rolling in around her in an almost suffocating flood of impressions. The scent of his expensive cologne drifted into her nostrils. She loved the smell of it, had only to catch a whiff of that citrus-based aroma to think of him. His strong jaw line was slightly rough with dark stubble and her fingers tingled with the need to touch him. Her body hummed in readiness as though he had thrown a switch. Every time he got close her reaction was stronger and more unnerving. She wanted him to kiss her; she wanted him to kiss her so badly that not being kissed *hurt*.

'I know, *piccola mia*,' Cesario purred soft and low, brilliant eyes bronze with sensual appreciation, a slight catch in his low-pitched voice. 'But we have company for lunch.'

Jess wasn't quite sure she had actually *heard* that assurance, for it implied that he had known exactly how she was feeling and the suspicion appalled her. Her face was flushed when she entered the drawing room to find a stockily built, balding man in his thirties with lively brown eyes advancing on her. His wife was a tall, slender blonde, so eye-catchingly lovely that Jess found that she was staring.

'I've been really looking forward to meeting you,' Alice di Silvestri confided with a warm friendly smile, these first words revealing that she was American.

And Cesario curved an entire arm round Jess, who stiffened before appreciating that her role of happy bride-to-be had acquired its first audience and found that she was smiling back. She cast off the weight of anger, anxiety and stress that had until that instant been weighing her down and crushing her spirits. She had come through and survived far worse than a convenient marriage, she reminded herself with stubborn resolution. Nothing that Cesario could throw at her was likely to trip her up...

CHAPTER FIVE

'YOU look as pretty as a picture,' Robert Martin pronounced, a betraying brightness to his eyes as he admired Jess in her wedding gown from the lounge doorway.

Restive in her unusually feminine finery, Jess peered at her reflection in the hall mirror, noting that the make-up artist had done a heck of a job in giving her a youthful, dewy look, while the hairstylist had worked a miracle transforming her teeming curls into soft shiny ringlets that fell round her bare shoulders. A splendid diamond tiara worthy of a princess glittered against the dark backdrop of her hair, courtesy of Cesario, who had sent it with the information that it was a family heirloom. She smiled wryly at the memory, wondering if he had been afraid she might think it was a personal gift, because she cherished no such illusions about her bridegroom.

Cesario di Silvestri had no plans to bring anything personal into their relationship. Her bridegroom was ruthless, ferociously self-disciplined and clever. When it came to his track record with women, he might have a very well-documented and volatile libido but in spirit Jess believed he was essentially cold. He might want a child. But that child, she was convinced, would have to look to her for the warmth of human kindness and affection. Cesario planned his every move, foreseeing every difficulty and then judging how best to deal with it. He was a control freak, a demanding personality with very high standards and expectations. Nothing less than the best would satisfy him in any field, which begged the question, why was a man who could have married any number of rich, beautiful, society women settling for a country veterinary surgeon from a much more ordinary background?

Was her winning factor her sex appeal? Her cheeks warmed. Or was it because she had once said no and refused to see him again? Could any guy be that petty? She could not see herself as a femme fatale, but what else but her looks could have sustained his ongoing interest? Was it offensive to be that desirable to a man? She found it hard to think of sexual desirability as an accolade. After all, being a man's object of desire had once long ago almost cost Jess her life and she shivered, suddenly chilled by traumatic memories that she very rarely allowed herself to recall.

Her niece and nephew, Emma and Harry, four and five years old respectively, looked adorable and were the perfect antidote to her briefly dark thoughts. Emma wore a floral-print bridesmaid's dress, while Harry was smartly dressed as a pageboy. Their mother, Leondra, who had married Jess's youngest brother when she fell pregnant at eighteen, had agreed to act as a matron of honour, although she had complained bitterly over the lack of a hen night to mark the end of Jess's life as a single woman. Jess had not had the nerve to tell her sister-in-law that she was expecting to be single again sooner than anyone other than her clued-up mother might expect.

'If only *he* could see you now,' her father proclaimed in a fond undertone while Leondra was talking to her children. 'He would immediately regret never having known you.'

'I don't think so.' Unhappily reminded of a rejection that had cut her in two when she was only nineteen years old, Jess stiffened defensively. The identity crisis she had undergone during that troubled period in her life had taught her not to build fantasy castles in the air. *Better the devil you know than the devil you don't,* she chanted inwardly, because she had learned to be grateful for the years of love and care she had received from the father she had once taken for granted. She would have hugged the older man had she not been afraid of spoiling her make-up. Just for once, she wanted to look perfect. There was nothing wrong with her self-esteem, she reflected impatiently, she was simply determined to grace her beautiful gown at the altar. For her own benefit, *not* for Cesario's.

After all, some day she would be showing the photos that would be taken of the occasion to her child. She had to believe in that, had to keep her thoughts firmly fixed on that ultimate all-important goal of having a baby. At the end of the day, a child would be what really mattered. Only it would not quite cover the wedding night and how she felt about sharing that kind of intimacy with a man who didn't love her.

Her tummy flipped when she thought about Cesario seeing her scars for the first time. In her opinion they weren't *that* bad. There was the chance that given enough darkness he mightn't even notice them. On the other hand, this was a guy accustomed to some of the world's most beautiful women and in every other way he was very much a perfectionist. And she was, by no stretch of the imagination, perfect any more. Stifling the kernel of panic deep down inside her, she struggled to overcome the sudden fear that he might be repelled by her flawed body. Some people were repelled by scarring and they probably couldn't even help reacting that way. As the car arrived to take her to the church she suppressed the rolling tide of insecure thoughts threatening to engulf her. Instead she scolded herself and acknowledged the futility of looking for trouble in advance.

Her heart was beating like thunder when she looked at the packed pews of the little flower-bedecked church of Charlbury St Helens, which lay only a hundred yards away from her parents' home. Lack of space in the nave had meant restricting the number of guests able to see the ceremony. When she caught a glimpse of Cesario standing so tall, dark and straight at the altar, she found it hard to get oxygen into her lungs. And then suddenly and without any warning at all, and in a spirit of sharp regret, she found that she was wishing that her wedding were for real, an occasion where two people in love shared their vows for a shared and productive future. The unemotional exchange of needs that she had agreed with Cesario was on another plane entirely and just then she felt incredibly lonely. A surge of over-emotional tears stung the backs of her eyes.

'Your bride looks gorgeous,' Stefano remarked admiringly at his cousin's elbow.

And Cesario stopped playing it cool and turned to get his own view. He felt the word didn't stretch anywhere far enough to do justice to the vision of Jessica in the full-skirted sparkling gown with a corset bodice that moulded her slim curves and defined her tiny waist. So stunning was she with her light grey eyes shining, her soft mouth unusually tremulous and full and her heavy mass of hair falling below the tiara that he barely registered the aggravation of her arriving at the altar on the arm of the man who had let thieves into his house.

Jess met Cesario's brilliant dark eyes and experienced a sizzling sensation in her pelvis that was unnervingly similar to an electric shock. Breathing rapidly, she averted her attention from him and concentrated studiously on the middle-aged priest's opening preamble. The ceremony was short and familiar, similar to a number of friends' weddings she'd attended in recent years, but she still could not quite accept that *this* time she was the bride. Her hand shook a little when Cesario first grasped it and she stopped breathing altogether when he slid the slim band of gold onto her wedding finger. His handsome mouth brushed her cheek in a light salutation and then they walked down the aisle, guests beaming at them as though they had done something terribly clever. She remembered to smile for the benefit of the congregation, which, aside of her mother, had no idea that she was not a normal, happy bride.

'You look amazing in that dress, *mia bella*,' Cesario commented during the drive back to Halston Hall where the reception was being held.

'And I picked it all by myself.' Jess could not resist

letting him know. 'The stylist wanted me to wear something plainer and more formal.'

'You made the right choice.'

Relaxing a little, Jess sighed. 'With all this fuss going on around us, it's hard to remember that it's all fake.'

Cesario frowned. 'It is *not* fake,' he contradicted.

Fake, fake, fake! she wanted to shout at him in defiant disagreement, but, suspecting such a response would annoy him, she managed to resist the impulse.

'We are now husband and wife and we will live as such.' Cesario delivered his different opinion in a tone of powerful conviction.

But Jess was stubborn and hard to impress and she wrinkled her nose. 'A temporary marriage could never feel real,' she said quietly, thinking of the very long, wordy legal contract she'd had to sign a couple of weeks earlier before the marriage could go ahead.

This prenuptial contract had made it very clear that the marriage was more of a commercial arrangement than anything else. The terms of the eventual divorce had been laid out with equal clarity with regard to income, property and the custody and care of any child born to them. No woman who'd had to sign such a detailed document could have cherished any romantic illusions about the nature of the marriage she was about to enter.

Cesario set his white even teeth together. 'Talk of that variety is premature. We don't know as yet when our marriage will end. That's not the aspect you should be concentrating on right now.'

But Jess was no more eager to think about the mechanics of getting pregnant. What if it simply didn't happen? What a nightmare that would be! For a start, it was the only reason he was marrying her and, from her own point of view, it was the only feature that made the whole agreement supportable. She wouldn't think about her wedding night, instead she would think about the baby she was desperate to hold in her arms. Only she discovered as she stood in line to greet their guests in the Great Hall of the Elizabethan house that she could not wipe Cesario's starring role in that future development from her mind and her nervous tension began to mount again.

The exhausting day continued and, having had little practice as a social butterfly, Jess found it a strain to laugh and talk and smile continuously with strangers, many of whom were undoubtedly curious to see what was so special about her that she had managed to get a male of Cesario's reputation to the altar. If only they'd had access to the truth, she thought wryly, standing behind a door in a quiet corner when she finally managed to escape the crush for a few minutes. At least the meal, the speeches and the first dance were over, she reflected ruefully, grateful that the spotlight of attention was no longer on the bride and groom quite so much. She gulped down a glass of champagne in the hope that the alcohol would help her to feel a little more relaxed and light-hearted, for Cesario had already suggested twice that she 'loosen up'. Her natural shyness and reserve seemed to be a disadvantage around him.

'I can't believe that Alice is being *so* two-faced,' Jess heard a female voice state with perceptible scorn. 'I don't believe for a moment that she is really pleased that Cesario has finally found a wife.'

'Oh, neither do I,' agreed another. 'After all, Alice was once utterly crazy about Cesario and she only married Stefano because *he* adores *her.*'

'I can understand why she did it, though. She'd been with Cesario for two years, there was no sign of him making a commitment and she wasn't getting any younger. Don't forget she's a few years older than he is and she didn't waste any time in having children with Stefano.'

'I heard that Cesario was devastated when she walked out on him for his cousin.'

The other woman laughed in disbelief. 'Can you imagine Cesario being devastated over a woman? If he'd cared about Alice that much he'd have married her when he had the chance.'

'Most men would consider a woman like Alice a keeper.'

'As you can see by his choice of bride, though, Cesario is *not* most men,' her companion said scornfully. 'Granted she's got the looks, but nobody had ever heard of her before the invitations arrived.'

'Why would we have heard of her? She looks after his horses!'

Jess moved away from the doorway in haste before she could be seen. Looks after his horses indeed, she thought in exasperation, recalling her long years of study and training for her career in veterinary medicine. She had no reason, though, to disbelieve what she had innocently overheard and she was taken aback to learn that Alice and Cesario had once been lovers. An affair that Cesario allowed to last for two years must have been serious, although the beautiful blonde had somehow ended up married to his cousin instead. Even more surprisingly, that development did not appear to have damaged the friendship between the two men.

'Have a drink,' her mother urged, pressing a champagne glass into her daughter's nerveless hand. 'You hardly ate anything of the wedding breakfast and you are as white as a ghost.'

'I'm fine,' Jess asserted automatically, her eyes anxiously scanning the knots of people in search of Cesario's tall dark head.

Ironically he was on the dance floor with Alice, the two of them so busy talking that they were circling very slowly. Stefano was watching his wife and his cousin from the top table, a troubled expression etching lines to his face

'What's wrong?' Sharon Martin prompted, reading her daughter's tension easily.

Jess continued to watch Cesario and Alice while sharing what she had overheard.

'I knew it—I told you how hard it is to keep your emotions out of things.' Her mother sighed. 'You haven't been married to Cesario for five minutes yet and you're already getting jealous and suspicious!'

Jess turned a hot guilty pink. 'Of course I'm not! I'm only curious to know if what I heard is true.'

'So ignore the gossip and ask your bridegroom for the real story. If you don't make a major issue out of it, he'll probably be quite happy to tell you what really happened,' the older woman opined.

Jess knew that was sensible advice, but it was frustrating advice because she couldn't imagine questioning Cesario about something that personal. She returned to her seat at the top table and sipped her champagne, still longing for the real fizz of fun and optimism to magically infiltrate her bloodstream and lift her mood. Her boss, Charlie, came up to talk to her about the locum vet he had engaged to cover for her while she was in Italy. In the end, after much debate, she had not opted for a partnership at the practice, reluctant to own a rise in status that could only be attributable to Cesario's wealth and influence and concerned that such a move would only burden her with even more responsibility than she already had. Since there was only so much of her to go round, she had decided that working part-time would suit her changing circumstances better, allowing her to continue her career and keep abreast of new developments while allowing her more free time in which to meet Cesario's expectations and to work towards her ambition of having her animal sanctuary registered as a charity.

Charlie was moving away when a tall young man with dark curly hair approached her. She didn't remember him from the guest line-up and she was surprised when he asked her to dance, although she stood up with good grace.

'I don't think I remember meeting you earlier.'

'You won't. I've only just arrived with some friends for the evening party,' he told her cheerfully, reaching out a hand to clasp hers with relaxed courtesy. 'I'm Luke Dunn-Montgomery.'

He was a member of the family that had once owned Halston Hall. Jess felt her mouth fall open in surprise and she swiftly cloaked her gaze, although she could not resist subjecting him to one intense appraisal to satisfy her curiosity, for she knew by his name exactly whose son he was.

'Obviously, I know who you are,' Luke remarked once they were safely on the floor and the music had ground conveniently to a halt so that they could talk briefly. 'You're the cat that's not allowed out of the bag for fear that my father might lose votes for his youthful indiscretion with your mother...'

At that irreverent explanation for her birth father's refusal to acknowledge her existence, Jess lifted startled eyes to his. 'I didn't realise anyone else in your family even knew I existed.'

'I heard my parents arguing about you when I was a teenager,' he confided. 'My mother was furious when she found out that you existed.'

'I don't see why. I was born long before your parents married,' Jess pointed out tightly.

'Actually, they were dating at the time you were conceived,' Luke explained in a suitably lowered tone, his eyes dancing with rueful amusement. 'I was sworn to secrecy about you.'

'I didn't think I was that important,' Jess confided a touch bitterly when she cast her mind back to the cold reception she had received on the one and only occasion when she had tried to make the acquaintance of her birth father.

Currently a well-known member of parliament with a political career that meant a great deal to him, William Dunn-Montgomery had refused to have anything to do with the illegitimate daughter born to Sharon Martin while he was still a student. He had even had a solicitor's letter sent to Jess warning her to stay away from him and his family. It was as if she might be the carrier of some dread social disease, she recalled painfully. She marvelled that she had ever expected any warmer a welcome from the man when he had given her teenaged mother the cash to pay for an abortion and had then considered his responsibility discharged even after he learned that he had a daughter.

'I've always been madly curious about you—my only sibling,' Luke told her. 'My word, with that hair and those eyes you do look very like Dad's side of the family, although you're a little on the short side!'

At that quip, Jess glanced up at him, saw that he was tall and she grinned, her tension suddenly dissipating. He was her half-brother, after all, and she was pleased that he'd had the interest to attend her wedding and introduce himself to her. 'I didn't even know there were any Dunn-Montgomerys on the guest list.'

'Your bridegroom got to know my parents when he bought this place and my father's very proud of his extensive connections with the business world. I'm sure Father made a very polite excuse for his and Mother's non-attendance. I imagine he was very shocked when he realised who Cesario was marrying. It'll be a challenge for him to avoid you now.'

'Cesario doesn't know about my background,' Jess admitted. 'And I have no plans to tell him.'

'I can understand why you would prefer to keep quiet about my father.'

'Some secrets are better left buried. I don't see the point of treading on anyone's toes now.'

Luke took the hint and dropped the subject, walking her off the floor while happily answering all her questions. He had all the assurance of a much-loved only child and explained that, in the family tradition, he was a pupil barrister as his father and grandfather had been before him.

Cesario glanced over Alice's shoulder and saw Jessica with her tall male companion. His dark golden gaze zeroed in on his bride, noting the happy glow she exuded, and his eyes widened in surprise when she laughed, showing more animation than she had shown throughout the whole of her wedding day. That she liked the company she was in was obvious and he could see that she was chattering away. Cesario, who had never yet got his bride to chatter, stared and frowned, wondering who the young man was because he didn't recognise him.

Sharon intercepted her daughter to ask in a worried undertone, 'What were you talking about with Luke Dunn-Montgomery?'

Jess laughed. 'He knows about me and he couldn't have been friendlier.'

'His family won't like that,' her mother pronounced.

'That's not my problem,' Jess replied, reaching for another glass of champagne and registering that she felt remarkably buoyant.

'Watch out,' Sharon said anxiously nonetheless. 'It's safer not to get on the wrong side of people like that.'

'Times have changed, Mum. The Dunn-Montgomerys are not lords of the manor any more and the locals don't have to bow and curtsy when they pass by.'

And, at that moment, Luke reappeared at her elbow and insisted on being introduced to her mother before sweeping Jess off to meet his friends. The champagne had loosened her tongue and made her more of a social animal than usual. Luke's friends were fun and she was giggling like mad over a silly joke when Cesario approached their table, spoke to everyone with rather chilling dignity and anchored a hand that would not be denied to Jess's elbow to raise her from her seat and walk her away.

Bristling at that high-handed intervention, Jess shot him a reproving look. 'What was that all about?'

'It's time for us to bow out of the festivities.'

'But we aren't leaving for Italy until tomorrow morning,' Jess protested, realising belatedly as she glanced at her watch that time had moved on without her awareness and that, at what felt like very little warning, she was about to embark on her much-agonised-over wedding night.

'It's after midnight and our guests are beginning to leave, a fact that seems to have passed you by while you were flirting—'

'I'm not Cinderella.' Jess froze, facial muscles tightening, slight shoulders stiffening as Cesario herded her out to the magnificent main staircase. 'And I wasn't flirting!'

'You've been flirting like mad with Luke Dunn-Montgomery for the past hour! *Maledizione*! I could hear you laughing across the dance floor.'

On the wide first landing, Jess slung Cesario a furious look and the truth trembled on her lips, but she wouldn't let it loose. Why should she admit that Luke was her half-brother and that she was thrilled he had sought her out and treated her like a sister? She didn't owe Cesario any explanations. He might have married her but he wasn't entitled to her deepest secrets, particularly not the wounding or embarrassing ones. Cesario was from an aristocratic privileged background similar to her estranged birth father's and she cringed at the thought of admitting that she was the former squire's unacknowledged child by one of the village girls. Even if it was the truth, it sounded hideously, mortifyingly like something out of a nineteenth-century melodrama. And when she was already struggling under the humiliation of Robert Martin having been responsible for the loss of Cesario's valuable painting, and having had to admit to having loan-shark, jailbird relatives as well, was it really her duty to lower herself further in his estimation?

'To be truthful it was good to have something to laugh about today!' Jess tossed back cheekily, clutching the full skirts of her gown in impatient hands as she mounted the stairs and struggled to keep up with his long impatient stride. 'I've not been in much of a laughing mood recently.'

'Believe me, I've noticed!' With that ringing indictment, which any woman would have taken as a direct criticism, Cesario thrust wide the door of a big bedroom, furnished with atmospheric pieces of antique oak and a fire flickering in the grate to ward off the chill of the late spring night air.

Jess stared wide-eyed and disorientated at the room; she had never been upstairs in the hall before. The Tudor magnificence of her surroundings was in stark contrast to the contemporary décor that embellished the ground floor reception rooms that she had seen.

'What's that supposed to mean?' Her tone was truculent as she questioned his censorious comment, but then she was assailed by dizziness as her head began to swim. She caught at the doorknob with her hand and leant on it to steady herself on knees that momentarily had all the consistency of jelly. Perspiration broke out on her short upper lip as she straightened up, wondering in dismay if she might have been a little too free with the champagne cocktails on offer at Luke's table. Depending on how much she narrowed her eyes, the vast oak four-poster bed that dominated the room seemed to be shifting and changing position rather like a boat on the edge of a whirlpool.

'That, in spite of the fact that I've done everything possible to accommodate your needs, you have been a very sulky bride!' Cesario condemned, still picturing her glowing face as she sparkled as brightly as a Christmas tree ornament while she talked, giggled and smiled for that toyboy, Luke Dunn-Montgomery's, benefit.

'So, I'm human and imperfect and you're surprised at this discovery?' Jess fired back, stumbling slightly in her high heels as she moved away from the door. She pushed the door shut too hard and it slammed, very loudly, closed behind her, making him frown and wince. 'It isn't that easy to marry a stranger and contemplate living with him…although I guess with all the one-night stands you've had it will be no big deal for you!'

Indignation lanced through Cesario at that unnecessary comeback. He was not promiscuous and, although he was willing to acknowledge that he could be arrogant and demanding, he had made a genuine effort to make the terms of their marriage more attractive for her benefit. Not only had he arranged without her knowledge to have her six moth-eaten dogs microchipped and transported out to Italy for their honeymoon, he had controlled his aggressive instinct to intervene and call every shot. And he was very far from being impressed by the response that his generosity had so far won from her. 'You shouldn't believe the nonsense you read about me in the newspapers. I left one-night stands behind when I was a teenager.'

'What about Alice? When did you leave her behind?' Jess heard herself throw at him out of the blue, not even aware that she was about to hurl those nosy questions until the driven words emerged from her lips.

His ebony brows knit in excusable surprise at that sudden change of topic. 'Why are you asking about Alice?'

'I heard a couple of the guests talking...I understand that you and she were an item before she married your cousin.' Having opened the subject, Jess discovered that she could not make herself back off from it again. She wanted to know, she *needed* to know more.

'That's true.' His lean, darkly handsome features taking on a forbidding aspect, Cesario compressed his wide sensual mouth into a hard, inflexible line, his dark golden eyes screened. 'But it's not a good idea to listen to malicious gossip. The truth is that I put Alice through hell and it's a wonder that she stayed with me as long as she did. I didn't realise I loved her until she was gone and by then she was with Stefano and it was too late. I wouldn't have come between them. They're very happy together.'

As she listened Jess had slowly lost colour to pale and
stiffen with discomfiture. She was horribly conscious
that she had asked what she should not have asked and
learned what she would sooner not have known. He
had *loved* Alice, maybe still loved her, even though he
couldn't have her. In fact, wasn't he exactly the sort of
high-achieving Alpha male who would want a woman
who was out of his reach all the more? He had stepped
back and done the decent thing for Alice and Stefano's
sake. It was not an explanation that pleased her or
soothed her worries. But why did she have worries on
that score? Why should it matter to her if Cesario was
in love with a woman married to another man? That
was none of her business. Their cold-blooded marriage,
their *project*, was not based on emotional ties or expectations, she reminded herself ruefully. And if he was
emotionally bonded to another woman, that could well
be why he had decided that only the most practical of
marriages would meet his requirements.

'I wasn't sulky today,' Jess fielded belatedly, lifting
her skirts to kick off her shoes and sink her bare soles
gratefully flat onto the Persian rug below her feet. At
least that was what she intended to do but, somewhere
in the midst of removing the second shoe, which neces-
sitated her standing on one leg like a stork, she lost her
balance and lurched sideways, knocking an occasional
table and the floral arrangement on top of it flying in a
noisy, tumbled heap.

'You were sulky and you've had too much to drink
as well,' Cesario contradicted between gritted teeth of
disdain, striding forward to haul her up out of the debris

of dripping flower stalks and greenery while lifting the table back up with one impatient hand.

'Maybe I'm a little tipsy but I wasn't sulking,' Jess persisted in stubborn denial. 'If you knew me better you would know that I'm quite shy and not a chatterbox at the best of times. I don't like crowds much either and today has been a big strain.'

Cesario closed the distance between them and raked long brown impatient fingers through his cropped black hair, gazing down at her with a dark intensity that made her nerve endings pull taut with shockingly sexual awareness. 'I thought all women loved weddings?'

Her tummy performed a nervous somersault while the buds of her breasts swelled and lengthened. Hot-faced, Jess viewed him with huge silvery eyes. 'But I don't love you and now I'm in a bedroom alone with you and you're *expecting*—' Her voice cut off abruptly as though she had bitten back dangerously unguarded words rather than cause offence. 'Well, you're expecting what you've got every right to expect as a new husband and that's all I've been able to think about all day and—'

'I too, but not, I think, for the same reasons, *piccola mia*,' Cesario incised, his dark golden eyes hot and hungry on her tense oval face, his long, lean, powerful body taut as he swooped on the vase still leaking water and set it upright on the rug.

He closed a lean hand round her wrist to tug her closer. He felt the resistance in her slight frame and expelled his breath in a slow measured hiss. 'I don't want you when you're intoxicated and unwilling...'

So tense she could barely catch her breath, Jess gazed

back at him and despised herself for playing that card when the flickering obstinate heat of arousal was shimmying through her pelvis like a mocking touch. In a movement that took him as much by surprise as it took her she shifted up against him, stretched up on tiptoe and pressed her soft mouth to his.

A masculine hand curved to her hip to crush her against him. Her heart thumping feverishly fast, she gasped as he drove his tongue between her lips in a delving, erotic assault that set up a jangling response throughout her entire susceptible body. Suddenly she wanted him more than she had ever wanted anything in her life and with a hot, sweet longing that came dangerously close to an edge of pain.

'There will be other nights,' Cesario quipped, lifting his handsome dark head, his dark eyes sardonic, and setting her back from him before walking to the door.

Trembling, senses awakened and cruelly crushed again, Jess studied the space where he had been and thought what a disastrous note she had chosen to begin their relationship on. *I don't want you when you're intoxicated and unwilling...* She cringed, despising herself for not being tougher. She had signed up for the marriage and cheating didn't come naturally to her. It didn't matter if Cesario loved Alice. It didn't even matter if he was convinced that Jess was a sulky, uptight bride and a flirt at her own wedding. They had had an agreement and she had just welched on the deal, and nobody could have been harder on Jess than she was on herself while she finally struggled free of her gown, washed off all her fancy make-up and climbed into the big bed alone.

There she lay with her eyes wide open because whenever she tried to close them the room revolved behind her lowered eyelids in the most nauseating way...

CHAPTER SIX

ALMOST unrecognisable in a stylish white linen skirt and top teamed with a bright turquoise jacket, sunglasses anchored firmly on her nose, Jess boarded Cesario's luxurious private jet in teeming rain the following afternoon. He had left the hall that morning to fit in a business meeting in the City before his departure.

Jess was still suffering from a hellish hangover and she had barely slept during the previous night. At some point during those slow-passing hours she had grudgingly acknowledged the truth of Cesario's criticism of her mood the day before. She had got the dream dress, the gorgeous groom and the fabulous ceremony, but she had not got the love, the caring or the happy-ever-after that brides looked forward to receiving. As a result, disillusionment and a horrid sense of being trapped had dogged her throughout her wedding day. It was as though the true cost of marrying Cesario di Silvestri had only really hit home after she and he had made their vows. But she had made an agreement with him and she would stick to it from here on in, she assured herself fiercely.

Cesario stepped onto the jet, his keen gaze shooting

straight to the petite brunette seated in a comfortable tan leather upholstered seat. 'Jessica...'

Tensing, Jess looked up warily, worried about the reception she might receive after events the night before. 'Cesario...'

'I think we can do without the sunglasses,' he said wryly, with a nod in the direction of the rain streaming down the nearest porthole.

Jess breathed in deep and removed the tinted spectacles, knowing her eyelids were pink and puffy in spite of the make-up she had applied.

'And please let your hair down. I love your hair, *mia bella*,' Cesario confided as though that were the most normal thing in the world for him to say to her.

'It'll be a mess,' Jess warned him, pink warming her cheekbones. Wanting to match his generosity in not holding onto any spite, she reached up and dragged the band out of her hair so that her curls tumbled free to her shoulders. 'I couldn't be bothered to do anything at all with it today, which is why I put it up.'

At that frank admission a slanting grin curved his wide sensual mouth. He bent down and fluffed her mass of curls round her anxious face with gentle fingers. 'It doesn't need anything. It looks great just as it is,' he contended. 'I like the natural look.'

But Jess didn't think Cesario would recognise 'natural' unless it hit him in the face; he had probably never been exposed to the real thing. She suspected that more than one woman had gone to bed with Cesario fully made up and just as many had sneaked out of bed early the next day to 'brush up' before he got a first look at them. She had noticed the very high levels of grooming amongst the female wedding guests and had appreciated that just to pass muster in such company she would have to make much more effort than she was accustomed to with her appearance.

'About last night,' she began awkwardly.

'Forget about it. Today we start again—fresh page, open book,' Cesario pronounced smoothly, sinking down in the seat opposite her and buckling up for the take-off. She found herself covertly watching his every fluid movement. The smooth bronzed planes of his high cheekbones framed his straight, strong nose and the sensual perfection of his full-modelled mouth. By the time his lashes lifted to reveal his dark golden eyes as he tilted back his dark head to address the stewardess, Jess was staring helplessly: he was a heartstoppingly handsome man.

'Tell me about where we're going,' she urged, keen to find out about their destination and talk to him for a change.

'Collina Verde...it means "Green Hill". It's the country house where I spent my earliest years with my mother. It's in the hills above Pisa and very beautiful,' he murmured softly.

Jess recalled him telling her that he had grown up without a mother and scolded herself for having made no attempt to learn more about his background. After all, it was on the basis of such little nuggets of information that most relationships were built and life would be easier for both of them if she made the effort to be more interested. 'What happened to your mother?'

Cesario compressed his lips, his dark eyes taking on

a grim light. 'She died from an overdose when I was seven years old.'

Jess was taken aback by that uncompromising admission. 'That is so sad. It must've been very hard for you to handle that loss at such a young age.'

'I blamed my father. He had had a string of affairs and they were living apart by then,' Cesario mused wryly. 'But he had a great line in self-justification: he said it was in the blood and that I would be exactly the same.'

Jess was too craven and too tactful to dare to comment on that issue. 'What was it like for you when you had to live with your father instead?' she asked curiously.

His dark eyes gleamed like polished bronze and he gave her a wry half-smile. *Dio mio.* He wasn't cut out to be a family man any more than he was fit to be a husband. He resented being tied down. He was very competitive with me and it got worse as he aged and had to face that his youth was gone. Nothing I achieved was ever quite good enough.'

In recognising that he came from a much less happy and secure background than her own, Jess had plenty to think about during that flight. After a light early supper they landed in Pisa at the Galileo Galilei airport. Though it was by now early evening, it was a good deal warmer than it had been in London and the sun was still shining by the time the waiting limousine wafted them in air-conditioned comfort deep into the Tuscan landscape. She had expected lovely countryside but she sank into another dimension of appreciation entirely at her first glimpse of the most distant rolling hills and the serried green ranks of the grapevines, softened here and there by the silvery clouds of foliage that distinguished the olive groves. All the buildings, fashioned of pale apricot-coloured stone, seemed ancient and the medieval towns and villages on the hilltops were impossibly picturesque.

Collina Verde sat on top of a hill ringed by woodland, and although its sheer size made it imposing it was a less formal property than she had expected. A fortified farmhouse composed of several rambling buildings, it sat with its castellated roof below a blue and gold evening sky and enjoyed the most breathtakingly timeless view she had ever seen. She got out of the car, still entranced by the outlook of the mountains and the valley below, and enjoyed the light breeze that lifted her hair back from her brow and cooled her warm skin.

'It is lovely,' she remarked, and then a chorus of familiar barks sounded and she jerked round in disbelief to see her six dogs pelting frantically across the paved courtyard towards her in noisy welcome. 'My goodness, how on earth did they get here?' Her attention flipped to Cesario. 'You arranged this?' she queried in visible disbelief.

'With the help of your mother. I know you planned to leave them behind with your rescue animals and I'm sure they would have been well looked after but I know how attached to them you are,' Cesario advanced, considering himself to be well rewarded by the shining look of appreciation etched in her face.

'I'm just…stunned!' Jess confided, hunkering down to be engulfed in a wave of wet noses, scrabbling paws and noisy greetings.

Cesario had suspected that the white outfit would have a limited shelf life with his bride and his worst expectations were fully met by the time Jess straightened again to head for the front door, her pack of dogs prancing round her. Her skirt had acquired dusty paw prints and damp patches and her top was speckled with dog hairs but she gave him a huge smile that let him know that, while the designer wardrobe worth many thousands had failed to impress, his gesture in flying her pets out to Italy had won him his highest yet approval rating.

'I mean, I know you're not a doggy person,' Jess pointed out breathlessly. 'Which is why it was such a particularly kind and thoughtful thing to do—'

'And not what you expect from me, *piccola mia*?' Cesario completed silkily.

'Well, no, it wasn't,' Jess agreed without hesitation. 'But I was wrong.'

Cesario was honest enough to feel a shade guilty, for all he had done was issue instructions to his staff, who had taken care of all the official hassle required to transport the dogs abroad on pet passports.

'Hugs gets so upset when he doesn't see me,' Jess explained, fondling the nervous wolfhound's ears while it gazed up at her adoringly. 'And Magic gets frustrated when he can't communicate.'

Cesario frowned, studying the Scottish terrier currently playing dead on the ground with four paws stiffly extended so that his tummy could be tickled. 'How does he communicate?'

'He's deaf and the man I hired to look after the sanctuary didn't know any doggy sign language,' she proffered, making a signal with one hand that made the terrier roll over and sit up, his little black beady eyes pinned to her.

Cesario was impressed by the demonstration. 'I've never really had a pet. My father disliked animals,' he told her, curving a hand to her elbow to walk her into the house. 'The closest I ever came to it was having a horse.'

They stepped over the greyhound, already fast asleep in the lengthening shadows cast by the wall. Weed, the thin grey lurcher, pushed his long narrow face into Cesario's hand and Jess stared in surprise. 'My goodness, Weed must like you. Someone once treated him badly and he rarely approaches anyone for attention.'

Resisting the urge to snap his fingers in dismissal of such notice, Cesario entered his Italian home with Weed sticking as close to him as a shadow. His housekeeper, Agostina, welcomed them all indoors, and as soon as introductions were over Jess surrendered to curiosity and wandered straight off alone for a tour. It was an atmospheric house, gently aged and respected and full of charm. Worn terracotta tiles that gleamed stretched underfoot, while wooden ceilings vaulted above big airy rooms furnished with light and colourful drapes, comfortable sofas and plain pieces of solid country furniture. A series of tall narrow doors stood wide open onto a terrace overlooking the valley and a table and chairs sat in the inviting shade of a big chestnut tree.

Pausing only to instruct the dogs to stay and not to follow her, Jess headed up the stairs. Their luggage had been parked in two different rooms, she noted, unsure whether she was pleased or not with the boundary that was being acknowledged. Business, not pleasure, she told herself resolutely, but it was an unfortunate thought, for she did not like to think that her body had anything to do with a business agreement. Seeking a distraction, she peered into the first of a set of magnificent marble bathrooms fitted out in opulent contemporary style. She took off her jacket and walked out onto a wrought iron balcony to enjoy the view.

'You will have to be careful not to get sunburned in this climate,' Cesario remarked, making her jump, for she had not heard his approach.

Jess swivelled round. 'It's an absolutely gorgeous house,' she told him with enthusiasm.

An indolent smile curved his darkly handsome lips. 'I'm glad we can agree on that. I had it updated last year and it is the perfect spot for a honeymoon.'

The colour of awareness flickered into her cheeks and he stretched out lean brown hands to clasp both of hers and ease her closer.

'Honeymoon…honeymoon…honeymoon,' he rhymed teasingly. 'It doesn't take much to make you blush, *moglie mia*.'

The setting sun cast still-heated rays on her skin, but not as hot and overwhelming as the hungry seal of his mouth over hers in a passionate kiss. The world went into a tailspin as the slow pulsating throb of arousal travelled all the way through her responsive body. Her nerve endings leapt, making every inch of her deliciously sensitive, so that even the hand he smoothed across the swell of her bottom was a source of pleasure and her legs shook beneath her.

His broad chest rising and falling and his breathing

fractured, Cesario gazed down at her rapt face, his dark eyes smouldering hot gold. 'I won't take anything for granted with you—yes or no?'

And Jess liked that he had still thought to ask the question. He was tugging her indoors out of the fading light and she blinked, long lashes sliding almost languorously up on her light grey eyes and there was no hint of reluctance there. Desire had dug unshakeable little talon claws into her, vanquishing the fear and uncertainty. Her body wanted to connect with his again and strain towards that distant source of satisfaction she sensed.

'Yes,' she told him shakily.

'Sì...your very first word in Italian, *moglie mia*.'

'Sì...but tell me what you are calling me,' she demanded as he drew her back to the bed.

'My wife,' Cesario translated with assurance, 'which you are.'

For some unfathomable reason, that was the first time Jess felt truly married. Those words achieved what the pomp and ceremony of the wedding day had not. She smiled, allowing herself to enjoy the warm hum of arousal in her pelvis. She refused to think about her scars, telling herself instead that most people had things they disliked about their bodies and that she was no different. So, she stood quiescent while he removed the linen top to reveal a pretty white and blue bra and then she moved forward and began without hesitation to unbutton his shirt. Her hands grew a little less dexterous as the edges of the shirt fell open to reveal the hair-roughened bronzed flesh beneath.

In acknowledgement of that wave of shyness, Cesario

tipped up her chin and crushed her raspberry-tinted mouth below his again, revelling in the sweet strength of her response and the way her fingers dug hard into his muscular shoulders. He kissed her and then he kissed her again, skilfully tasting the voluptuous curve of her lips and the honeyed secret corners of her tender mouth and still he wanted more, wanted everything she had to give with a raw edge to his hunger that was refreshingly new to him. She trembled against him, enslaved by the sexual probe of his tongue darting inside her mouth and the urgent masculine erection she recognised when his hand closed to her hip to crush her against his big powerful frame. Her whole body rejoiced in the effect she was having on him.

As he released the zip on her skirt and it pooled round her feet Cesario lifted her clear of its folds and brought her down on the big wide divan bed crisply dressed in linen. Before he removed his hand he brushed the roughness of the skin on her back and he glanced down in surprise at the long pale scar there.

'Did you have surgery there?' he asked.

Jess froze and angled away from him to present him with a defensive spine, only now his attention was fully engaged and he saw the furrow of scar tissue marring the pale skin and he touched it with his finger.

'Per l'amor di Dio,' Cesario exclaimed in surprise. 'What the hell happened to you?'

Jess flipped back to him and lay flat. She pressed two fingers to the final scar on her midriff and said fiercely, 'You missed one!'

Cesario focused on that final pale line cruelly bisecting her creamy skin. 'Those must surely have been life-threatening injuries?' he breathed starkly, black brows pleated as he studied her with questioning dark eyes that for once had no gleam of mockery.

'A…knife attack while I was at university. I almost bled to death,' Jess responded jerkily, and then she folded her lips closed and stared at him and in the depths of her pale glittering eyes he saw her fear that he would persist in his questions.

Cesario contrived to shrug a broad shoulder as though he saw knife wounds on his lovers every day and he half turned away to remove his shirt and kick off his shoes. His expressive gaze was veiled to conceal the true strength of his reaction from her because he was enraged by the image of her being slashed by a knife and helpless. She was so small, so feminine, but maybe those traits had made her a more appealing target, he reflected with grim cynicism.

'Sorry, I just don't like to talk about it,' she said unevenly, one hand curling into a fist on the sheet as if even saying that much was a major challenge. 'Maybe I should've warned you—I know my scars are ugly…'

Having shed his trousers, Cesario came down on the bed beside her and bent his tousled dark head to the scar on her abdomen. Her heart hammered with tension, butterflies fluttering loose in her tummy as he pressed his mouth gently to the slightly puckered skin. 'Not ugly, just part of you. I'm sorry you suffered an experience like that and I certainly didn't need warning, *piccola mia*.'

He was rarely at a loss for the right thing to say, she thought enviously, only half convinced by his words and gesture that he was not repelled, but the worst of her tension had evaporated. The ferocious tightness of her muscles eased and she rested her head back on the pillow and breathed again. 'You see, I'm really not a perfect doll.'

'You're talking to a guy who wanted you even when you sported a dirty waxed jacket, muddy boots and a team of misfit dogs,' Cesario reminded her lazily.

'I'm surprised you didn't have the dogs booked into the local beauty spa for some grooming,' Jess teased, balancing on her elbows to stretch up and tilt her parted lips in invitation as though a piece of elastic were pulling her to him to rediscover that warm, sexy mouth of his for herself again.

And that next kiss ravished and seduced and left her dizzy and breathless, wondering where he had been all her life, for no other man had ever made her feel that way. She was already finding out that Cesario was not the guy she had believed him to be. He had much greater depth than she had ever been willing to concede when she reflected on their often spiky exchanges in the stable yard. She had repeatedly failed to look beyond the rich sophisticated façade to the male beneath that glossy patina of worldly success.

Her bra melted away during the kissing and, while he palmed the small pert mound of her breasts, he stroked her pointed nipples and captured them between his lips and sucked until the tingling buds were hard and swollen. Until then, she had not known that she might be so sensitive there. He caressed her until she was gasping for breath and a pool of liquid warmth had infiltrated her pelvis.

'I want this to be really special for you,' Cesario husked. 'But it might hurt.'

'So, get it over with,' she urged apprehensively.

Cesario gave her a wicked grin that squeezed her heart inside her chest. 'Shame on you—that's the wrong attitude to take. A good lover never rushes a woman.'

He tugged up her legs and skimmed off the white and blue matching knickers, sliding a hand between her slender thighs to find the engorged bud below the black curls on her mound. He teased her with the ball of his thumb and her hips rose off the bed in sensual shock at the sweet erotic surge of arousal. It was almost too intense for her to bear and she was hugely conscious of the surge of moisture there.

Cesario pulled back from her and she studied him with sensually lowered eyelids, taking in the hard sleek contours of his broad chest and the muscles flexing across his flat stomach as he leant back and removed his boxers. He was magnificent and more than a little daunting to inexperienced eyes. He pulled her back to him and studied her with a hint of amusement in his beautiful eyes. 'I promise to be gentle,' he intoned, carrying her hand down to his bold shaft and encouraging her to explore his dimensions.

Her hand closed round him, for she was full of desire and curiosity, and she learned that he was strong and smooth, velvet over steel. Answering heat flowered between her legs so that when he took her mouth again with hungry urgency she more than reciprocated the feeling. He began to explore her most secret and responsive flesh, tracing the delicate folds, teasing the nub of her desire and then the damp little entrance. It wasn't long before little whimpers of sound were escaping her throat, the strength of her wanting making her legs tremble while the unbearable craving and the ache at the heart of her grew stronger by the second. She had not known that anything could feel that powerful and least of all that it might be him who introduced her to the powerfully addictive force of desire.

He taught her to want what she had never learned to want, only wondered about, what she had truly believed she might go to her grave without experiencing, and she had honestly thought that it wouldn't matter because she wasn't really missing anything important. So he taught her differently, stroking her with skilful fingers, licking at the wildly sensitive buds of her nipples while he surely, gently prepared her for the ultimate pleasure. But the yearning inside her for more steadily grew intolerable, sharp-edged, greedy and impatient so that she bit in impatient reproach at his lower lip and let her trembling fingers close tight into his luxuriant black hair.

Fluid and strong, he came over her, sliding between her thighs when she was shaking and desperate with pent-up need. She was wildly eager for that first gentle thrust, feeling the stretch of her inner tissue struggling to contain him and then the surge of his hips against her as he drove deeper. It hurt a little more than she had expected and she could not suppress a cry of pain. Instantly he stopped, gazing down at her with those drowningly dark and golden eyes of his that were so beautiful they made her ache.

'I'm sorry, *moglie mia*,' he whispered, brushing her

tumbled curls from her brow to press a benediction of a kiss there. 'It will ease...I hope.'

Her inner muscles tightened round him and he groaned with an uninhibited sensuality that thrilled her and he shifted lightly, slowly, sinking into her by erotic degrees until she didn't know where he ended and she began. But it was an overpoweringly good feeling and she moved sinuously beneath him, angling up her hips to encourage him, all discomfort forgotten. As he withdrew and came back into her, her excitement began to build. Excitement laced with deep, deep pleasure at the motion of him in her and over her. His slow, steady rhythm ensured that the tight feeling low in her pelvis began to expand and spread outward, sucking her into a vortex of intense driving sensation. And then without even knowing where she was going and simply blindly allowing the force of her response to carry her with it, she reached a peak and the incredible waves of pleasure gathered her up and threw her down again on the other side. In a daze she floated back to earth again.

Cesario was watching her with dark, dark eyes when she recovered her senses again and his hand was closed over one of hers, his body hot and damp and intimately masculine against her thigh. She looked back at him with light eyes that still reflected some of her wonderment at what had just transpired. His strong jaw line squared.

'Don't look at me like that. Don't forget our agreement,' he breathed suddenly, his keen gaze narrowed on her feverishly flushed face. 'I didn't ask for your love and I don't want it. We will share a bed, nothing more, until a child is born, *piccola mia*.'

It was like an unanticipated slap in the face for Jess and she went straight into shock, recognising that he, of all men, would recognise when a woman might be getting a little too attached, a little too serious. Her facial muscles tightened, her expression carefully schooled to blankness as a wave of anger and pain broke inside her like a tide crashing on the shore. She would not give him the satisfaction of knowing that he had hit pay-dirt with that cold-blooded warning. She would not respond with the angry resentment that would reveal that he had wounded her.

'I don't have love to give you,' Jess fielded flatly as she deliberately shifted away from him, rejecting that deceptive togetherness for the pretence that it so clearly was. 'I love my family and my pets and some day I will love my child, but I'm afraid that's it. I am a very sensible person when it comes to my emotions.'

A slight darkening of skin tone over his cheekbones hinted that she might have touched him on the raw. He screened his gaze and murmured levelly, 'I just don't want you to be hurt.'

'I'm strong, much stronger than you seem to think,' Jess countered, and then, in a tone of polite enquiry calculated to underline that declaration for his benefit, 'Are you staying here for the night? Or do we sleep separately?'

Cesario sat up as though she had elbowed him in the ribs. 'My room is next door.'

'Goodnight,' Jess told him sweetly.

'*Buone notte, ben dorme*...sleep well,' he breathed, springing out of the bed, pausing only to pick up his clothes before he vanished through the connecting door.

Sleep well? Jess might almost have laughed at that piece of advice until she cried. She freshened up with a shower in the superb adjoining bathroom, went downstairs briefly to take care of her dogs and then finally crawled back into bed, the slight persistent ache at the very heart of her as much a reminder of what had changed in her life as the lingering scent of his cologne and his body on the pillow beside hers. Breathing that aroma in, she groaned out loud and shut him out of her head.

Her thoughts came in a kind of vague shorthand because she was blocking out so much of what she was feeling and denying the pained sense of loneliness, loss and rejection she was experiencing. Her husband had introduced her to sex. He was good at sex and she was very lucky that that was so, she told herself determinedly. He had tried to pretend that theirs was a normal marriage but he had lied. He didn't want her to care about him. But she was a proud and clever woman and she would respect his warning. She would not make the foolish mistake of falling in love with a man who'd made it clear from the outset that he could never love her back...

She also wondered dully if it was true that he was still in love with Alice. That would give him a very good reason to make a marriage of convenience in an effort to produce the heir he required to gain legal title to his family home. If he was already in love with another woman, a businesslike arrangement was his only real hope.

Jess told herself that it made no odds to her whether or not Cesario loved another woman. Such subtleties, such secrets, were beyond her remit and immaterial in terms of a marriage already openly acknowledged to be one of pure practicality. Why should she give a hoot if he cherished another woman in his heart? On that challenging thought, sheer mental and physical exhaustion dragged Jess down into a deep, dreamless sleep…

CHAPTER SEVEN

CESARIO was suffering from an appalling headache. He had taken his medication but it had yet to kick in. Actually, he wanted a drink, but knew that alcohol was a bad idea with powerful painkillers. He massaged his brow and tried to loosen his taut neck muscles while studiously endeavouring to suppress all the negative thoughts threatening his equilibrium. He had been warned about headaches and this was as bad as he had been promised: so far, so normal...

He knew his bride thought that he was a cold, callous bastard, but he had said what he'd had to say and drawn a necessary line in the sand. He didn't want her on his conscience. He didn't want to hurt her either. It struck him as strange that he had not foreseen that possibility *before* he married her. Was he really so single-minded and selfish that he had not considered the damage he might inflict? Evidently, he was.

Determined to stay grounded, he reminded himself that the marriage was a project, a business agreement and little more. His bride might seem vulnerable and naïve, but it would be unwise to overlook the fact that he had paid a fat price for her services when he accepted the loss of that painting and dropped the chance to prosecute her father. And obviously he wanted Jessica to find pleasure in his bed, since it might well take months for a conception to take place. The big seduction scene that he had unintentionally staged could only have been motivated by subconscious common sense, he reasoned grimly. It was then that he got himself the stiff drink he knew he shouldn't have and still lay awake until dawn broke the skies.

The following morning Jessica awoke to the chink of china rattling and sat up to be served breakfast in bed on a tray complete with a linen napkin and a pretty flower in a bud vase. So, *this* was what it was like to be spoiled, she thought ruefully, pushing her wild tumble of black curls out of her eyes as the smiling maid chattering in broken English opened the curtains and threw open the doors onto the balcony, inviting in fresh air and sunshine. Jess discovered that she was ravenous and she washed down pancakes and fresh fruit with juice and cappuccino coffee.

A slim figure in floral shorts and an emerald green T-shirt, her black curls bouncing on her shoulders, she descended the stairs. A door stood open wide onto a rear courtyard and, with a hail of excited barks and yelps, her doggy posse came charging through it. All her pets, with the exception of Weed, were present, and as she straightened from her greeting session Cesario appeared in a doorway, Weed lurking shyly to one side of him.

Self-conscious, Jess tensed and tried not to stare but it was a tough challenge. Cesario was less formally clad than she had ever seen him, in a casual shirt that clung to his wide shoulders and powerful chest and linen trousers that accentuated the long muscular strength of his legs and the lean tautness of his hips. But while informal it was still cutting-edge Italian designer style he sported, and his ruffled black hair and the shadow of stubble round his handsome mouth only roughened the edges of his usual perfect grooming to ensure that he looked even more masculine and sexy than he normally did.

Her mouth ran dry, the colour in her cheeks heightening as she briefly relived the intensity of her pleasure with him the night before and her tummy flipped, her legs trembling below her.

'Where have you been, Weed?' she asked her stray pet, concentrating her attention on him because it was safer than focusing too much on the sleek predator by his side.

'He just wandered in and went to sleep under my desk,' Cesario told her with a shrug that disclaimed all responsibility for the development.

'My goodness, you start work early! I'd better go and feed the dogs...'

'They've already been fed. I employ a dog handler in my security team and he's been taking care of the practicalities.'

Taken aback by that assurance, Jess gave him a disarmingly natural grin. 'I can't get over the novelty of having people do things for me—I mean, breakfast in bed, what a treat!'

'Every day can be a treat for you now,' Cesario murmured, enchanted against his will by that sudden flashing smile that lit up her oval face. During the night he had thought about the knife attack she had mentioned.

Belatedly recalling what had surely been a defensive wound on her hand, he had wanted to know the whole story, but he was reluctant to risk traumatising her by asking her to satisfy his curiosity. She had said she might have died and then he would *never* have known her. His lean strong face shadowed as he forced that gloomy thought out.

'No, I don't like being spoiled. I'm not helpless and I'm too used to doing things for myself,' Jess fielded briskly, suddenly wanting and needing to hold onto what was familiar lest her life become subsumed entirely by his.

'You're on your honeymoon.'

Her nose wrinkled. 'Call it a holiday, not a honeymoon. By no stretch of the imagination could we be like a honeymoon couple,' she pointed out drily.

'What I said last night wasn't meant to offend you,' Cesario drawled. 'It was intended to—'

'Save you the hassle of dealing with a lovesick bride who wants to hang onto you a few months down the road?' Jess trilled quick as a flash. 'Relax, that's not going to happen. I'll be looking forward to getting my freedom and my own life back.'

For a split second Cesario looked as though he might have been about to argue with that assessment, but then he closed his handsome mouth, watching her with screened liquid dark eyes that gave away nothing. Jess, however, had few illusions about the warning she had received the night before. The very fact she was still a virgin had probably given him commitment-phobia. She was, after all, dealing with a man accustomed to women who fell madly in love with him and his lifestyle and then were reluctant to let go of him and the luxury again. But she had no intention of becoming one of that undistinguished crowd. Jess had fought many a fight against poor odds in her life and had emerged triumphant. There was nothing of the loser in her genes. Hopefully she would walk away from Cesario di Silvestri with a child, but only because that was her choice as well as his, she told herself fiercely.

'So, how do we spend the first day of this holiday?' Jess enquired brightly.

Cesario slung her a wicked grin full of sexuality and fantasy, his dark golden eyes dancing with amusement, and hot pink drenched her cheeks.

'Okay...' Jess conceded between gritted teeth. 'But in between times I want to see Tuscany.'

'Your wish is my command, *delizia mia*.'

'Again?' Cesario husked as a slim hand wandered across his hair-roughened thigh with an intent he knew all too well only to discover that he was ahead of her and already primed and ready for another bout of lovemaking. Being with a woman who wanted him as much as he wanted her, he had discovered as the days of their honeymoon had unfolded, was a very invigorating experience.

This particular day, though, had started off on a purely cultural note with a trip to the beguiling hilltop town of San Gimignano, dominated by its thirteen medieval towers. Cool as a spring flower in a pale blue skirt and white lace top, Jess had admired the Ghirlandaio frescoes in the Renaissance chapel of Santa Fina and she had succumbed to highly infectious giggles when

Cesario compared her profile to one on the wall. They had enjoyed a leisurely lunch in a thirteenth-century town house followed by vintage wine served in the piazza. There, slowly but surely, intelligent conversation had faltered as their eyes had met and other rather more basic instincts had taken over.

But it was Jess who had taken Cesario by surprise when she had ultimately leant across the table to whisper feverishly, 'Get us a room...'

They had barely made it through the door of the airy tower room of a nearby hotel he had hurriedly taken for them before, still almost fully clothed, they were enjoying each other up against the wall with a scorching raw-edged passion that Cesario had never before dared to unleash on a woman. The looks they had shared in the piazza over the wine had acted as the most arousing session of foreplay he had ever experienced. Even now, lying naked and bronzed in a tangle of sheets, he was still reliving the hot, tight, wet seal of her body round his and the gasping sounds of unashamed pleasure that had rung in his ears even as she tried to stifle them for fear of being overheard. He had already had her three times and he knew it would not be the last time that day. As those delicate fingers of hers enclosed his bold erection and she lowered her luscious mouth to caress him, Cesario just lay back and closed his eyes, literally drunk on pleasure. Being married was turning out to be a whole lot more enthralling than he had ever dared to hope.

Jess loved to plunge Cesario into that rich well of sensuality where she held sway. It was a power-play, a runaway triumph for a woman who had been a virgin a mere six weeks earlier and pretty ignorant of what it took to be an equal bed partner. But that aside, touching Cesario, making love with Cesario, just *being* with Cesario was also the biggest source of pleasure Jess had ever known. Telling herself that it should not be that way hadn't worked as a defence against feeling things she knew she shouldn't be feeling with him. Only in the realm of sex and physical expression could she let her barriers down, freely showering him with the physical hunger he ignited and sealing her mouth and her mind shut on the thoughts and the emotions that accompanied the desire.

Sharon Martin had spoken wisely when she'd warned her daughter that it wouldn't be easy to live with a man without her emotions getting involved. But Jess didn't blame herself for failing to maintain her defences, she blamed Cesario for transforming himself into the perfect new husband, a fabulous lover and all-round fantastic companion, whom pretty much any woman would have found irresistible.

In the aftermath of yet another session of hot, satisfying sex, Jess lay with her heart racing and her body aching in the circle of Cesario's arms. He was still holding her, stroking her spine, his mouth gently brushing her temples. He was doing that fake caring thing again and part of her wanted to slap him for it. She had tumbled headlong in love with him but she still had her brain and she didn't need the pretences, didn't want them. It was just sex they shared and she could handle that reality—she had never been a coward when it came to the hard realities of life!

'Sex with you sizzles every time,' Cesario told her appreciatively. 'You could make me monogamous.'

Her grey eyes flashed silver and she lifted her head. 'If I thought for one minute that you would stray while I was still living with you, I would probably kill you!' she swore shakily, passion betraying her.

Cesario stretched back against the pillows with predatory grace and no small amount of male satisfaction at what he took as a compliment. 'I do believe you would, *moglie mia*. You're not the sort of woman any man would dare to take for granted.'

'I'm not a proper wife…don't talk as though I am!' Jess warned him waspishly. 'A proper wife wouldn't drag you off to a bedroom in the middle of the day and shag you half to death…'

Cesario shifted again and grinned wickedly like the cat who'd got the cream while he curved a strong arm round her to hold her close. 'The wife of my dreams certainly would…'

'I'm not the wife of your dreams either.' Her fingers spreading defensively across his hair-roughened pectorals as she lay against him, Jess could hear the flat note in her delivery and prayed that he couldn't.

Jess was fully convinced that Alice, the beautiful American former fashion model married to Stefano, would have been the true wife of Cesario's dreams. Alice and Stefano and their two gorgeous little boys lived only a few miles away from Collina Verde and they were regular visitors. While the men had happily talked politics, business and the intricacies of producing award-winning wines, Jess and Alice had got to know each other. Jess genuinely liked Alice and admired her talent as an amateur artist. But she was also always painfully aware of Alice's extensive list of appealing traits. Alice was gentle and kind, a shining example of a woman who was as lovely on the inside as she was on the outside, and Jess was convinced that no man who had lost a woman of Alice's worth could have easily recovered from the experience and moved on. She was not surprised that Cesario had once loved Alice or that Alice and Cesario remained very close. Jess had yet to see anything she could object to in their behaviour but in their presence she was always conscious of how well they knew each other and of how new her own relationship with Cesario truly was. It was a struggle not to be jealous of his bond with the other woman.

As Jess shifted her hand down to his flat, hard stomach Cesario closed his fingers over hers and his thumb smoothed gently and consideringly over the scar on her hand, his lean, powerful body tensing in response. 'Tell me who did this to you,' he urged tautly. 'I need to know what happened to you.'

After a moment of silence, Jess slowly released her breath in a rueful sigh. 'I attracted the attentions of a stalker in my first year at university. An unemployed loner whom, as far as I know, I'd never actually met or even spoken to,' she explained reluctantly. 'When the police showed me his photo after the attack it was a challenge to even recognise him—'

'A stalker?' Cesario was already frowning. 'I assumed you'd been the victim of some random robbery.'

'There was nothing random about it and no theft involved. I began getting cards and little gifts in my accommodation mailbox and I had no idea who they were on British television made her raise her brows. 'I didn't even know that you and she—'

'We didn't—she was always drunk. A couple of casual dates and I'd had enough of her falling out of chairs, cars and doorways!'

'But my opinion of you wasn't formed by anything I read in the newspapers,' Jess confided, giving him a deliberately mysterious glance that was pure provocation. 'To be honest, I had a source of information much closer to home.'

'Who?'

'I'm not telling.' Throwing back the sheet, Jess pulled playfully free of his hold and slid off the bed. 'Just for once I'm going to grab the first shower.'

'I'm feeling lazy. We could stay here tonight, dine out and go home tomorrow. It is our last week.'

'I would love that.' Padding into the compact en suite bathroom, Jess was ridiculously pleased that he appeared to be as aware as she was that their honeymoon idyll was almost at an end. It touched her that he was keen to make the most of what time was left.

If she had not known that they had married simply to conceive a child, she would have described the last six weeks they had shared as a magical time of discovery and joy. As it was, she knew she had to keep her feet firmly pinned on the ground and pour cold water on her more fanciful thoughts and reactions for, within days, she would be returning to England, her job and usual routine. And since she was beginning to suspect that she might already have conceived she was wondering just how much she could hope to see of Cesario in the future.

Did he too suspect that she might have conceived? Had he noticed that her menstrual cycle had not once kicked in since they'd became lovers? Surely he must have noticed even though he hadn't said anything? Perhaps she should visit the local doctor when they got back to Collina Verde. Could it have happened so fast? Her face warmed as she towelled herself dry and stood back to allow him access to the shower. They had had sex a lot. Some days they had barely got out of bed. And even now she could hardly keep her hands off him. It shocked her how much she craved him, how often they could make love and for how little time that fierce hot arrow of desire would remain satisfied. So, it was not beyond the bounds of belief that she might already have fallen pregnant. She was excited and apprehensive— excited at the prospect of a baby, but apprehensive that conception would mean the end of all intimacy between her and Cesario. After all, once a baby was officially on the way, their 'project' would be complete and there would no longer be a reason for them even to live below the same roof.

From the bedroom window, she looked out over the textured terracotta roofs that lent such warmth and colour to the panoramic view of the old town as the medieval houses beneath them stepped down the hillside. Her memory served up cherished images of the relationship they had created between them. He had bought her a gilded image of a saint in the market at Castelnuovo di Garfagnana, which he had insisted reminded him of her. She thought the resemblance was in his imagination alone. Possibly that was the first thing he had said and done that he should *not* have in the first forty eight hours of their stay in Italy, she mused unhappily. There was no room for such frills and fancies in a practical marriage of convenience.

But then there had been very little practical about the experiences they had shared. In the tour of Tuscany that Cesario had treated her to, he had walked hand in hand with her like a lover through winding streets and alleyways, happy to shop in tiny traditional workshops and sample the freshest of food in the picturesque restaurants. The same male who had warned her not to fall in love with him had moved the goalposts without telling her and she had been afraid to remark on it lest it change the wonderful ambience between them. They'd had picnics amongst the wildflowers on deserted hillsides and long chatty romantic evening meals on the elegant loggia at the house listening to the classical music she loved. She had adored Florence and Siena, but had found both cities too hot and crowded at this time of year and he had promised to bring her back once the height of the tourist season had passed. Now, she wondered if he would ever keep that promise.

She had learned that he was human too, once she came to appreciate that he occasionally suffered from shockingly bad migraines, which he flatly refused to talk about. Indeed he seemed to look on any admission of feeling unwell as the behaviour of a wimp and his ridiculous stoicism brought a tender smile of remembered amusement to her lips. Somewhere along the line, she acknowledged ruefully, their holiday had turned into a proper honeymoon.

He had bought her a fabulous designer bag in Florence and a painting that she found so ugly she had threatened to dump it while he believed it would grow on her and refine what he saw as her unsophisticated taste in art. And then there was the jewellery…he really loved to give her jewellery and to see her wear it. Her fingers touched the delicate choker of golden leaves that curved round her throat like an elegant question mark. He had bought it for her thirty-first birthday, which he had remembered without any prompting from her. He had also insisted that she had to have a diamond pendant and earrings if she was not to look only half dressed beside Alice when they dined out with the other couple.

He had shown her Etruscan tombs and magnificent palazzos and taught her to distinguish a good wine from an indifferent one. He had laughed when she'd told him that she had not known what cutlery to use on that disastrous first dinner date and she'd had to explain how intimidating she had found that because, born into wealth and fine dining as a way of life, Cesario had not initially understood the problem.

She had fallen in love with her husband and did not know how she could possibly have *avoided* doing so, because Cesario di Silvestri had somehow succeeded in making himself indispensable to her comfort and happiness.

Over dinner that evening, Cesario was still demanding that she name her mole concerning his reputation and she finally took pity on him and confided that her parents lived next door to his former housekeeper.

Cesario frowned. 'She signed a confidentiality agreement. All my staff have to. I can't believe she's gossiping about my private life…'

Jess winced. 'I should have kept quiet and I probably shouldn't have listened either. Dot does seem to cherish a certain resentment over being put into retirement before she was ready to go.'

'Because an audit revealed that she was helping herself to the household cash and selling off wine on the sly,' Cesario chipped in drily. 'That's why she was put out to grass and Tommaso was brought in.'

Jess was shocked by that explanation. 'But you didn't prosecute her?'

'She's quite an age and had worked for the Dunn-Montgomery family all her life. Rather than make an example of her in my role was still a game, but even then I didn't lie about it or make promises I couldn't keep,' Cesario answered. 'Growing up with my father, who always had more than one woman on the go, I saw the cost of that kind of deception time and time again. I've never wanted to live my life the same way. Screaming rows, jealous scenes and bitter break-ups are better avoided.'

'Deception is the one thing I couldn't forgive,' Jess confessed. 'Honesty is incredibly important to me.'

Cesario screened his gaze, his lean, strong face hollowed by unmistakeable tension. Glancing up at him in the small hotel foyer, she surmised that she had got _____ made him feel uncomfortable. Were _____ It was an as the new owner of the ⅃raiston estate, I thought it best to just write it off to experience and replace her.'

They walked hand in hand back to the little hotel. Three quarters of the way across the moonlit piazza he paused and kissed her with a slow, deep hunger that made her heart crash against her breastbone.

'I misjudged you,' she confided in a guilty rush. 'I believed all the bad stuff. I thought the very worst of you from the moment we met.'

Cesario looked down at her in the moonlight, dark eyes gleaming above classic high cheekbones. 'But you don't now.'

'Are you a love cheat like the tabloids say?' Jess asked abruptly, allowing her need to know free access to her deepest insecurities.

Cesario groaned out loud in dismay at that blunt query. 'Is my answer going to be held against me?'

'Probably,' Jess declared.

'I did cheat sometimes when I was younger and sex

too serious and made her standards of behaviour too high for him. It was an unsettling suspicion. Perhaps he even suspected that she was trying to get him to make her promises and the notion brought colour to her cheeks, for she wanted nothing from him that he did not choose to give her of his own accord.

Long after Cesario went to sleep that night, Jess lay awake by his side and wondered what their future held. Or even how far that fragile future might extend in front of her.

CHAPTER EIGHT

A DAY and a half later, on the eve of her return to England, Jess stared down in consternation at a pregnancy test wand and its indisputable result.

There it was, ironically, the outcome she had secretly come to fear most. Seemingly it had taken hardly any time at all for Cesario to get her pregnant and it was a discovery that ripped Jess into emotional shreds and plunged her into violent conflict with herself. She hadn't expected to conceive so quickly and had simply assumed that it would take at least a year. One half of Jess wanted to get up and dance round the room and tell everyone and anyone who was willing to listen that she was expecting her first child. For so long she had dreamt of becoming a mother and now the opportunity had finally come her way and she knew that she ought to be feeling ecstatic.

But the other half of Jess was cast into complete turmoil by the positive result. Would this result mean that her marriage to Cesario was now effectively over? Confronted by that threatening fear, it was impossible for her to be ecstatic or even accepting. She loved Cesario, she was not yet ready to lose him, could not see when she would ever be ready to. Would she now be returning to Halston Hall alone, there to wait out the course of her pregnancy with nothing more than occasional phone calls from the man who had fathered her child? In the circumstances, how much more involved could she expect Cesario to be in her life? The whole point of their marriage had been to conceive a child, she reminded herself bleakly. He would not have married her otherwise. Now that the baby had become reality Cesario would be free to return to his former lifestyle of wine, women and song, a possibility that made Jess feel quite sick with apprehension.

Of course, it was perfectly feasible that the result was wrong, Jess began to reason frantically, surveying the discarded packaging and deciding all of a sudden that it looked like a cheap and unreliable testing kit. Her bowed shoulders began to rise again. She just knew that Cesario wouldn't be overly impressed by the news that she had run her own test. She really would need to see a doctor to get a proper diagnosis and it would be much simpler just to wait until she got back to England where she could easily make an appointment at the village surgery. Her frown of worry ebbed. It would be crazy to burn all her boats at once, so she would keep the unconfirmed result of the test to herself until she had irreproachable proof of her condition, she decided, her spirits recovering from their temporary dive into the doldrums. She really couldn't be *too* cautious. Wouldn't it be dreadful to tell Cesario that she was pregnant and then discover that she had made a ghastly mistake?

Of course, in the short term, she would be careful to take every possible precaution with her health in case she did receive a positive confirmation, Jess reflected.

At the very least she would stay off alcohol and be careful of what she ate. To date, however, she was feeling her normal healthy self. Admittedly she was tiring a little more quickly than usual, but that tiredness and the tenderness of her breasts were the only physical changes she had noted and nothing she couldn't live with. Torn in two by her conflicting feelings, she rested a hand against her still-flat belly and wondered if there really was a baby growing in her womb.

Attired in a simply cut crimson dress that flattered her slender curves with a close fit, Jess went downstairs for lunch. Agostina, their housekeeper, mentioned that Alice was with Cesario. Jess was about to go in the rambling main reception area to join them when she was startled to hear Cesario exclaim angrily, 'No! That's out of the question!'

'But I can hardly meet her eyes as it is,' Alice was arguing in a tone of distress. 'Jess deserves to know the truth, Cesario. How is she going to feel if you don't tell her?'

Round a corner and hidden from the view of her husband and his companion, Jess was frozen to the spot by the dialogue she had almost interrupted. Now her imagination was flying free and she was eavesdropping, wanting and desperately needing to know what they were talking about that had got both of them so worked up.

'What Jess doesn't know won't hurt her. It's a fallacy that the truth is always preferable or kinder.'

'But I feel so guilty whenever I'm with her—'

'You won't be with her again for quite some time. We're leaving for England tomorrow morning—'

'It doesn't matter how you wrap it up. What we're doing is wrong,' Alice argued emotively. 'She's being cheated!'

'I refuse to discuss this with you any more, Alice,' Cesario cut in with icy finality.

What we're doing is wrong. She's being cheated. Oh, my goodness, *Oh. My. Goodness!* Jess thought sickly as she stumbled blindly back to the hall and headed like a homing pigeon for the stairs again to take cover in privacy. They were having an affair behind her back and Alice was feeling guilty? Alice, it seemed, actually wanted to come clean about the affair, but Cesario was all for keeping their adultery a secret. Of course, he had excellent reasons for wanting to keep quiet, didn't he?

Had he owed her such an honest explanation of where his heart really lay when they first embarked on their marriage of convenience? Possibly not, for fidelity and deeper emotions had not featured in what she had innocently believed that marriage would entail. What was in his heart had been nothing to do with her when he had only married her to ensure that any child they conceived was born within wedlock. And he still needed a child to ensure he could inherit Collina Verde, so naturally he wouldn't want Alice to rock the boat with ill-judged confessions of unfaithfulness just at this moment.

It all made perfect sense to Jess and she felt dizzy and sick with shock and disillusionment. She dropped down on the edge of the bed. Her skin was clammy and her tummy was on a nauseous roll. On every level of her being she was appalled by what she had just discovered because she had expected better of the man she had married. For a start, Cesario and Stefano were as close as brothers. Both were only children and had grown up together; Cesario, in particular, had spent a lot of time with Stefano's family following his mother's premature death. Jess would have sworn that Cesario was deeply attached to his cousin, and that Stefano was a doting husband who would be devastated to find out that the wife he adored was sleeping with his best friend. How could Cesario betray Stefano like that? Jess called herself a fool, a blind, trusting fool, for not being more suspicious of a woman who, having once been Cesario's lover, still remained on such openly warm terms with him. How often were such continuing friendships purely platonic? And Alice was an extremely beautiful woman...

Jess squeezed her eyes tight shut and knotted her fists. Maybe she should not have been so quick to dismiss the daunting tabloid reports of Cesario's sexual exploits and heartless nature. Having fallen in love with him, she had wanted only to think good things of him and had happily assumed such rumours to be lies couched to entertain readers who enjoyed being shocked by the shameless shenanigans of the rich and famous. Cesario had certainly misled her, so it was hardly surprising that he had also misled his cousin into believing that his relationship with Alice was innocent.

Jess asked herself what she did now. As the saying went, she was neither fish nor fowl and really had no idea what her status was as Cesario's wife. Was he currently sleeping with Alice? Or was that intimacy being reserved for when his relationship with Jess ended? Or was she kidding herself in thinking that the lovers might be practising that kind of respectful restraint? At the same time, Jess had spent almost every waking hour with Cesario since their wedding and she could not think when Alice and Cesario could have had the opportunity to cheat. He had enjoyed no unexplained absences or trips anywhere and had never failed to answer his mobile phone when she had called him; if he was having an affair with Alice it was an incredibly discreet one and he was being unbelievably careful not to rouse suspicions. Was it possible that there was another explanation for the mysterious conversational exchange she had overheard?

Wondering if she was being silly even to think that she might be mistaken, Jess went back downstairs. Cesario entered the dining room at almost the same time.

'Isn't Alice joining us?' Jess asked, to let him know that she was aware of the other woman's visit.

Cesario gave her a level look that carried not a shred of discomfiture. 'No. I asked her to stay but she has guests arriving this afternoon for the weekend. Before I forget, she left a gift for you. I believe it's a belated birthday present,' he advanced, striding out of the room and reappearing a minute later with a package, which he extended.

Jess frowned. 'What is it?'

'I think she's painted something for you,' Cesario said carelessly.

Jess removed the wrapping paper and the bubble-wrap beneath and found she was looking at a very charming framed drawing of her dogs lying in a group on the shaded loggia. She did recall Alice sketching out there one day but had simply assumed that she was drawing the magnificent view. 'It's really beautiful,' she remarked in shock at the generosity of the gift, noting how Alice had carefully managed to capture the traits of each animal. 'She's very talented.'

'You're much more impressed with that than you were with the painting I bought you,' Cesario noted with an incredulous lift of his expressive ebony brows.

Jess studied the delightful drawing of her pets, which she would cherish, and guilty discomfiture engulfed her. She could not credit that the woman who had taken the time and effort to give her such a well-chosen, personalised present could, at the same time, be having an affair with her husband. Did that make her foolish and naive? However, now Jess could not believe that Alice was capable of such dishonesty while simultaneously behaving like a caring, considerate friend. She had no idea what Alice had been arguing with Cesario about, but she was increasingly convinced it could not relate to the two of them being involved in a secret affair. Was it possible that she herself was guilty of being just a little bit paranoid about Cesario? Was she more jealous of his bond with Alice than she had any reason to be? Seemingly she had leapt far too fast to the wrong conclusion and envy was the most likely cause. Her face warmed at the idea.

'You're very quiet this afternoon, *piccola mia*.'

'It's very hot. I'm kind of sleepy,' Jess said truthfully.

'You do look tired. But then I never leave you to sleep the night through in peace,' Cesario remarked with a rueful hint of discomfiture. 'But tonight I will—'

'No, you won't,' Jess objected before she could even

think about the bold statement she was making when she disagreed. 'I'll have a nap now.'

A potent sexy grin curled Cesario's mouth at that offer, his lean dark features reflecting his amusement. 'I like being in demand very much, *moglie mia*.'

But if he knew she might already be pregnant, would he still want to be in demand? Or would he suddenly appreciate that all his options were open again and that the intimate phase of their marriage was over and done with? In spite of those misgivings, Jess fell asleep within minutes of lying down on the bed in the shaded bedroom and she slept the afternoon and early evening away.

When she got up again, she tracked Cesario down in the room he used as an office. Glancing up, he saw her hovering in the doorway, bright as a butterfly in a lilac top and skirt. 'Come and see this,' he urged with a frown.

Jess wandered over and stared down at the sheet of paper he was poring over. 'What is it?' she prompted uncertainly.

'Rigo sent a scan of it to me this afternoon.'

Jess stared down at the sheet of paper. Jumbled letters cut from a newspaper had been put together to form a note. But the spelling was so appalling that it was hard to work out the words, although she was quick to register that it had been put together in English. 'Where did this come from? And who is Rigo?'

'Rigo Castello looks after my security and the original of this communication arrived at Halston Hall this morning. It's offering to return my stolen painting for a finder's fee...'

'Your painting…the one that was stolen? A *finder's* fee?' Jess exclaimed in disbelieving repetition.

'I think we can safely assume that the thieves sent this demand,' Cesario contended, his hard, handsome face sardonic. 'Presumably they have found it impossible to sell the painting for the kind of money they were hoping to receive and are now hoping to ransom it back to me.'

Jess was still struggling to decipher the jumble of misspelt words on the sheet. Helpfully, Cesario read it out, right down to the concluding assurance that further instructions would follow as to where the money was to be left. 'What on earth are you going to do?' she muttered in bemusement.

'Well, I'm not going to pay for the return of my stolen property,' Cesario declared with derision. 'I refuse to be held to ransom by criminals!'

Jess shifted uneasily where she stood, all too well aware that he might well have got his art work back had he been able to approach the police, but of course that would incriminate her father in the robbery. She was beginning to feel very uncomfortable because adolescent memories were also stirring and it was impossible to forget the mortifying involvement of her mother's relatives in the crime. At that instant she was one hundred per cent convinced that she knew exactly who was responsible for the theft of Cesario's painting.

'When I was a teenager, my cousins, Jason and Mark, once sent a letter like this to intimidate a neighbour who had complained to the police about them,' she told him ruefully. 'The spelling in the letter was dreadful. I think this could be from them and that they must have your painting.'

Cesario surveyed her with hooded eyes. 'I must say that I have married into a very interesting family.'

Her face flamed. 'Look, don't make a joke of it. Think of how you would feel if you were related to people like that!' she urged.

'You're right, *moglie mia*. That was a cheap crack and undeserved, particularly when you've just given me useful information. We will not discuss this again,' he completed, his strong jaw line clenching.

'I'm sorry about the painting. I know how much you valued it,' she said awkwardly.

His lean, darkly handsome features softened. 'It's not your fault and I don't hold you responsible in any way. Don't blame yourself because your father got in over his head and did something stupid.'

Jess felt that that was a generous response in the circumstances and she had cause to remind herself of that during the hours that followed. Over dinner Cesario seemed preoccupied and he excused himself to catch up with work afterwards and did not join her in bed that night. It was the first time in weeks that she had slept alone. She lay awake thinking about their return to England in the morning while trying not to wonder if Cesario was keeping his distance because he was repulsed by her thieving relatives. It was all very well for him to tell her that she was not to blame, but she could not forget that she was only married to him and possibly even carrying his child because of that robbery.

In the morning, Jess could hardly keep her eyes open and she made more use of make-up than she usually did in an effort to lift her wan appearance. She did not see Cesario until after breakfast and he still seemed distant. Determined not to waste any time in finding out whether or not she was pregnant, she phoned to make an appointment to see her GP in Charlbury St Helen's before they even left for the airport and caught their flight home to the UK. Her dogs would already be at Halston Hall waiting to greet them.

'This is your home now, *piccola mia*,' Cesario pronounced as the limo drove through the turreted gates of the Elizabethan property. 'Make whatever changes you please to the house. I want you to be comfortable here.'

It was a generous invitation and it warmed her uneasy heart and steadied her nerves about the future, until it occurred to her that Cesario had made no such open-handed comments in relation to his other homes round the world. Collina Verde in Italy, it seemed, had been her home only for the honeymoon. She tried hard not to read any significance into that fact. If Cesario was rather cool in her radius it was probably only the natural result of the robbery fiasco, because when the thieves had offered to sell his own painting back to him they had undoubtedly added insult to injury.

'By the way, I've bought you a new vehicle to get about in,' Cesario informed her as they travelled down the drive to the hall. 'Your car was ready for the scrap heap.'

'But I don't need a new car!' Jess protested.

'There it is—the blue one parked out front,' Cesario informed her as smoothly as if she hadn't spoken.

It was a brand-new, top-of-the-range Range Rover,

ten times more expensive then her elderly four-wheel drive and embellished with the most sumptuous cream leather upholstery Jess had ever seen. 'I gather this is part of my new swanky image,' she said tartly, turning her head to look at him after she had walked all the way round the luxury car.

'No, not in this case. I didn't think that wreck you were driving was very safe and I didn't want it breaking down and stranding you somewhere lonely late at night,' Cesario contradicted silkily, making her feel ungracious.

Jess was on the brink of protest about his interference until she registered that she actually liked the fact that he was concerned about her safety. It was a satisfyingly husbandly concern and allowed her to feel more like a real wife than she usually dared to feel. 'It's not going to look clean and perfect for very long with me and the dogs using it,' she warned him ruefully.

As Tommaso appeared beaming at the front door a canine flood surged out to acknowledge their arrival with a flurry of barks and scrabbling paws. Cesario strode off towards the garages after telling Jess that he had an urgent appointment to keep. Weed raced round the corner in his wake—the skinny lurcher, whose confidence had grown by leaps and bounds in Italy, had become her husband's shadow, and Magic bounced along after them.

Jess changed into more comfortable clothing and went out to keep her medical appointment at the local surgery. Thirty minutes later she had the confirmation she had sought and, feeling somewhat shaken by the news that she would have a child by the following spring, she went to visit her mother.

'Cesario called in an hour ago,' Sharon Martin told her daughter when she arrived. 'He spoke to your father at work and then came here to ask me some questions about your uncle Sam.'

Jess fell still and grimaced at that information. 'What's he up to?'

'Your husband wants his painting back and he's determined to get it,' her mother confided ruefully. 'He told your father that he would try to keep him out of things but that he can't guarantee it—'

'That's not fair!' Jess gasped in consternation. 'I have an agreement with Cesario...'

'And he wants the agreement *and* he wants his painting back. Typical man,' Sharon Martin quipped. 'He wants it all and sees no reason why he shouldn't have it.'

Jess breathed in deep. 'You're going to be a grandmother again next year.'

Initially taken aback by the change of subject, her mother stared at her and then, with an exclamation of pleasure, she rushed forward and gave her daughter a warm hug. 'My goodness, that didn't take long! Are you pleased?'

Squashing her doubts and insecurities about Cesario and keen to ensure that her mother didn't worry about her, Jess fixed a smile to her lips. 'I'm over the moon! I haven't told Cesario yet, so keep my secret for me.'

Before returning to the hall, Jess called in at the veterinary surgery to check the work rotas. She went straight to talk to her boss because her pregnancy would mean there had to be a good deal of reorganisation at the practice. She would have to take extra safety precautions and consider the kind of jobs she took on. She thought it said a lot for Charlie that, even after taking all that approaching hassle into account, he was still able to offer her his hearty congratulations and happily reminisce about his early days as a new father.

When she got back to Halston Hall, Tommaso was in the hall supervising the placement of a very large canvas of what looked like a desiccated tree twisting in a storm. Rigo Castello, a heavily built older man, was poised nearby wearing a large approving smile. Jess gaped at the painting and recognised it at once from Cesario's description of it. She asked where Cesario was and raced breathlessly into his office with her dogs accompanying her. 'You got it back? How on earth did you do it?'

Cesario straightened his long, lean, powerful body fluidly from his lounging position on the edge of the desk and made a hand signal to Magic, which made the deaf and excitable terrier sit down and stop barking. 'Your Uncle Sam is a sensible man.'

And then without any warning at all, and as if someone had suddenly pulled a rug from beneath him, Cesario lurched sideways and crumpled down into a heap on the floor. 'Tommaso!' Jess shouted in shock, dropping to her knees by Cesario's side and noting that he was ashen-faced, with perspiration gleaming on his brow.

His security chief, Rigo, joined her first. 'Let me deal with this, *signora*.'

'I'll call the doctor!' Jess exclaimed because Cesario appeared to be unconscious.

'That won't be necessary, *signora*. Mr di Silvestri is already coming round.'

Jess watched Cesario's lashes lift on dazed dark golden eyes. He blinked several times. Her heart was pounding with adrenalin inside her ribcage. Rigo addressed his employer in rapid low-pitched Italian and, raking a trembling hand through his cropped black hair, Cesario responded.

'I'll call the doctor,' Jess said again.

'No—I don't want a doctor!' Cesario asserted with what struck her as quite unnecessary force. As he struggled to get up she noticed that he leant heavily on Rigo's arm.

Jess was concerned enough to argue with her husband. 'You're obviously not well! You need to see a doctor…'

'I tripped on the corner of the rug and I must've struck my head,' Cesario countered, dismissing Rigo, who shot him a troubled look before leaving the room.

Her brow indented as she glanced at the rug, which seemed to be lying perfectly flat. She had only seen him fall and it had looked more like a collapse or a faint to her than a moment of clumsy inattention. Not only did his interpretation not make sense, she could think of no reason why he should lie about it. She studied him worriedly, grateful to see that he had regained colour and looked more like himself. It shook her to recall that just months ago he had meant very little more to her than a stranger in the street, while now he meant the whole world to her.

'You said you had spoken to my uncle?' she prompted, her curiosity about the painting overtaking her concern now that he seemed to have made a recovery.

'Yes, and he didn't want any trouble. He was even less keen on the idea of the police being called in. He told me that if his sons had my painting he'd have it back here within the hour and presumably they did,' Cesario pointed out drily.

'You intended to bring in the police if you didn't get anywhere with him?' she pressed.

'Rather than let your cousins get away with robbing me blind? *Yes*,' Cesario confirmed without hesitation, his lean strong face stamped with resolve. 'I warned your father but, fortunately for him, I've got my property back and the matter can be forgotten about now.'

'Well, I'm glad you got it back but you didn't really play fair, did you?' Jess commented, light grey eyes full of reproach. 'To keep my father safe, I married you and agreed to give you a child, which was a pretty tall order. But in spite of that, today you were ready to sacrifice my father.'

'Why worry about what didn't happen, *piccola mia*?' Closing the distance between them, Cesario spread his long fingers either side of her anxious face and gently smoothed her skin in a soothing gesture. 'Your father is innocent of any criminal intention and he was not at risk. I accepted that after speaking to him personally following the robbery and if the police had got involved they would have reached the same conclusion that I did, *moglie mia*.'

Jess trembled, more affected than she was prepared to admit by his proximity and words of understanding.

He'd called her 'my wife' and instantly everything seemed lighter and brighter. She wrapped her arms round his neck and within seconds he was kissing her with a hot, driving hunger that left her dizzy with its intensity. Her body quickened, desire rising embarrassingly fast so that she pushed against his hard, muscular frame, her breath ragged in her throat, her nipples tight and throbbing.

'Bed,' Cesario muttered thickly, grasping her hand and urging her out of the room and up the stairs.

'It's time for dinner,' she muttered.

'*Non c'è problema!* Tommaso won't let us starve, *bellezza mia.*'

And the hunger he roused in her with his second kiss was fierce and relentless, every plunge of his tongue sending a responsive quiver through her slight body. It was as if there were a flame desperate for fuel burning at the heart of her as she hauled off his jacket and pulled open his shirt. He laughed softly and then crushed her mouth almost savagely beneath his. As he removed her clothes with impatient hands she knew that, somehow, the same overwhelming urgency and need for fulfilment was driving him.

He sank into her hot, wet sheath hard and fast and released a groan of pleasure that acted like an aphrodisiac on her. She felt wild as she craved every thrust of his lean, muscular hips, her body jolting and straining towards a climax even while he paused to savour the moment. She came apart in the circle of his arms, ravished by the exquisite pleasure that washed through her in a sweet drowning tide, so that even afterwards all she was conscious of was the race of his heartbeat against her breast and the damp, reassuring solidity of his big powerful body against hers.

'I've never needed anyone the way I just needed you, *cara mia*,' Cesario framed heavily, both arms wrapped round her as though he was still reluctant to let her go.

And in the fading light she smiled and touched a loving hand to his shadowed jaw line, admiring his fabulous bone structure and the inky darkness of the long lashes that framed his bronzed eyes. She loved to be needed, lived to be needed by him, and his passion for her made her feel special. It would have been the perfect moment to tell him that she was pregnant but she was quick to discard the idea, preferring to concentrate on their togetherness rather than on an announcement that might well bring their current living arrangements to an end. She would share her news in the morning instead, she decided, and she stayed silent, even though they later got out of bed to enjoy a late dinner.

What remained of the night was long, since they made love until dawn. Cesario was tireless and his hunger for her seemed both ravenous and unquenchable. When exhaustion finally overcame her, she slept deeply and wakened to find that she was alone. She had planned to make her announcement over breakfast with Cesario but the morning was already well advanced.

Clad in cropped trousers and a silk top, she hurried across the imposing landing of the mansion that was now her home and sped downstairs. She found Cesario in his office talking in Italian on the phone. Weed and Magic were curled up together below his desk. Eyes tender with love, she watched Cesario unnoticed from the doorway for the space of minute, revelling in the memory of the closeness they had shared and proud of the intimate ache that was the penalty for such passion...

CHAPTER NINE

'JESSICA…' Cesario perceptibly tensed the instant he saw her there, his lean strong face pulling taut and shuttering. 'I'll be with you in a moment.'

A little hurt by the reserve she sensed in him, Jess asked Tommaso to bring them coffee and took a seat. 'I've got something to tell you,' she said as soon as Cesario had finished his phone call.

Tommaso created a welcome hiatus with his return with a tray and Cesario wandered over to the window with his cup cradled in one lean hand, sunshine glinting over his black hair and adding reflected light to his charismatic dark eyes. 'What is it?' he asked casually.

Jess lifted her head high. 'I'm pregnant,' she told him quietly.

Cesario looked revealingly stunned, as though that was the last piece of news he had expected to hear. His ebony brows pleated in a questioning frown. 'You can't be…'

'I am.' A confident smile of achievement illuminated her face. 'I saw the doctor yesterday and had it confirmed, so there's no mistake.'

'But so soon, so, er, *quickly*?' Cesario breathed in stilted English, his surprise still lingering in spite of her explanation. 'We're both in our thirties and I believed it might take months.'

'No. We'll be parents by the end of January next year,' Jess told him excitedly, wanting to infect him with some of her enthusiasm because he was standing there so still and quiet.

'January next year,' Cesario repeated slowly.

She thought he looked pale beneath his bronzed skin and more like a man who had been dealt a severe shock than a man given news he should have been eager to hear. His strong facial bones were clearly defined, his brilliant eyes hooded so that she had not the slightest idea what he might be thinking. It was the most complete non-reaction that she had ever experienced and very far from what she had hoped to receive.

'You're not pleased,' she breathed unevenly.

Cesario unfroze and took a hasty step towards her, only to come to a halt again and then hover with uncharacteristic uncertainty. 'Of course, I'm pleased!'

Jess could feel herself turning stiff and defensive, for any hint of the warm intimacy of the night hours had been well and truly scuppered by his attitude. 'No, you're not pleased and I don't understand why you're not. Isn't this what you wanted? Didn't you marry me so that I could give you a child?' she prompted, her voice getting more shrill without her meaning it to, and for a horror-stricken instant she was afraid she sounded whiny.

'*Che cosa hai*…what's the matter with you?' Cesario chided, pulling her resistant body to him with firm hands. 'Does falling pregnant make a woman shockingly cross, *bellezza mia*?'

'No, of course, it doesn't!' she rebutted tightly, gazing up into his breathtakingly handsome features with bewildered eyes. 'It's the way you're behaving that's making me feel like this. You've changed your mind, haven't you? You don't want a baby any more!'

Cesario closed his larger hands firmly over hers. 'I have never heard such nonsense. If you are having my baby—'

'I *am*,' Jess slotted in truculently.

'Then naturally I am overjoyed, *piccola mia*,' Cesario insisted, his beautiful dark eyes intent on her troubled face as if he was willing her to believe what he was telling her. 'But I am very concerned that I should hear this wonderful news and then have to tell you that, owing to a business emergency, I have to fly to Milan this afternoon and leave you alone here.'

Although her heart sank at the prospect of him leaving and she could barely credit that he should already be returning to Italy when they had only left the country the day before, she was relieved by his clarification. Her cherished announcement had clearly suffered from bad timing when he was already preoccupied with business problems and his imminent departure.

'I'll be absolutely fine here. My family are within reach if I need company. But, to be frank, I have a good number of hours to catch up at work and I'll be very busy as well.'

His hold on her hands tightened. 'Now that you're carrying a baby you'll have to rest more.'

'I'll be sensible. I am only contracted to work part-time now,' she reminded him. 'I also need to get the accommodation here and staffing sorted out for my rescue animals. I've got plenty to do while you're away.'

And she maintained that upbeat outlook until he took his leave a couple of hours later. The last impression she wanted him to leave with was that of her being irritable and difficult. But even as she set off for work wearing sensible clothing and driving her opulent new car with her dogs confined behind a special screen in the boot area, she was conscious that, no matter how she looked at it, Cesario's response to the news of their baby had still fallen very far short of her fondest hopes.

Jess was convinced that Cesario had not been pleased. Something had altered since their marriage. Had he changed his mind about having a child with her? Admittedly she had conceived more easily and quickly than either of them had expected and he had been unprepared for her announcement. But could that simple fact have caused him to have second thoughts about fatherhood? She kept on picturing his expression at the instant she had given him her news. He had looked bleak, disturbed...*guilty*? Her brow furrowed. From where had she received the impression that he felt guilty? That had to be her imagination because why on earth would he feel guilty about her having fallen pregnant just as he had planned?

Over the next four days Jess was exceptionally busy both at work and at the sanctuary. She received an influx of unwanted dogs from the council dog pound. People often surrendered pets because they weren't allowed to keep them in rental accommodation and, these days, more and more because they couldn't afford to feed them or cover veterinary care. Cesario rang her twice, brief, uninformative calls that might have come from an acquaintance rather than a husband. Jess tormented herself with recollections of the reality that theirs was not a real marriage and never had been and maybe only now was she seeing proper evidence of the fact. Possibly the passionate nature of their relationship had blurred the boundaries and confused them both, only Cesario did not appear confused any more, she acknowledged unhappily. Cesario now seemed to be putting more than physical distance between them because he was treating her with detached and impersonal formality. She felt as if she was losing him and it unnerved her, for intelligence warned her that she had never had a normal claim to him. He had never loved her and lust was not an advantage now that she was carrying his baby.

On the sixth day after his departure, the estate manager called up to the hall to ask her to get in touch with Cesario on his behalf as he was having trouble reaching him. Jess could not get an answer on Cesario's mobile phone, which went automatically to his messaging service, and finally she rang his head office in London, only to be told by his PA that he had taken a few days off and would not be back at work until the start of the following week.

'Is he still in Milan?' Jess pressed.

'Mr di Silvestri is in London, *signora*,' the woman responded in audible surprise. 'I'll let him know that you want to speak to him.'

Jess was shaken. Cesario had allowed her to believe that he was in Italy when he was actually in *London*? Her heart sank at that awareness because she could not think of an innocent explanation for such behaviour on his part.

'There's no need for you to contact Cesario now. I'll see my husband before he receives any message you could give him.' Frowning, Jess replaced the receiver and then she used her mobile to try and contact Alice. The other woman's phone also went straight to voice-mail and when she called the landline at Stefano and Alice's Italian home she was told that Alice was visiting friends in England.

For the second time in the space of two weeks, Jess was eaten alive by cruel and wounding suspicions. Fear flung her mind wide open to the worst possibilities. *Was* Cesario having an affair with Alice? Were her husband and his former girlfriend together in London? The sheer gut-wrenching pain of that apprehension ripped through Jess and suddenly she could not bear not knowing the truth. Blinking back tears she couldn't hold back, she decided that she would go to London immediately, visit Cesario's apartment and confront whatever she found there head-on. Would she find him there with Alice? She *had* to know what was going on. How could she live otherwise? How could she even get out of bed tomorrow if she didn't know whether or not their marriage was still alive?

Although Jess was aware that Cesario owned an apartment in London, she had not previously had a reason to visit it. She drove to the local station and caught the city-bound train, thinking it was ironic that she felt nauseous for the very first time during that journey. Her emotional state of mind seemed to be seeking a physical outlet. She took a taxi to an ultra-modern apartment building and travelled up in the lift, squinting at herself in the reflective steel walls, wondering if she could possibly be as pale and miserable as she looked.

Rigo Castello let her into the apartment and there was no sign of reluctance or discomfiture on his part, which warned Jess straight off that she was not about to surprise Cesario *in flagrante delicto*. Straightening her spine and throwing back her stiff shoulders, she told herself that she had every right to ask awkward questions of the father of her unborn child before she walked into the airy reception room with splendid views over the city.

Cesario was outside on the rooftop terrace, striding towards the sliding doors that were wide open at the far end of the room. His black hair was blowing back from his lean, darkly handsome face. Unusually he was not wearing a business suit, but jeans and a black T-shirt that enhanced the sculpted lines of his lean, muscular body. He did not seem surprised by her sudden appearance, a reality that led her to assume that his PA had given him prior knowledge of her phone call.

'Jessica...' he murmured, his rich accented drawl rather flat in tone and delivery, brilliant dark eyes shrewd and distinctly wary.

'I guess the phrase, "Fancy seeing you here" really belongs to me!' Jess quipped loudly, determined not to show her distress either through tears or temper. 'After all, I was still under the impression that you were working eighteen hour days in Milan!'

Cesario surveyed her levelly. 'I'm sorry that I lied to you—'

'But why did you lie? That's what I want to know.'

'I don't think you *will* want to know once I explain,' Cesario countered. 'And that's the main reason why I kept you out of the situation.'

Refusing to engage with that baffling forecast and assurance, Jess snatched in a steadying breath and then asked bluntly, 'Were you ever in Milan?'

'No. I've been in London throughout the week.'

'With Alice?' she prompted jerkily.

Cesario regarded her with frowning force and a tangible air of bewilderment. 'Why would Alice be here?'

'I thought perhaps you were having an affair with her,' Jess advanced rather reluctantly, because it was so patently obvious from his pained expression that sexual shenanigans with his cousin's wife had played no part in his pretence about his whereabouts.

'No,' he proclaimed in blunt dissent. 'You thought wrong.'

'Maybe not with Alice, but possibly with someone else?' Jess persisted, unable to quite let go of her suspicions regarding his fidelity.

'*Dio mio*, sex with anyone other than you has to be the last thing on my mind right now,' Cesario responded with an impatience that dispelled her concerns in that field better than any heated denial would have done.

'Well, I don't know what goes on in your mind, do I?' In reaction to the sudden release of her tension, because the spectre of Alice and that past affair had loomed like a very large threat in her mind, Jess threw up her hands in an unusually dramatic gesture and stalked over to the window. Ebony curls danced on her slim shoulders as she swivelled back to look at him, her profile taut and pale. 'You told me you were in Milan and you were lying!' she reminded him fiercely.

'I have to confess that since we met I have kept a lot from you, *piccola mia*,' Cesario declared.

'Stop hinting and start telling!' Jess flung in direct challenge, angry grey eyes bright as silver stars above her flushed cheekbones.

'I really thought we could do this without anyone getting hurt,' Cesario breathed in a raw undertone. 'But with hindsight I can see now that I was depressed when I asked you to marry me. I was looking for a way out and a means of distraction—'

'Just get to the point, Cesario!' Jess cut in furiously, wondering what on earth he could have been depressed about, while bristling at the suggestion that marrying her had been a means of distraction. That made her sound insultingly like an entertainment act he had hired for his amusement.

'Eight months ago, I had a series of medical tests and, with the diagnosis, life as I knew it came to a sudden end,' Cesario revealed in a driven undertone, his strong facial bones taut beneath his bronzed skin. 'I had been suffering from intermittent problems with my balance and vision and also severe headaches. A scan revealed that I had a brain tumour.'

Totally unprepared for the startling turn that the dialogue had taken, Jess simply stared at him and parroted weakly, 'A brain tumour?'

'Although the tumour is benign, I learned that surgery could leave me seriously disabled and that was a risk I was not prepared to take. I decided that I valued the quality of the life I had left more than the quantity, and I refused further treatment,' Cesario revealed quietly.

Shock had drained the blood from Jess's face and made her tummy flip a somersault. She was struggling to absorb what he had told her and it was so far removed from what she had expected that she was utterly stunned. 'Your migraines...your fall last week...'

'Caused by the tumour,' he confirmed, his jaw line clenching at the reminder. 'My condition has been worsening faster than I had expected and becoming unpredictable, which is why I came to London to undergo more tests this past week—'

'You're telling me that you knew you were *dying* when you asked me to marry you,' Jess almost whispered as she finally put that scenario together for her own benefit and reeled from the ramifications of it. 'When you asked me to have a baby with you, you must have known that you wouldn't be here for that child while it was growing up. How could you deceive me like that?'

Beneath her hail of accusing words, Cesario had lost colour. 'I only appreciated how selfish I was being last week when you told me that you had conceived...'

'Selfish and irresponsible!' Jess slammed back loudly at him, outraged and bitterly hurt that he could have kept her in ignorance of such a crucial if unpalatable fact from the outset of their relationship. 'I knew you weren't planning to stay married to me for ever, but I did believe that you would be available to act as father to our child...you allowed me to believe that!'

In addition, Jess was already working out that while

Cesario had kept secrets from her she had been in a minority. Clearly Stefano and Alice had known that Cesario had a brain tumour. Now she understood the often anxious looks she had seen Stefano angling at his cousin. Now she knew exactly what Alice had been getting at when Jess had overheard the other woman arguing with Cesario. Alice, bless her heart, had been trying to persuade Cesario that day that he ought to tell his wife about his condition, Jess registered belatedly. Of course, she was fairly sure that Alice had no idea that Cesario's was a marriage of convenience built on practicality rather than love and trust. And Cesario's revelations had just blown Jess and all her misconceptions about him and their relationship right out of the water and left her floundering in alien territory.

'Tell me everything,' Jess urged grittily.

'It was not a complete lie when I said I needed a child to inherit Collina Verde,' Cesario continued grimly. 'My grandfather did leave a complex will and to inherit I did have to name Stefano and his son as my heirs because I didn't have a child of my own. But I used that inheritance claim as an excuse when all I really wanted was a child to leave my wealth to—without a child, everything I had worked for all my life suddenly seemed so shallow and pointless.'

And with a shrug of a broad shoulder on that grudging admission, Cesario half turned away from her. He spread expressive lean brown hands in a gesture of frustration that appealed for her understanding. 'I thought I was seeing clearly, but my rationale was warped and short-sighted. I believed I was doing something good, something worthwhile...'

'How could it possibly have been worthwhile?' Jess couldn't think straight. She had come to London to find out where she stood with the man she loved and he had thrown everything she thought she knew about him and their marriage on its head. Her heart thudding fast behind her breastbone, she studied him in growing disbelief as he unwound the tangle of falsehoods he had spread to lay the truth bare for her.

'I saw a child as a worthwhile investment for the future I didn't have,' Cesario extended heavily. 'But I was kidding myself—I was really only thinking about what *I* wanted, not about what truly mattered. And I wanted you from the first moment I saw you.'

But Jess was not prepared to listen to that line of argument. In concert with what he was telling her, she felt as though her own life were shattering and falling down around her in broken irreparable pieces. Nothing was as she had thought, nothing was as it had seemed. The fabulous honeymoon in Italy had been a mere passage out of time—*a means of distraction*—and essentially meaningless. Cesario had cruelly deceived her from the start. He wasn't going to be there for her as a husband, or as a father for their child, or even as a former partner in another country, she registered sickly. He wasn't going to be there for her at all.

'Everything you told me was a lie,' she began in condemnation.

'And honesty is very important to you...I know,' Cesario returned with a sardonic edge to his voice. 'I'm not trying to minimise the effect of what I did to you. It was wrong.'

Jess settled embittered eyes on him. 'But it's too late for regret now. I'm married to you and pregnant!'

Cesario stared at her with deep, dark bronzed eyes and it was as if she was seeing him clearly for the first time. He was so handsome and so sexy, but he was also unfathomable, with depths that she had not even come close to plumbing, she acknowledged unhappily, feeling her ignorance bite to the very foot of her soul.

'We can separate right now if you like. It's not a problem,' Cesario informed her quietly. 'I'm prepared for that.'

Jess flinched as if he had jabbed a red-hot branding iron near bare skin. She wanted to shout and scream back at him like a fishwife in response to that offhand statement, which set such a low and casual value on their marriage. It was a direct reminder of the practical agreement on which their union was based. Only fierce pride kept the tide of her rising emotions taped down and under control. He was offering her her freedom back as though their marriage had indeed only been a temporary diversion for a man whose future would be taken from him when he least expected it. He was showing her the door. He was politely letting her know that, although he had lied to her and kept her in the dark, it didn't ultimately matter because he didn't care enough even to try to hang onto her.

'The baby,' she mumbled sickly.

'I'm sorry, I'm very sorry that I got you involved in this,' Cesario muttered roughly. 'I know that's not good enough but, apart from money, it's all I've got to give you right now.'

Jess lifted what shreds of dignity remained to her and

dealt him a scornful smile of dismissal. 'I don't need your money!'

'I'm signing the Halston Hall estate over to you this week.'

Jess was trembling; appalled by the way he was concentrating on financial arrangements for their separation when her heart was breaking up inside her and her sense of loss was dragging her down so deep and so fast she felt as if she were drowning. 'Oh, goody, I'll own the Dunn-Montgomery ancestral home—how fitting!' she exclaimed with a brittle laugh, desperate to hide her pain and spinning around in an unchoreographed half circle to conceal her emotion from his keen appraisal.

'What are you talking about?'

'I never got around to telling you but I'm actually an illegitimate Dunn-Montgomery,' Jess told him in an artificially bright voice. 'Robert Martin married my mother when I was ten months old but I wasn't his child. My father is the member of parliament, William Dunn-Montgomery, although he will never admit the fact. He was a student when he got my mother pregnant—'

'And that's why Luke was so taken with you at our wedding—he knows he's your half-brother!' Cesario guessed, frowning at her in sudden comprehension as he made that familial connection. '*Madre di Dio!* Is that why you married me? To get Halston Hall?'

Thunderstruck by that suggestion, Jess stared blankly back at him.

'I can see that my ownership of the house would have been a major attraction to someone in your circumstances,' Cesario said drily.

Jess had turned pale. 'Someone in my circumstances?'

'You said yourself how fitting it would be that you should own the former ancestral home of the Dunn-Montgomerys, when your birth father refuses to even acknowledge your relationship,' Cesario extended. 'I don't mind. In fact it's a relief if Halston Hall can in some way compensate you for the way in which I've screwed up your life.'

There was a note of finality to that assurance. His dark golden eyes were cool, his stubborn sensual mouth composed in a firm line. For the first time since her arrival she knew exactly what he was thinking: he had said all he had to say to her and now he was ready for her to leave. For several seconds she withstood the steady onslaught of his gaze, because a crushing sense of rejection was holding her in a near state of paralysis, and then she moved away on feet that felt as if they didn't belong to the rest of her body.

Cesario was making a phone call in his own language but both his voice and actions seemed to be happening far away at the end of a long dark tunnel. Jess felt detached from her surroundings and horribly light-headed.

'You'll be driven home...no, don't argue with me,' Cesario urged as her lips parted. 'You're pregnant. I don't want you struggling to find a seat on a packed train during the rush hour.'

With enormous effort, Jess focused on him. She dimly recognised that she was in a state of shock so profound that she could barely think, but there was one question that she could not suppress. 'You said your condition had got worse...how long?' and her voice ran out of steam altogether and just vanished in the awfulness of what she was saying.

'They're not quite sure. Not more than six months,' he proffered with unnatural calm. 'I do have one favour to ask...'

'What?' Jess prompted shakily, for the number six was whizzing round and round inside her head as if someone had turned on a manic mixer.

'Would you mind if Weed and Magic lived with me? For as long as that's practical,' Cesario extended tight-mouthed.

Jess felt as if someone had their hands squeezing round her throat: it was that hard to breathe and there was a pain building in her chest. She was recalling the patient way he had learned hand signals so that he could communicate with the deaf terrier. 'No problem,' she said, schooling her voice to control it. 'No problem at all.'

Rigo Castello escorted her in silence down to the basement car park and tucked her into a limousine. She remembered the older man's behaviour when Cesario had collapsed and realised that he had been in on the secret as well. It seemed that of all the people close to Cesario she had been just about the only one kept in the dark. Deceived, lied to, shut out of the charmed circle and, although he wanted her dogs for company, he didn't want her...

CHAPTER TEN

THE instant Jess laid eyes on her mother that evening she started to cry. Once she had let that flood of pent-up grief and despair flow freely there was no stopping it.

Shaken by the state her daughter was in, Sharon Martin took some time to grasp the situation that her daughter was describing between heartbroken sobs. When Jess had finally mopped her eyes dry, her eyelids were so swollen she could hardly see out of them. But she had only to think of Cesario and more moisture trickled down her quivering cheeks.

'You're the first person in my family ever to go to university and yet when it comes to a real crisis you act as if you're as thick as two short planks!' Sharon pronounced, shocking her daughter right out of her self-preoccupied silence.

'How can you say that?' Jess gasped.

'The man you say you love is dying and you're still whinging on about how he lied to you! What are you thinking of?' the older woman demanded.

The man you love is dying. And there it was, the simple fact that had frozen Jess's ability to reason at source. That news had torn her apart, both angering and terrifying her, for she did not know how to handle something so enormous and threatening that it affected her entire world and destroyed even the future.

'Cesario lied to protect you and, by the looks of it, he knew what he was doing when he lied, because you're sitting here being useless!' Sharon scolded. 'Where is your brain, Jess? He doesn't want you to feel that you *have* to stay with him because you're his wife and he's ill. He knows you didn't sign up for that and he clearly never intended to tell you. Obviously he thought he was going to have more time with you. He doesn't want your pity. That's why he told you that you could have a separation right now, so that you are free to do whatever *you* like.'

Blinking rapidly, Jess stared back at her mother. 'What *I* like?' she echoed.

'A week ago you were in Italy with Cesario and you were both very, very happy, weren't you?' Sharon voiced that reminder gently.

'Yes, but—'

'No buts. Cesario can't have changed that much in the space of a few days. He's just giving you the chance to escape getting involved in his illness.'

'You honestly believe he's trying to protect me rather than get rid of me?' Jess whispered shakily.

'I think that's the only reason he lied all along. He's trying to be a tough guy and deal with his condition alone.'

Jess swallowed the thickness in her throat and stared down at her feet with glazed eyes. 'I don't think I can handle losing him,' she framed gruffly.

'Then don't give up. By the sound of it, he's already given up, so he doesn't need more of the same from you. There may still be room for hope. You tell him he has to give the treatment a go—for your sake and the baby's,' the older woman proffered briskly. 'With any luck, it won't be too late for him to change his mind.'

Jess grasped that thought like a mental lifeline and held fast to it. 'I've been stupid, blind, self-obsessed...'

'You were in shock and now you've had the chance to think things through. You have to fight for most things in life that are worth having.'

'I'll go back to London...'

'Tomorrow. Right now you're exhausted and you need a good night's sleep before you do anything,' Sharon told her firmly. 'You have to look after yourself and the baby now.'

The next morning Jess had a routine surgery to carry out and it was the afternoon before she had the leisure to think. A deep longing for Cesario's presence clawed at her, filling her with fear of the future all over again, but also hardening her resolve to take action. She drove back to the hall, gazing out at the gracious old house, and while marvelling that it was now her home she frowned at the sight of the pair of vans already parked outside.

It was an unpleasant surprise to walk into the big hall and see a stack of boxes piled up. Looking beyond them, she could see the amount of activity going on in Cesario's office, people moving about busily while desk and cupboards were cleared and packed. Her heart sank to the soles of her feet and she felt sick: he was already moving out!

Without any warning, Cesario appeared in the doorway, Weed and Magic at his heels. That he looked so healthy with his vibrant golden skin tone hit her like a slap in the face, while the cloaked and unrevealing darkness of his gaze simply hurt her. Once again she felt excluded, on the outside when she wanted to be involved in everything he did.

He strolled fluidly closer, as elegant as he always was in a pearl grey business suit, only the absence of a tie striking a less formal note. He looked gorgeous. In spite of the pain Jess was fighting to hold at bay, her heart started to pound very, very fast inside her.

'I'm sorry—this isn't how I planned this. I intended to be gone before you got back from work,' he admitted levelly.

'It won't do you any good,' Jess told him tartly. 'I'll just follow you to London and camp out on your doorstep.'

His brow indented and he gave her a bemused look. 'I'm sorry?'

'I want to be with you. I *need* to be with you,' Jess said boldly. 'Blame yourself for that. You dragged me into this.'

'We'll talk in the drawing room,' he breathed tautly, lush ebony lashes lowering to screen his gaze from the intrusion of hers.

'Nothing you could possibly say will change my mind,' Jess warned him, lifting her chin as he closed the door on the hall and the bustle of the packers.

'You're taking an emotional view of this situation and that's wrong.'

'Maybe it would be wrong for you, but it's not wrong for me,' Jess cut in with assurance.

'You're thinking of me the way you think of your

rescue animals—all starry-eyed compassion and do-gooding instincts to the fore,' he condemned, his lean, strong face rigid with censure. 'I don't want that. I can't live with that.'

'And I can't live with you dealing with this alone and away from me, so it seems that we're at an impasse,' Jess pronounced, taking in the disorientated look starting to build in his beautiful dark golden eyes and the anger that she was behaving in a way he had not foreseen. 'We're also about to have a major argument.'

A black brow lifted. 'About what?' he challenged, an aggressive angle to his strong jaw.

'You have to go for that treatment you refused—'

'No.' The rebuttal was instant.

'Stop thinking about you and think about this baby you decided to bring into this world.' Jess shot that fiery advice back at him without hesitation. 'Our baby deserves that you fight this by any means open to you. If there's the smallest chance that you can survive this, you *owe* it to us to take it!'

Cesario gazed back at her with unflinching force but he had lost colour. 'Strong words...'

'Strongly felt,' Jess traded, holding that look with intent grey eyes that willed him to listen, for she felt as if she was fighting for both their lives. When the tumour had first been diagnosed he had taken a stance and, in her opinion, he had taken the wrong one.

'And what of the consequences if the surgery doesn't go well?'

Jess squared her slim shoulders. 'Then we'll deal with that when and if it happens. We'll manage. You're luckier than most people in that you can afford the best medical care and support if you need it.'

'But what if I'm not prepared to live with the risk of being maimed?' Cesario pressed darkly.

'Life is precious, Cesario. Life is *very* precious,' Jess whispered vehemently, longing for him to accept that truth. 'I can tell you now that our child would rather have you alive and disabled than not have you at all.'

'I'm not going to ask you how you feel!' Cesario shot back at her in a derisive attack that cut a painful swathe through her anxiety. 'I'm talking to a woman with a three-legged, half-blind dog and a deaf dog and several others with what you might term a "reduced quality of life", so I already know your liberal views. But I'm not a dumb animal and my needs are a little more sophisticated!'

'But you are also putting your pride and need to be independent ahead of every other factor and you're assuming that the worst case scenario will result,' Jess condemned in a determined attack on his outlook. 'Why so pessimistic? What happened to hope? What's wrong with having hope? We have a child on the way. I'm asking you to think about what having a father will mean to our baby as he or she grows up.'

Cesario compressed his lips. 'I'm not the right person to discuss that with because I had a rotten father.'

'All the more reason for you to think this over now, because you could do the job better. I had a rotten birth father as well. He gave my mother the money for an abortion and considered his responsibility to us both concluded. But Robert Martin was a wonderful father to me,' Jess declared with passionate sincerity. 'He's not educated and he's not clever or successful like my birth father, but I love him very much for always being there to love, support and encourage me. What's in your heart is what matters, not the superficial things.'

'You were fortunate.'

Her face took on a wry expression. 'But sadly I didn't appreciate just how lucky I was to have Robert, until William Dunn-Montgomery had a solicitor's letter sent to me warning me to stay away from him and his family.'

Cesario frowned, taken aback by that admission. 'When did that happen?'

'When I was a student of nineteen and I tried to meet my birth father. It was after I got out of hospital following the stalker attack. I was going through a difficult time emotionally and I was madly curious about my beginnings and rather naïve in my expectations. Sadly, William Dunn-Montgomery took fright at my first approach and made it very clear that he wanted nothing to do with me,' she explained with a grimace. 'It took that experience of rejection for me to realise how privileged I'd been to have a stepfather like Robert, who always treated me as a daughter he was proud of.'

'I can understand the depth of your loyalty to him now,' Cesario conceded heavily. 'I wish I hadn't taken advantage of it.'

'Never mind that now. Having a father enriched my life. All I'm asking is that you try to give our child the same advantage.'

Dark eyes bleak and without a shade of gold, Cesario breathed curtly, 'I'll bear that in mind, but I have thought long and hard about this and I have already made my decision.'

Jess released her breath in a slow hiss, the ferocious tension holding her taut draining out of her again to leave her feeling limp and wrung out. 'Decisions can be changed!' she argued.

'But that decision was made six months ago. Surgery may not even be an option any more.'

That risk hadn't really occurred to Jess. Up until that point all she had focused on was getting him to change his mind and consider treatment. Now all she could think about was how cruel it would be if Cesario was destined to die because he had met her too late.

Cesario searched her distraught face. 'You and that baby have me over a barrel.'

'That's not how I want you to feel.'

'I'm meeting with my doctors tomorrow—'

Her eyes widened fearfully. 'I'm coming too. From now on, you don't shut me out any more.'

'This was supposed to be a practical marriage. I never wanted you to get involved in this!' Cesario derided in a sudden burst of very masculine frustration.

'I decide what I want to get involved in,' Jess responded squarely.

'You'll regret it,' he told her grimly. 'At any time, feel free to walk away from this and me.'

'I'm not going anywhere,' Jess informed him stubbornly. 'And, by the way, I didn't marry you to gain the right to live in this house because it once belonged to the Dunn-Montgomery family. Nor did I marry you purely to save my stepfather's skin. I also wanted a child of my own—you and I had the same agenda.'

His lush lashes cloaked his gaze and the lean hands he had coiled into fists loosened again. He released his breath on a sigh. 'I know that, but it doesn't alter the fact that I used your stepfather's plight to put you under unfair pressure to marry me.'

'That's not how you felt about it at the time,' Jess reminded him. 'And if we're staying together, please tell your staff to put the office contents back.'

A faint touch of colour edging his high cheekbones, Cesario went to speak to his staff and the moving operation went into sudden reverse. Jess started to breathe a little easier when the first box went back through the office doorway instead of out of the house.

Taking off his jacket, Cesario strode back to her side, beautiful dark eyes lustrous, rousing a tiny scream of pain and fear inside her. How could he look so well and yet be so very far from well? Suppressing that negative thought, she sensed his uncertainty and she reached for his hand in an instinctive gesture of unity.

'Let's go upstairs where we'll get some peace,' he urged in the midst of the bustle around them, and he directed her towards the magnificent staircase.

'There are things I have to say to you, *mia bella*,' Cesario said very seriously before they reached the bedroom they invariably shared. 'Things that I wanted to say weeks ago in Italy but which I felt then were better left unspoken.'

'So, get them out of the way now,' Jess urged, wondering in some apprehension what he had held back from saying to her. 'We shouldn't have any more secrets from each other.'

Cesario studied her intently. 'I blackmailed you into

marrying me, *moglie mia*,' he intoned with regret. 'I wanted you and I didn't care how I got you. But no matter how you feel about it now, it was incredibly selfish of me to plunge you into this situation.'

'You'd be surprised how resilient I am.' Jess lifted her head high, her grey gaze soft and strong as it rested on him. 'And, yes, you blackmailed me, but I was attracted to you as well and without the pressure you put on me I would never have done anything about it. Never mind what happens in the future; I'll always be glad we did get together,' she completed gruffly.

'But I feel like I've trapped you now. You're way too nice to put yourself first and walk away from a dying partner,' Cesario derided in a frustrated undertone.

'You may not die. You *must* look at the more positive angle,' Jess breathed feelingly. 'And I'm not too nice. If I didn't want to be with you, I wouldn't be here now because I couldn't fake it, I couldn't pretend...'

He touched her damp cheek with a gentle forefinger and looked down into her open gaze. 'No. I don't think you could fake what you feel either and it's one of the things that I love most about you. What you see is what you get, but I'm still taking advantage of your good nature and loyalty—'

Jess was so tense that she might as well have been poised on a cliff edge. 'Did you just say that you loved me?'

'I am hopelessly in love with you—didn't you guess?' Cesario vented a rueful laugh. 'I thought I was kind of obvious.'

Jess was trembling. 'I can be a bit slow on the uptake

sometimes,' she said shakily. 'When did you realise you felt that way?'

'In Italy when it was a challenge just to be away from you for a couple of hours,' Cesario confided huskily. 'I've never felt like that before.'

'Not even about Alice?' Jess heard herself ask, and then she winced, wishing she had not let that petty jealous question escape her lips.

'Jess, you have never had any reason to worry about the relationship I once had with Alice. I like and respect Alice a great deal but we were a mismatch. When I was with her, I was too young to want to settle down and even though I was unfaithful she never stood up to me.' Cesario shared those uncomfortable truths and grimaced. 'I'm not proud of the way I treated her. I only realised that I did care about her when she was gone from my life. But I never loved her the way Stefano loves her and I wouldn't have married her because my feelings didn't go deep enough for that.'

'I'm sorry to keep on going on about Alice,' Jess said ruefully as she linked her arms round his broad shoulders, her fears about the other woman finally laid to rest by his candour. 'But when I overheard you and Alice talking the night before we left Italy it did make me wary of your friendship with her.'

Cesario frowned. 'What did you overhear?'

And once Jess had explained, he heaved a groan of comprehension. 'Alice and Stefano have known about my condition from the start, and Alice was correct when she said that I wasn't being fair to you in not telling you. But those weeks we shared in Italy were some of the happiest of my life…and I didn't want to sacrifice a day of that to the reality of my condition.'

That declaration made her eyes prickle with tears. But she swiftly blinked the betraying moisture back because she knew he would take the wrong message from it and return to believing that he was the worst thing that had ever happened to her when in fact he was the best. 'I fell in love with you in Italy as well.'

'I was ahead of you there,' Cesario claimed, tipping up her chin with his fingers to look down into her silvery grey eyes. 'I probably fell for you at the moment I saw you in your wedding gown at the church—you looked like my every dream come true. And that's from a guy who never thought he was romantic.'

Jess had never felt that, for a thousand and one little and large romantic gestures had made their honeymoon special. But she smiled up at him with her heart in her eyes. 'I love you so much…'

'I'm never going to stop wanting you, *amata mia*,' Cesario pronounced with driven sincerity, brilliant dark eyes pinned to her with adoring intensity. 'But I didn't want to do this to you. I wanted to make you happy, not sad.'

'And whatever happens you *will* make me happy,' Jess told him with confidence. 'Every day we have together now is a day we wouldn't have had, if you had succeeded in scaring me off yesterday.'

'But it's not fair to put you through this with me,' Cesario groaned, unable to hide his guilty look of concern.

Jess smoothed gentle fingertips across the taut line of one high masculine cheekbone. 'How would you feel if it was me that had the tumour? Could you just walk away?'

'*Infierno!* Are you joking?' Cesario demanded incredulously.

'Well, then, don't expect me to be any different. I love you too,' she reminded him. 'I want to be with you, whatever happens.'

And in a flood of passionate appreciation that he could not hide from her, Cesario covered her mouth with his and kissed her breathless. She trailed his jacket off in the midst of it, embarked on undoing his shirt buttons and spread loving hands over the warmth of his hair-roughened torso. His lean, strong body was urgent and aroused against hers and she shut out the negative thoughts that lurked ready to threaten her happiness.

The man she loved loved her back with the same heat and passion and, for now, that was enough for her. She would take happiness where she could find it and make the most of every moment with him.

Rio, named Cesario at birth after his father, kicked the ball and it hit a window with a loud thump followed by the noise of shattering glass.

'*Mamma!*' he yelled in dismay.

Jess, who had been sitting in the shade of the loggia, rose to her feet and hurried along the terrace to ensure that her son stayed well away from the broken glass while shooing away the dogs at the same time. She checked his clothing for tiny shards, moved him well clear of the debris and then smiled at Tommaso. Having returned the ball, the older man, a long look of calm resignation on his face, was already advancing with a brush and shovel to clear up the mess. It was expected that a lively little boy would practise his football moves and, at five years old, boys didn't come much livelier than Rio.

He was blessed with his father's lustrous dark eyes and his mother's black curls; his decided appeal made it very likely that some day he would be a heartbreaker as well. Born a week after his due date in a straightforward delivery, Rio had delighted his mother from the first moment he'd drawn breath and motherhood had more than lived up to all her expectations, though been rather more tiring than she had appreciated. Although Rio had been a very good-natured baby he had also required little sleep and after more interrupted nights than she still cared to recall Jess had been glad to have the support of a good nanny. Having inherited his parents' stubborn streak, determination and intelligence, Rio could be a handful.

Her entire family enjoyed a long summer holiday at Collina Verde every year. Her parents were currently attending evening classes in Italian and working hard to learn the language. Her half-brothers still worked on the Halston estate, but her father had surprised them all by finding a new job at a local garden centre where he was happily employed as a deputy manager. Jess was also in regular contact with her other brother, Luke Dunn-Montgomery, and the previous year he and his girlfriend had joined her for a winter break at Cesario's opulent villa in Morocco. She had heard nothing more from her birth father but was content with that situation. Alice and Stefano and their children were regular visitors, and Alice had gradually become

Jess's best friend. The couples shared family events and celebrations.

Soon after Rio's birth, Jess had opted to buy into the veterinary practice as a partner and she still worked part-time hours. That same year, her animal sanctuary had won charitable status. Full-time employees, assisted by a rota of volunteers, now kept the rescue facility running efficiently and many animals had been happily rehomed since the sanctuary had reopened on the Halston estate. Dozy, her narcoleptic greyhound, was asleep by the wall next to Johnson, her collie. Harley the Labrador and Hugs the wolfhound had passed away due to old age, but their places had since been filled by Owen, a lively Jack Russell, who acted as a seeing-eye guide to his friend, Bix, a blind Great Dane. Weed and Magic, however, were now scampering cheerfully in the wake of the two little girls running across the terrace.

Graziella, an adorable three-year-old, with her mother's light grey eyes, rushed to show Jess the painting she had done at the summer playgroup she attended. Her little sister, Allegra, an apple-cheeked toddler of eighteen months with an explosion of black curls, bowled along behind Graziella like a shadow.

Jess gathered both girls into her arms with a grin but her whole face lit up when Cesario, her tall, dark and very handsome husband, strode out of the house. He bounced a new football across the terrace to Rio, who gave a whoop of pleasure and grabbed both ball and father in his enthusiasm, chattering in ninety-mile-an-hour Italian about the window he had broken.

'Daddy didn't play music in the car like I wanted,' confided Graziella crossly. 'We had football.'

From beneath the vine-covered loggia, Jess surveyed the man she loved with amused eyes. He made a special effort to take time off and spend it with his family during the long summers they usually spent at Collina Verde. Although she rarely thought back now to the period when she had feared she would lose Cesario, because she felt it was good to move on mentally, she valued the happiness she had found with him and her children all the more from the knowledge that she could so easily have lost him.

Having changed his mind and finally agreed to accept treatment, Cesario had benefited from the latest neurosurgical techniques. Stereotactic surgery, in which CT images were used to pinpoint the location of the tumour and target it with carefully controlled doses of gamma radiation, had been utilised and this non-invasive method had protected all healthy tissue from damage. He had spent only three days in hospital and, after a successful procedure, had experienced neither complications nor subsequent problems. The tumour was gone and follow-up scans remained reassuringly clear.

'Do you think we're spoiling Graziella?' Cesario remarked as their nanny, Izzy, put in an appearance to take the children indoors for lunch. 'She's a real little bossy-boots.'

'I wonder who she gets that from,' Jess commented tongue in cheek, since she had noticed that her elder daughter could twist her father round her little finger with just the suggestion of tears or disappointment. 'Or do you think it could be that maybe she just doesn't like football radio commentaries?'

A wickedly appreciative grin slashed Cesario's wide sensual mouth. 'She takes after her *mamma* then, her very beautiful, very much loved—'

'And very pregnant *mamma*,' Jess completed, hopelessly conscious of the size of her pregnant body on such a warm day. She was within weeks of her delivery date for their fourth child. She already knew that she was carrying a second boy, who would very probably be christened Roberto after his doting grandfather. Their children had given them both so much joy that they weren't quite sure when they would consider their family complete.

Cesario splayed a protective hand across the proud swell of her belly. 'Very beautiful, very pregnant *mamma*,' he traded huskily as he pulled her back against him, 'whom I was extremely lucky to find and marry in my hour of greatest need.'

Jess leant back against the support of his big powerful body and sighed in blissful relaxation, enjoying a moment of perfect peace without the children providing a distraction. 'We found each other and once I had had a taste of you and Italy I knew you were the man for me. I love you so much.'

Cesario turned her slowly round in the circle of his arms and looked down into the silvery grey eyes he still found so enthralling. 'The love of my life,' he breathed and kissed her with tender loving care...

A RICH MAN'S
WHIM

CHAPTER ONE

MIKHAIL KUSNIROVICH, RUSSIAN oil oligarch and much feared business magnate, relaxed his big body back into his leather office chair and surveyed his best friend, Luka Volkov, with astonishment. 'Hiking...*seriously*? That's truly how you want to spend your stag weekend away?'

'Well, we've already had the party and that was a little high octane for me,' Luka confided, his good-natured face tightening with distaste at the memory. Of medium height and stocky build, he was a university lecturer and the much admired author of a recent book on quantum physics.

'You can blame your future brother-in-law for that,' Mikhail reminded him drily, thinking of the lap and pole dancers hired by Peter Gregory for the occasion, women so far removed from his shy academic friend's experience that the arrival of a group of terrorists at the festivities would have been more welcome.

'Peter meant it for the best,' Luka proclaimed, instantly springing to the defence of his bride's obnoxious banker brother.

Mikhail's brow raised, his lean, darkly handsome face grim. 'Even though I warned him that you wouldn't like it?'

Luka reddened. 'He does try; he just doesn't always get it right.'

Mikhail said nothing because he was thinking with regret of how much Luka had changed since he had got engaged to Suzie Gregory. Although the two men had little in common except their Russian heritage, they had been friends since they met at Cambridge University. In those days, Luka would have had no problem declaring that a man as crude, boring and boastful as Peter Gregory was a waste of space. But now Luka could no longer call a spade a spade and always paid subservient regard to his fiancée's feelings. An alpha male to the core, Mikhail gritted his even white teeth in disgust. He would *never* marry. He was never going to change who and what he was to please some woman. The very idea was a challenge for a male raised by a man whose favourite saying had been, 'a chicken is not a bird and a woman is not a person'. The late Leonid Kusnirovich had been fond of reeling that off to inflame the sensibilities of the refined English nanny he had hired to take care of his only son. Sexist, brutal and always insensitive, Leonid had been outraged by the nanny's gentle approach to child rearing and had been afraid that she might turn his son into a wimp. But at the age of thirty there was nothing remotely wimpy about Mikhail's six-foot-five-inch powerfully built frame, his ruthless drive to succeed or his famous appetite for a large and varied diet of women.

'You'd like the Lake District...it's beautiful,' Luka declared.

Mikhail made a massive effort not to look as pained as he felt. 'You want to go hiking in the Lake District? I assumed you were thinking of Siberia—'

'I can't get enough time off work and I'm not sure

I'd be up to the challenge of the elements there,' Luka admitted, patting his slight paunch in apology. 'I'm not half as fit as you are. England in the spring and a gentle workout is more my style. But could you get by *without* your limo, luxury lifestyle and your fleet of minders for a couple of days?'

Mikhail went nowhere without a team of security guards. He frowned, not at the prospect of existing without the luxuries, but at having to convince his protection team that he didn't need them for forty eight hours. Stas, his highly protective head of security, had been taking care of Mikhail since he was a little boy. 'Of course, I can do it,' he responded with innate assurance. 'And a little deprivation will do me good.'

'You'll have to leave your collection of cell phones behind as well,' Luka dared.

Mikhail stiffened in dismay. 'But why?'

'You won't stop cutting deals if you still have the phones in tow,' Luka pointed out, well aware of his friend's workaholic ways. 'I don't fancy standing on top of a mountain somewhere shivering while you consider share prices. I know what you're like.'

'If that's really what you want, I'll consider it,' Mikhail conceded grudgingly, knowing he would sooner cut off his right arm than remove himself, even temporarily, from his vast business empire. Even so, although he rarely took time out from work, the concept of even a small physical challenge had considerable appeal for him.

A knock on the door prefaced the appearance of a tall beauty in her twenties with a mane of pale blonde hair. She settled intense bright blue eyes on her employer and said apologetically, 'Your next appointment is waiting, sir.'

'Thank you, Lara. I'll call you when I'm ready.'

Even Luka stared as the PA left the room, her slim hips swaying provocatively in her tight pencil skirt. 'That one looks like last year's Miss World. Are you—?'

Mikhail was amused and his wide sensual mouth quirked. 'Never ever in the office.'

'But she's gorgeous,' Luka commented.

Mikhail smiled. 'Is the reign of Suzie wearing thin?'

Luka flushed. 'Of course not. A man can look without being tempted.'

Mikhail relished the fact that *he* could still look at any woman and be tempted, a much more healthy state of affairs in his opinion than that of his friend, he reflected grimly, for Luka clearly now felt forced to stifle all his natural male inclinations in the holy cause of fidelity. Was his old friend so certain that he had found everlasting love? Or should Mikhail make use of their hiking trip to check that Luka was still as keen to make the sacrifices necessary to become a husband? Had Luka's awareness of Lara's attractions been a hint that he was no longer quite so committed to his future bride? *Forsaking all others…in sickness and in health*? Not for the first time, Mikhail barely repressed a shudder of revulsion, convinced that it was unnatural and unmanly to want to make such promises to any woman, and as for the what's-mine-is-yours agenda that went with it—he would sooner set fire to his billions than place himself in a financially vulnerable position.

Kat tensed in dismay as the sound of the post van crunching across gravel reached her ears. Her sister, Emmie, had come home late and unexpectedly the night before and she didn't want her wakened by the doorbell. Hastily setting down the quilt she was stitching, she flexed stiff fingers and hurried to the front door. Her stomach hollowed in fear of what the postman might be delivering. It was a fear that never left her now, a fear that dominated her every waking hour. But Kat still answered the door with a ready smile on her generous mouth and a friendly word and as she signed for the recorded delivery letter with the awful tell-tale red lettering on the envelope she was proud that she kept her hand steady.

Slowly she retreated back inside the solid stone farmhouse, which she had inherited from her father. Birkside's peaceful setting and beautiful views had struck her as paradise after the rootless, insecure existence she had endured growing up with her mother, Odette. A former top fashion model, Odette had never settled down to live an ordinary life, even after she had children. Kat's father had married her mother before she found fame and the increasingly sophisticated Odette had found the wealthy men she met on her travels far more to her taste than the quiet accountant she had married at too young an age. More than ten years had passed before Odette chose to marry a second time. That marriage had produced twin daughters, Sapphire and Emerald. Odette's final big relationship had been with a South American polo player, who had fathered Kat's youngest sister, Topaz. When Kat was twenty-three years old, her mother had put her three younger daughters into care, pleading that the twins in particular were out of control and at risk. Touched by the girls' distress, Kat had taken on sole responsibility for raising her half-sisters and had set up home with them in the Lake District.

Looking back to those first halcyon days when she had had such high hopes for their fresh start in life now left a bitter taste in Kat's mouth. A deep abiding sense of failure gripped her; she had been so determined to give the girls the secure home and love that she herself had never known as a child. She tore open the letter and read it. Yet another to stuff in the drawer with its equally scary predecessors, she reflected wretchedly. The building society was going to repossess the house while the debt collection agency would send in the bailiffs to recoup what funds they could from the sale of her possessions. She was so deep in debt that she stood to lose absolutely everything right down to the roof over her head. It didn't matter how many hours a day she worked making hand stitched patchwork quilts, only a miracle would dig her out of the deep financial hole she was in.

She had borrowed a small fortune to turn the old farmhouse into a bed and breakfast business. Putting in en suite bathrooms and extending the kitchen and dining area had been unavoidable. The steady stream of guests in the early years had raised Kat's hopes high and she had foolishly taken on more debt, determined to do the very best she could by every one of her sisters. Gradually, however, the flow of guests had died down to a trickle and she had realised too late that the market had changed; many people preferred a cheap hotel or a cosy pub to a B&B. In addition, the house was situated down a long single-track road and too far from civilisation to appeal to many. She had still hoped to get passing trade from day trippers and hill walkers but most of the walkers, she met went home at the end of the day or slept in a tent. The recent recession had made bookings as scarce as hens' teeth.

A tall beautiful blonde in a ratty old robe slowly descended the stairs smothering a yawn. 'That postman makes so much noise,' Emmie complained tartly. 'I suppose you've been up for ages. You always were an early riser.'

Kat resisted the urge to point out that for a long time she had had little choice with three siblings to get off to school every morning and overnight guests to feed; she was too grateful that Emmie seemed chattier than she had been the night before when the taxi dropped her off and she declared that she was too exhausted to do anything other than go straight to bed. During the night, Kat had burned with helpless curiosity because six months earlier Emmie had gone to live with their mother, Odette, in London, determined to get to know the woman she had barely seen since she was twelve years old. Kat had chosen not to interfere. Emmie was, after all, twenty-three years of age. Even so, Kat had still worried a lot about her, knowing that her sister would ultimately discover that the most important person in Odette's life was always Odette and that the older woman had none of the warmth and affection that every child longed to find in a parent.

'Do you want any breakfast?' Kat asked prosaically.

'I'm not hungry,' Emmie replied, sinking down at the kitchen table with a heavy sigh. 'But I wouldn't say no to a cup of tea.'

'I missed you,' Kat confided as she switched on the kettle.

Emmie smiled, long blonde hair tumbling round her lovely face as she sat forward. 'I missed you but I didn't miss my dead-end job at the library or the dreary social life round here. I'm sorry I didn't phone more often though.'

'That's all right.' Kat's emerald green eyes glimmered with fondness, her long russet spiralling curls brushing her cheekbones in stark contrast to her fair skin as she stretched up to a cupboard to extract two beakers. More than ten years older than her sister, Kat was a tall slender woman with beautiful skin, clear eyes and a wide full mouth. 'I guessed you were busy and hoped you were enjoying yourself.'

Without warning, Emmie compressed her mouth and pulled a face. 'Living with Odette was a nightmare,' she admitted abruptly.

'I'm sorry,' Kat remarked gently as she poured the tea.

'You knew it would be like that, didn't you?' Emmie prompted as she accepted the beaker. 'Why on earth didn't you warn me?'

'I thought that as she got older Mum might have mellowed and I didn't want to influence you before you got to know her on your own account,' Kat explained ruefully. 'After all, she could have treated you very differently.'

Emmie snorted and reeled off several incidents that illustrated what she had viewed as her mother's colossal selfishness and Kat made soothing sounds of understanding.

'Well, I'm home to stay for good this time,' her half-sister assured her squarely. 'And I ought to warn you... I'm pregnant—'

'*Pregnant*?' Kat gasped, appalled at that unexpected announcement. 'Please tell me you're joking.'

'I'm pregnant,' Emmie repeated, settling violet-blue eyes on her sister's shocked face. 'I'm sorry but there it is and there's not much I can do about it now—'

'The father?' Kat pressed tautly.

Emmie's face darkened as if Kat had thrown a light switch. 'That's over and I don't want to talk about it.'

Kat struggled to swallow back the many questions brimming on her lips, frightened of saying something that would offend. In truth she had always been more of a mother to her sisters than another sibling and after that announcement she was already wondering painfully where she had gone wrong. 'OK, I can accept that for the moment—'

'But I still *want* this baby,' Emmie proclaimed a touch defiantly.

Still feeling light-headed with shock, Kat sat down opposite her. 'Have you thought about how you're going to manage?'

'Of course, I have. I'll live here with you and help you with the business,' Emmie told her calmly.

'Right now there isn't a business for you to help me with,' Kat admitted awkwardly, knowing she had to give as much of the truth as possible when Emmie was basing her future plans on the guest house doing a healthy trade. 'I haven't had a customer in over a month—'

'It's the wrong time of year—business is sure to pick up by Easter,' Emmie said merrily.

'I doubt it. I'm also in debt to my eyeballs,' Kat confessed reluctantly.

Her sister studied her in astonishment. 'Since when?'

'For ages now. I mean, you must've noticed before you went away that business wasn't exactly brisk,' Kat responded.

'Of course, you borrowed a lot of money to do up the house when we first came here,' Emmie recalled abstractedly.

Kat wished she could have told her sister the whole truth but she didn't want the younger woman to feel guilty. Clearly, Emmie had quite enough to be worrying about in the aftermath of a broken relationship that had left her pregnant. Kat did wonder if some people were born under an unlucky star, for Emmie had suffered a lot of hard knocks in her life, not least the challenge of living in the shadow of the glowing success and fame of her identical twin, who had become an internationally renowned supermodel. Saffy had naturally suffered setbacks too, but not to the extent Emmie had. Moreover, Saffy, the twin two minutes older, had a tough independent streak and a level of cool that the more vulnerable Emmie lacked. Already damaged by her mother's indifferent approach to raising her daughters, Emmie had been hurt in a joy-riding incident when she was twelve and her legs had been badly damaged. Getting her sister upright and out of a wheelchair had been the first step in her recovery but, sadly, a complete recovery had proved impossible. The accident had left Emmie with one leg shorter than the other, an obvious limp and significant scarring, a reality that made it all the harder for Emmie to live side by side with her still physically perfect twin sister. Emmie's misery and the unfortunate comparisons made by insensitive people had caused friction between the two girls and even now, years later, the twins still barely spoke to each other.

Yet, happily, Emmie no longer limped. In a desperate attempt to help her depressed younger sister recover her self-esteem and interest in life, Kat had taken out a large personal loan to pay for a decidedly experimental leg-lengthening operation only available abroad. The surgery had proved to be an amazing success, but it was that particular debt that had mushroomed when Kat found herself unable to keep up the regular repayments, but she would never lay that guilt trip on Emmie's slim shoulders. Even knowing the financial strain it would place on her family, Kat knew she'd do it all over again in a heartbeat. Emmie had needed help and Kat had been willing to move mountains to come to her aid.

'I've got it,' Emmie said suddenly. 'You can sell the land to settle any outstanding bills. I'm surprised you haven't thought of doing that for yourself.'

But Kat had sold the land within a couple of years of settling in the area, reasoning that a decent sum of cash would be of more use to her at the time than the small income that she earned from renting out the land that she had inherited with the house. Raising three girls had unfortunately proved much more expensive than Kat had initially foreseen and there had been all sorts of unanticipated expenses over the years while Odette, who was supposed to pay maintenance towards her daughters' upkeep, had quickly begun skipping payments and had soon ended them altogether. To add to Kat's problems during those years, her youngest sister, Topsy, who was extremely clever, had been badly bullied at school and Kat had only finally managed to solve the problem by sending Topsy away to boarding school. Mercifully, Topsy, now in sixth form, had won a full scholarship and although Kat had then been saved from worrying about how she would keep up the private school fees she had still had to pay for that first year and it had been a tidy sum.

'The land was sold a long time ago,' Kat admitted reluctantly, wanting to be as honest about the facts as she could be. 'And I may well lose the house—'

'My goodness, what have you been spending your money on?' Emmie demanded with a startled look of reproof.

Kat said nothing. There had never been much money to start with and when there had been, there had always been some pressing need to pay it out again. The front door bell chimed and Kat rose eagerly from her seat, keen to escape the interrogation without telling any lies. Naturally Emmie wanted the whole story before she committed herself to moving back in with her sister. But it was early days for such a decision, Kat reminded herself bracingly. Emmie was newly pregnant and a hundred and one things might happen to change the future, not least the reappearance of the father of her child.

Roger Packham, Kat's nearest neighbour and a widower in his forties, greeted Kat with a characteristic nod. 'I'll be bringing you some firewood tomorrow... Will I put it in the usual place?'

'Er...yes. Thank you very much,' Kat said, uncomfortable with his generosity and folding her arms as the bitingly cold wind pierced through her wool sweater like a knife. 'Gosh, it's cold today, Roger.'

'It's blowing from the north,' he told her ponderously, his weathered face wreathed in the gloom that always seemed to be his natural companion. 'There'll be heavy snow by tonight. I hope you're well stocked up with food.'

'I hope you're wrong...about the snow,' Kat commented, shivering again. 'Let me pay you for the wood. I don't feel right accepting it as a gift.'

'There's no call for money to change hands between neighbours,' the farmer told her, a hint of offence in his tone. 'A woman like you living alone up here...I'm glad to help out when I can.'

Kat thanked him again and went back indoors. She caught a glimpse of herself in the hall mirror and saw a harassed, middle-aged woman, who would soon have to start thinking about cutting her long hair. But what would she do with it then? It was too curly and wild to sit in a neat bob. Was she imagining the admiring look in Roger's eyes? Whatever, it embarrassed her. She was thirty-five years old and had often thought that she was a born spinster. It had been a very long time since a man had looked at her with interest: there weren't many in the right age group locally and in any case she only left the house to buy food or deliver her quilts to the gift shop that purchased them from her.

If she was honest, her personal life as such had stopped dead once she took her sisters in to raise them. Her only serious boyfriend had dumped her when she accepted that commitment and in actuality, once she was engulfed in the daily challenge of raising two troubled adolescents and a primary-school genius, she hadn't missed him very much at all. No, that side of things had died a long time ago for Kat without ever really getting going. It struck her as a sad truth that Emmie was already more experienced than she was and she felt ill-qualified to press her sister for details about her child's father that she clearly didn't want to share. Kat knew little about men and even less about intimate relationships.

As she walked back into the kitchen, Emmie was putting away her mobile phone. 'May I borrow the car? Beth's invited me down,' she explained, referring to her former school friend who still lived in the village.

Guessing that Emmie was keen to confide her problems in a friend of her own age, Kat stifled an unfair pang of resentment. 'OK, but Roger said there'll be heavy snow tonight, so you'll need to keep an eye on the weather.'

'If it turns bad, I'll stay over with Beth,' Emmie said cheerfully, already rising from her chair. 'I'll go and get dressed.' In the doorway she hesitated and turned back, a rueful look of apology in her eyes. 'Thanks for not going all judgemental about the baby.'

Kat gave her sister a reassuring hug and then steeled herself to step back. 'But I do *want* you to think carefully about your future. Single parenting is not for everyone.'

'I'm not a kid any more,' Emmie countered defensively. 'I know what I'm doing!'

The sharp rejection of her advice stung, but Kat had to be content, as it appeared to be all the answer she would get to her attempt to make Emmie take a good clear look at her long term future. She suppressed a sigh, for after eleven years of single parenting she knew just how hard it was to go it alone, to have only herself to depend on and never anyone else to fall back on when there was a crisis. And if she lost the house, where would they live? How would she bring in an income? In a rural area there was little spare housing and even fewer jobs available.

Ramming back those negative thoughts and a rising hint of panic, Kat watched the snow begin to fall that afternoon in great fat fluffy flakes. When the world was transformed by a veil of frosted white it made everything look so clean and beautiful but she knew how treacherous the elements could be for the local farmers and their animals and anyone else taken by surprise, for the long-range weather forecast had made no mention of snow.

Emmie rang to say that she was staying the night with Beth. Kat stacked wood by the stove in the living room while the snow fell faster and thicker, swirling in clouds that obscured the view of the hills and drifted in little mounds up against the garden wall. A baby, Kat thought as she worked on her latest quilt, a baby in the family. She had long since accepted that she would never have a child of her own and she smiled at the prospect of a tiny nephew or niece, quelling her worries about their financial survival while dimly recalling her paternal grandmother's much-loved maxim, 'God will provide.'

The bell went at eight and as she started in surprise it was followed by three unnecessarily loud knocks on the front door. Kat darted into the hall where the outside light illuminated three large shapes standing in the small outer porch. Potential guests, she hoped, needing to take shelter from the inclement weather. She opened the door without hesitation and saw two men partially supporting a third and smaller man, balancing awkwardly on one leg.

'This is a guest house, right?' the tall lanky man on the left checked in a decidedly posh English accent, while the very large black-haired male on the right simply emanated impatience.

'Can you put us up for the night?' he said bluntly. My friend has hurt his ankle.'

'Oh dear...' Kat said sympathetically, standing back from the door. 'Come in. You must be frozen through. I've nobody staying at the moment but I do have three en suite rooms available.'

'You will be richly rewarded for looking after us well,' the biggest one growled, his heavy foreign accent unfamiliar to her.

'I look after all my guests well,' Kat told him without hesitation, colliding with startlingly intense dark eyes enhanced by spiky black lashes. He was extremely tall and well built: she had to tip her head back to look at him, something she wasn't accustomed to having to do, being of above average height herself at five feet ten inches tall. He was also, she realised suddenly, quite breathtakingly good-looking with arresting cheekbones, well-defined brows and a strong jawline, an alpha male in every discernible lineament.

He stared down at her fixedly. 'I'm Mikhail Kusnirovich and this is my friend, Luka Volkov, and his fiancée's brother, Peter Gregory.'

Mikhail had never been so struck by a woman at first sight. Spiralling curls the rich dark colour of red maple leaves rioted in an undisciplined torrent round her small face in glorious contrast to porcelain-pale perfect skin with a scattering of freckles over her small nose and eyes as luminous and deep as emeralds. Her mouth was full and pink and unusually luscious, provoking erotic images in his brain of what she might do with those lips. He went instantly hard and his big powerful body stiffened defensively because he was always in full control of his libido and anything less than full control was a weakness in his book.

'Katherine Marshall...but everybody calls me Kat,' she muttered, feeling astonishingly short of breath as she began to turn away on legs that suddenly felt heavy and clumsy. 'Bring your friend into the living room. He can lie on the sofa. If he needs medical attention, I don't know what we'll do because the road's probably impassable—'

'It's only a sprained ankle,' the man called Luka hastened to declare, his accent identical to the larger man's. 'I simply need to get my weight off it.'

Mikhail watched her cross the room, his attention gliding admiringly down over the small firm breasts enhanced by a ribbed black sweater, the tiny waist and the very long sexy legs sheathed in skinny jeans. Aside of the fluffy pink bunny slippers she sported, she was gorgeous, a total stunner, he thought in a daze, disconcerted by the level of his own appreciation.

'What a hottie...' Peter Gregory remarked, predictably following it up with a crude comment about what he would like to do to her that would have had them thrown out had their hostess had the misfortune to overhear him. Mikhail gritted his even white teeth in frustration. So far, Peter's unexpected inclusion in their disastrous weekend of hiking remained the worst aggravation Mikhail had had to bear. Always at his best in a crisis, Mikhail functioned at top speed under stress and enjoyed a challenge. The sudden change in the weather, Luka's fall and losing battle to tolerate the freezing temperatures, their lack of mobile phones and inability to call for help had all played a part in the ruin of their plans, but Mikhail had dealt calmly with those setbacks. In contrast, having to also tolerate Peter Gregory's crassness downright infuriated Mikhail, who had virtually no experience of ever having to put up with anyone or anything he didn't like.

The two men lowered the third to the sofa where he relaxed with a groan of relief. Kat thoughtfully provided Luka with a low stool on which to rest his leg while the tallest man went back out to the porch to retrieve their rucksacks. He returned with a small first aid kit and knelt down to remove his friend's boot, a process accompanied by several strangled groans from the injured man. They conversed in a foreign language that she did not recognise. Without being asked Kat proffered her own first-aid kit, which was better stocked, and he made efficient use of a bandage. Kat then fetched her father's walking stick and helpfully placed it next to them before noticing that Luka was shivering and dragging a woollen throw off a nearby chair to pass it to the man tending to him.

'Have you any painkillers?' the hugely tall one, Mikhail, asked, glancing up at her so that she could not help but notice that he had the most ridiculously long, lush black eyelashes she had ever seen on a man. Eyes of ebony with sable lashes, she thought, startling herself with that mental flight of fancy.

Her cheeks pink, Kat brought the painkillers with a glass of water, noticing that the younger posh man had yet to do anything at all to help. He had also at one point complained bitterly that the other two men were no longer speaking English.

'I'd better show you your rooms now. I've got one downstairs that will suit you best,' she informed Luka with a reassuring smile, for he was obviously enduring a fair degree of discomfort.

'I need to get out of these filthy clothes,' Peter Gregory announced, storming upstairs ahead of Kat. 'I want a shower.'

'Give the water at least thirty minutes to heat,' she advised.

'You don't have a constant supply of hot water?' he complained scornfully. 'What kind of guest house is this?'

'I wasn't expecting guests,' Kat said mildly, showing him into the first available room to get rid of him. She had dealt with a few difficult customers over the years and had learned to tune them out and let adverse comments go over her head. There was no pleasing some folk.

'Ignore him,' Mikhail Kusnirovich told her smoothly. 'I do…'

The deep vibrations of his accented drawl raised

goose bumps on Kat's skin, made her feel all jumpy and she swung open the door of the next room, eager to return downstairs.

CHAPTER TWO

KAT SCANNED THE messy room she had entered in frank dismay, having totally forgotten that Emmie had slept there the night before and had left the bed unmade and every surface cluttered with her belongings. Unfortunately she had no other room available.

'I forgot that my sister slept here last night. I'll tidy up and change the bed,' she assured Mikhail as she began to snatch up Emmie's possessions in haste, gathering up an armful to carry it across the corridor and deposit it in her own bedroom.

Mikhail wondered why she was so nervous around him. He could feel the nerves leaping off her in invisible sparks, had noticed how she carefully kept a distance between them. No, this was not a woman who was going to butt into his space like so many of her sex tried to do, drawn like magnets to his power and wealth with little understanding of the man who went with those attributes. Yes, he was used to rousing many female reactions—lust, jealousy, greed, anger, possessiveness—but nervousness had never once played a part and was novel enough to attract his attention. It amused him that she had not the slightest idea who he was: he had noticed her total lack of recognition of his name when he introduced himself. But then why should a woman who lived in the backend of nowhere know who he was? That sense of anonymity was strangely welcome to the son of a billionaire who had never known a way of life that did not classify as A-list and exclusive.

Kat returned for a second bundle of her sister's belongings. Mikhail tossed her a bra that was dangling from the lampshade by the bed. Kat flushed to the roots of her hair, feeling embarrassingly like a shocked maiden aunt, and sped back across the corridor, pausing on her return trip to grab fresh bedding from the laundry press. She was so self-conscious when she walked back into the room that she couldn't bring herself to look at him. 'Are you and your friends on holiday here?' she enquired stiltedly to try and fill the dragging silence.

'A weekend break from London,' he advanced wryly.

'Is that where you live?' she prompted, allowing herself a quick upward glance in his direction as she began stripping the double bed, already reckoning that it would be a few inches too short for him and then forgetting the fact entirely as her gaze locked onto him like a guided missile that was out of her control. Her regard clung to the stunning symmetry of his features, collided with eyes that glittered like black diamonds and it was as if her mind blew a fuse. Next thing she was remembering that symmetry was supposed to be the most powerful component in the definition of true beauty...and he had it in spades with his exotic cheekbones, perfect nose and wide, wondrously sensual mouth. She was staring and she couldn't stop staring and the knowledge sent a shard of pure panic through her because she didn't know what was the matter with her.

'*Da*...yes,' he qualified in husky English. 'Luka and I are Russian.'

Suddenly released from her paralysis while he blinked, her face hot and red with chagrin, she fought with the bottom sheet, spreading it, tucking it in, wishing he were the kind of guy who would offer to help so that she could do the job more quickly. But judging by his arrogant stance as he watched from by the window, he had probably never made a bed in his life.

Mikhail dug his hands into the pockets of his trousers to conceal his erection. He was hugely aroused. She was bending over right in front of him, showing off a perfect heart-shaped bottom and the shapely length of her slender thighs as she stretched energetically across the mattress. He was picturing those legs wrapped round his waist, urging him on as he rode her, and perspiration dampened his upper lip, sent his temperature rocketing. He felt like a man who had been deprived of sex for years, and as that was far from true, he could only marvel at the wildly exciting effect she had on him. Thankfully she had stared back at him with a look he knew all too well on a female face: an openly acquisitive look of longing and hunger. Satisfaction gripped him. She wore no rings and she was clearly available...

Having dealt with the pillows in a silence that threatened to suffocate her, Kat glanced at him again, feeling as awkward as a schoolgirl, knowing she ought to be chatting the way she usually did with guests. Except normal behaviour was impossible around him and she cringed that even at her age she could still be so vulnerable. His expressive mouth quirked with sudden humour and she blushed again and tore her attention from him, thoroughly ashamed of herself. She might not be a naive teenager any more but she was acting like one. That near smile, though, had lightened his darkly handsome features, which in repose had a grim, brooding quality, and her heart had leapt inside her like a startled deer; she was seeing another layer of him and greedy to see more.

'Can you provide food for us this evening?' Mikhail asked levelly, watching her slot the duvet into the cover with frantic hands. She was nervous, clumsy, and agitated and it was astonishing how much he enjoyed seeing that rare vulnerability in this particular woman. She had no sophisticated front to hide behind. He believed he could read her like a book and he relished the idea. She wouldn't be that experienced, he guessed, wondering why that thought didn't put him off because he was accustomed to women who were more likely to introduce *him* to new techniques in the bedroom, women as practised as whores but a good deal less honest in the impression they liked to make.

Kat turned her head, glossy russet curls flowing back over a slim shoulder, and refused to look directly at him, focusing on his flat midriff instead. 'Yes, but it won't be fancy food, it will be plain.'

'We're so hungry it won't matter.'

She shook out the duvet, hurried into the bathroom to check it, gathering up her sister's toiletries to tip them into a bag and snatch up the used towels. 'I'll come back up and clean it,' she said, crossing the bedroom.

But Mikhail wanted to keep her with him. He spread out an Ordnance Survey map on the top of the dressing table. The *dusty* dressing table, Kat noticed in consternation, shocked by how much she had neglected her once thorough cleaning routine since guest numbers dwindled and daily financial stress took its place.

'Could you show me where this house is?' he asked although he knew perfectly well. 'I want to work out how far we are from our four-wheel-drive...'

'Give me a minute,' Kat urged, leaving the room to dump the remains of her sister's belongings and extract clean towels from the laundry press. Drawing in a deep steadying breath, she settled the fresh towels on the bed and returned to his side. He was uncomfortably close: she could feel the heat emanating from his lean, powerful body, hear the even rasp of his breathing and smell a hint of cologne overlying an outdoorsy male scent. It was a wickedly intimate experience for a woman who had long since closed the door on such physical awareness around men and it made her every treacherous sense sing. Her body quickened as though he had touched her, a chain reaction running from the sudden heaviness of her breasts to the clenching sensation low in her belly.

With fierce force of will she stabbed a finger down on the map, for she had often studied maps with walking guests to offer them advice on the best routes and view points. 'We're right *here*...'

His hand covered hers where it rested on the map, warm, strong, ensnaring, a thumb lightly enclosing and massaging her wrist as though to soothe the wild pulse beating there. 'You're trembling,' Mikhail murmured in a roughened undertone, using his other hand to turn her round to face him, long fingers firm on her slight shoulder.

'Must be c-cold...' Kat said jerkily, terrified that she was guilty of encouraging a complete stranger to touch her and shocked that she was allowing it to happen. He could hardly have failed to notice her staring, but she was convinced that a male with his stunning looks had to be used to that kind of attention. In a minute he would surely be laughing at her shaking and stuttering like an old maid afraid of her own shadow in his presence.

And it was that last thought, that terror that he had to be seeing her as a figure of fun, that made her compose herself and lift her head high in a determined display of control. It was a mistake for he was gazing down at her, black eyes blazing like fireworks flaring against the night sky, utterly riveting, utterly inescapable. Her throat tightened, her breath entrapped there and a shot of pure driving heat raced through her tall slender body like a living flame. Cold was the very last thing she was feeling, but then she had never before felt anything quite that painfully intense. It was as if time stopped and in the interim he lifted his hand from her shoulder to trace the plump pink line of her lower lip with the tip of a long forefinger and her entire skin surface tightened over her bones in response.

'I want to kiss you, *milaya moya*,' he breathed thickly.

And his words freed her as nothing else could have done, so lost was she in what she was experiencing while she also tried to withstand the hurricane force of his strong personality. She reeled back in sudden shock from him, seriously alarmed by her loss of control and common sense, no matter how brief that moment had been. 'No…absolutely not,' she framed jaggedly, her heart still accelerating like a racing car while his face hardened and his black-diamond eyes turned to crystalline black ice instead. 'For goodness' sake, I don't even know you—'

'I don't usually ask for permission to kiss a woman,' Mikhail retorted with chilling cool. 'But you should be more careful—'

Suddenly the tables were being turned with a vengeance on Kat and she was hopelessly unprepared for the tactic. 'I beg your pardon? *I* should be more careful?' she gasped blankly.

'It's obvious that you're attracted to me,' Mikhail countered with a rock-solid assurance that glued Kat's tongue to the roof of her mouth in sheer horror. 'I saw that and reacted to it... You're a very beautiful woman.'

The humiliation he inflicted with that first sentence was enough to burn Kat up from inside out with shame. So, it was *her* fault he had made a pass at her? That was certainly putting a new spin on an unwelcome approach from a man. He was quick of tongue and even faster to take advantage, she registered with seething resentment. As for that old flannel he had tossed in about her being a 'very beautiful' woman... Who did he think he was kidding? Did she look as if she had been born yesterday? Was that piece of outrageous flattery supposed to mollify her and remove her embarrassment? Furious as she was, Kat clenched her teeth together tight because in some remote corner of her brain she was very much afraid that in some mysterious way she *had* encouraged his advances and that he might have a right to reproach her for the mistaken impression she had evidently given him.

Kat hurriedly shut down her troubled thoughts in the brooding silence; her most pressing desire was to escape the scene of her apparent crime. 'I need to cook,' she said succinctly like an automaton and, spinning round, she walked straight out of the room.

I need to cook? Mikhail was as astounded by that unfathomable declaration as he had been moments earlier when she had backed away from him as though a desire to kiss her were the equivalent of an assault.

He *knew* women—he knew women well enough not to make a move on an uninterested one, he reflected angrily. What the hell was she playing at? Was this stop-start nonsense her idea of flirtation? Was he supposed to want her more because she held him at arm's length? He swore long and low in Russian, still taken aback by what had happened: the absurd and unthinkable, the impossible. For the first time in Mikhail's adult life a woman had rejected him.

Kat dug meat out of the freezer and set about defrosting it. A basic beef stew was the best she could offer her guests. She still hadn't cleaned *his* bathroom but no way was she going back up there to face him again! It was not that she was scared—she was simply dying a thousand deaths of embarrassment with that accusation still ringing in her ears. *It's obvious that you're attracted to me.* The wretched man had turned her knowledge of herself upside down and inside out within the space of an hour. For the first time in more years than she cared to count she had been attracted to a man. He was right on that score; she certainly couldn't deny it to herself. But the last time she had reacted to a man that way she was working as a conservation trainee in a London museum, light years back in her past when she had still been young and full of dreams, hopes and ambitions. And even then, even when she had got all silly and tingly about Steve, her one-time boyfriend, it had not hit her anything like as hard as the explosive effect of Mikhail Kusnirovich had! No, back in those days in a similar situation she had still found it possible to act normally and not like a brainless idiot!

But my goodness, how had *he* known how she felt?

How had she shown herself up? Her ignorance of what might have betrayed her infuriated her, making her feel suddenly like a child in an intimidatingly adult world. It *must* have been the way she looked at him, so she would make sure not to look at him again, not to speak to him, not to do anything that might be misinterpreted. The sheer shock value of having such responses roused in her again would have been quite sufficient for her to handle. She had not needed to find herself trapped below the same roof as the man as well! So, she was not too old to react like that, not past those hormonal urges in the way she had blithely assumed. Well, that didn't make her feel one bit better. And where did he get off calling her beautiful? Did he think she was stupid as well as a slut? After all, only a slut would be kissing a complete stranger within an hour of meeting him for the first time!

A knock sounded and she glanced up from her task of angrily slicing vegetables and blinked at the sight of Luka standing there in the doorway, leaning heavily on the stick she had given him. She had totally forgotten the poor man was in the house!

'Sorry to interrupt but—'

'No, I'm sorry…I forgot to show you to your room,' Kat said for him while she washed and dried her hands.

'I fell asleep in the chair,' Luka told her wryly as he shuffled along beside her. 'Never been so tired in my life yet Mikhail didn't even break a sweat when he was virtually carrying me the last mile. I can't believe this weekend was *my* idea…'

'Accidents happen, no matter how careful you are,' Kat told him soothingly while she gathered up the only remaining rucksack in the hall for him on her way past and opened the door to the room he was to occupy.

* * *

There was an atmosphere at the dining table no matter how hard Kat strove to ignore it. There might as well have been a giant black hole cocooning the chair in which Mikhail sat, for Kat refused to acknowledge his presence. The men ate hungrily and with pleasure and when she served up apple tart and ice cream for the dessert, the compliments came thick and fast.

She could cook like a dream. Mikhail, who had never thought about such a talent before, was reluctantly impressed, although he was anything but impressed to find himself eating in a kitchen. Nor was he enamoured of the childish manner in which she was treating him, although it gave him every opportunity to examine her and admire the way her bright hair glimmered below the lights with her every mercurial movement, note the elegance of her pale slender hands as she shifted them and the dainty silence of her table manners. More and more the depth of his interest in her irritated him for it was not his style. Indeed a volcanic growl of frustration began to swell in his chest when she dared to enjoy a light-hearted conversation with Luka.

'What are you doing living all the way out here alone?' Peter Gregory interrupted to ask Kat abruptly. 'Are you a widow?'

'I've never been married,' Kat replied evenly, all too accustomed to being asked that kind of question by her guests. 'My father left me this house and turning it into a guest house made sense at the time.'

'So, is there a man in your life?' Peter prompted with an assessing, too familiar look that she didn't appreciate, particularly not now that Mikhail had put her on her guard.

'I think that's my business,' Kat countered, feeling that politeness only went so far.

Another man? Why hadn't that possibility occurred to him? She might be attracted to him but she had backed off because she had someone else in her life, Mikhail reflected in an increasingly aggressive mood that was steadily beginning to knock him off balance. He felt angry, edgy, quite unlike himself, his vibrant energy too confined by the walls threatening to close up around him. Being cooped up was giving him cabin fever, he decided broodingly. He had always taken his space, his privacy and his complete freedom for granted. In a sudden movement he plunged upright.

'I'll walk back to the car and collect our phones. Leaving them behind wasn't such a good idea, Luka,' he told his friend shortly.

Kat blinked in astonishment at that declaration.

'You can't go back out there,' Luka objected in dismay. 'There's a blizzard blowing and the car's miles away.'

'I would have returned to it earlier if you hadn't been hurt,' Mikhail replied drily.

'I'd really like my phone back,' Peter Gregory said cheerfully.

Kat turned her attention to Mikhail for the first time since he had entered the kitchen. It had taken considerable control to stave off her insatiable need to look at him again but genuine concern now gripped her. After an instant of hesitation, which gave him time to don his waterproof jacket in the hall and open the front door, she jumped up and chased after him.

The snow was falling thick and fast, the road beyond her gates so deeply engulfed with furrowed drifts of snow that she could no longer see it. A split second before Mikhail stepped off the doorstep with the casual confidence of a male about to go for a stroll in a sunlit park, she shot out her hand and closed it around his arm to stop him. 'Don't be an idiot!' she exclaimed, shivering violently in the freezing air. 'Nobody risks their life to go and collect phones—'

'Don't call me an idiot,' Mikhail growled in rampant disbelief at her interference, his handsome features clenched with derisive incredulity. 'And don't be a drama queen…I am not risking my life if I choose to take a walk in little more than a foot of snow—'

'Well, if I didn't have a conscience I'd be happy to leave you to die of frostbite and exposure in a drift somewhere down the road!' Kat let fly back at him, her temper breaking through. Of all the stupid male macho idiots she had ever met, he surely took the biscuit.

'I am not about to die,' Mikhail fielded with sardonic bite, black eyes full of arrogant scorn. 'I am wearing protective clothing. I am very fit and I know exactly what I'm doing in such terrain and weather—'

'I'm afraid that's not a very convincing claim coming from a guy who had to have *me* show him where this house was on the map!' Kat whipped back at him without an ounce of hesitation. 'Use the landline here and be sensible.'

Mikhail gritted his perfect white teeth, caught out by the reminder of the little game he had played with her. He gazed down at her in furious frustration, her bossiness an unwelcome surprise. She was virtually shouting at him as well and that was a novelty he had never met with before and liked even less in a woman. But her green eyes still gleamed like the richest emeralds in her heart-shaped face while the breeze whipped her torrent of curls round her narrow shoulders and made of skim her pale cheeks. She provided an alluring vision, even for a male who had long since decided that, like children, he pretty much preferred women to be seen and not heard. And that fast Mikhail switched from wanting her silence into an infinitely more intoxicating mood, all conscious thought suspended while his body thrummed taut with powerful sexual need and tension.

Later, Kat would tell herself that he behaved like a caveman and that the way she found herself staring up at him had nothing to do with the manner in which, black predatory eyes glittering, he hauled her up against him with alarmingly strong arms and kissed her. And then the memory of what happened next went completely hazy because she fell into that kiss and almost drowned in the overpowering onslaught of the hungry passion he unleashed. Full of virile masculine power and devouring demand, his hard lips captured hers and thrust them fiercely apart so that he could penetrate the tender interior with his tongue and with a shockingly erotic thoroughness that racked her slender body against his with a helpless shudder of response. All control vanquished, she let the excitement rage over her and through her, tightening her nipples into bullet points, while flashing a jolting sensual wake-up call to her core. She shook in reaction, icy snowflakes melting on her cheeks in contrast to the smoulderingly hot burn of his carnal mouth on hers. It was a connection she had never made before and it was inexplicably and all at once wonderful, magical and terrifying.

'I'll be a couple of hours, *milaya moya*,' Mikhail imparted thickly, staring down into her dazed face with the strongest sense of satisfaction he had experienced in a long time because she was finally behaving the way he wanted her to. 'May I hope that you'll wait up for my return?'

And just as quickly, in receipt of that manipulative invitation that naive sense of wonder and magic that had briefly transformed Kat into a woman she didn't recognise shrivelled up and died right there and then on the doorstep.

'Not unless you've got a death wish,' Kat countered tartly, rubbing at her swollen lips with the back of her hand as though he had soiled her in some way, making his stunning dark eyes blaze like fireworks all over again above her head. 'When I say no, Mr Whoever-you-are, I *mean* it and the answer hasn't changed—'

'You're a very strange woman,' Mikhail gritted, outraged by her and yet curiously drawn by the challenge of her defiance.

'Because I'm not saying what you want to hear? Well, do I have news for you?' Kat told him angrily. 'I'm not the Sleeping Beauty and you're not my prince, so the kiss was a waste of effort!'

Kat watched him stride off in the snow and she stalked back into the house and shut the door with the suggestion of a slam. Wretched, stubborn, *stupid* man! She turned and saw Luka staring at her wide-eyed from the lounge doorway as if she were an even stranger creature than his friend. His mouth curved with sudden unmistakable amusement. 'Mikhail has done trekking in the Arctic and in Siberia,' he delivered in a I-know-this-is-going-to-embarrass-you tone of apology.

Freakin' typical, Kat thought tempestuously, her face colouring at the information: macho man had genuine grounds to believe that he was a superior being in the fitness field. *The Arctic*? Wincing, she went back into the kitchen to tidy up. That kiss? Her first in over ten years? No way was she going to think about that for even ten seconds! That would be awarding the Russian the kind of importance that he already so clearly believed to be his due and she had more backbone than that!

While Kat cleared the dishes from the kitchen table, Peter Gregory talked continuously about his big city apartment and the size of his last whopping banking bonus while dropping the names of several well-known clients, which she vaguely recognised from magazines. Grudgingly she conceded that he was so conceited that he made Mikhail look and sound positively humble.

CHAPTER THREE

KAT WAS PEERING round her bedroom curtain when she finally saw Mikhail returning, ploughing through the snow with his long powerful stride. He was *safe*. She had not been able to sleep for worrying about him and now, although she no longer had an acceptable reason to hover or pry, she very quietly opened her bedroom door to listen to the voices drifting upstairs from the hall below.

'We'll be back in London by lunchtime,' Luka was saying with satisfaction.

'Are you sure you want to leave so soon, Mikhail?' Peter Gregory enquired in a salacious tone of amusement. 'Isn't our hostess hottie waiting up for you? Bet you five grand you can't get her into bed before tomorrow!'

Wishing she hadn't chosen to eavesdrop, Kat turned paper pale and her stomach lurched. In haste, she closed her bedroom door softly shut, afraid that the smallest sign that she was still awake might be taken as proof of some sleazy invitation. There was no doubt about it: men could think, talk and behave like repellent beasts, she thought in disgust. Peter Gregory and his dirty mind certainly fitted into that category. Were the three men really agreeing a bet on the odds of her sleeping with

Mikhail tonight? Clearly that kiss had been witnessed and misunderstood. A rolling riptide of shame and mortification assailed Kat. She had never been more aware of how inexperienced she was in the field of sex. A truly confident woman would have overheard that bet being proposed and sauntered downstairs to make a smart comment that would deflate Peter's ego and show how little she cared for such coarse sexist nonsense. But Kat just felt hurt and humiliated and, unable to think of a smart comment, she paused only to turn the key in the lock before scrambling into bed.

And that was when she thought about that kiss; the recollection of her foolish surrender to it hit her like a slap in the face. She had *let* him kiss her, hadn't made the slightest attempt to prevent him. Even worse, she had revelled in every insanely exciting second of his mouth on hers. Maybe all the years of self-discipline and repression had left her sex-starved and pitifully vulnerable to such an approach; maybe she was every bit the spinster figure of fun that she had feared she was, she conceded wretchedly. She tensed as she heard a slight noise outside her door, her imagination making an unpleasant deduction as a light knock sounded on her door. She froze in an agony of shame, did nothing, said nothing, her face burning as though it were on fire. It crossed her mind that she was being very heavily punished for allowing a single kiss and that she was old-fashioned and badly out of touch with modern mores not to have appreciated that even that small amount of intimacy had evidently encouraged expectations she would never have dreamt of fulfilling.

The following morning that restive night of self-recrimination and regret had etched shadows below her eyes and left her pale and out of sorts with the world in general. She rose early to prepare the full breakfast her guests would expect. She heard Mikhail's deep drawl before she saw him and busied herself by the stove, the nape of her neck prickling, stark tension leaping through her slim, taut length.

A hand touched her arm and she jerked her head around, colliding with his stunning dark eyes.

'I expected to see you last night,' Mikhail informed her with a candour that disconcerted her.

'Sorry, you lost your bet,' Kat framed with dulcet scorn.

His level black brows pleated and he swung back to her, surprisingly light on his feet for all his size. '*What* bet?' he shot back at her.

Her cheeks flamed. 'I overheard your friend offering you a bet last night—'

'Oh...*that*,' Mikhail breathed with a sardonic tightening of his handsome mouth, his spectacular dark eyes meeting hers without a shade of discomfiture. 'I'm a little too mature to bet on such outcomes.'

Kat glanced past him to note that only Luka was at the table while Peter Gregory was still chatting on his phone in the doorway. Kat moved a step closer to Mikhail and lowered her voice. 'You knocked on my door,' she murmured that dry reminder, pleased that she managed to achieve a tone of complete unconcern.

A sardonic laugh was wrenched from the tall, powerfully built Russian. '*So*?' he challenged. 'What does that have to do with anything?'

Kat dealt him a cold appraisal and without another word whisked the hot plates out of the warming oven in the range to serve the breakfast.

'*Ne ponyal*...I don't get it,' Mikhail extended impatiently, determined to win a response.

Kat planted a rack of toast on the table along with a pot of coffee and stood at the window, watching Roger Packham drive a tractor in the field beyond her garden, only vaguely wondering what he was doing there in the snow while she struggled to keep a hold of her temper. She didn't care whether Mikhail *got* it or not. Thankfully he was leaving and she wouldn't have to see him again and recall how degraded he had made her feel. He had assumed that she was so easily available, so free with her body that she might invite him into her bed within hours of meeting him, and that was an insult. He would have slept with her too, had she been willing, Kat thought grimly, and that told her all that she needed to know about him and his outlook on life. Most probably, he was what Emmie called a 'man whore', the sort of guy who slept around, who probably kept a tally of his sexual scores and prided himself on his high success rate with women.

In the continuing silence, Mikhail ground his teeth together. She infuriated him without even trying. 'I want to see you again,' he said flatly, not an ounce of appeal or gentleness in that statement.

'*No!*' Kat told him sharply, her soft full mouth rounding on the vowel sound in a manner that sent his hormones jumping.

'And that is all you have to say to me?' Mikhail growled, outraged by her attitude, luminous black eyes glittering like falling stars.

'Yes, that is all I have to say to you. I'm not interested,' Kat completed with a little toss of her head that sent her fiery curls snaking round her taut cheekbones.

'Liar,' Mikhail contradicted with complete derision and the thwack-thwack noise of a helicopter coming in low above the house almost drowned him out.

But Kat heard him and squared up to him, antagonism splintering from her. 'You really do think you're
God's gift to the female sex, don't you?' she condemned,
her scorn unhidden. 'I'm not interested and I can't wait
for you to leave!'

'Never thought I'd see the day that *you* got the brush
off,' Peter Gregory murmured somewhere in the background while Luka, glancing in every direction but at
Mikhail, urged his future brother-in-law to keep quiet.

In a rush, Kat served the breakfast. Two helicopters
were engaged in landing in Roger's field beyond her
garden. The older man must have been clearing the
snow for them to land. She turned back to discover that
Mikhail had still not sat down.

'Eat,' she urged him.

'I'm not hungry,' he breathed curtly, colour scoring
his exotic cheekbones to accentuate the clean sculpted
lines of his darkly beautiful face.

An unexpected stab of remorse assailed Kat, who
wondered if she had been unreasonably outspoken and
spiteful. Hadn't she made assumptions about him in the
same way she assumed that he had made assumptions
about her? What if she was wrong? But she had not
been wrong in her conviction that he had knocked on
her bedroom door the night before, she reminded herself
impatiently, wondering where that inappropriate attack
of conscience had come from. Soft pink mantled her
cheeks just as a loud series of knocks sounded on the
back door. Mikhail opened it and suddenly her kitchen
was awash with large men in overcoats all speaking
Russian at one and the same time. An older man with
greying hair greeted him with perceptible warmth and
relief. In the free-for-all of competing male voices, Kat
concentrated on offering everyone coffee and biscuits.

Evidently, Mikhail was important enough to have a helicopter sent to pick him up to facilitate his swift return to London. *Two* helicopters? Had he arranged that means of transport the night before? Was he a flash high-earning banker like Peter Gregory? Or some big businessman with more money than sense?

Luka was digging through his pockets to extract money to settle the itemised bill she had left on the table. Mikhail swept the bill up, glanced at it and shot Kat a sardonic look. 'You don't charge enough,' he told her forcefully, digging the bill into his pocket, leaning down to thrust his friend's money back into his hand. He tugged out his own wallet and slapped several banknotes on the table.

'Thanks,' Kat said in a voice that conspicuously lacked gratitude.

Mikhail dealt her a hard-eyed look, his superb dark eyes glittering with hauteur and arrogance. 'I will *not* thank you,' he delivered with succinct bite. 'As yet you have done nothing to please me...not one single thing.'

And she almost burst out laughing because he sounded remarkably like a sultan informing a humble harem girl of his displeasure while cherishing the belief that she would naturally wish to improve on her performance. But when she clashed unwarily with his striking black eyes and the inescapable chill etched there, any sense of amusement vanished and a touch of dismay and foreboding somehow took its place.

The men filed out to head for the gate that still led from her garden to the field and the parked helicopters. Mikhail waited to the last while the older man awaited him just beyond the door. 'I'll be in touch,' he murmured huskily, surveying her downbent coppery head in frustration.

Kat studiously avoided looking at him. 'Don't bother,' she could not resist saying.

'*Look at me*,' Mikhail ground out between clenched teeth.

Against her will, affected more by that tone of command than she expected to be, Kat glanced up. Soft pink flushed her delicate cheekbones while a pulse beat out her nervous tension like a storm warning just above her collarbone. Involuntarily captivated by the brilliance of her green eyes against her pale perfect skin, Mikhail studied her with a frown. He watched the tip of her tongue slide out to moisten her lower lip and he went hard as a rock just imagining even the tip of that tongue on his body. Expelling his breath harshly, he turned his handsome head away.

'I'll be in touch,' he said again in a tone of decided challenge.

Kat closed the door, shutting out the freezing air. As Mikhail reached the boundary of the gate he addressed the older man by his side. 'Katherine Marshall. I want a background check done on her. I want to know everything there is to know about her...'

Stas stiffened. 'Why?' he dared as if he had not noticed that very interesting hostile exchange at the back door.

'I want to teach her some manners,' Mikhail grated with a brooding glance back in the direction of the house. 'She was rude!'

Astonished by that outburst, Stas said nothing. As a rule Mikhail never got worked up over a woman. Indeed his marked indifference to the many women who pursued him and even the chosen few who shared his bed was a legend among his staff and Stas could not begin to imagine what Katherine Marshall could have done to arouse such a strong reaction in his employer.

Kat was grateful to be busy once the helicopters had gone. She stripped the beds and in the act of filling the washing machine found herself pressing the striped sheet that had been on Mikhail's bed to her nose, catching the elusive scent of him from the cotton before she even realised what she was doing. Her face hot, she stuffed the sheet into the machine, poured powder into the dispenser and turned it on. What the heck had he done to her? She had sniffed his sheet... She was acting like a loon! It was as though Mikhail had switched on some physical connection inside her and she couldn't switch it off again. She was embarrassed for herself.

Roger Packham called that afternoon with the firewood he had promised her and she invited him in for a cup of tea. With satisfaction he told her the outrageous sum he had charged to clear the snow for the helicopters to land that morning. 'City boys must make easy money,' he remarked with scorn.

'I was grateful to get three guests out of the snow,' Kat admitted, knowing she would use that money to stock up on food because, with the current state of her finances, getting hold of ready cash was a problem. 'Business has been anything but brisk recently.'

'But it must have been difficult for you to have three strange men staying here,' Roger remarked disapprovingly. 'Very awkward for a woman living on her own.'

'I didn't find it awkward,' Kat lied with a determined smile, keen not to play up to the older man's preferred image of her as a poor, weak little female. 'And Emmie's back from London, so I won't be alone any more. She stayed in the village last night.'

Mikhail was gone and he wouldn't be back. She could bury all those squirming, inappropriate feelings and reactions that he had aroused, forget the mortification they had caused her, forget *him*...

'Don't use it,' Stas advised, sliding the file onto Mikhail's desk. 'You've never been the kind of man who would use this kind of stuff against a woman...'

His appetite whetted by the rare event of Stas coming over all moral and censorious, Mikhail lifted the file and flipped it open. He read the extensive information about Katherine Marshall with keen interest, noted the figures, raised a black brow in surprise and knew exactly where Stas was coming from. She was on the edge of bankruptcy, struggling to hang onto the house, a sitting duck of an easy target. Now he knew why he had never seen a smile on her face. Serious financial problems caused stress and might that explain why she had blown him off that weekend? He knew he could act on such information, employ it like a weapon against her. It was what his father would have done with an unwilling woman. Mikhail's handsome mouth hardened, his eyes darkening, for the most unwilling woman of all had been his own mother, a living doll ultimately broken by his father's rough handling. But he was *not* his father and Katherine Marshall was *not* an unwilling woman, simply a defiant screwed-up one, he mused impatiently.

What was it about her that had kept her image alive for him? He frowned, frustration gripping his big powerful frame, for he was suspicious of anything he didn't immediately understand. Three weeks had passed yet he still thought about her every day, hungering for that elusive image even as more immediately available woman

failed to ignite the same urgency. His stubborn desire
for Kat Marshall was obsessional and impractical and
that he could see that and still feel that way greatly disturbed him. He wanted his head back in a normal place
and he didn't believe he could achieve that without seeing her again. But while she might be in debt and he was
rich enough to solve her every difficulty, there was still
one insurmountable problem on Mikhail's terms: his
own unbreakable rule that, no matter what happened,
he didn't buy women. Exactly where did that leave him?

The next day, Kat received a devastating letter informing her that her house would be repossessed at the end
of the month. As she had received copious warnings
on that score it was not a surprise. A week after that,
she answered her phone and frowned when her solicitor asked her to come and see him as soon as possible.
What more bad news lay in store for her? Mr Green
could only want to see her about her financial situation,
which he had become aware of some months earlier
when she had first approached him for advice. He had
urged her to sell up, settle what she could of her debts
and start again, but she had been desperate to hang
onto the house that still counted very much as home
for both her and her sisters. Birkside was their safe
place, their security blanket, the place to which all her
siblings ran to for cover when life got too tough in the
outside world. Once it had worked that magic for Kat
as well. Losing the house would be like losing a chunk
of herself and now, after months of fruitless anxiety, it
was finally happening.

'I received this letter yesterday.' Percy Green extended
the single sheet to Kat. 'It contains an extraordinary

offer. Mikhail Kusnirovich is willing to settle your out-standing debts in full and buy your home. He is also giv-ing you the chance to remain at Birkside as his tenant—'

Kat had turned pale. 'Mikhail...K...?'

'Kus-niro-vich,' the older man sounded out helpfully. 'I checked him out and I'm afraid I haven't the faintest idea how he became involved in your debt situation. He's an oil billionaire, not a loan shark.'

'B-billionaire?' Kat stammered incredulously. '*Oil*? Mikhail's rich?'

Astonishment made the solicitor stare at her. 'You actually *know* this man—you've met him?'

In some discomfiture, Kat explained briefly how the three men had taken shelter with her in the snow the previous month. 'And you say he's suggesting that he pay off my loans and purchase Birkside? Why on earth would he do something like that?' she whispered shakily.

'A rich man's whim?' Percy Green shook his head slowly, his incomprehension unconcealed. 'From your point of view, it's a miracle and a timely one. Obviously since the repossession order would leave you homeless you'll accept this offer.'

'Obviously,' Kat parroted unevenly.

The letter dug into her bag, Kat drove back to Birk-side in a growing stew of incomprehension. Mikhail was richer than sin and she was staggered by the dis-covery. Mikhail was offering to pay off her debts and buy her house. But why would he do such a thing? What did he want from her in return for such expenditure on her behalf? Wealthy men didn't give their money away or waste it. She wasn't a charitable cause he could claim as a tax deduction either. So, what *was* he after? Was he showing off his power? Punishing her for her rejection? But how could saving her from becoming home-less be considered a punishment?

She called the lawyers' office responsible for sending the letter and requested the phone number she needed to get an appointment with Mikhail. Whoever she was speaking to went all cagey and uninformative until her call was eventually passed on to someone else. Once she had identified herself, the attitude changed and the phone number was finally advanced. But the difficulties she had had getting that number from the legal office were as nothing to the challenge of getting past the secretarial watchdogs who were determined to know her business before even considering her request to see their employer. Hot with chagrin, Kat finally admitted that Mikhail owned her home and that she wanted to discuss the matter with him. She was offered an appointment four days away.

Emmie dropped Kat off at the railroad station and showed little curiosity about her sister's unusual desire to visit London. Kat smothered a yawn on the train, her early start to the day soon making itself felt. Clad in a tailored dark trouser suit that she had last worn to attend a neighbour's funeral, she felt overdressed as well as deeply apprehensive and angry. What was the wretched man playing at? What did he want from her? Surely not the obvious? She could not believe that Mikhail would not have far more exciting sexual options than she could possibly offer.

When she finally reached the reception area on the top floor of the impressive office block that functioned as Mikhail's London base, a dazzling Nordic blonde came to collect her and walk her down a corridor. The blonde's curiosity was unhidden. 'So, you are Katherine

Marshall and Mikhail owns your house,' she remarked rather curtly. 'How did that come about?'

'I haven't a clue,' Kat fielded. 'But I'm here to find out.'

The blonde subjected her to another assessing look, her bright blue eyes cool. 'Don't take too long about it. He has another appointment in ten minutes.'

Kat gritted her teeth on a sharp retort and smoothed anxious hands down over her slim thighs to dry the nervous dampness from her palms. A door swung open in front of her. She passed over the threshold and into bright blinding sunlight that prevented her from seeing anything.

CHAPTER FOUR

MIKHAIL TOOK FULL advantage of the sunlight that blinded her, striding forward to seize the initiative and, in a gesture that disconcerted her, he reached for both her hands. 'Kat...it's good to see you here, *milaya moya...*'

He was so tall, so dark and so arrestingly handsome in the sleek formality of a tailored black business suit that he had instant overwhelming impact. Her heart thumping inside her ribcage, Kat gazed up into ravishing dark eyes enhanced by thick black lashes and blinked rapidly, thoroughly disorientated by his unexpected smile of welcome and sudden proximity. A feeling of warmth spread through her, a disturbing sense of security holding her still. In a conscious rejection of that treacherous response, Kat snatched her hands angrily free of his. 'Of course I'm here—what choice did you give me? You're buying my house!'

'It's already done. Technically, I now own a house with a sitting tenant,' Mikhail fielded smoothly. 'A landlord is surely a far less alarming prospect than homelessness and the threat of bailiffs removing your belongings and selling them?'

His reminder of how dire her circumstances had been before he stepped in clamped down like steel girders of restraint on Kat's unruly temper. She was furious with him and deeply resented his interference in her private affairs, but she could not have put her hand on her heart and honestly sworn that she wanted the threat of repossession and the prospect of bailiffs back in her life. In truth it was an enormous relief for her not to be dogged day and night with those fears, afraid to answer the phone in case it was the debt collection agency ringing with demands for repayment, afraid to answer the door bell as well. She breathed in deep and slow to calm herself and reorganise her thoughts.

'Why don't you sit down?' Mikhail indicated a couch in one corner of the vast room. 'I'll order coffee.'

'That's not necessary,' Kat told him, dragging her attention from his bold bronzed profile and energy-zapping presence to examine his office. Large in both size and personality, he had an unnerving ability to utterly dominate his surroundings.

'I decide what's necessary,' Mikhail contradicted and he lifted the phone to order coffee.

Kat had not required that reminder of how domineering he could be and her generous mouth tightened as she sat down on the couch, determined to behave normally and betray no hint of her nervous tension. A wonderfully vibrant abstract painting adorned the far wall, the only splash of colour in a room furnished with cold contemporary steel, leather and glass and everything cutting edge technology had to offer. Mikhail Kusnirovich as her landlord? That was a ridiculous euphemism for him to employ when he had repaid substantial cash sums on her behalf. No longer in debt to the loan company or the building society, Kat now considered herself to be in debt to him instead. Of course, he owed her an explanation for his astonishing intervention.

'Why did you do it?' Kat prompted tautly.

Mikhail compressed his wide sensual mouth and shrugged a broad shoulder. It was not an answer but it was the only one he was prepared to give her. He had no socially acceptable altruistic reason to offer in his own defence. What had driven him had been a great deal more basic and selfish: having seen her vulnerability, he had immediately wanted to ensure that he was the only person with access to it. He was a territorial male and he wanted her more than he had wanted any woman in a long time. And only free of debt could she be free to be with him.

His arrogant dark head turned, his striking deep-set dark eyes winging to her lovely face. He watched her colour beneath his stare, soft pink surging below that pale skin to highlight her bright eyes and taut cheekbones. He liked the fact that she blushed, could not recall ever being with a woman who still had that capability. His keen gaze lingered on her lush pink lips and the shadowy vee of white skin revealed by the neckline of the shirt she wore beneath her jacket. That fast, that easily the pulse at his groin reacted and he wanted to touch her and discover if her skin felt as soft and smooth as it looked. Soon he would know one way or another, he told himself soothingly.

The tension in the atmosphere thrummed through Kat as well. His scrutiny of her lips felt like a physical touch. Recalling the hunger of his mouth on hers, she quivered, her breasts full and heavy inside her bra, the tender tips pinching tight while unwelcome heat surged at the heart of her. With ferocious determination, she reined back that tide of debilitating physical awareness, refusing to be either sidetracked or silenced. 'I asked you why you did it. I mean, you hardly know me,' she continued doggedly. 'It's not normal to go out and dig up a person's debts and offer to settle them. You've put me under a huge sense of obligation to you—'

'That was not my wish,' Mikhail lied, for he liked the fact that he had created a link between them that she could not reject. That he had not given her a choice in the matter didn't bother him because he had protected her home for her when she stood to lose it.

In receipt of that guarded reply, Kat felt her growing sense of frustration surge up another notch and she scrambled upright, her russet-red hair streaming in trailing spirals across her narrow shoulders as she threw them back and straightened her slender spine. Getting an explanation out of him was like trying to pull teeth, she thought in exasperation. 'There's absolutely no point in you telling me that that was not your wish when I'm now in debt to you to the tune of thousands and thousands of pounds!'

'But you're not in debt if I refuse to acknowledge that there *is* a debt requiring repayment,' Mikhail imparted with quiet emphasis. 'I saved your skin. All you need to do now is say thank you.'

'I'm not going to thank you for your interference in my life!' Kat snapped back at him without hesitation, galled by his stinging reminder that he had dug her out from between a rock and a hard place. 'I'm not so stupid that I don't appreciate that if something seems too good to be true, it probably *is*. I'm here to ask you what you want from me in return.'

'Nothing that you're not inclined to give,' Mikhail retorted drily.

Kat was very tense, interpreting that statement in only one way. 'Are you hoping that I will become your lover?' she asked him baldly, lifting her chin as she voiced that embarrassing question.

Without warning, Mikhail laughed, startling her, his lean dark features creasing with genuine amusement. 'Should I not? Like most men, I enjoy female company, nothing more complex.'

That might be so, Kat reasoned, unimpressed, but he had not denied that he had a sexual interest in her. If only he knew, she thought ruefully, if only he knew how inexperienced she was he would probably be a great deal less interested in an era when most men expected women to be equal and adventurous partners between the sheets.

'And I'm prepared to make you an even better offer,' Mikhail imparted huskily, dark eyes narrowing to gleaming jet chips of challenge.

'An offer I can't refuse?' Kat quipped, reckoning that he was finally going to get down and dirty with her and admit what she had suspected all along. He wanted her to sleep with him while pretending that she wasn't just doing it because he had paid off her debts. He was a blackmailer with touchy principles, she thought angrily—in other words a total hypocrite. What bad taste she had in men! How could she possibly be attracted to someone as ruthless as him?

'Agree to spend a month on my yacht with me and at the end of that month I will sign the house back to your sole ownership,' Mikhail proposed in a harsh undertone, for even going that close to his unbreakable rule riled him, reminding him that he had not been himself since he met her. He was *too* hot for her, he decided grimly. It was risky to want a woman as much as he wanted her but it was also exciting to meet with a woman who challenged him, and, while his sane mind told him that no woman could really be worth the amount of time and effort she demanded, it was still the excitement that took precedence every time.

'A month…on your yacht?' Kat repeated dizzily, shaken by the sheer shock value of that suggestion. 'But there's no way I would sleep with you!'

'I find you very attractive and I would be happy to take you to my bed, but I've never forced a woman into anything she doesn't want and I never will. Sex would only feature in the arrangement with your agreement,' Mikhail informed her huskily, his deep dark eyes locked to her startled face with satisfaction. 'I want your companionship for a month, a woman on my arm to act as an escort when I go out and a hostess when I entertain on board.'

Kat could not believe her ears, could not credit that he could offer her the equivalent of a luxury holiday with a big bonus at the end and not demand the assurance of sex in return. She had always assumed that all men wanted sex any way they could get it, but he appeared to be telling her that, if she didn't want to sleep with him, it wouldn't be a deal breaker. 'Why would you make me such an offer?' she pressed.

'If I insisted on including sex in our agreement, it would be sleazy,' he pointed out levelly, loving the way she was still challenging him with her suspicions rather than avidly snatching at his very generous proposition. 'I don't treat women like that.'

'I could do the companionship thing but I would never agree to sleep with you as part of the arrangement,' Kat warned him shakily, her colour high, her level of discomfiture intense. 'I mean that. I wouldn't want any misunderstandings on that score.'

Mikhail said nothing because he could see no advantage to arguing with her. But when all was said and done, the same desire that burned in him burned in her as well. She would sleep with him, *of course* she would, she wouldn't be able to help herself when they were together for hours on end. He was absolutely convinced that no matter what she said she would end up with her glorious long legs pinned round his waist, welcoming him into her lithe body. When, after all, had a woman ever said no to him? Kat had taken fright when he had first approached her in her home, that was all, he reflected wryly, reckoning that he had been too spontaneous and aggressive with her. She would want him to make a fuss of her first and if that was what it would take to win her surrender he was, for once, willing to go that extra mile. The background check he had had done on her had made it clear that it was a long time since she had had a man in her life. Naturally she would have reservations and insecurities. He could even understand that she might be a little shy, but ultimately he believed that she would satisfy his driving need to possess her. Women were invariably flattered rather than repelled by the strength of a man's desire.

The gorgeous blonde who had escorted Kat into Mikhail's office also delivered the coffee, her bright blue eyes skimming left and right with keen curiosity as she picked up on the tension in the room. Stiff with self-consciousness and with her own gaze carefully veiled, Kat lifted the cup and saucer and struggled to sip hot coffee with her throat muscles so tense that she could barely swallow. Intelligence and growing caution warned her not to betray weakness in Mikhail's radius. He would use it against her: he was a ruthless man. In her ignorance weeks earlier, she had had no idea of the extent of Mikhail's power and influence and even less grasp of his inflexible drive. Her rejection had clearly challenged him and dented his pride. What else was she to think? Why else would he have come after her? And he had, without a doubt, come after her all guns blazing, Kat conceded in a daze, still stunned that he had gone to such lengths to exert his dominance over her. Yet he had done so. Having identified her financial vulnerability, he had employed it as a means of bringing her to heel. He owned everything that mattered to her lock, stock and barrel and there was nothing she could do about that.

Well, option one was to walk away, acknowledging that losing her home had been on the cards anyway, Kat reasoned feverishly. That would create a stalemate that would certainly surprise and disappoint Mikhail, but ultimately it would gain Kat nothing. Yet what was the alternative? She had not the slightest desire to play the victim and whinge about his callous blackmailing tactics. On the other hand, Kat thought on a sudden strong surge of adrenalin, if she had the gumption to fight Mikhail on his own playing field and *win* she would have her home as a prize at the end of it all. And wasn't a secure base what she really needed, especially now with Emmie pregnant and both of them currently unemployed? Birkside meant so much more to Kat than mere bricks and mortar. It was in every sense the only home she had ever had and very much at the heart of the family she had created with her sisters. How could they still be a family if she no longer had a home her sisters could visit in times of need?

Mikhail was engaged in a dangerous game of one-upmanship, Kat mused thoughtfully, studying his stunning dark features with innate suspicion from below her lashes, for she recognised that he was a clever, sharp-as-tacks operator. He said he didn't expect sex as part of his arrangement but while Kat might be sexually untried she was no fool. She had read all about Mikhail and his ever-changing harem of readily available women on the Internet. This was a guy who didn't do relationships, he only did *sex*. Mikhail was accustomed to easy conquests seduced by his spectacular dark good looks, incredible wealth and dominant personality. Without a doubt, he was assuming that Kat would be just the same as her predecessors and that secluded with him on his yacht she would ultimately succumb to his undeniable sexual charisma. But in that assessment he was wrong, *very* wrong. Kat, dragged up by a mother who was a pushover for every wealthy man who looked her way, had formed her own very effective defences. She had learnt at too young an age that the average man would promise a woman the moon if he wanted her in his bed badly enough. Time and time again Odette had fallen for such promises only to be betrayed once the man involved gained the intimacy that he craved. For that reason, trusting men had never come naturally to Kat, which was why she was still a virgin at thirty-five. She had always wanted commitment before she put her body on the line. Steven had talked the talk but hadn't stuck around long enough to prove that he could walk the walk as well.

'Share your thoughts with me,' Mikhail urged in the charged silence.

He was a class act, Kat conceded with bitter amusement, stealing a glance at his riveting, darkly beautiful face, lingering on the glittering eyes that added threat and vitality to those lean tough features. Her biggest mistake would be to forget that they were essentially enemies, set as they both were on opposing goals. For one of them to win, the other had to lose and she doubted that Mikhail had much experience of being in the loser's corner or that he would be gracious in defeat. She tilted her chin with determination and said quietly, 'If I was to seriously consider your proposition, I would first need legal guarantees.'

Surprise momentarily assailed Mikhail, who had not anticipated such a cool, rational response from her. 'Guarantees with regard to what?' he queried with complete calm, once again relishing the fact that she could still have the power to disconcert him.

'Primarily a guarantee that regardless of what does or doesn't happen on that yacht of yours, if I put in the required time with you, I still get the house back,' Kat proposed dry-mouthed, knowing that that was the most crucial safeguard she required.

'Of course,' Mikhail conceded, affronted by her terminology, his sculpted jaw line clenching with all-male disdain. He had offered her a month of unimaginable luxury on his yacht, *The Hawk*, an invitation that countless women would kill to receive, and she talked about 'putting in her time' with him as though she were referring to a prison stretch? Even worse, she was questioning his word of honour. 'But I too would expect guarantees...'

Kat dragged in a sustaining breath, almost mesmerised by the intensity of his scrutiny and the slow heavy thud of her heartbeat. Her mouth ran dry, a flock of nervous butterflies unleashing in her tummy and clenching the muscles in her pelvis tight. 'Of what kind?'

'That you would fulfil the role of hostess and companion as directed by me,' Mikhail extended coolly, the beginnings of a smile of satisfaction starting to curl the corners of his expressive mouth. 'I didn't think you would agree to this so easily—'

'Only a fool would look a gift horse in the mouth!' Kat quipped in protest, colour firing her cheeks at the calculating mercenary role she was forcing herself to play, not only to protect herself, but also to grab at the chance to get her much-loved home back. 'You're offering me a month of work to regain ownership of my home. From any angle, that's a golden opportunity for me.'

It was the truth and yet making such a declaration, so clearly motivated by greed, made Kat want to cringe with shame. What on earth was she doing? Hadn't she raised her sisters to put principles and conscience ahead of financial success? Yet had Mikhail not deliberately yoked her to that financial obligation, she would never have thought or acted in such a way. Playing him at his own game was self-defence, nothing more, she told herself uncomfortably. He was only going to get the disappointment he deserved for putting her in such an impossible position in the first place.

Mikhail crushed the disturbing pang of dissatisfaction that her candour awakened in him. After all, he motivated employees with bonuses and thought nothing of the practice. Why should Kat Marshall be any different from all the other women attracted by his great wealth? He was *not* buying her; he was *not* paying for her time…hell, he hadn't even slept with her yet! Suppressing the uneasiness stirring inside him, Mikhail chose to think instead of having her all to himself on *The Hawk,* his ocean-going yacht, and the hunger took over again, wiping away every other thought and impression with startling efficiency.

* * *

That evening, Emmie was thunderstruck when her older sister told her why she had gone to London. While intellectually Emmie knew her sister was a beautiful woman, neither Emmie nor her siblings had ever considered Kat in that light, having always been content to accept their sister's claim that she had moved past the age where she still wanted a man in her life. For that reason she simply could not begin to imagine how Kat's supposed charms could have ignited as much interest in a Russian billionaire as some celebrity sex kitten might have done.

Wide-eyed with shock, she stared at her older sister. 'Are you sure this guy hasn't somehow got you mixed up with Saffy?'

'No, he never mentioned Saffy except to ask why she hadn't helped me with my financial problems.'

Emmie grimaced. 'Because Saffy, our drop-dead perfect supermodel sister, may earn a fortune but she is too selfish to think that her own family might need help more than that African orphan school she supports.'

Kat gave the younger woman a pained appraisal. 'Saffy would have helped if I'd asked but I didn't feel it was her responsibility,' she said awkwardly.

Kat didn't want to admit that since most of the debt had been caused by the cost of Emmie's surgery she had been reluctant to approach Saffy for assistance. Emmie would have felt horribly guilty and Saffy could have reacted with angry resentment and the bad feeling between the twins might well have increased.

Emmie continued to stare at Kat. 'So, this guy will do just about anything to get you onto his yacht?' she prompted, still unflatteringly incredulous at the idea that any man could be attracted to her older sister to that extent. 'Doesn't that scare you?'

Kat resisted a sudden urge to confide that Mikhail's fierce desire for her company had to be the biggest ego boost she had ever experienced, but that was a truth that had only recently occurred to her. Even so it was a fact: no man had ever wanted her that much, certainly not Steve, who had taken fright and bolted the minute she agreed to give a home to her younger sisters.

'It surprises me,' Kat admitted. 'I suspect it has a lot to do with the fact that Mikhail's not used to meeting women who say no.'

'But will he continue to take no for an answer?' Emmie prompted anxiously. 'If you're marooned on some yacht with him, can you trust him to keep his hands to himself?'

Kat's tummy somersaulted as she recalled the flash-fire heat of Mikhail's mouth on hers and the silken tangle of his thick hair between her fingers. Yes, Mikhail would keep his hands to himself as long as she kept her hands off him, which she would, of course she would. His kiss on the doorstep had taken her by surprise. If he touched her again she would be better prepared and ready to deal with that weakening surge of temptation that emptied her mind of all sensible thought. After all, it would be very unfair if she encouraged him without having any intention of ultimately going to bed with him.

'Yes, in that line I do think I can trust him. He's too proud to put pressure on a woman who doesn't want him.'

'But he's still willing to pay richly just for the pleasure of your company?' the younger woman queried distrustfully.

'It's only a job...a stupid macho whim on his part,' Kat argued.

'But you know if you *were* sleeping with him this particular job would bear a close resemblance to prostitution.'

Kat paled. 'I'm not going to sleep with him and I've already warned him about that upfront...'

Emmie grinned at that blunt admission. 'Some men would see that as a challenge.'

'If he does, that's his problem, not mine,' Kat pointed out. 'But what's a month out of my life if it secures this house for us again?'

'I take your point,' Emmie conceded thoughtfully.

'You'll stay on here to look after Topsy when she comes home from school for the Easter holidays?' Kat checked.

'Of course. I've nowhere else to go.' Emmie hesitated. 'Just promise me that you won't go falling for this bloke, Kat.'

'I'm not that much of a fool—'

'You're as soft as butter, you know you are,' Emmie responded ruefully.

But during the following week when Kat learned exactly what was entailed in the role of acting as an escort for a Russian oligarch, she felt anything but as soft as butter. First of all, she sustained a nerve-racking visit from a smooth London lawyer bearing a ten-page document, which he described as 'an employment contract' and which delineated in mind-numbing detail what Mikhail would expect from her: perfect grooming, courtesy and an unstinting readiness to please Mikhail and his guests in her role either as companion or hostess, good timekeeping, minimal use of alcohol and no use whatsoever of drugs. In return for successfully fulfilling those expectations for one calendar month, Birkside would be signed over to her.

The reference to grooming mortified Kat, but on reflection she could not even remember when she had last done her nails, and when Mikhail's PA phoned her to tell her that she had an appointment to keep at a London beauty salon on the same day that she was to present herself for her new role, she saw no good reason to argue. It was all part and parcel of the position she had accepted, she told herself comfortingly, and it was not unreasonable that he should want her to look her best. As her slender wardrobe was in no way up to the challenge of a stay on a luxury yacht, she could only assume that he was planning to take care of that problem as well. Sixth sense warned her that Mikhail Kusnirovich left very little to chance and she wondered what would happen when he finally appreciated that she was not supermodel material and was actually very ordinary. After all, he somehow seemed to have formed an image of her very far removed from reality and clearly imagined that she was more fascinating and desirable than she truly was. When that false impression melted away and he was disappointed would he send her home early? She could not believe that he would seek to retain her presence on his wretched yacht for an entire month. In her own opinion he would quickly get bored with her.

On the same day that Kat was collected off the London train by a car that ferried her to an exclusive beauty salon, Mikhail registered that he was in an unusually good mood. He could not concentrate on business: his mind kept on wandering down undisciplined paths as he wondered which of the many outfits he had personally selected for Kat she would wear that evening to dine with him. Only the nagging reminder that he had virtually *paid* for her presence by dangling that shabby little house on the hillside like a carrot to tempt her took the edge off his anticipation and satisfaction. He looked forward to the day when she would try to cling to him as all women did and he would send her on her way, bored with what she had to offer. His face hardened at that desirable prospect: the day of his indifference would come, it always did. In the end he would discover that she was no different from and no more special than any other woman he had taken to his bed and the kick of lust that even the thought of her roused would die a natural death.

Kat was surprised to discover that she enjoyed the grooming session at the beauty salon, although she was just a little shocked by some of the waxing options she was casually offered. That obstacle overcome, she took pleasure in the new arch in her brows and the pretty pale pink of her perfectly manicured nails, not to mention the silky, glossy shine of her curls once the stylist had finished fussing with her hair. She wasn't terribly keen on the professional make-up session that transformed her face but she tolerated it, noting that it gave her cheekbones she had not known she possessed, rather Gothic dramatic eyes and ruby red lips. She thought she looked a bit like a vampire but assumed it was fashionable and resisted the urge to rub a good half of the cosmetics off again. Presumably this was the look *he* wanted and expected.

The limo delivered her to an opulent city hotel where she was wafted straight up to a spacious suite and shown into a bedroom with closets and drawers already packed with what appeared to be her new wardrobe. She blinked in shock, catching her unfamiliar reflection in a mirror and batting her false eyelashes

for effect. A vampire or maybe even that wicked Cru-
ella de Ville character from the Dalmatians book? Keen
to embrace a new persona that seemed infinitely more
exciting than her more average self, she chose a black
lace dress from the packed closet. She was sliding her
feet into perilously high red-soled designer shoes, the
hem of the dress frothing silkily above her knees, when
the phone by the bed buzzed.

'I'm waiting in the lobby for you,' Mikhail told her
with audible male impatience roughening his deep dark
drawl. 'Didn't you get my message?'

'No, I didn't…I'm sorry!' Kat muttered in a bit of a
panic, tossing some essentials into a tiny bag and already hurrying towards the door as she recalled that
clause about good timekeeping. He didn't like to be
kept waiting. The show, she recognised giddily, was
finally going *live*.…

CHAPTER FIVE

MIKHAIL SAW KAT step out of the lift. She looked stunning but oddly different in a way he didn't like. His keen gaze narrowed as she moved towards him and he absorbed the theatrical make-up that spoiled the natural quality she had had and which he had not even realised until that moment had made her so appealing to him. His dark brows drew together in a frown of displeasure.

Kat couldn't even breathe when she saw Mikhail staring across the foyer at her, almost six and a half feet of lean powerful male with his arrogant dark head held at an imperious angle. He was shockingly good-looking, spectacularly sexy and the dark masculine intensity of his appraisal sent a shard of high-voltage heat shooting down through her tummy. She swallowed hard, mouth running dry, perspiration dampening her short upper lip, the tiny hairs at the nape of her neck standing erect as a frisson of fierce physical awareness tightened the skin over her bones.

'The car's waiting outside for us,' Mikhail told her as the four men she recognised from their visit to her house closed around them, opening the exit door, checking the street in advance before striding across the pavement to open the passenger door of the waiting limo.

'Are those men security guards?' Kat enquired, sliding along the sumptuously upholstered leather back seat, striving not to gape at the opulent fittings surrounding her.

'*Da*...yes,' Mikhail confirmed. 'Why are you wearing so much make-up?'

That directness of the question startled Kat. She blinked. 'I didn't put it on,' she responded. 'The make-up girl at the beauty place did it—'

'Why did you allow it?'

Her smooth brow creased. 'I didn't know I had a choice. I assumed this was the one-size-fits-all look you like your companions to have.'

His mouth set into a harsh line. 'You are not expected to conform to some ludicrous identikit female appearance for my benefit. I have no such preference. I respect individuality and I expect you to make your own choices about such things. I also liked you the way you were.'

'Understood.' Her generous mouth tilted in amusement at his honesty. He was very blunt but she found that remarkably refreshing in comparison to the polite and often meaningless fictions that people spouted. 'So, I'll take off the false eyelashes the first chance I get. It feels like I'm wearing fly swats on my eyelids.'

Unexpectedly, Mikhail laughed, black eyes gleaming with appreciation as he lounged back in the corner of the limo, long powerful thighs spread in relaxation, and scrutinised her slender figure in the fitted black dress: the small high breasts, the tiny waist and slim shapely knees. Arousal hummed through him. 'Talk to me,' he urged lazily. 'Tell me why you took on responsibility for your half-sisters.'

Naturally Kat had accepted that Mikhail had to know a good deal about her life when he had discovered how much she was in debt, but that question made her green eyes flash with annoyance, for she did not like the idea that she had surrendered the right to all privacy. 'I'm sure you're not really interested.'

'Would I have asked if I wasn't?'

'How would I know?' Kat replied flippantly, shooting him a look of barely concealed resentment. 'It's quite simple. My mother couldn't cope with my sisters and she put them into foster care. They were very unhappy when I visited them and I wanted to help—I was the only person who *could* help.'

'It was a generous act for so young a woman—you sacrificed your freedom—'

'Freedom's not always the gift people like to think it is. Family's important to me and I never really had that security when I was a child. I also wanted my sisters to know that I cared about them,' she admitted grudgingly.

Dense black lashes framed the shrewd gaze still welded to her, his dark eyes lightening with male appreciation. 'Why do you always want to argue with me?'

'Do you want an honest answer?' Kat enquired.

'*Da*,' he confirmed huskily, but in that moment he was mental miles away, engaged in imagining her graceful length adorned with pearls and nothing else. No, not pearls, he decided, rubies or emeralds to enhance that porcelain-pale complexion.

'You're so sure of yourself and so arrogant that you irritate me,' Kat confessed, lush red-tinted lips pouting as she framed the words.

Mikhail's body tensed because he very much wanted to nibble at that full lower lip, but for the first time in his life with a woman he hesitated to do exactly what he wanted. He didn't need to dive at her like a starving man being offered a last meal. He could practise restraint, couldn't he?

'I can't understand why a man acting like a man should irritate you,' Mikhail told her with amusement, his healthy and exuberant ego gloriously impervious to her criticism, for he had never known what it was to doubt that he knew best in every situation. 'Unless you prefer weaklings…in which case I could never hope to please you.'

Involuntarily studying him, taking in the amusement illuminating his dark as night eyes and the tug of a smile pulling at the corner of his stubborn mouth, Kat stiffened, resisting his potent masculine charisma with all her might. Companion, she reminded herself staunchly, not his lover or one of his admirers. 'You do realise that you're going to get bored with me?' she warned him.

'How could you bore me when you're quite unlike any other woman I've met before?' Mikhail countered with lazy assurance. 'I never know what strange thing you will say next, *milaya moya.*'

As Kat was not aware that she had ever said anything that might be considered strange to him she was, not unnaturally, silenced by that statement. The limo drew up in a quiet street and they alighted, Mikhail clamping his big hand to her slim hip to draw her below the shelter of his arm when she would have put greater distance between them. Disturbingly conscious of his proximity and the familiar scent of his cologne, not to mention the weight and position of his hand near her derriere, Kat had to fight the desire to pull away from him, knowing it would be as welcome to him as a slap in the face. She had to be more tolerant and relaxed, she instructed herself sternly. She was a grown woman and there was no need for her to behave like a jumpy teenager around him.

His security team ushered them into a low-lit restaurant. They were greeted at the door by the proprietor, who bowed as low as if royalty had arrived. A sudden hush fell among the other diners and heads swivelled in their direction. Mikhail addressed the proprietor in his own language. They were shown to a table and menus were presented with much bowing and scraping. Yes, it was very like being out in public with royalty, Kat decided ruefully, glancing down at her menu only to discover that it was incomprehensible to her.

'Is this a Russian restaurant?' Kat enquired.

Mikhail nodded calmly. 'I often eat here.'

'The menu's in Russian—I can't read it,' Kat pointed out stiffly a couple of minutes later because he still hadn't noticed that she was having a problem.

'I'll choose for you,' Mikhail announced rather than offering to play translator for her benefit.

Kat gritted her teeth again, wondering how she would get through the month without trying to kill him at least once. He existed in his own little bubble of supreme confidence, King of all he surveyed, blithely, unashamedly selfish and stubborn. *Her* needs, *her* wants did not exist as far as he was concerned. Suddenly she wondered if that meant that he would be rubbish in bed and hot-pink chagrin flooded her complexion at that uncharacteristic thought on her part. As she had no intention of going to bed with him, she would never know the answer to that question, she reminded herself irritably.

'What's wrong?' Mikhail asked, recognising the tension in her fine-boned features while at the same time wishing she would go and wipe off all the metallic grey make-up obscuring her beautiful eyes.

'Nothing…' Kat forced a valiant smile while he ordered their meals in Russian without consulting her preferences or even telling her what he had chosen for her to eat. She was doing this to regain her family home and she could put up with being treated like a piece of inanimate furniture for the sake of the house, she told herself staunchly.

Mikhail signalled Stas and gave him an instruction that startled the older man into glancing in surprise at Kat.

The first course arrived and it was caviar served with strips of hot buttered toast. Kat had never liked fish—in fact even the smell of anything fishy made her tummy roll. Mikhail failed to notice how little she ate and was equally impervious to the fact that she only took a few mouthfuls of the equally fishy soup that followed. Stas then approached her with a package, which he handed to her.

'The make-up…you can remove it now,' Mikhail informed her with satisfaction as she glanced into the bag in disbelief and discovered a pack of wipes.

Taken aback by the request that she remove her make-up while she was out in public, Kat vanished to the cloakroom and carefully peeled off the false eyelashes before wiping off the dramatic eye shadow. The effort left her eyelids slightly swollen, not that she supposed that that little consequence would matter to Mikhail, whose main goal in life always seemed to be getting exactly what he wanted from those around him. He didn't seem to respect or even notice the normal boundaries that other people observed. After only a couple of hours Kat was reeling in shock from the challenge of dealing with such a force of nature. She dug into her bag for her own small stock of cosmetics and

applied some foundation and lip gloss to banish the bare
look from her face.

'Much better,' Mikhail told her approvingly when
she reappeared, looking more as he remembered her.
He was as comfortable with her transformation and
his determined control of it as she was not. 'I can see
you again.'

Mercifully, a giant succulent steak arrived for Kat's
main course and she was finally able to satisfy her appetite with something she could eat. The dessert was
something cheesy covered with honey. After that no-
holds-barred introduction to Mikhail's national cuisine,
dutifully drinking down the special vodka he praised
to the skies and ending on coffee seemed almost tame
in comparison.

He then asked her if she wanted to visit a club and
Kat felt like a party pooper when she admitted that it
had been a long and very busy day and that she was
tired.

As they stepped out of the restaurant onto the shadowy street, a dark shape lunged at her without warning and a shocked cry of fear erupted from Kat. Just as
abruptly, Mikhail thrust her behind him and stepped between her and her apparent assailant with what sounded
very much like an oath. In the scuffle that followed,
men seemed to jump from all directions and she fell
back into the doorway breathless and full of alarm,
her heart thundering in her eardrums as she appreciated that Mikhail already had the man pinned down in
a pretty threatening manner. Stas, the head of his security team, was intervening and he and Mikhail momentarily seemed to be engaged in some sort of a dispute.
Mikhail's anger was audible in his dark deep voice.
Shaking the terrified-looking man he still held as a

terrier might shake a rat, Mikhail released him with a sound of disgust and swung round to retrieve Kat.

'Are you all right?' Mikhail demanded thunderously.

'I got a fright…that's all,' Kat framed shakily.

'I saw the street light gleam on something in his hand—I thought he had a knife,' Mikhail grated, shepherding her with determination towards the limo where the passenger door already stood open. 'But it was just a camera—he's only an idiot paparazzo trying to steal a photo!'

Still trembling from the shock of the incident, Kat settled into the passenger seat and marvelled at the way in which her attitude to Mikhail Kusnirovich had been turned on its head within the space of a minute. He might have neglected to ask what she liked to eat at dinner but he had, without the smallest hesitation, put himself in the path of what he thought might be a knife to protect her. Kat was stunned but hopelessly impressed that he could even have considered putting himself at risk for her benefit.

'Wouldn't your security have taken care of him?' she prompted in bewilderment.

'Their primary task is always to protect me, not those I am with. It was *my* duty to protect you, *milaya moya*,' Mikhail growled between compressed lips, a lean brown hand clenching into a fist on his thigh, his adrenalin charge still clearly running on a high.

'For what it's worth, thanks.' Kat concentrated on breathing in deep and slow to still her racing heartbeat.

'You were in no danger—it was only a camera,' Mikhail reminded her dismissively.

But *he* hadn't known that when he had instinctively acted to ensure that she was not hurt, Kat conceded, suddenly plunged deep into her own thoughts and ashamed of the speed with which she had been willing to label Mikhail as selfish and arrogant. What had just happened revealed that there was far more depth and many more shades to the Russian billionaire's tough character than she had been prepared to believe.

When Mikhail stepped into the lift with her back at the hotel, however, Kat's nervous tension mushroomed afresh. She wondered why he was coming up to the suite with her. He lounged back in one corner of the lift, brilliant black eyes pinned to her with glittering intensity, and her legs went all woolly and her head swam, nerves fluttering in her tummy as she fumbled for something casual to say to dispel the dangerous drag in the atmosphere.

'What birth sign are you?' Kat heard herself ask inanely.

Mikhail gazed back at her blankly. No, she wasn't going to get any horoscope chit-chat out of him, she registered in fierce embarrassment.

'I'm a Leo...I was asking when were you born?' Kat explained in the hope that he would appreciate that she wasn't a crackpot.

Mikhail, taken aback by the random nature of the conversation and still not grasping what she wanted from him, breathed tentatively, 'Thirty years ago?'

In receipt of that unexpected information, Kat froze in horror. 'Are you telling me that you're only thirty years old?' She gasped.

Exasperated, Mikhail, who had been thinking that kissing her would hardly be breaking the rules because it was essential that she became accustomed to being touched by him, raised level black brows in enquiry. '*Ya ne poni' mayu*...I don't understand. What's the problem? What are we talking about?'

Kat's back was so stiff she might have had a poker welded to her slender spine and her colour remained high. She stepped out of the lift, dipped the key card into the lock on the suite door and stalked into the big reception room, switching on the lights.

Mikhail followed her, a frown hardening his features as he studied her. 'Kat?' he pressed impatiently.

Kat spun back to him and settled furious green eyes on him. 'You're younger than me...*years* younger!' she launched at him in angry consternation. 'I can't believe that I didn't see that, that I didn't even consider the possibility!'

Unmoved by the same conflict of emotion that powered Kat, Mikhail gazed steadily back at her. '*Da*... you're a few years older. And the problem *is*?'

Outrage shimmering through her slender taut figure, Kat stared back at him accusingly. '*That's* a big problem as far as I'm concerned.'

Women were strange, Mikhail reflected, but he was utterly convinced in that instant that she was more strange than most. She had been born five years in advance of him. It was an age difference so minor in his opinion that it was barely worth commenting on, but the look of aversion stamped in her beautiful green eyes warned him that she was not so accepting of the fact. Anger stirred in him because he immediately recognised that she was grabbing at yet another reason to hold him at bay and no woman had ever put up such sustained resistance to him before.

'It's not a problem for me,' Mikhail countered curtly, black eyes brooding as he struggled to work out why he still wanted her in spite of all the discouragement she offered. In fact the more she tried to move away, the faster he wanted to haul her back in a kneejerk reaction that felt natural enough to disturb him.

An older woman with a younger man, Kat was thinking in painful mortification. People always found that combination both funny and objectionable. Remarkably older men seemed to get away with relationships with very young women without attracting similar derision. But the knowledge that Mikhail was a full five years younger than she was simply underscored Kat's conviction that she should not be with him at all.

'It's wrong, distasteful…inappropriate that you're younger than I am,' Kat spelt out jerkily. 'I've read in the newspapers about women christened "cougars" for getting involved with younger men and I'm afraid I've never wanted a toy boy…'

A smouldering silence spread between them.

'A toy boy? You are calling *me* a toy boy?' Mikhail echoed in rampant disbelief that she could have *dared* to apply that offensive term to him. Dark blood marked the arch of his high cheekbones. It was one of the very few occasions in his life when he was rendered almost mute by a shock backed by a surge of the volatile rage that he virtually never let anyone see. 'Take that back… that term,' he instructed rawly. 'It is an insult that no man would tolerate!'

The scorching heat of his dark eyes blazing with indignation clashed with Kat's defiant gaze. She was very still because although he had not raised his voice she had never seen that much anger in anyone: it burned off him like a shower of sparks in darkness, acting on her like a menacing wave of warning that shortened the breath in her lungs and convulsed her throat.

'You're years younger than me,' Kat responded in shaken self-defence, pained by that discovery, not even understanding why it should matter so much to her. 'It's not right—'

'Take it back,' Mikhail breathed wrathfully. 'It is unacceptable that you should say such a thing to me.'

Kat swallowed hard. Her knees felt wobbly: he really could be the most downright intimidating male. 'All right, I'll take it back,' she muttered ruefully. 'I didn't intend to insult you but I was shocked.'

'I would be no woman's toy boy,' Mikhail delivered harshly.

It was a ludicrous label for a six-foot-five-inch male exuding aggression, Kat conceded numbly as she sank down boneless with stress on a sofa and nodded weakly, still shaken by the inexplicable emotions that had erupted inside her. 'Well, that's OK because I wouldn't make a very good cougar,' she confided in a pained undertone.

'Why not?' Mikhail enquired, his tension dispersing as he studied her. She looked exhausted, her russet head drooping on her slender neck like a broken flower, as if it was too much effort to hold it upright, and a sense of blame assailed him because he had almost lost his temper with her and he knew he had frightened her. He recalled his father's infamous violent rages too well to allow himself any comparable outlet. Indeed the main bastion of his character was self-control in every mood and in every situation.

Kat was all shaken up. She could not recall ever having been in such turmoil before or understanding herself less. He was only thirty-years old and she was thirty five, way too old for him, in fact even being attracted to him was practically cradle-snatching, she decided desolately.

'Why not?' Mikhail asked again, curious about what

made her tick in a way he had never been curious about a woman before.

'Cougars are experienced women…I'm not,' Kat admitted dully, convinced that she was an oddity in such a day and age and wondering in despair how she could possibly have done things differently. Her mother had put her sisters through so much with her ever-changing parade of men and Kat knew that for the sake of her siblings' welfare she needed to lead a very different life from Odette. Unfortunately ten years earlier she had not appreciated that that would mean celibacy because in those days she had still dimly assumed that eventually she would meet a suitable man and enjoy a serious relationship. Only it hadn't happened; the opportunity had just never arisen.

His level black brows drew together. 'I don't understand.'

Kat released a bitter laugh that was discordant in the quiet room and lifted scornful green eyes to say, 'I'm still a virgin. How's that for seriously weird?'

In the immediate aftermath of that admission, it would have been hard to say which of them was the more shocked: Kat that she had told him something she had never told any other living person, or Mikhail, who could not have been more stunned had she confessed that she was a serial killer. Physical innocence was way beyond his experience and even further removed from his comfort level.

CHAPTER SIX

ENSCONCED IN THE spectacular luxury of Mikhail's private jet the following day on a flight to Cyprus where they were to board his yacht, *The Hawk,* Kat pretended to read a magazine.

So far, Mikhail had not required much in the way of companionship. He had worked industriously since they boarded mid-morning. If he wasn't talking on his phone, he was doing something on his laptop or rapping out instructions to the employee who had boarded with him. Kat was relieved by his detachment because she was still cringing over her behaviour with him the night before. How on earth had she lost the plot like that? Why the heck had she randomly announced that she was a virgin? That was none of his business and totally extraneous information to a male she had no plans to become intimate with. She would live to be a hundred before she forgot the stunned expression he had worn in receipt of her gauche admission. Aghast at having embarrassed herself to that extent, Kat had simply fled afterwards, muttering goodnight and taking refuge in her bedroom.

A *virgin*? Mikhail was still brooding on that astounding information. It explained a lot about her though, he conceded grudgingly; it made sense of things he hadn't understood. No wonder she had been so edgy and had overreacted to his approach in her home, no wonder she had felt the need to insist that she would not sleep with him! But he was still strongly disconcerted that a beautiful, sensual woman with so vital a spirit could have denied herself physical pleasure for so many years. His suspicion that she might be trying to play games with him as so many of her predecessors had done by using his desire for her as a bargaining chip had died then and there. Furthermore, far from being daunted by what she had told him, he had discovered that he wanted her more than ever. Was that because she had never been with another man? The novelty of the situation? It was yet another question he couldn't answer. He studied her covertly, taking in the taut delicacy of her profile set against her rich russet curls and the long slender legs crossed at the knee with a humming tension he could feel. Although he knew that she wasn't one bit happy about being on his jet en route to his yacht, hunger laced with satisfaction roared through Mikhail like a tornado. For the moment, she was here and she was *his*. Pushing his laptop aside, he dismissed the PA hovering at his elbow to do his bidding.

Kat stole a covert glance at Mikhail, yielding to the terrible secret fascination that literally consumed her in his presence and tugged at her every nerve-ending. She sensed his preoccupation, wondered if he was thinking about her and despised herself for it. She didn't want his attention, had never wanted his interest, she told herself staunchly. Yet how did that belief tie in with her treacherous satisfaction that he should find her so attractive? There was something within her that rejoiced in his awareness and her own, something she didn't know how to root out, something that scared her because it seemed outside her control.

'Would you like a drink?' Mikhail asked smoothly.

'Water, just water, please…' Kat responded, mouth running dry as she collided with glittering black eyes enhanced by luxuriant lashes. Alcohol would not be a good idea when she needed to keep her wits about her. He had the most *stunning* eyes and the reflection made colour stream like a banner across her cheekbones.

Mikhail pressed the bell and the steward appeared to serve them. Restive as a prowling jungle cat, Mikhail leapt upright and watched her sip almost frantically at the water, the glass in her slender hand trembling almost infinitesimally. She could fight it all she liked, he thought with dark triumph, but she was every bit as aware of him as he was of her. He reached down, deftly removing the glass from her clinging fingers to set it aside, closing a big hand over hers to lift her to her feet. She raised startled eyes to his lean strong face, her beautiful eyes as verdant a green as a spring leaf.

'*What*?' Kat gasped, nerves now leaping about like jumping beans inside her as she looked up at him, feeling dwarfed by his height and width, the sheer hard power of his tall, well-built frame.

'I'm going to kiss you,' Mikhail murmured huskily, his dark deep drawl roughening.

Totally unprepared for that approach, her lashes flickered in shock. '*But—*'

'I don't need permission for a kiss,' Mikhail derided. 'Only to take you to bed. That gives me a fair amount of leeway, *milaya moya*.'

Kat was very much shaken by that catastrophic interpretation of their agreement. She had assumed that if he could accept she wouldn't sleep with him, he wouldn't touch her at all, for why would he want to waste time and energy on foreplay when the main event was not on offer to close the deal? She was stung by the realisation that he was bending the rules and by the belief that she should have known in her bones how devious he would be.

'But I don't want this,' Kat told him feverishly, her slender body rigid as steel in the imprisoning circle of his arms.

'Let me show you what you want,' Mikhail husked with unassailable cool, long fingers closing into a handful of russet curls to draw her head back.

And he kissed her with soul-shattering intensity, his lips hungrily demanding entrance to her mouth, his tongue tangling erotically with hers and stabbing deep enough to send streamers of liquid fire snaking through her trembling body. She had had kisses, but nothing had ever come close to comparing to that explosive assault. That kiss was utterly decadent and deeply, compellingly sexual in nature. Suddenly her bra felt too small and tight to contain her swelling breasts. Her nipples were almost painfully stiff and the tingling awareness there tugged as though a piece of elastic connected her breasts to her groin. The tender flesh between her legs felt hot and damp and unbearably sensitive.

A big hand splayed across her bottom, gathering her closer, so that her breasts were crushed by the wall of his chest and she could feel the bold, hard ridge of his erection against her. A dulled ache gripped her pelvis, heat pulsing at her feminine core, and her knees turned weak and boneless beneath her.

His black hair tousled by her fingers, Mikhail lifted his dark head to stare down at the hectically flushed triangle of her face. 'You see...' he murmured raggedly, reining back his overwhelming need with fierce self-discipline, determined not to destroy the moment. 'There's nothing to be scared of.'

Breathless, Kat reeled away from him again, shattered by the effect he had had on her and the mindless clamour of a body suddenly unplugged from the source of energy and excitement that he had taught her to crave. Nothing to be scared of? Was he joking? Every natural alarm she possessed was screaming panic at full volume. Purebred predator that he was, he was toying with her as a cat might play with a mouse, his confidence in his own powers of seduction supreme. And why shouldn't he feel like that? Kat castigated herself furiously. Telling a guy like Mikhail that she was a virgin had been the equivalent of throwing down a red carpet to welcome the enemy.

Let me show you what you want. How dared he? As if she didn't know what she wanted; as if she were so confused it would take a *man* to show her anything! She already knew that he attracted her but she wasn't prepared to act on the fact. Her choice, her decision! Trembling with rage and frustration, she sank back into her seat and refused to look at him again. He would use her own weakness against her without conscience but she was stronger than that, much stronger. Her teeth clenched together hard as she bit back angry defensive words that would only tell him how rattled she was. He had done that to her. With one scorching kiss he had pulled the rug out from below her feet.

Mikhail savoured his vodka, blithely unconcerned by the furious silence emanating from his companion. So, she was angry, but he had expected that: she was a fiery, independent woman too accustomed to having her own way. He wasn't going to back off like a little boy who had had his wrist slapped and it was better that she knew the score from the outset. He had trod on glass around her for long enough. That wasn't his style with a woman and now it was time for him to be himself.

When the jet landed in Cyprus, they transferred to a helicopter. The noise of the rotor blades on board made conversation impossible. As the unwieldy craft came in to land on the pad on the prow of the huge yacht below them, Kat was wide-eyed with wonderment. *The Hawk* was much bigger than she had expected and infinitely more elegant, different decks rising in sleek tiers rimmed with gleaming metal balustrades. There was already another pair of helicopters parked nearby.

'I wasn't expecting anything this size,' Kat confessed as Mikhail urged her away from the landing area with a predictably bossy hand planted to her spine.

A grin slashed his wide mobile mouth and he told her what length *The Hawk* was and the maximum speed it travelled at. His zeal and pride of possession were patent and Kat listened graciously to the story of where the yacht was built, who he had chosen to design it and why as well as the exact specifications he offered. Although Kat had very little interest in such matters and much of it was too technical for her, she did have a fond memory of her late father giving her equally enthusiastic and unnecessary details about a new lawnmower he had once bought. The comparison almost made her laugh, for she knew that Mikhail would hang, draw and quarter her if he knew she had likened his precious yacht to a piece of garden machinery.

After a man in a captain's cap greeted Mikhail and a brief introduction was performed, Kat moved away a few feet to stand by the guard rail, the breeze blowing her hair back from her face as she took in the impres-

sive view of the sleek prow scything smoothly through
the turquoise depths of the Mediterranean sea. It was
an undeniably beautiful day: the sky was blue and the
sun was shining down to pour welcome warmth on
her winter-chilled skin and, annoyed as she still was
with Mikhail, she could only feel glad to be alive on
such a day.

A stewardess in uniform appeared at her elbow, told
Kat that her name was Marta and offered to show her
to her cabin. Leaving Mikhail chatting to the captain,
Kat followed the stewardess down an incredible curving glass staircase, which Marta informed her lit up and
changed colours once darkness fell. Quite why anyone
would want a staircase that changed colour escaped Kat,
but the sheer opulence of the guest suite impressed her
to death. The bed in the big room sat on a shallow dais
and doors led off to an incredible marble bathroom, a
dressing room and a private furnished balcony. A steward arrived with Kat's luggage and Marta proceeded
to unpack it.

'When do the other guests arrive?' Kat enquired.

'In about an hour, Miss Marshall,' Marta told her.

Positively relieved by the news that she and Mikhail
were not to be left alone together for even a day, Kat
decided to get changed to ensure that she was ready
for her hostessing duties. Choosing a simple but elegant toffee-coloured shift dress from her new wardrobe, she freshened up in the bathroom, emerging just
as another door opened on the far side of her room and
Mikhail strode in.

'You're dressed…excellent,' he pronounced approvingly.

Through the door he had left open behind him she
could see another bedroom, which she surmised to be

his and her colour heightened as dismay flashed through her. 'There's a connecting door between your accommodation and mine?'

A wickedly amused smile slashed his expressive mouth. He stood there, big and bold and brazen, daring her to object. 'Did you expect me to have it bricked up for your benefit?'

Her small white teeth scissored together. 'Of course not, but for future reference...I'll be keeping it locked—'

'I have a master key for every compartment on board but you don't need to be quite so protective of your privacy—I'm equally keen on my own,' Mikhail informed her drily while simultaneously awarding her slender figure a slow, lingering appraisal that ran from the top of her head down to her curling toes. Beneath that relentless dark and shameless gaze, fresh heat sprang up in her face and her discomfiture increased. 'That colour suits you—I knew it would.'

Kat was already very tense. 'You chose my clothes... *personally*?'

'Why not? I've been buying clothes for my women since I was eighteen,' Mikhail fielded with lazy assurance.

It was just another piece of his control freakery, Kat told herself in exasperation, not something she needed to get worked up about. Unfortunately there was something alarmingly intimate about the idea that he had personally selected the very clothes she wore to suit his tastes. That was way too intimate. She had assumed some hired help had selected the garments. And she really didn't want to know that he had been buying clothes for women since he was a teenager. That both shocked and alienated her. The very thought of him with other women was offensive to her and the discovery filled her with consternation. Surely she couldn't be developing possessive feelings about him?

'I'm not *your* woman,' Kat told him with icy emphasis, green eyes glimmering with hauteur and resentment.

'Then what are you?' Mikhail countered levelly, one ebony brow slightly elevated as if he was looking forward to the prospect of her trying to explain her exact role in his life.

'Your hostess…er, your companion,' Kat quantified stiltedly.

A charismatic smile of amusement crossed his face. His spectacular eyes glittered like black diamonds in sunshine, his potent sexual appeal making her mouth run dry and her blood run hot in a way she was starting to recognise. With great difficulty she dragged her gaze from his, struggling to control the race of her heartbeat and the edge-of-her-seat excitement he could induce so easily.

'I'm not *your* woman,' Kat told him stubbornly again.

'But never doubt that that's my ultimate goal, *milaya moya,*' Mikhail imparted silkily just as a knock sounded on the door.

It was the dynamic blonde, Lara, from his London office. Her bright blue eyes ping-ponged assessingly between her employer and Kat before she extended a file to Mikhail, which he immediately passed to Kat. 'The profiles of the guests I've invited,' he explained.

Kat's fingers tightened round the file while she told herself that Mikhail's goal was not a threat to her as long as she kept a steady head on her shoulders. This holiday on his yacht was an interlude in her life, not a real part of it. 'Thanks. I'll study them.'

And with a decisive jerk of his chin, Mikhail swung

round and returned to his own room. Kat followed him at speed and snapped shut the lock on the door before walking out to the balcony and sitting down on a comfortable wicker seat to open the file.

There were twenty guests in all, more than she had expected. There were several business tycoons with their partners and adult children as well as a well-known entrepreneur and his actress girlfriend. Some of the names were familiar to her, most were not. The presentation of the file, however, had calmed her nerves because it was a welcome reminder that she was on *The Hawk* to fulfil a function and she intended to do it to the best of her ability as she memorised the useful information she had been given.

An hour later, Lara reappeared to usher her upstairs to welcome Mikhail's guests, who had arrived on the helicopters sent to collect them. Lara had changed into a very short silver dress more akin to a cocktail frock than anything else and it had the effect of making Kat feel severely underdressed. She reminded herself that Mikhail had approved what she wore but that was a humbling recollection that could only irritate her. After all, she was not *his* woman; she did not belong to him in any way and she had no intention of changing her mind on that score.

The salon was a large light-filled space ornamented with spectacular seating arrangements and paintings. Lara hovering at her elbow, Kat spoke to a well-preserved blonde in a reassuringly restrained dress. Even so, a glance around the gathered cliques revealed the fact that all the younger guests were wearing party gear, displaying legs, cleavage and glitzy jewellery. A slight hush fell in the chatter and the hair at the nape of Kat's neck prickled a sixth-sense warning. She turned her

head to see Mikhail stride in, dressed in tailored chino
trousers and an open shirt. The sheer impact of his size,
black hair and golden skin was undeniable and set up
a sizzling chain reaction deep in her tummy that made
her shift her feet uncomfortably. She saw the women
present look at him as though he were a tasty dish on a
banqueting table and move almost as one towards him
until he was literally surrounded.

'Women always act that way around the boss. You'll
get used to it,' Lara cooed in her ear in a saccharine-
sweet tone of sympathy.

'It doesn't bother me,' Kat fielded softly, pride making her chin tilt, and stiffening her spine. Mikhail was
breathtakingly handsome and sexy in a way she had
never seen in a man before but she could cope, yes, she
could cope because looks and sex appeal were only a
superficial blessing. She had no intention of getting
involved in a shallow affair with a man who was only
interested in her body.

Lara gave her an unconvinced look and said, 'Most
women are prepared to put up with a lot to stay in the
boss's life.'

'I'm quite content,' Kat responded evasively, uneasy
with the conversation and how personal it was becoming
because she wasn't sure whether or not any of Mikhail's
staff were aware that she was simply a woman hired
to do a job and she did not want to be indiscreet. After
all, Birkside hung in the balance and, while Mikhail's
ultimate goal seemed to be sexual, Kat's sole goal was
to reclaim her home. And she *would* achieve that, she
told herself bracingly, without sex playing any part in
the arrangement.

'That's Lorne Arnold over there,' Lara whispered,
evidently having taken the hint that her curiosity was

unwelcome. 'I would pay him some special attention. He looks bored.'

Kat nodded, her brain summoning up the details she had carefully memorised. Lorne Arnold. At thirty-three years of age, he was a very successful London-based property developer and he was currently involved in a high-profile development scheme with Mikhail. He was an attractive man with blond hair almost long enough to hit his shoulders and his partner, Mel, a top financial analyst, was nowhere to be seen. Possibly the woman had decided to change before she joined them, Kat surmised, directing her steps into his path while she moved a hand towards a waiter standing by the wall to encourage him to bring his tray of drinks over.

Mikhail's brooding gaze swept the room and snapped to a sudden halt when he finally located his target. His big powerful frame went rigid. Kat was laughing and smiling up at Lorne Arnold. He watched in growing disbelief as Lorne planted a hand to Kat's arm to draw her attention to a painting on the wall and guided her over to it, and his handsome mouth compressed into a harsh line, rage lashing through him like a whip. What the hell did Lorne think he was playing at when he flirted with Kat of all people? And why was Kat encouraging him like that? That was certainly not the way she behaved in Mikhail's company when she had never yet deigned to laugh or smile. Kat still treated Mikhail like a queen trying to repel an over-familiar commoner and it galled him. The only time he was happy with her response to him was when she was in his arms and her reserve was shattered, ripped away by the passion she could not suppress.

'*Ty v poryadka*...are you OK?' Stas murmured to one side of him.

Eyes bright as golden stars in his lean strong face, Mikhail was pale with dark fury and he didn't trust himself to speak. Kat was engaged in animated conversation with Lorne: her expressive hands were sketching vivid word pictures while she studied the painting with the other man. Lorne now had an arm clasped round her waist and the sight of that familiarity was so offensive to Mikhail that he could happily have wrenched the couple apart and tossed his business partner off the side of the yacht. Kat was *his*. She's *mine* screamed every fibre of Mikhail's tautly muscled body and he was ready to break Lorne's arms for daring to touch her. Damn art, Mikhail thought bitterly, thrusting his passage through the crush around him. That had to be the common denominator that had brought down the barriers between Kat and Lorne because Lorne was involved with the Arts Council and *she* had a degree in Fine Arts. Mikhail's vast and much-admired art collection was solely investment-based and he couldn't have talked about any of it, for his interest had never gone much beyond that level. And for the first time in his life he was in no mood to admit to being a total philistine.

An arm locked round Kat's waist from behind, anchoring her back into the powerful strength and heat of a large male body. Disconcerted at being touched without warning even though she knew immediately who it was who held her, Kat jerked and froze even as Mikhail murmured her name above her head and addressed Lorne Arnold. Hot pink swept her cheeks as the other man tensed, unable to hide his surprise at Mikhail's revealing embrace. Long lean fingers brushed her torrent of russet curls back off one slim shoulder and male lips slowly grazed the slender column of her throat, pressing in at one point in a fleeting kiss that sent a lightning bolt of sizzling sexual awareness shooting through her unprepared body. Her breasts peaked and sliding heat clenched every muscle in her pelvis. Even as angry resentment roared through Kat she found herself leaning back into Mikhail for support to compensate for the sudden paralysing weakness of her legs.

'Excuse us,' Mikhail purred like the predator he was, holding Kat below one arm like a piece of booty he had reclaimed and urging her across the room while at the same time refusing to allow any of his attentive guests to intercept him.

Stas yanked open the door in readiness and Kat recognised the glimmer of amusement in the older man's eyes even though his expression was politely impassive. That glimpse stoked her own temper even more and that was the only reason she did not protest Mikhail's domineering behaviour. She did not want to have a row with Mikhail in front of an interested audience.

Thrust into another room across the corridor furnished like an office, Kat barely paused to draw breath before she whirled round to confront him. 'How dare you touch me like that in public?' she raked at him in an uncompromising attack.

Mikhail was utterly taken aback by that defiant demand, and his darkly handsome features hardened even more. 'You shouldn't have been flirting with him and encouraging him to take liberties—'

'I wasn't flirting with him!' Kat flung back at him hotly. 'We were just chatting—'

'*Nyet*…no, you were flirting like mad, batting your eyelashes…smiling…*giggling*!' Mikhail condemned in a raw undertone of accusation, eyes full of derision at her plea of innocence.

Belatedly recognising that he was entirely serious

in his misapprehension, Kat compressed her lips. 'We were in a room surrounded by people—'

'And I saw in his face that until I touched you he didn't even realise who you were!' Mikhail grated. 'He would never have laid a finger on you had he known you were here with me. You should have been by my side—'

Kat tilted her bright head to one side, green eyes sharp as lasers with offence. 'Sticking to you like glue, so that you didn't feel the need to mark your territory like a wolf? I have never been so embarrassed in my life.'

Black eyes blazing at her accusation, Mikhail bit out ferociously, 'Don't exaggerate! I only kissed your neck—I didn't touch you anywhere intimate!'

Still all too aware of the fast-beating pulse at the precise spot he had *only* kissed, Kat went rigid with resentment at the memory of the practised manner in which he had demolished any possible resistance she might have raised to protect herself. That place on her throat was clearly an erogenous zone she had not even known she possessed and he was a man capable of demonstrating many more such tricks. Well, he wouldn't be doing that to her again—not if she had anything to do with it!

'I wasn't flirting,' she said again in a cutting tone and she watched him pick up on that tone as if she had thrown a flaming torch at him: his black eyes suddenly burning jewel-bright, his exotic cheekbones slashing taut. 'Why would I have flirted with him? Lorne has a girlfriend and I was expecting her to appear at any moment—'

'When he arrived, he told me they'd broken up a few weeks ago. He's looking for a replacement and he had his eye on you,' Mikhail delivered grimly.

Refusing to be intimidated, Kat tossed her russet

curls back and sighed. 'So? I smiled at the man. I was only being friendly. I don't giggle…I never ever giggle,' she told him drily. 'And you didn't like it? Why do you think that is? Because I don't smile and laugh with you? Ask yourself if you have ever done or said *anything* likely to encourage such a relaxed response from me.'

Infuriated by the charge that laid fault at his door when it was her unacceptable behaviour that had provoked him into warning off Lorne, Mikhail gritted his perfect white teeth and almost snarled. He reached out for her with determined hands.

Kat backed off so fast that she would have fallen over, had she not had the support of the desk behind her. 'You're such a caveman,' she muttered helplessly. 'And you're not touching me in that mood.'

Mikhail stayed where he was mere inches from her but he dropped his hands, disconcerted by her words and equally disturbed by the level of his own anger. 'I would never ever hurt you.'

And reading the look of reproach in his stunning eyes, Kat believed him, but he was never going to be a pussycat of the domestic variety either. He was one-hundred-per-cent primal male laced with aggression. 'I know but unfortunately for both of us that legal agreement didn't go far enough—'

'Kat…?' Mikhail began darkly, exasperated by the change of subject.

'No, please let me have my say for once,' Kat cut in in a resolute plea that ignored the taut silence smouldering around her. 'You want something from me that I'm not prepared to give and now you're judging me unfairly. I wouldn't flirt with one of your guests. I'm not that sort of woman, I'm not even sure that after so long I even know how to flirt any more—'

'You *know*,' Mikhail contradicted without hesitation. 'Lorne couldn't take his eyes off you.'

'But I was only trying to make him feel welcome. There was no subtext and nothing else intended,' Kat told him quietly. 'I wouldn't do anything to embarrass you either but you *do* need to be aware of the boundaries of that agreement.'

'In what way?' Mikhail prompted, marvelling that against all odds she had managed to talk him down from his rage, somehow cutting through all the aggro to make him think clearly again. Even so, he didn't like the explosive, unpredictable effect she had on his mood; he didn't like it at all. Lorne was a business partner and a friend, but, if the other man had gone even one step further with Kat, Mikhail knew he would have struck him. The sight of Lorne's hand on Kat had enraged him and that disturbed him as well. In all fairness, what could have happened between Lorne and Kat in a room full of people? Nothing, his logic answered. He had never been a possessive man when it came to women but Kat roused unsettling reactions in him. He didn't want another man anywhere near her. But where did she get off calling him a caveman? He was a highly sophisticated, educated guy, who had never treated a woman in a less than civilised manner. Had he been the barbarian she suggested he would already have seduced her and dragged her off to his bed, instead of which he was, for the first time in his life, practising restraint with a woman and giving her the chance to get to know him… for all the good that that was doing him, he reflected broodingly as he recalled the caveman insult.

Mikhail shifted an infinitesimal distance closer and her big green eyes widened. Beautiful eyes but not doe's eyes. Kat's eyes were wide, wary, and suspicious. He lifted a hand and ran his forefinger gently down the side of her face. 'In what way do I need to be aware?'

Kat blinked. For a split second her entire mind was a terrifying, disorientating blank. The touch of his finger had whispered down her cheekbone like a teasing caress and he was so close her nostrils were flaring on the spicy tang of the cologne he wore and the underlying scent of clean warm male. Butterflies broke loose in her tummy, her nipples tightening and lengthening below her clothing. 'Aware?' she queried uncertainly.

'You said I had to be aware of the boundaries of our legal agreement,' Mikhail reminded her, black-lashed dark eyes turned a mesmeric gold as they connected with hers.

Like a doll re-equipped with a new battery, Kat's brain suddenly switched back on. 'Oh, yes, the agreement. I think you need to be reminded that you don't own me. I don't belong to you in any way—'

'Nor do you belong to anyone else,' Mikhail pointed out with lethal cool. 'You're up for grabs—'

'No, I'm not!' Kat countered speedily, keen to kick that idea to the kerb. 'I'm not interested in a relationship with anyone—'

'Except with me,' Mikhail slotted in silkily, as stubborn as a mule in pursuit of his goal.

Oh, my word, those long curling eyelashes went for her every time he got close, a quite unnecessary dramatic embellishment to his stunning dark gaze, Kat reflected dizzily. Her mouth was running dry, her brain on overload, physical impressions flooding her and washing away logical thought.

'You want me,' Mikhail told her with a deep roughened edge to his powerful voice that shimmied down her taut spine and made her tremble.

Without any warning that she picked up on, he framed her face with long splayed fingers and kissed her. It was drugging, wildly intoxicating, like an adrenalin shot straight into the veins. One minute she was thinking no, this *can't* happen, I must stop it here and now, and the next the hungry and continuing pressure of that wide sensual mouth was what she wanted and needed most in the world.

With a muffled sound thrumming deep in his broad chest, Mikhail gathered her up into his arms and sank down in the chair behind the desk. For a split second he appraised her flushed and lovely face, the dazed expression in her eyes for once empty of defiance and censure, and it grabbed hold of every base male instinct in his body. He wanted her so much more than he had ever wanted any other woman. He wanted her under him, over him, in every possible position. He wanted her to accept that she was *his*. He wanted to see that look of bliss on her face for him again and again and again. Tamping down his ferocious hunger to possess, he lifted her up to him and darted his tongue between her lips in a rhythmic invasion, revelling in the sweetness of her response and the little moan she could not hold back.

'*Ti takaya krasivaya*...you are so beautiful...' he translated his own first words for her '...but *ti svodishme nya suma*...' You drive me crazy.' He didn't translate that last admission.

As he bent over her Kat's fingertips feathered through his thick black hair even while she was wondering what she was doing, but, strangely enough, she felt extraordinarily safe and at peace in his arms. There was something definitely to be said for a male big enough and strong enough to pick her up. 'What am I doing?' she framed with a sudden frown.

'For once? Exactly what you want,' Mikhail husked and kissed her again with all the hungry fervour of his high-voltage temperament.

With one hand he nudged her knees apart and she tensed, a choky little sound of dismay escaping her throat.

'I won't do anything you don't want me to do. I won't take you.' Mikhail was determined to keep her where she was on his lap and within reach of intimacies he had hitherto only been able to dream about.

The tension in her slender frame began to ebb and he nibbled enticingly at her full lower lip before plunging his tongue deep within again. The taste of him went to her head like fine wine and another flush of arousal travelled through her, stiffening her nipples and making her achingly aware of an even more private place. He pushed up the hem of her skirt and she jerked while he made soothing sounds she could not have believed he was capable of making. His hand smoothed over her inner thigh, temptingly close to the unbearable heat and sensitivity there, and she had never wanted so badly in her life to be touched. The need for more was screaming through her every skin cell like nothing she had ever imagined and so strong was that need she consciously stopped trying to fight it. Curiosity had awakened along with the longing.

He stroked a finger over the stretched taut fabric of her knickers, heat rippled through her and her hips rose and her slender thighs parted without her volition. 'Just do it…w-whatever,' she murmured shakily from between clenched teeth for she truly didn't know what he was planning to do and didn't much care at that moment. If he could satisfy the desperate pulsing craving inside her, it would be enough.

Mikhail almost laughed at that command she had issued but the strangest shard of something tender burnished his hard dark eyes. He didn't know what it was about her but she touched things in him that nobody else ever had and right then she needed him. He closed his lips to her wonderfully swollen and tempting mouth and wrenched the surprisingly strong barrier of her underwear down her legs, even sparing a frowning glance in the item's direction as it fell on the floor in a sensible heap of white cotton, for it was certainly not anything that had featured in his lingerie choices for her wardrobe.

One moment Kat was mortifyingly aware of how damp she was down below and the next as a fingertip very delicately traced the tiny entrance to her body she was shivering and mindless with a flood of hunger like nothing she had ever felt before. There was not a thought in her head—there was no room for it: excitement had driven out everything else. He stroked her clitoris and it was as if an electric shock ran through her, her back arching, every muscle tightening. He circled that tiny bundle of nerve-endings and it was like being set on fire, for the tormented shivers of arousal were assailing her ever more strongly. The heat in her pelvis and the extreme sensitivity at the heart of her were almost unbearable. His tongue flicked against the roof of her mouth and she gasped round it as he eased a finger into her, answering a need she had not even known she had until he showed her. She bucked. Erotic pulses of agonisingly strong sensation were gathering at her feminine core and she couldn't stay still, couldn't find her voice to tell him that she needed *more* and *faster*. And almost as though he was attuned to her needs as she was, his fingers plunged deeper within her while his thumb pressed against her clitoris.

'Come for me, *laskovaya moya*,' Mikhail husked, a tremor she had never heard before threading his voice.

And there was nothing Kat chose about what happened next, for her body had long since taken charge of her. It was as if white lightning cracked inside her, throwing her high and tearing her apart while wave after wave of shudderingly intense pleasure engulfed her.

But Kat didn't float back to planet earth again, she fell with a resounding crash when coherent thought returned and she grasped exactly what she had allowed. And she wanted to scream and thump herself, was already wondering if she was a split personality to tell him to stay away, to tell herself that she wanted him to stay away and then to engage in such intimacy!

'I want so much more from you,' Mikhail confessed huskily, both arms banded round her so firmly that she would've had to fight to escape.

Kat couldn't look at him, knew the power of those eyes of his to sway her into stupidity and recklessness. 'Please let go of me,' she whispered unevenly, desperate to find the right words to explain herself but meeting only a mortifying emptiness in her brain. Confusion assailed her. Only the awareness that it had been a very one-sided episode restrained the anger she usually used to keep him at a safer distance.

Mikhail expelled his breath in a thwarted hiss and released her with exaggerated immediacy. Dragging the hem of her dress down over her thighs, Kat scooped up the undergarment on the floor with crimson cheeks. 'I don't know what to say to you—'

'Say nothing at all,' Mikhail advised in a dry tone

that made her wince. 'You're not very tactful. Go and change for dinner. I'll see you later.'

Later...as in her bedroom? Kat wondered wildly. Well, she could hardly blame the guy for expecting something in return for such encouragement as she had given him! Nor could she imagine managing to tell him that lust wasn't enough, for her, would never be enough for that, she was convinced, was what was wrong with her. She lusted after him like a shameless hussy, lost all control the minute he looked at her in a certain way or made physical contact!

Mikhail swore long and low in Russian. She was nuts, way too mixed-up for him. How had he avoided seeing that for so long? What *was* he doing with her? He should have her flown home, allow Lara to take over... That would be the rational thing to do. And Mikhail was nothing if he was not rational.

CHAPTER SEVEN

FIVE DAYS LATER, Mikhail stood on the terrace outside his office on *The Hawk* sharing a drink with Lorne Arnold.

His other guests were swimming and sunbathing down below on the main deck. He was so accustomed to half-naked women that he spared the exposed bodies barely a glance, awarding his attention only to a slender redhead moving in the shadows. As willowy and graceful in her leggy delicacy as a gazelle, Kat burned in the sun, but her smooth light skin made her stand out all the more from his fake-tanned and sun-bronzed guests.

'Kat's a real find,' Lorne remarked carefully, watching Kat sit down with a book to read.

Mikhail gritted his even white teeth. If only you knew, he thought in frustration. He had backed off from Kat and that hadn't worked either. She was like a jig-saw puzzle with several missing pieces: incomprehensible and infuriating.

'Very natural, warm, unspoiled...' Lorne could not hide his appreciation

'Very unspoiled,' Mikhail fielded tongue-in-cheek.

'You don't seem to pay her much attention...'

'Kat thrives on neglect,' Mikhail told him grittily, wondering why he had had the misfortune to land the only woman in the world who didn't react to such an approach. Mikhail, more used to women who crowded him and clung, eager to please and entertain him, was at a rare loss with one who chose to keep her distance.

Lara settled down beside Kat in the shade. 'I'm too hot,' the svelte blonde complained.

Kat knew better than to suggest that the topless blonde in her minuscule bikini briefs take a dip in the inviting pool. Most of the female guests, including Lara, avoided the water to conserve their hair styling and make-up while Kat continued to swim several times a day, frustrated by the laziness of sitting around doing very little. It had made her hair a little frizzy but with a fully staffed beauty salon on board that was hardly a problem.

'Tonight is the guests' last night,' Lara reminded her. 'What are you wearing to the club in Ayia Napa?'

'I'll find something,' Kat responded lightly, watching Mikhail stand with a drink on his office terrace with Lorne. Very tall, very dark and very handsome and infuriatingly inscrutable and unpredictable. He had virtually ignored her since that fatal encounter in his office. While he was polite and gracious in company just as though they were a couple, he had not tried to touch her again and she didn't blame him for that, having looked back repeatedly to what she had done and cringed. She had *said* one thing to him but had *done* another. If he had had enough of that, so had she. It was as if she were a split personality, one half recalling her turbulent childhood with her man-hungry mother and the other half recalling the strict moral limits she had tried to instil in her sisters while always setting her siblings a good example. Sex to scratch an uncomfortable itch of lust didn't figure anywhere between those parameters and she was not ashamed of resisting the urge and standing by her principles.

'I hope you don't mind but I thought you might want to borrow something and I left a dress on your bed,' Lara told her with a bright smile.

In recent days, Kat had learned to relax more with the other Englishwoman, who had made a real effort to offer her useful advice. Gradually it had dawned on Kat that Lara usually hosted Mikhail's guests and could have bitterly resented being supplanted by Kat. For that reason the other woman's sociability had proved a pleasant surprise, particularly when compared to Mikhail's cool detachment.

'But I'm sure I've got—' Kat began in disconcertion.

'You haven't got anything suitable to wear to a nightclub,' Lara assured her confidently. 'You'll want to fit in…for a change.'

'My clubbing days are behind me,' Kat commented quietly, ignoring that less than tactful comment on her style. 'I'm thirty-five, Lara.'

Lara's eyes widened in apparent disbelief. 'But that means you're older than him! I'm only twenty-six.'

And probably much more suitable, Kat reflected wearily, wondering why that should bother her. Lara was beautiful and bright and posing there topless and uninhibited, infinitely more likely to please Mikhail than Kat ever could. Behind her sunglasses Kat focused on Mikhail, sunlight gleaming off his carved cheekbones and stubborn jaw line, and her heart seemed to twist at the very idea of him with Lara…with *any* woman. It was because she was dreaming about him every night, embarrassingly erotic dreams that made her wake up perspiring in a tangle of bedding.

A few hours later, garbed in Lara's short red dress

and buffed and polished within an inch of her life by
the beauty salon, Kat scanned her reflection and grimaced. In her own opinion she was showing too much
flesh because the dress bared her back and a good deal
of her legs, but what was her opinion worth? She was a
fish out of water in Mikhail's exclusive world and she
didn't want to go clubbing with the younger, livelier
members of the party and stick out like a sore thumb...
like an older woman got up in absurdly teenaged clothing? Mutton dressed as lamb? Kat cringed at the fear
that she might look foolish in the dress. A tide of homesickness suddenly engulfed her, accompanied by distaste for the superficial existence she was leading where
appearance and amusement appeared to be all that truly
mattered. Right at this very minute, her youngest sister,
Topsy, was home from boarding school and staying at
the farmhouse with Emmie, and although Kat phoned
her sisters most days it wasn't the same as seeing them
in the flesh and catching up on the gossip. Three more
weeks marooned on Mikhail's giant floating palace
threatened like a prison sentence.

Kat sat beside Lara in the VIP chill-out room where
several yards away at another table Mikhail appeared
to be holding court like a reigning king. Surrounded
by bottles of champagne and beautiful girls vying for
his attention, he was in his element.

'Is it always like this for Mikhail?' Kat heard herself
ask her blonde companion.

Lara made no pretence of not grasping the question.
'You must understand that even when he was a boy he
was very much in demand. He excites women because
very rich, handsome and still *young* men are rare. They

all want to be the one he marries but he doesn't want to get married.'

'That doesn't surprise me,' Kat responded, sliding upright to go to the cloakroom, glancing back over her shoulder at Mikhail to note that two young women in very revealing outfits were performing some ridiculous form of suggestive belly dance for him and his companions. Their giggling display of their nubile bodies set her teeth on edge and made her feel about a hundred years too old for such nonsense. Mikhail's arrogant dark head lifted and turned as though he could sense her watching him. Dark eyes gleaming, he summoned her with a lean brown hand to join him…as if she were a waitress or a pet dog or something! Stiffening at that suspicion, Kat reddened and ignored the signal. Her earlier attack of homesickness and alienation returned with even greater force. She didn't want to be in Cyprus at an exclusive club for the rich and bored. She didn't want to go back to Mikhail's yacht either. She didn't belong in either place and she missed her sisters.

She had persuaded herself that regaining the ownership of her home was worth any sacrifice and only now was she finally questioning that conviction. Mikhail was upsetting her. She could never remember feeling more unhappy than she currently felt and her self-esteem had sunk to an all-time low. Earlier he had scanned her in the crimson dress, had frowned but said nothing. The absence of his admiration, however, had been blatant and from that moment on the red dress had felt like a colossal unflattering mistake. But why was she allowing Mikhail's opinion to matter so much to her? The means to stop the process of what felt like humiliation dead had always been within her own hands and perhaps it was past time that she acted. Her fingers tightened on her envelope purse, which contained her passport. Stas was poised by the exit doors and she walked over to him, her head high, eyes alight with sudden energy again.

'Could you arrange a taxi to take me to the airport?' she asked, knowing she couldn't just walk out and disappear without causing an inexcusable furore.

Momentarily, Stas seemed to freeze. 'Of course,' he told her nonetheless. 'Give me five minutes to organise it.'

Her decision made to fly home as soon as she could get a flight, Kat felt loads happier, as if a giant weight had fallen from her shoulders. She would go home, find a job and somewhere else to live, she reflected as she freshened up in the cloakroom. She didn't *need* to look to Mikhail to do anything for her, certainly not to give her a house she had lost through her own mistakes and done nothing to earn!

When Kat reappeared Stas was waiting to show her through the double exit doors and then he surprised her by throwing open another door off the corridor and she hesitated with a frown. 'Where are you taking me?'

Mikhail filled the doorway like a big dark storm cloud. 'You're not walking out on me.'

Kat settled outraged green eyes on him. *'Watch me!'* she advised.

'We'll discuss it first, *milaya moya,*' Mikhail declared, blocking her path with his tall lean body and pressing the door wider.

Kat supposed she owed him some sort of an explanation. Possibly it had been unrealistic to believe that she could just leave without a confrontation because Mikhail Kusnirovich would never accept anything less blunt. But he didn't own her and she hadn't signed away her life or anything stupid when she signed that wretched agreement with him.

'I'm not your prisoner,' Kat told him, lifting her chin. 'I can leave any time I like—'

'And where are you planning to go at this time of night in a foreign country?' Mikhail demanded harshly.

'I can wait at the airport until there's a flight. I believe the London flights are quite frequent,' Kat pointed out, swallowing so hard in the smouldering silence that her throat muscles ached. In truth she didn't have enough cash in her bank account to pay for a flight home, but she had planned to phone Saffy and ask her sibling to buy a ticket for her.

Mikhail counted slowly and internally to ten but it didn't work any magic on his aggressive mood. The realisation that she was prepared to simply walk out on him had struck him like a punch in the gut and he was genuinely stunned by the concept. A woman had never walked out on him before but he thought it was typical that she would be the first to try and do it. There she stood, her slim figure rigid with resolution, beautiful green eyes defiant and angry, pointed little chin at a combative angle, just daring him to argue. She was as unstable as gelignite, he told himself grimly. Maybe he *should* have paid her more attention in recent days instead of shelving her like a difficult project, he thought furiously, maybe he should have talked to her sooner… but talked to her about what exactly? The number of serious chats Mikhail had enjoyed with women outside business hours couldn't have covered a postage stamp. He didn't do the talking thing; he wasn't in touch with anyone's feelings, least of all his own, and he didn't do serious…which meant there really wasn't much left to talk about.

'I don't want you to leave,' Mikhail spelt out in a harsh undertone, spectacular dark eyes pinned to her with driving tenacity.

'Let's face it…without Stas's warning you, you would barely have noticed my absence,' Kat countered drily. 'You are surrounded by loads of other women tonight—'

'But I don't want any of them,' Mikhail grated without hesitation. 'I want you.'

Kat was grimly amused by that frank admission. 'Then you were going the wrong way about attaining me.'

'There *is* no right way with you. If even you don't know what you want, how am I supposed to deliver it?' he shot at her with stormy impatience.

'I know exactly what I want—I want to go home,' Kat declared, throwing her head back, spiralling russet curls falling back from her heart-shaped face.

'Isn't that just typical of a woman?' Mikhail growled. 'You light a fire and then you run away!'

Outrage rolled through Kat's slender body in an energising wave and she took an angry step forward. 'I am *not* running away!'

'Of course you are,' Mikhail fielded with biting assurance. 'You want me and I want you but evidently you can't cope with something that simple.'

'It's not that simple!' Kat launched back at him furiously, inflamed that he was confidently arguing with her when she was being plunged into ever deeper turmoil.

'It is. You can't handle your own sexual inhibitions. Call yourself a *cougar*?' Mikhail hitched an ebony brow, his derisive amusement unconcealed at the term as applied to her. 'You're more like a toddler in the sex stakes. One step forward, two steps back. If I didn't know there was no malice intended by your behaviour, I'd call you a tease—'

'How dare you?' Kat raked at him, enraged by his censure. 'I warned you that I wouldn't sleep with you!'

'While you continue to respond to my every look and touch,' Mikhail reminded her doggedly. 'You're terrified of having a normal sexual relationship with a man—that's the only reason you're still a virgin!'

'No, it's not!' Kat argued vehemently, high spots of colour burning in her pale cheeks, green eyes raw with rage that he could dare to say such a thing to her when he still didn't know anything about the person she was. 'I refuse to let any man use me for sex the way men used my mother!'

'Your...*mother*?' Mikhail's brows drew together in a frown of incomprehension because, while he might have paid to have an investigative report carried out on Kat, he had paid very little heed to her past. 'What the hell has she got to do with anything?'

Kat blinked rapidly, almost as surprised as he was that she had voiced that comment out loud. It was based on a fear that ran all the way back to her unsettled childhood when Odette had frequently complained that as soon as a man got her into bed, he lost interest in her again. 'I don't want to be used just for my body. Sex is all you're interested in,' Kat protested stiltedly.

Mikhail vaguely appreciated that he had stumbled into one of those 'relationship' talks he always avoided like the plague. Obviously sex was what he was interested in, but what was wrong with that? He had always regarded sex as a normal healthy appetite until he met her and desire became an endurance test.

'I've been used by many women,' he traded with

cool cynicism. 'For sex, for money, for my connections. It happens to all of us. You can't protect yourself from such experiences and it's spineless to run away from them—'

'I'm not spineless!' Yet Kat was starkly disconcerted by his admission that he had also been used by the opposite sex for what he could offer. But she was equally disconcerted by the admission she had made to him and feared that he might be about to make the same deduction that she had for herself. Could she have made it more obvious that she wanted *more* than sex from him? Suddenly she was praying that he didn't think too deeply about what she had said, for the emotions that had urged her to run far and fast in self-defence were too private and new to share with anyone, least of all him.

Scanning her pale taut face, Mikhail expelled his breath in a hiss and strode forward. In a disturbingly sudden movement, he lifted her off her startled feet and ignored her dismayed gasp to settle her down firmly on the leather sofa behind her. 'Sit down and talk to me, then… Tell me what possible influence your mother could still have over you…'

Mikhail felt benevolent as he offered that unparalleled invitation. If it stopped Kat walking out, he would listen to anything, while on another level he was surprisingly keen to know why she gave him so many conflicting messages.

While Kat watched Mikhail open the door to speak to Stas before he sank lithely down opposite her, her mind was already filling with uneasy images. Drinks arrived while she struggled to suppress her unfortunate memories of her childhood. Her mother, Odette, the woman Kat had loved without return until she too became an adult, was someone Kat rarely let herself think about because, even after all this time, Odette's essential indifference to her daughter could still hurt. Odette had always liked to play the victim and, as Odette's biggest audience, Kat had often witnessed more than she should of her mother's tangled love life. Long ago she had buried those distressing memories deep and moved on with her life and it was only now, as she was forced to dig those memories out again, that she appreciated that everything now looked rather different. Reality no longer matched up with the facts, she conceded ruefully. Suddenly she felt exceedingly foolish for not having seen the obvious much sooner.

'Kat.?' Mikhail prompted, surveying her highly expressive face and deeply troubled eyes with frowning force, exasperation clawing at him when they were interrupted by the arrival of the drinks he had ordered.

Kat moistened her lips with the bubbling champagne, grateful for something to hold in her trembling hand. 'My mum, Odette, was a successful model but probably not a very nice person. Our lives were unsettled because her relationships were always breaking down,' she admitted stiffly, reluctant as she was to reveal any vulnerability to him. 'She married my dad for security and then divorced him when her career took off. She deserted the twins' father when he went bankrupt, but still all she ever talked about while I was growing up was how men let *her* down and *used* her. It's only now that I can see that in most cases she was much more of a user than they were.'

Mikhail lowered lush black lashes over his bemused gaze. 'And how does that comparison apply to us?'

'It doesn't,' Kat conceded, ashamed that she had let her mother's self-pitying conditioning influence her outlook without her awareness for so many years. Odette had believed that simply engaging in sex with a man constituted a relationship and that having his baby would make him commit, she reflected wryly, and it was that shallow short-sighted outlook that had ensured that none of her mother's relationships had prospered.

'Do you still want to go back to the UK?'

Her tummy gave an apprehensive lurch as she looked into brilliant dark golden eyes, still the most beautiful she had ever seen in a man's face. He was a very dangerous man, she conceded dizzily, for he had chosen the perfect moment in which to ask that leading question and she could not believe that the timing was accidental. She didn't *want* to leave Mikhail now, she acknowledged guiltily, wasn't yet ready to close the door on what she might still discover about him. Without even realising it, she had been running away, forced into a corner by her mother's brainwashing during her impressionable adolescence and her own terror of being hurt. But logic told her that life was to be lived, mistakes included, and that in any case she was not following her mother's example.

Kat lifted her bright head. 'Not just yet...' she confessed and drained her glass.

'Let's get back on board *Hawk*,' Mikhail urged huskily, as mystified as ever by the strange way in which her mind worked but satisfied by the result. He closed a hand over hers and tugged her up from the sofa.

'What about your guests?'

'They're too busy partying on their own account to notice my absence,' he replied dismissively, long brown fingers tightening resolutely round hers, his breath fanning her cheek as he bent over her. The warm scent of his body tinged with the exclusive cologne he wore infiltrated her. A little quiver of almost painful sexual awareness engulfed her slim length and tensed her muscles.

Kat reddened when she saw Stas study their linked hands but she knew that there wasn't a romantic edge to that connection for Mikhail. No indeed, for once she could read her Russian billionaire's mind. As long as he kept a physical hold of her she couldn't go anywhere he didn't want her to go: he really was that basic. If only she could be as cool-headed and practical as he was, she ruminated worriedly as he tucked her on board the tender that would whisk them out of the harbour and back to the yacht. He had fallen in lust but she was falling in love…

As he pushed open the door of her suite Kat was scarcely breathing from nervous tension and anticipation, but once again he surprised her by stepping back to head for his own accommodation next door.

'Decision time, *milaya moya*,' he quipped, glancing back at her from heavily lidded dark sensual eyes. 'If you want me, you know where to find me.'

CHAPTER EIGHT

KAT LEANT BACK against her door, her heart hammering inside her chest… *You know where to find me.*

On the other side of the door she had locked. Could she really blame him for telling her to take the initiative for a change? She had made such a deal over *not* sleeping with Mikhail and, without ever meaning to be unfair, she had allowed him to touch her and then had withdrawn that licence at the last possible moment. But then right from the first minute she had laid eyes on Mikhail Kusnirovich, she had wanted him, wanted him more than she had ever thought she could want any man, and, unhappily for both of them, desire had decimated her common sense and control.

And common sense and control, Kat recognised, had absolutely nothing to do with the way she felt about Mikhail. Desire was a much more primitive feeling it was an unquenchable craving that it literally hurt to deny. With impatient hands she shed the green dress and her underwear and left her clothing lying in a heap, defying her instinctive urge to put every item tidily away. For too long she had lived by a rigid set of rules and she had questioned nothing. Instead she had blindly obeyed those rules like an obedient little girl.

Now all of a sudden she was looking back at the last

conservative decade of her life and she was finally *done* with playing safe and even more sick of always trying to do the right thing to set a good example! What gains had her good example achieved? It hadn't stopped Emmie from getting pregnant outside marriage any more than it had stopped Emmie's twin, Saffy, from getting married and divorced too young.

But it was still that conviction that she had to set a good example that had ensured that Kat hadn't had a man in her life for more years than she cared to recall. How dared Mikhail call her a coward? Cowardice had had nothing to do with it! There had been no arbitrary decision to remain a virgin. Instead she had consciously chosen to put her sisters' need for stability ahead of her own needs as a woman.

But would it really have damaged her siblings so much had she enjoyed intimacy with a lover? Now her sisters were moving on, making their own lives and leaving her behind, still ridiculously ignorant for a woman of her age. Continuing such self-denial was pointless. It really didn't matter if she only slept with Mikhail to satisfy her curiosity about sex, she thought painfully. It didn't even matter if she loved him and hoped for more than she would ever receive from him. A mistake was a mistake and not a disaster, and she was strong enough to survive making mistakes. Never again would she run away from the unknown like a frightened child or use her mother's errors of judgement as her safety valve.

Clad in a gossamer-thin silk nightgown, Kat unlocked the door between her suite and the master suite to push it wide with an unsteady hand. Mikhail appeared in the bathroom doorway, only a towel linked round his lean bronzed hips. His black diamond eyes settled on her and a smile of satisfaction instantly curved his wide sensual mouth. Half naked he was an imposing sight, his black hair spiky and damp from the shower, water droplets scattered across his powerful hair-roughened pecs and rock-hard abdominal muscles. He had a fabulous body, she acknowledged helplessly, and her face coloured as she tried very hard not to stare at his potent male perfection.

'I feel as though I've been waiting for you for ever,' Mikhail husked, moving forward to scoop her up in his arms and settle her down on the wide divan bed.

'And I can't believe I'm here,' Kat confided jerkily.

'Believe, *moyo zolotse.*' His mouth swooped down on hers in a kiss as evocative as rough velvet brushing her parted lips, his tongue spearing between and tangling with her own. The intoxicating taste of him was more than enough to chase the goose bumps of nervous tension from her skin and she shivered helplessly against him. Her fingers curved to his broad brown shoulders while damp heat surged between her thighs and she could feel her breasts swelling, the nipples tingling as she pushed the sensitive mounds into the hard muscular wall of his chest. Even through the thickness of the towel she could feel the hard wedge of his erection against her thigh and she trembled at the thought of him pushing inside her to sate the tormenting ache stirring in her pelvis.

He pulled back, remarkably beautiful eyes skimming her hectically flushed face while his hands roamed over her silk-clad curves, cupping her breasts before rising to slide down the straps on her shoulders and bare her tender flesh. The gown slid to her waist and he captured her distended nipples between finger and thumb and tugged to send arrows of longing shooting down into her groin.

'Mikhail…' She was breathless, quivering, almost frightened by the powerful surges of response assailing her.

'Your breasts are so sensitive that I want to torture you with pleasure,' Mikhail growled.

His mouth captured a rosy beaded tip and she gasped, jerking at the response that travelled straight down to heat her pelvis and making no protest as he lowered her down against the pillows. With his tongue and the edges of his teeth he played with the engorged buds while easing the nightie from round her hips to cast it aside. In the lamp light the porcelain purity of her slender figure glowed like polished alabaster. Big hands cupped her hips, parted her thighs and traced a trail to the silken heart of her where she was so desperately wet and swollen.

Pure undiluted hunger fired Mikhail's eyes and he pulled lithely back from her to draw her down towards the foot of the bed. She was limp with surprise and uncertainty, tensing when he pushed her knees apart and freezing into rigidity when he spread her wide to expose that part of her that she usually kept hidden. 'What are you doing?' she demanded strickenly.

'Trust me…relax,' Mikhail soothed. 'I want tonight to be the best night you've ever had with a man—'

'It'll be the only night,' she reminded him shakily while she fought the urge to snap her thighs shut like scissors and blanked her overpowering awareness that she was naked and exposed.

'Not *our* only night,' Mikhail forecast with confidence. 'But I'll make it good, *moyo zolotse…*'

'Promises, promises…' Her voice shook uncontrollably as she dared to voice that sally.

He sank his hands below her hips to lift her and his tongue swiped across her clitoris. That instant pleasure was almost too intense to be borne and her hands clawed convulsively into the bedding beneath her as he teased her tender flesh. She tried very hard to swallow back the noises rising in her throat but his unnerving skill at heightening her responses made that an impossible challenge. Her back arched, her hips rose and she cried out as his fingers penetrated her in the way she most needed to be touched, giving her just a little of what she helplessly craved. She went out of control so fast then that she had no idea of what was happening to her. She was shaking, alternately rigid and then weak before the great surge of irresistible pleasure shockwaved through her with almost brutal force and she was crying out and splintering and shuddering with the intensity of her climax.

Blinded by that all-encompassing pleasure, she looked up into his face and he gazed down at her through a veil of thick dark lashes as flattering as a fringe of ebony lace and muttered hungrily, 'I love watching you come…'

Her face burned and she tensed as he rose over her and she felt his bold shaft ease into her. He was thick and amazingly hard and he felt like an incredibly tight fit while her muscles slowly stretched to accommodate his size. His groan of uninhibited pleasure sent a jolt of delight darting through her. The raw tension in his lean, powerful muscles told her of the care and control he was exerting, but there was no escape from the brief but sharp sting of pain that assailed her when he sank deeper into her and broke through the final barrier of her innocence.

'I'm sorry,' Mikhail growled, stunning black diamond eyes glittering with the raw excitement he could not hide. 'I was trying not to hurt you.'

'It's all right… It's not hurting any more,' Kat confided, lifting her hips up to him in an instinctive movement and moaning as he drove deep into her again.

'You feel so good I don't think I could stop,' Mikhail groaned, pulling out of her receptive body and then plunging back into her hot slick depths again with a rough growl of satisfaction.

He taught her that rhythm very quickly and the constant physical stimulation fed into the overwhelming excitement he had unleashed. Her slim body rose below his again, her eyes like stars as the ripples of her second orgasm pulsed through them both, so that he drove even harder into her and shuddered over her with a shout of satisfaction he could not restrain.

Her heart was thumping so fast that even lying down she felt dizzy and breathless and utterly unlike her usual sane and sensible self. Her arms closed round him. 'Is it always that exciting?' she whispered shyly.

Mikhail pinned her to his hot damp body. 'Rarely. It's the best sex I've ever had, *milaya moya.*'

And for a split second she was pleased by the compliment and the overpowering sense of intimacy that she was enjoying while she lay in his arms. But the feeling of peace and relaxation didn't last once she thought about the label of having given him the best sex he'd ever had. Somehow instead of making her feel complimented that made her feel cheap, as if she had supplied just another novelty experience to a male who had already enjoyed a wide variety of experiences in the field of sex.

'Time for a shower,' he breathed, rolling her to the side of the bed with him and urging her in the direction of the bathroom.

Her legs felt as collapsible as a deckchair's and she clung to a muscular male arm, wincing when she felt the dulled ache at the heart of her.

'You're sore…' Mikhail husked, studying her expressive face, laughing when she blushed crimson. 'Well, what did you expect?'

'I should go back to my room,' Kat muttered, pulling back from the big tiled wall he was about to step around.

'No, I want you to stay,' Mikhail confided, hauling her up against his big powerful body as he switched on the water.

'Thought you liked your privacy,' Kat reminded him tautly, disconcerted by the amount of intimacy being forced on her all at once, uneasy with her nakedness below the strong overhead lights.

'But I like the thought of you in my bed first thing in the morning even more,' Mikhail growled against her throat as he pinned her to the tiled wall, dropped his hands to her hips to hold her there and crushed her lush mouth with hungry urgency beneath his.

Imprisoned by his big powerful body, Kat couldn't breathe for excitement and she discovered that even the tenderness between her thighs couldn't stop her wanting him again with a level of hunger that shook her. 'Now my hair's wet,' she complained prosaically.

'You'll survive,' Mikhail breathed, letting his tongue delve between her lips in an urgent rhythmic foray that mimicked the act of intercourse so closely that she quivered with spellbound yearning, the distended tips of her breasts grazing his hard pectoral muscles. Against her stomach she could feel him rigid and urgent again and she marvelled at his speedy recovery.

And Kat, who never would have dreamt of going to bed with wet hair forgot about her hair, and forgot to worry about what it would look like the next morning. In the grip of passion, Mikhail was too determined to withstand. He strode from the shower with her wrapped round him and seated her on the granite vanity counter. It was the work of a moment for him to snatch a contraceptive from a drawer, tear the packet open and don a condom. He stepped between her spread legs to ease into her honeyed softness again with a sigh of profound relief.

'Thought you were going to wait until tomorrow,' Kat reminded him, her teeth gritting on a spasm of erotic pleasure so devouring it resembled pain because he was being extraordinarily cautious and gentle and slow. Little tremors of exquisite excitement made her clench tight around him.

'Never was any good at waiting,' Mikhail growled, fighting to stay in control as he rocked against her, fearful of hurting her but wanting her so desperately it was like a mounting fever in his blood.

The ball of his thumb circled the little nub of nerve-endings at the swollen heart of her and she moaned wildly under his mouth, her arms tightening round him, her nails digging into his shoulders as he quickened the pace of his possession.

In the morning he took her again, his mouth tracing the corded delicacy of her throat to awaken her before he sank his thickness into her receptive body over and over again until she screamed her explosive release into the pillow beneath her head.

'Shower with me,' he urged afterwards.

Kat knew he wasn't to be trusted in the shower and reluctantly laughed. 'I'll use my own.'

'Breakfast in ten minutes,' he told her firmly.

Kat didn't move until he had vanished safely into his bathroom. The ache of overindulgence was so strong that she gritted her teeth when she got out of bed and returned to her own room to freshen up. A cry of horror was wrenched from her when she looked in a mirror and saw her curls all standing on end in a wall of frizz. She looked like a rag doll who had been tortured. With no time to do anything with her recalcitrant curls, she scraped the messy russet torrent back and secured her tumbled hair with a clip. Showered, she dabbed on a little light make-up, trying to conceal the swollen contours of her mouth and the evidence of his stubble marking her with a beard rash across her cheeks and throat. She pulled on underwear and yanked a sundress from the dressing room, hurrying because she knew he was so impatient that he would come looking for her if she didn't appear on time.

So *that* was sex, she reflected in a daze, so much more than she had expected: more exciting, more intimate, more everything really. And she had loved everything he had done to her, had swiftly got over her shyness and uncertainty to appreciate that he was a good lover and that she was lucky to have had so considerate and skilled an introduction to intimacy. But now she was wondering if she had lived up to *his* expectations or whether at the end of the day he could be wondering what all the fuss had been about.

Breakfast was served on the extensive private deck beyond Mikhail's suite. Sunlight glancing off the tur-

quoise waters of the Mediterranean sea, Kat sipped her
coffee and tried to stop smiling, indeed to cram a lid
down on the bubbling happiness welling up inside her.
Happiness wasn't fitting. They didn't have a relationship for her to celebrate or pin hopes on. All they had
was an affair and now that they were actually having
an affair that agreement they had made had to become
history, Kat thought ruefully.

'You can't give me the farmhouse back now,' Kat
told Mikhail squarely.

An ebony brow quirked. 'Why not?'

'It would be inappropriate now that we're sleeping
together,' Kat pointed out flatly as she took a seat.

'According to whose book of sexual etiquette?'
Mikhail queried very drily.

'If I accepted the house back now, it would be like
accepting payment for sex—'

'Don't look for trouble where none exists. I don't
offer payment for sex, never have, never will.'

'I wouldn't feel comfortable now letting you return
the house to me,' Kat explained stubbornly.

'Tough,' Mikhail remarked, unimpressed. 'We made
that agreement and I see no reason to deviate from it.
That house is your home.'

'That house belongs to you now,' Kat retorted in
crisp disagreement.

Mikhail vented a sound of exasperation. '*Zatk'nis!*
Shut up!' he told her impatiently. 'You're talking nonsense.'

Her green eyes flared. 'Think about what I'm saying... You know it makes sense!'

'But I'm not listening,' Mikhail responded with an

imperious shift of a lean brown hand that dismissed the discussion in its entirety.

Her teeth gnashed together.

'I tell you what to do...you *do* it,' Mikhail drawled softly. 'That was also in the agreement and I wouldn't like you to lose that talent now.'

Sheer frustration sent Kat up out of her seat again and she rested her slender forearms on the rail to stare out to sea. 'You sound like a Neanderthal again.'

Strong hands skimmed down her spine to curve down over her hips. 'Whatever turns you on—'

'*That* doesn't,' she told him succinctly.

Long fingers inched up her skirt and glided up the silken length of her thigh and she froze. 'What the heck are you doing?' she exclaimed in consternation.

Masculine fingertips flirted with the lacy edge of the knickers interrupting his exploration. 'Take them off,' he said.

'Of course I'm not taking them off!' Kat protested in disbelief. 'Have you gone insane?'

'Just the thought of you naked below that dress excites me,' Mikhail purred, pressing his lips to a delicate spot just below her ear in a caress that left her hot and breathlessly eager for more. 'What's wrong with that?'

'I wouldn't feel right without them on,' Kat muttered tautly while shamelessly angling her head back to provide easier access for his wide sensual mouth.

In answer, Mikhail hauled her up against him and kissed her with a hungry fervour that thoroughly unsettled her. With her cradled in his arms he sank down into his seat with her again, long caressing fingers stroking her slim thighs below the skirt of her dress. Recognising that he really didn't know how to take no for an answer but simply pursued another path when he met with opposition, Kat slapped a hand down on the hem of her dress to prevent it from rising any further and to restrict his clever hands. 'No,' she told him flatly. 'I'm keeping my underwear on!'

'You're so stubborn,' Mikhail growled in complaint against her lush mouth.

'You're even worse,' Kat complained, idle fingers brushing through his luxuriant black hair while her languorous gaze admired the exotic slash of his cheekbones, the arrogant jut of his nose and the strength of his jaw line. 'But luckily for you, you're also incredibly sexy...'

Mikhail tilted his imperious dark head back and laughed out loud. 'Am I?'

Barely able to credit that she could already be so relaxed in his company that she could tease him, Kat grinned. 'I think so...but shouldn't we be joining your guests for a farewell breakfast?'

'Stop being so sensible,' Mikhail urged with a frown.

'I'm *always* sensible,' Kat told him ruefully.

'If you were that sensible you would have avoided me like the plague,' Mikhail asserted with conviction.

And that he could coolly issue that warning sent a cold shiver down Kat's vulnerable spine. It was sex, only sex, that had brought them together, she reminded herself urgently, nothing more involved or dangerous. He was fantastic in bed and that was that: she didn't *have* any other feelings for him. No, not one single tender feeling or stab of womanly curiosity, she reflected, and on that soothing thought she dragged her fingers out of his hair and shifted off his lap as though someone had harpooned her with a flaming arrow. After all, she didn't want to give him the impression that he was sleeping with a clinging vine.

* * *

'My mother died when I was six years old,' Mikhail admitted grudgingly.

'What did she die of?' Kat prompted, ignoring the I-don't-want-to-talk-about-this signals he was emanating in a defensive force field. He never ever mentioned his family or his childhood and, considering that he knew everything there was to know about her, his determined reticence was starting to annoy her.

'Being pregnant. She went into labour at home. Something went wrong and she bled to death. The baby died as well,' Mikhail spelt out grimly.

'That must have been very traumatic for you and your father,' Kat said quietly, disconcerted by the tragedy he had revealed.

'If she'd had proper medical attention, she probably would have survived but my father didn't want her going into hospital.'

Her brow furrowed. 'Why not?'

Lean, darkly handsome features taut, his black diamond eyes glittered and his handsome mouth compressed into a hard line of dissatisfaction. 'I don't want to talk about this. It's not my favourite topic of conversation...*vy menya panimayete*...do you understand me?' he bit out with harsh emphasis, swinging round and striding away.

Kat suppressed a sigh. Three weeks of unparalleled exposure to Mikhail had taught her that she apparently had the tact of an elephant in hobnail boots. She was no good at pussyfooting round the things he didn't want to discuss. Indeed the minute she realised he was holding back on her that topic became what she most wanted him to talk about. Secrets nagged at her. What was wrong with curiosity? Surely it was natural for her to be curious?

The problem was that in recent weeks she had begun to feel misleadingly close to Mikhail. They had spent so much time together. Another party of guests had come and gone midway through the cruise. Barbecues had been staged on deserted beaches, trips organised to exclusive clubs and designer shops. He had complimented her on her skills as a hostess but she hadn't had to make much of an effort. She liked meeting different people and loved to ensure that they enjoyed themselves and relaxed. After all, those same traits had once persuaded her to open a guest house. But on a more personal level she could not afford to forget that the man who slept beside her all night long was only a lover and not a partner. There were limits to their relationship and evidently she had just breached them and caused offence. Unfortunately for her, she was continually battling the desire to break down Mikhail's reserve.

In the office on the upper deck, Mikhail opened his laptop. Kat would sleep in her own bed tonight. He could get along without her for one night. He had never been dependent on a woman in his life and she was no different. Well, she was different in one aspect: he wasn't tired of her yet, hadn't yet had enough of that slender, soft-skinned body of hers that melted into his as if she had been created to be his perfect fit. Sex was amazing with her, everything he had ever wanted, everything he had never dreamt he might find with one woman. The pulse at his groin stirred, the stubborn flesh swelling and hardening behind his zip even at the thought of her. Three weeks and she was *still* turning him on hard and fast. He didn't like it—he resented her power over him, loathed it when she tried to plunge him into the kind of meaningful dialogue he never had with women. In a sudden movement he snapped the laptop shut again and rose lithely upright, six feet five inches of powerfully frustrated and aggressive male.

'Where is she?' he asked Stas, who was hovering by the door.

'Still out on deck,' the older man confirmed.

He found Kat leaning against the rail looking out to sea, her dress fluttering against her slim curves in the breeze. His hands came down on her shoulders and she jerked in surprise.

'Stop snooping,' Mikhail told her, tugging her back into the hard heat of his big body.

'I wasn't snooping!' Kat argued vehemently without turning her head. 'I'm not a snoop!'

'My childhood wasn't exactly a bowl of cherries,' Mikhail breathed curtly.

'Neither was mine but you accept that and move on...'

'I don't think about it, so there's nothing to move on from, *milaya moya*.' Mikhail pressed her up against the rail and buried his mouth hungrily in the soft sensitive curve of flesh where her neck joined her shoulder. She shivered, imprisoned by his body, achingly aware of her own and the hunger he could ignite so easily.

'The fact you don't think about it and won't talk about it says it all,' Kat quipped. 'Why all the secrecy?'

'I have no secrets,' Mikhail fielded.

And not for one moment did Kat believe that claim, for he was a fascinatingly complex man, who revealed very little about himself on a personal level.

'My mother was from a tribe of nomadic herders in Siberia,' he volunteered with startling abruptness. 'My father was trying to buy up oil and gas rights in the region when he saw her. He said it was love at first sight. She was very beautiful but she didn't speak a word of Russian and she was illiterate—'

'It sounds very romantic to me,' Kat said defiantly.

'He had to marry her before her family would let her go. He took her from life in a herders' tent and put her in a mansion. He was obsessed with her. He enjoyed the fact that she had to depend on him for everything, that she understood nothing about the life he led or the world he lived in as a wealthy businessman. He liked her ignorance, her subservience,' Mikhail breathed scathingly. 'He never took her out. Behind closed doors, he treated her like a domestic slave and when she got things wrong he beat the hell out of her!'

Kat twisted round and focused stricken green eyes on his lean, strong face. 'Did he beat you as well?'

'Only when I tried to protect her,' Mikhail replied, his handsome mouth twisting at the recollection. 'I was only six when she died, so I might have got in his way a few times but I wasn't physically capable of preventing him from hurting her. He suffered from violent rages yet she worshipped the ground he walked on because she didn't know any better. She thought it was her duty to make her husband happy and if he wasn't happy she believed it was her fault.'

'It was probably the way she was raised. It's hard to shake that kind of conditioning,' Kat muttered soothingly, sensing the pain that he refused to express. There had been violence in his childhood. He had loved and pitied his mother and had been powerless to help her. She could imagine the wound of regret and frustration that that must have engraved on his soul.

'You fight me every step of the way,' Mikhail pointed out.

'Maybe you would have preferred a subservient woman—'

'*No!*' The interruption was harsh, unequivocal. 'I wouldn't want you if you were scared of me or always trying to impress or please me.'

'I never really understood why you do want me,' Kat murmured truthfully.

Mikhail flipped her round and stared down at her with smouldering dark eyes. 'You don't need to understand.'

Long fingers were gently smoothing her upper arms, awakening her to the hunger she couldn't restrain. He mightn't scare her but the hunger *did*. It overpowered her will, made her desperate and needy, two things she always hid from him. Even now, when he simply looked at her, arousal ran like a current of fire through her body as her breasts swelled and peaked and liquid heat curled between her thighs.

'I want you now, *moyo zolotse,*' he husked and the dark rough edge of his voice slid over her senses like silk.

'Because I upset you—'

'I wasn't upset—'

Her winged brows arched in disbelief at the claim. 'You were furious!'

An appreciative laugh was wrenched from Mikhail. His face etched with amusement. He really was a breathtakingly handsome man, she conceded dizzily. He pulled her up against him, fingertips brushing a slender thigh as he lifted her skirt.

'I was about to say that you'll never make diplomatic status but perhaps I was wrong. You're bare and you know how much I like that.' Mikhail breathed a little raggedly as he scooped her off her feet and carried her back indoors.

Her face was burning with colour. She was a shameless hussy who rarely wore a full set of underwear in his radius. Three weeks as this man's lover had changed her and she didn't think she could ever go back to the prim and cautious woman she had been before. Although she was always waiting to see him betray some sign of boredom or lack of interest, he never seemed to get enough of her.

He settled her down on the bed and stood over her, ripping off his shirt to expose the six-pack abs that she so admired and unzipping his chino pants to reveal a very healthy erection. She reached out to touch him, stroking his thick hardness with gentle fingers, watching his eyes narrow below his lush lashes and shimmer with unashamed desire. He came down on top of her and kissed her with hungry driving urgency, his tongue stabbing between her parted with lips with an erotic skill.

He wasn't prepared to free her for long enough to remove her dress in the proper fashion and as he attempted to impatiently extract her from its folds fabric ripped and she gasped, 'Mikhail! I liked this dress—'

With a stifled curse he concluded the struggle by pulling it over her head and finally flung it aside. '*Ti takaya valnuyishaya*...you are so exciting. I can't wait—'

'We only got out of bed a couple of hours ago,' Kat reminded him, swiping the tip of her tongue over his wide full lower lip, loving the scent and the taste of him.

'Obviously you should have given me more attention while we were there,' Mikhail quipped speciously, his hands cupping the soft full mounds of her breasts and rubbing her straining pink nipples, so that her breath caught in her throat and the smart answer on the tip of her tongue got lost somewhere in the passage from her brain.

Her eyes drifted closed as he kissed her again and stroked between her legs. She quivered, hips rising as he pleasured her with consummate sizzling ease, touching her where she needed to be touched, setting alight every nerve ending in her writhing body until an uncontrollable ache built at the heart of her.

'You're so hot and tight,' Mikhail growled against her throat, pushing back from her to close his hands round her waist and turn her over onto her stomach. 'I need you now.'

He tugged up her hips and sank into her in one long deep thrust that made her cry out in shock and delight. Her level of pleasure went into overload as he took her hard and fast. Intense sensation laced with wild excitement seized hold of her. The slam of his body into hers kicked off a chain reaction of spellbinding heat in her pelvis. The excitement surged to an unbearable level and she was gasping, whimpering, begging until the skilled brush of his thumb over her clitoris sent her rocketing into a blazing paradise of erotic pleasure that splintered through her quivering length like an explosion. She collapsed down on the bed as he groaned his own release into her shoulder.

'You're crushing me,' she protested, struggling desperately to catch her breath again.

Mikhail expelled his breath and released her from his weight, rolling onto the bed beside her before pulling her back into his arms to kiss her with lingering appreciation. 'You set me on fire,' he muttered thickly. 'But the moment I stop I only want to do it again—'

'Forget it…I won't be capable of moving again this side of midnight,' Kat mumbled, her body still pulsing and thrumming from the intensity of her climax, her limbs resting so heavily on the mattress that they felt like iron weights.

'I'm ready and willing to do all the work.' But then, in a disconcertingly sudden movement, Mikhail fell back from her and swore in Russian. 'I didn't use a condom!'

Consternation gripped Kat. She sat up, seriously startled by that admission, for he never took risks in that department. No matter when or where they made love he was always careful to use contraception to protect her. Being in a relationship where pregnancy could even be a risk was, however, still so new and surprising to Kat that her mind refused to even estimate the possibility of an unplanned pregnancy.

'And if my calculations are correct we may have chosen a bad day to be careless,' Mikhail breathed tautly, his strong jaw line hardening at the prospect. 'Less than two weeks have passed since your last period, which puts us slap bang in the middle of your fertile phase.'

His intimate grasp of the workings of her female body embarrassed Kat, but there was no hiding such facts in a relationship such as theirs. 'But I'm at an age where my fertility is probably going downhill,' she told him thinly, not really wanting to be reminded of that possibility but keen to stop him worrying.

'These days lots of women are giving birth in their forties,' Mikhail fielded drily. 'I doubt that you have any grounds to assume that you're infertile.'

'Well, let's hope we don't have cause to find out

whether I am or not,' Kat muttered ruefully, sliding off the bed and heading into the bathroom because all of a sudden she needed a moment alone and unobserved.

The Kat she saw reflected in the mirror was all shaken up, her eyes dazed, her face pale and troubled. An affair seemed trouble free until the real world threatened and there could be nothing more real world than an accidental pregnancy. For goodness' sake, her sister Emmie was pregnant and hadn't she disapproved, deemed her irresponsible and feared for her sibling's future? How much less excuse did she have at her age? She should have taken care of birth control even before she got on the yacht. Better safe than sorry should have been her guiding principle. She had been so sure she wouldn't end up in Mikhail's bed and where had that belief got her?

Mikhail joined her in the shower. He ran a reproving fingertip along the anxious line of her compressed lips. 'Stop worrying about it. If you conceive, we'll handle it together. We're not frightened teenagers,' he pointed out levelly.

But the day after tomorrow she would be leaving the yacht and he would no longer be part of her life. He had said nothing to make her think otherwise and she preferred that. She didn't want him promising to phone and then not bothering. She had fallen in love with him but that wasn't his fault. He had made her no promises and told her no lies. So, how had she managed to fall for him?

Was it when he first ensured that she got her favourite chocolate breakfast drink every morning even though he thought it was a disgustingly sweet concoction? When he started teaching her simple words of Russian? When he tolerated her obsession with a certain television reality show and let her watch it even though it bored him to death? Or was it when he most unexpectedly ran her a hot bath when she found herself suffering one evening from embarrassing cramps? Or even when he treated her as though she was the only woman in the world for him, angling his head down to catch her every word, offering advice on the way she handled her sisters, telling her where she had gone wrong with her guest house? No, Mikhail's full attention was not all a source of joy, she conceded with wry amusement, for he thought he knew everything and that there was no problem he could not fix.

Sometimes she lay awake in bed beside him, studying his lean bronzed profile and the black lashes almost hitting his spectacular cheekbones, and she would try to remember what life had been like without him. Unhappily for her, she didn't want to remember that time or the absence of fun and passion that had made her life so colourless and predictable. Life was never that predictable in Mikhail's radius. It shocked her that she could have lived so many years without ever discovering such joy and delight in another person.

CHAPTER NINE

'WHAT DO YOU want to do today?' Mikhail prompted Kat the following morning as he wrapped a fleecy towel round her dripping figure.

'I thought you had work to do—'

'On your *last* day?' A black brow slashed up.

Her heart thudded as though he had pulled a knife on her, dismay reverberating through her slender body. She had actually thought he might not be aware that the month and the agreed amount of time was up. What a fool she had been! Clearly he had an internal calendar every bit as accurate as her own and it was a timely reminder that she had something she really did need to discuss with him *before* they parted.

'Could we be ordinary people for a change?' she heard herself ask, thinking that it would be easier to talk to him away from the yacht as he was highly unlikely to stage a row with her in a public place.

'Ordinary?' he queried blankly.

'Walk down a street without an escort that attracts attention, window-shop, go for coffee some place that isn't fancy...' she extended uncertainly. 'Simple things.'

Dark as night eyes widening in surprise at the request, Mikhail shrugged a broad shoulder. 'I'm sure I can manage that.'

The tender dropped them at the boarded promenade walk that skirted the coastline of the resort. Stas and his companions followed them but kept their distance. Casually clad in shorts and an open-necked shirt, Mikhail urged her into the town and, closing a hand over hers, he walked her down the main street. She checked out shop windows and went into a gift shop where she insisted on paying for a small glass owl that she knew Topsy would happily add to her collection.

'I've decided I don't like independent women,' Mikhail imparted, watching her study a display of sparkling dress rings in a jeweller's window. 'There's nothing here worthy of your interest... At those prices it's all fake.'

'I'm not a snob—'

'I am,' Mikhail interposed without hesitation. 'Which one do you like?'

'The green one,' she confided, surprised he had asked.

'I couldn't bear to look at that on your finger,' Mikhail derided and he tugged her on down the busy street at a smart pace. 'Where are we going for coffee?'

Kat picked a quiet outdoor café set above the beach with comfortable seats and a beautiful view of the sea. A resigned look on his strong face, Mikhail folded his big powerful frame down into a chair that creaked alarmingly. 'So what's so exciting about coming here?' he enquired, keen for her to spell out the source of the attraction.

'That's the point. It's not exciting or fancy, it's just plain and peaceful,' she told him lightly, knowing she had a thorny subject to broach before she departed and wanting to get that little discussion over and done with somewhere where Mikhail was unlikely to lose his cool.

Kat was so far removed from his usual style of lover that his fascination with her was understandable, Mikhail conceded impatiently, striving tolerantly not to frown with disapproval as she sipped at yet another sickeningly sweet chocolate drink, which could only be bad for her health. Didn't she care about her well-being? Or the fact that she was currently as poor as a church mouse? Any other woman he had slept with would, at the very least, have thought nothing of marching him out to some designer retail outlet so that he could reward her generously for her time with the goodbye gift of a new wardrobe...

So, it had finally come: the moment to say goodbye. He would miss Kat, he acknowledged reluctantly, and not only in bed. He would miss her ability to challenge him, her refusal to be impressed by what his money could buy, even her easy friendliness with his staff and his guests, although he would not miss her ridiculous obsession with reality shows that portrayed a lifestyle that ironically she appeared to have no interest in acquiring for herself. And missing a woman, even rating a woman as being capable of giving him more than a few weeks of amusement, was not a familiar experience for Mikhail. He had always believed that for every woman he left behind another even more appealing would soon appear and experience had borne out that trusty conviction. He would move on as he always did, of course he would.

And no doubt she would move on quickly as well, he reflected darkly, for he was convinced that Lorne would track her down once he knew that Mikhail had ditched her. Lorne Arnold had been very taken with Kat... Lorne was waiting in the wings ready to pounce. Mikhail gritted his teeth, trying not to imagine Kat in bed with Lorne, parting those wonderfully long legs for him and making those throaty little cries when she climaxed. He felt sick to the stomach. But why should that imagery bother him so much? He wasn't possessive about women, never had been, wasn't sensitive either. When it was over, it was over. He wasn't unstable and irrational like his father, the sort of man who obsessed over one special irreplaceable woman and drank himself to death when she was gone. He didn't *do* emotion, he didn't get attached...or hurt or disappointed either. That was the bottom line: he never ever made himself vulnerable. That was a risk that only the foolish ran and he had never been a fool.

'What are you thinking about?' Kat prompted, having noted the grim set of his strong jawline and the flinty hardness of his eyes as he gazed out to sea. 'You look angry.'

'Why would I be angry?' Mikhail enquired, irritated that she watched him so closely and read him so accurately. She got under his skin in some way and wrecked his self-control. Only a few hours had passed since he had forgotten to use a condom for the first time in his life but that single little instant of shocking forgetfulness had shattered his equilibrium. How could any woman excite him that much? He needed a little distance from her; he *needed* to send her home for his own peace of mind.

'I don't know but you certainly don't look happy,' Kat remarked gingerly, picking up on his irritation as well. She would never work out what made Mikhail tick. She did recognise that he had a dark side, a core he never exposed, but he was not, as a rule, moody or bad-tempered. Quick-tempered, yes, bad-tempered, no.

'I'm fine,' Mikhail insisted while mentally engaged

in drawing up a list of what he *didn't* like about Kat. She asked awkward questions and refused to back off even when he made his dissatisfaction clear. She snuggled up to him in bed, which was actually rather endearing, he conceded grudgingly. He might not be a touchy-feely kind of guy, but he did not find the natural warmth and affection she showed him objectionable in any way. On the other hand, she liked the shower a lot hotter than he did and also liked to eat disgustingly sweet things— were those flaws too petty to consider? Since when had he been petty? Since when had he had to think of reasons why he should ditch a woman? He would buy her a fabulous jewel to show his appreciation. He dug out his mobile phone to make the arrangements.

Kat sighed the minute she saw the phone in his lean hand. 'Is that call really necessary?' she asked gently.

Recognising the reproof for what it was, Mikhail ground his teeth together and added another score to her tally of flaws. '*Da*...it is.'

Kat nodded, wishing his mind weren't always one hundred per cent focused on business. Was it naive of her to have hoped that he would let his guard down a little on her last day and engage in meaningful conversation? Mentally she winced at that pathetic hope. Had she really thought Mikhail might come over all romantic and tell her that he wanted her to extend her stay? What a silly dream that would be for her to cherish when she badly needed to go home and pack up her belongings in the farmhouse! After all, Emmie had already established that a little terraced house in the village would soon be available for rent. It wasn't like Kat to be so impractical and it was past time that she told Mikhail what she had decided about Birkside. She studied his bold bronzed profile while he talked on his phone and her eyes warmed, any prospect of practicality draining away. She adored those eyelashes, thick as fly swats, the only softening element in his lean dark face. But there was more to her feelings than the fact that he was an incredibly handsome man and a breathtakingly passionate and exciting lover. She loved his strong work ethic, his open-handed generosity for the right charitable cause, his bluntness, his essentially liberal outlook.

'We have something to talk about,' Kat said stiffly.

'We can talk when we get back on board,' Mikhail murmured abstractedly as he dug his phone back in his pocket.

'You want to leave already? You haven't even touched your coffee yet,' Kat pointed out.

'There's a chip in the cup,' Mikhail informed her drily. 'I don't do ordinary very well...I'm sorry.'

In a forgiving mood, Kat shrugged a narrow shoulder. 'That's OK. You're not on trial. I do need to talk about that legal agreement we made though—'

Mikhail frowned. 'That's water under the bridge—'

'No, it's not. I can't accept the house from you now,' she said with a tight little grimace of discomfiture. 'In the circumstances it would feel too much like payment for services rendered in the bedroom.'

'Don't be ridiculous!' Mikhail told her bluntly. 'I offered the house and you accepted it—it's a done deal.'

'I haven't accepted it and I'm not going to,' Kat protested stubbornly. 'The house is worth thousands and thousands of pounds and far too big a payment for the amount of hostessing I've done for you.'

'That's my decision, not yours,' Mikhail traded curtly, dark eyes now cool as rain on her sun-warmed skin; indeed she actually felt physically chilled by that look.

Kat's spine was rigid with tension but she was determined not to surrender because for once she knew that she was right and he was wrong. 'I won't accept you signing the house back to me. I've thought about this and I mean what I'm saying, Mikhail. Everything's changed between us since we made that agreement and it would be wrong to stick to it.'

Mikhail thrust back his chair and sprang upright to stare down at her with intimidatingly cold, dark and angry eyes. 'You're getting your house back...*end of*!' he framed with a growling edge of ferocity.

Out of the corner of her eye she watched Stas rush to pay the bill while simultaneously keeping a wary eye trained on his employer. She reddened when she saw the diners at the next table staring at them.

Kat hurried over to Mikhail's side before he could stride off without her. 'I had to tell you how I felt,' she told him ruefully.

'And now you know how *I* feel,' he countered grimly. 'Stop messing me around, Kat! It annoys the hell out of me!'

'I'm not doing that,' Kat protested in sharp disconcertion.

But that they had differing opinions on that score was clear when the tender whisked them back to *The Hawk* and Mikhail strode away from her the minute they boarded. She had said what she had to say and she was not taking it back, she told herself squarely, and she went downstairs to her suite to pack her case so that she would be ready to leave in the morning. She walked next door into Mikhail's suite to retrieve her wrap, two nightdresses and the toiletries that had taken up residence in his bathroom. When she returned to her own room, she was taken aback to find Mikhail lodged in the doorway like a big black-haired thunder cloud.

'You're packing,' he noted flatly.

Kat nodded uneasily, her mouth running dry as he stared in level challenge back at her.

'This is for you...' Mikhail tossed a jewellery box carelessly on the bed where it landed beside her suitcase. 'A small token of my...my appreciation,' he selected with cool precision.

Her heart beating very fast, Kat lifted the box and flipped it open to display a breathtaking emerald and diamond pendant. 'It's hardly small,' she told him, taken aback by the sheer size of the emerald and its deep glowing colour. 'What on earth do you expect me to do with this?'

'Wear it for me tonight. What you choose to do with it afterwards is entirely your business.'

'I suppose I ought to have said thank you straight away but I was rather overwhelmed by you giving me something so expensive,' she said apologetically.

An ebony brow rose. 'You expected something cheap and tacky to go with this ordinary kick you're suddenly on?'

'Of course not, but it's not a kick—*I'm* ordinary, Mikhail. And tomorrow I'm going back to my own life and it's ordinary as well,' Kat countered with quiet dignity as she set the jewellery box down on the dressing table and studied it with a sinking heart and a growing sense of desolation.

That spectacular emerald was his way of saying goodbye and thanks. She knew that so why was the fact that he was treating her exactly as she had expected him to treat her hurting her so much? Had she somehow thought that she might be different from her predecessors in his bed, that she might mean a little more to him? Pallor now spread below her fair complexion, her tummy succumbing to a nauseous lurch. Well, if she had thought that she was more special, she was being thoroughly punished for her vanity. He had just proved that she meant little more to him than a willing body on which he could ease his high-voltage sex drive. She had fulfilled his expectations and pleased him and now it was time for her to leave: it was that simple. She was no longer flavour of the month. She spun back to look at him, lounging in her doorway in an open-necked shirt and jeans, six feet five inches of unadulterated alpha male, absolutely gorgeous with his black hair ruffled by the breeze and a dark covering of stubble accentuating his handsome jaw line and wide expressive mouth. Tension screamed from him and she dropped her gaze, belatedly appreciating that he was not enjoying the process of putting her back out of his life any more than she was.

'I'll see you at dinner,' he told her and he walked away.

Hearts didn't break, Kat told herself as she clasped the pendant round her throat a couple of hours later. Hearts dented and bruised. She would head home tomorrow, sell the emerald to buy some security for her and her sisters and find a job. In truth, a new life awaited her, for the loss of the guest house was forcing her to strike out in an alternative direction. Where was her eagerness to greet that fresh start? She smoothed down the folds of the maxi dress, a colourful print that accentuated her bright hair and light skin. The emerald glowed at her throat, the surrounding diamonds twinkling to catch the light.

A knock sounded on the door. It was Lara, studying her with languid cool to say, 'Dinner is ready...I see you're packed and ready to go.'

Kat nodded. Lara had abandoned her friendly approaches once it became obvious that Kat and her boss had become lovers. 'Yes...'

'Are you upset?' Lara asked, disconcerting Kat once again.

Kat shrugged a bare shoulder as she concentrated on climbing the colourful glass staircase without tripping over her long skirt. 'Not really. Staying on *The Hawk* has been an experience but it's hardly been what I'm accustomed to. I'm looking forward to getting home, pulling on my jeans and gossiping with my sisters,' she fielded, pride lifting her head high, for she would have sooner thrown herself down the stairs than reveal just how cut up she truly was at the prospect of leaving Mikhail.

'The boss will be a hard act to follow. I hope you don't find that he's spoiled you for other men,' Lara commented.

'Who knows?' Kat quipped. Not for the first time it occurred to her that Mikhail's PA was a little too impressed by her boss and the unattainability factor he was famed for. The girl was gorgeous, Kat acknowledged, and perhaps it annoyed the beautiful blonde that Mikhail could remain impervious to her appeal while choosing to spend time with a woman who had neither Lara's glossy perfection nor her youth.

'The chef has really pushed the boat out tonight with the meal. Everyone knows you're leaving tomorrow,' Lara remarked laconically before she left her.

Lara had not been joking, Kat registered as her attention fell on the impressive dining table festooned in

crisp pastel linen, sparkling candles and a light scattering of artistic pearls and rosebuds. Her brows rose
as Mikhail strode out of the salon chatting on his cell
phone in Russian. He put away the phone while studying her with shrewd assessing eyes. Was he looking for
evidence of tears or sadness? Her chin tilted and a resolute smile softened Kat's tense lips as she took a seat.

'You look stunning this evening,' Mikhail said, startling her, for he rarely handed out compliments. 'The
emerald brings out the remarkable green of your eyes,
milaya moya.'

Bellini cocktails were brought to the table and then
the meal was served and Kat's mortification began to
climb, for the starter arrived cooked in a heart shape
and every edible aphrodisiac known to man featured on
the menu, accompanied by a good deal of chocolate. It
was like an over-the-top Valentine's Day meal, wholly
inappropriate for a couple on the brink of parting for
ever. Mikhail, furthermore, preferred plain Russian
food and a good deal of it, not the dainty elaborate por-
tions he was being served.

'I suppose all this is in your honour,' he said drily,
watching Kat bite into a chocolate truffle. 'Clearly my
chef is your devoted slave.'

'Hardly that. François understands that I appreciate
his efforts,' Kat countered lightly, for while Mikhail
paid his staff well and rewarded them for excellence,
he generally only spoke to them about their work when
they did something to displease him, an attitude that Kat
had combatted with praise and encouragement.

Sadly, on this particular occasion François' wonderful food was wasted on her because she was sitting there
thinking that she would never dine with Mikhail again.
He had treated her as he always did, with engrained

good manners and light entertaining conversation. If he was ill at ease with the situation, it didn't show.

Kat, on the other hand, felt increasingly gutted by his steady self-control. She watched him, hungry for every last imprint of him, her troubled gaze winging constantly back to the remarkably beautiful eyes that illuminated his handsome face, the strength that dominated his features, and there was not a sign that he was experiencing an ounce of the regret that was torturing her. The remnants of the glorious truffle turned to ashes in her mouth. For a dangerous moment she wanted to cry and rail at the heavens for what Mikhail did not feel for her.

'I'm pretty tired tonight,' she admitted, although she already knew she would not enjoy a single wink of sleep.

'Go to bed. I'll join you later,' Mikhail breathed, his husky dark drawl smooth as a caress.

Halfway out of her chair, Kat froze, for it had not occurred to her that he might expect her to share his bed as usual. Had he no sensitivity, no comprehension of how she felt? Stifling her anger, she lifted her russet head. 'I hope you don't mind but I'd prefer to be on my own tonight.'

Mikhail frowned, for he had cherished a fantasy of seeing her reclining on his bed, those pale soft curves embellished only by the emerald he had bought her.

'It wouldn't feel right to be with you tonight,' Kat muttered in harried explanation, her pale face flushing with self-conscious colour. 'We're over and done now and I couldn't pretend otherwise.'

Mikhail was taken aback by that candid assessment and the insulting suggestion that she might have to *pretend* anything in his arms, and his stubborn mouth clenched hard. *Let it go*, logic dictated. A celibate night might not be what he wanted or even what he felt he deserved when he had handled her with kid gloves and all the respect he could muster, but even less was he in the mood for feminine drama. Not that Kat looked likely to offer him tears: her heart-shaped face was as still as a pond surface. With an odd little smile and a nod she walked away fast.

Dinner had felt like the condemned woman's last meal, Kat conceded wretchedly as she got ready for bed, but she wasn't going to cry about him. It was over and she would pick herself back up and go on. From the first moment they had met this hour of hurt and rejection had awaited her as surely as disillusionment. He said all the right things, he did all the right things, but he didn't *feel* them. There was only a superficial bond between them and it meant a lot less to him than it did to her. And so Kat tormented herself with wounding thoughts that kept her tossing and turning until she put the bedside light on at about two in the morning and dug out a magazine in the hope of quieting her overactive brain.

When a light knock sounded on the door that communicated with Mikhail's suite she froze as if a thunderclap had sounded and then slid out of bed in a rush. She had locked the door earlier, not because she feared he might ignore her desire to spend the night alone, but because she wanted to underline for her own benefit that their intimacy was now at an end. Now, with her heart beating very fast, she unlocked the door and opened it.

'I saw the light. You can't sleep either?' Mikhail had stepped back a couple of feet from the door, his lean, powerfully muscular body clad only in light boxer shorts.

'No, I can't.' Her palm sweated against the door, her heart thumping in her ear drums at an accelerated rate as she noted, really could not have avoided noticing, that he was sporting a hard-on that tented his boxers. Her mouth ran dry and she tore her gaze from him, heated colour burnishing her cheekbones.

'*Pridi ka mne*…come to me,' Mikhail murmured slightly raggedly, black eyes smouldering like fire-brands over her, lingering on the generous curve of her soft mouth.

And it was as if that one look lit a fire inside her treacherous body because her breasts stirred, the nipples tightening, and moist heat made her uncomfortably aware of the ache at the heart of her. She froze in denial of those lowering sensations. 'I *can't*,' she muttered tightly. 'It's over now. We're finished.'

Kat closed the door fast, shot the lock closed again and rested back against the cold unyielding wood to support her weak lower limbs. She had resisted him and she was proud of her self-discipline. Another bout of wildly exciting sex was not going to cure what ailed her heart and it would only make her feel ashamed of herself. It was one thing to love a man, another thing entirely to drop one's self-esteem in pursuit of him. Her teeth clenched, she moved back to the bed, doused the light and clambered below the sheet with hot tears stinging her eyes. She ignored the tears, determined not to let go of her control, determined not to greet him in the morning with swollen reddened eyes that would destroy her pride.

Cursing below his breath, Mikhail went for another cold shower. It was sex, that was all, he told himself. It was nothing to do with the fact that the bed felt empty without her and he missed her chatter. It was logical to end it, logical to guard against getting involved. When it came to a woman, he was far too clever and disciplined to give weight to illogical feelings and irrational and undoubtedly sexual promptings.

After a sleepless night, Kat asked for breakfast in her room, seeing no reason why she should put herself through another nerve-racking meeting with Mikhail. Indeed the less she saw of him before she left, the better, she told herself urgently. She dressed with great care in a smart blue shift dress and cardigan and used more make-up than usual to conceal the shadows below her eyes.

Lara phoned down to tell her that the helicopter that would take her to the airport for her flight was powering up. There was a note of satisfaction in the glamorous blonde's voice that even Kat could not have missed. Lara, without a doubt, was glad to see Kat leaving, Kat acknowledged ruefully, marvelling that she had for a while felt quite warm towards the young woman, for it was obvious to her now that Lara could never have honestly returned that friendliness. Had Lara been jealous of Kat's relationship with her boss? Was Lara in love with Mikhail?

Her cases having already been collected, Kat climbed the glass staircase for the very last time. She wouldn't miss the fancy stairs, she thought glumly. They were a colourfully confusing nightmare to use safely at night. From above her she could hear the calls of the crew as they made preparations for the helicopter to take off. As she emerged into the bright sunlight of a beautiful day Mikhail appeared, shocking her, for she had honestly believed that she would not see him again before she left. Sheathed in a lightweight designer beige suit

Kat was thoroughly bemused by his forceful behaviour. 'But you *can't* simply change your mind like that at the last minute.'

Shrewd black eyes gazed down in challenge at her. 'If I recognise a wrong decision, should I not put it right? Kat—have you any idea how rarely I admit to being in the wrong?'

Kat had an excellent idea, but he had plunged her into turmoil. She had hyped herself up to leave him and it had taken every ounce of her strength to retain her composure in the face of that challenge. His sudden change of heart, however, had steamrollered over her defensive barriers as nothing else could have done. 'I can't just stay with you,' she said again, her voice shaky and lacking its usual energy. 'I've got a life and a family to get back to, Mikhail.'

Her lips parted again. 'You were finished with me. It was over…that's what you wanted—'

'If it was genuinely over, I'd have let you leave. Keeping you was a gut instinct,' Mikhail confessed harshly.

A gut instinct? Where did that leave her? One minute he was getting rid of her, the next he was snatching her back from the brink. 'But what happens now?' she whispered unsteadily, suddenly cold and shivering even in the protective circle of his arms.

His powerful chest expanded as he breathed in deep. 'I take you home with me.'

Her brows climbed. 'You take me *home* with you? Am I a pet all of a sudden?'

'I'm asking you to move in with me. I've never asked a woman to do that before,' Mikhail revealed quietly.

Kat examined the idea, taken aback by it and then alarmed by how much she liked the images springing to mind. But it was a commitment, far more of a commitment than acting as a man's companion and lover on board a yacht for a month. Yes, it was definitely a commitment, she registered dizzily, and suddenly her eyes were overflowing with the tears she had held back with such tenacity.

'What's wrong?' Mikhail demanded, a long forefinger skimming the glistening trail of moisture marking her cheek.

'Nothing! I'm just leaking!' Kat gasped defensively, dashing the tears away with an impatient hand. 'But I *can't* just move in with you. I have commitments too—'

'Your sisters? I will look after them as if they were my own flesh and blood,' Mikhail told her with a sudden expansive smile.

'But I've to sort out the farmhouse, make arrangements—'

'You will leave all such responsibilities to me. You will move in with me, take care of me and my home and that is *all* you need to worry about in the future. Is that understood?'

Kat closed her eyes tight because the tears were still welling up and she was biting back a sob and loving and hating him simultaneously: loving him for recognising that they had found something special, hating him for springing it on her in such a last minute way that she couldn't be fully convinced by it. 'What if you change your mind again?' she asked in a wobbly undertone. 'What if this isn't what you want in a few weeks' time?'

'That's a risk I'm prepared to take. I will always be honest with you and I don't want to lose you.'

Kat swallowed back the thickness in her throat and struggled to breathe at a regular rate again. She supposed she couldn't expect him to say much more, for they would both be on the same learning curve together.

He didn't want to lose her yet he had very nearly let her go. How very close he had come to doing that would probably always haunt her. If she had left on that helicopter, would he have come after her?

'I own a country house that I believe you will like,' Mikhail volunteered. 'You can invite your sisters there, treat it as though it was your own home and next week you can attend Luka's wedding with me as my partner.'

Her restive fingers clenched on the edge of his silk-and-linen-mix jacket, wet clogged eye lashes lifting on drenched green eyes as she stared up into his handsome face, her heart pounding like a piston engine.

His forefinger gently traced the generous curve of her lower lip. 'It will work beautifully...you'll see,' Mikhail forecast with his usual invincible confidence, and then he kissed her with passionate urgency and thought took a hike from her head.

At the end of that day she lay in his bed, her body weak and sated from the hungry demands of his, and she wondered if she had been foolish to agree to stay with him. Was she merely putting off the heartbreak that awaited her? Extending her suffering? She loved him like crazy, but was very much afraid that he was simply in lust with her and not yet ready to give that pleasure up.

CHAPTER TEN

MIKHAIL LISTENED TO the lawyer's advice only because
he paid generously for all advice that offered him
greater financial protection. But he was immoveable
when it came to the issue of presenting Kat with another legal agreement, on this occasion one relating to
her status as his live-in lover. No way was he making
that mistake again! He had still to hear the last from
her lips regarding the previous agreement, and in any
case he was convinced that Kat didn't have a mercenary bone in her body. Time and time again she had
spurned the chance to enrich herself at his expense.
Even though she had been desperate for money to settle her debts when they first met, her bill for that one
night of accommodation in her former home had been
ridiculously modest.

'My girlfriend is not a gold-digger,' Mikhail murmured levelly. 'I am not that much of a fool. I can scent
a gold-digger at a hundred yards.'

'Situations change, *people* change,' the smooth-talk-
ing legal eagle pointed out speciously. 'It is of crucial
importance that you consider the future and protect
yourself.'

Mikhail reckoned that he had been protecting himself all his life in one way or another, so there was

nothing new in that idea. Protecting himself was second nature. He was well aware that he was still feeling punch drunk at the roaring success of letting Kat into his life on a less temporary basis. That had proved to be an excellent move and he was certainly reaping the benefits on the home front. If it was possible to bottle the essence of Kat, he would be constantly drunk. An abstracted smile curled his handsome mouth as he thought of Kat in his hot tub, Kat in his bed, Kat at his dining table, Kat…whenever and wherever he wanted her. After a mere six weeks he was happy to judge his new living arrangements as the essence of perfection. Even better, he had worked out exactly where his father had gone wrong in his relationships with women. The true secret was moderation. He didn't allow himself the pleasure of Kat *every* night; he carefully rationed himself to ensure that she did not become too necessary to his comfort. Sometimes he stayed over quite deliberately in the city and pleaded the pressure of work. Sometimes he didn't phone her, although she was getting remarkably good at phoning him to ask why he hadn't phoned, which rather put paid to the point of that attempt to set out his boundaries. As long as he stayed in control, however, he foresaw no problems.

'Are you considering marriage?' the lawyer asked in a bald enquiry.

Mikhail frowned and compressed his lips at the question.

'Do you think your Russian is considering marrying you?' Emmie was asking her sister at that exact same moment as she zipped up the frock Kat was trying on in the spacious cubicle. 'You know…is the living with him a trial for the ultimate commitment in his eyes?'

'No. Mikhail seems quite happy with where we are now,' Kat pronounced thoughtfully. 'He's very cautious... What do you think of this dress?'

'The silver metallic one has the most impact. I already told you that,' Emmie repeated, smoothing an abstracted hand over the obvious swell of her own pregnant stomach as she too looked in the mirror at their combined reflection. 'I just don't want you to be hurt, Kat...and goodness knows, you're not getting any younger—'

'Like I need that reminder!' Kat quipped with a wry laugh.

'Yes, but it is something you need to seriously consider. If you do want children some day you haven't got much time left to play with.'

'Emmie, only a few months ago there was no man in my life,' Kat reminded her ruefully. 'I certainly can't expect the first one who comes along in years to want to start a family with me. That would be a big ask for a guy who shies away from serious commitment.'

'Have you discussed the subject with him?' Emmie asked.

Kat stiffened, her thoughts hurtling back several weeks to the evening she had received the proof that their contraceptive oversight on the yacht had not resulted in conception. Mikhail had absorbed the news without comment, revealing neither relief nor regret, but Kat had been shocked by the stark wave of disappointment that had consumed her. As she had spent so many years raising her siblings she had always assumed that she would never crave the added responsibility of having a child of her own. Unfortunately for her, somehow even being with Mikhail had given her a powerful yearning for a baby, but she was utterly convinced that nothing would ever come of it.

Mikhail had brought her into his life but he wasn't building his life around her, Kat reflected sadly. He had moved her into Danegold Hall, his impossibly impressive Georgian country house, and urged her to make whatever changes she thought necessary there, only that was not an invitation to take too much to heart when the male giving it really didn't give a damn about his surroundings as long as he was comfortable. He had made the move easy for her by sending professional packers to Birkside. Her belongings and the pieces of furniture that Emmie didn't want were now stored in a barn on the estate for her to go through at her leisure. Emmie was living in the farmhouse now, drawing up plans to open a business while earning a living from the pedestrian job she had found locally. But on her days off, Emmie regularly got on the train and met up with her sister in London for a shopping trip. On this particular occasion the sisters were looking for a dress for Kat to wear to Luka Volkov's wedding.

'Kat?' Emmie persisted.

'Look, Mikhail's only thirty. He's got years and years ahead of him when he can choose to have a family and naturally he's not in any hurry,' Kat said lightly.

'But if he loves you—'

'I don't think he loves me. I don't think I'm in a for-ever-and-ever relationship with him,' Kat confided truthfully, lifting the silver dress off the hook and heading gratefully off to pay for it with one of the string of credit cards that Mikhail had insisted she accepted from him.

Even so, Kat disliked feeling like a kept woman and she would have preferred to look for employment. But

Mikhail wanted her to be available when he was free and able to travel if need be and there was no way she would be able to manage that feat and him and his vast Georgian home and even larger staff there if she had a job to go to every day. She had had to ask herself which was more important: her pride and independence or her love. And love had won because when Kat wasn't being tormented by her various sisters' awkward questions about her relationship with Mikhail, she was deliriously happy, certainly much happier than she had ever thought she could be. He was the sun, the moon and the stars for her, but she knew that she had to accept that outside the bounds of marriage many such relationships eventually came to an end.

Her phone buzzed. It was Mikhail.

'Meet me at the office and we'll go for lunch, *milaya moya,*' he suggested huskily, his dark deep drawl sending a responsive tremor down her spine.

Kat smiled into the phone, delighted that he was so eager to see her. He had stayed in his city apartment the night before and she had missed him. Possibly he had missed her as well, she reasoned with satisfaction, for otherwise he would have been willing to wait until he got back to the hall later that evening to see her.

Emmie gave her a stern look. 'He owns you…that's what I don't like.'

Kat's eyes widened in dismay. 'What on earth do you mean?'

'You're like…*addicted* to him,' Emmie pronounced with unhidden distaste and disapproval. 'Even Topsy noticed that weekend she stayed with you that when Mikhail enters the room, you can't see anyone else but him.'

'I do love him and I don't think it does Topsy any

harm to see that I care deeply for the man I'm living with,' Kat said gently, wishing she knew more about the background to Emmie's pregnancy, for with every week that passed Emmie seemed to be becoming more of a man hater.

A limo whisked Kat to Mikhail's London headquarters. She was accompanied by Ark, Stas' kid brother. Mikhail, from Kat's point of view, appeared to be obsessed by the idea that she might be mugged or attacked and had insisted she accepted Ark's presence when she was out in public. Only when she had recognised that that risk was a source of very genuine concern for him had she finally agreed, but she often felt sorry for Ark, reduced to hanging around bored while she shopped or sat gossiping over lengthy coffee sessions with her sisters.

Mikhail was in a meeting when Kat arrived and she stowed her shopping by the wall and sat down in Lara's office to wait while Ark hovered in the corridor.

Lara glided across the room to greet her with a rather tight smile of welcome and bent down to study more closely the emerald pendant that Kat wore. 'May I see it?' the other woman prompted politely.

Kat flushed with self-consciousness and nodded uneasy agreement as Lara minutely examined the emerald. She guessed that the other woman probably thought the pendant was far too ostentatious to wear out on a shopping trip and Kat could actually have agreed with her on that score. But the sticking point was how Mikhail felt about it. Mikhail *loved* to see Kat with the emerald round her neck and Kat wore it frequently to please him.

'The jewel is magnificent,' the gorgeous blonde commented thinly, overpowering envy souring her flawless features as she stepped back from her examination.

'The word is that the boss has never spent so much on a gift for a woman—you must feel very pleased with yourself.'

Kat's fine brows pleated in surprise and she flung the blonde a startled glance, not quite sure if Lara could have meant that comment the way it had sounded. 'No, that's not how I feel. I'm just…happy,' she breathed in a discomfited tone, offended at the suspicion that Lara could suspect that she might only be with Mikhail for his wealth.

'Of course you're happy. Why would you not be? *Suka!*' Lara snapped sharply, at which point, unnoticed by either woman, Ark put his head round the door to peer into the room. 'But I could tell you something that would wipe that smug smile right off your face!'

No longer suffering the misapprehension that her understanding was at fault, Kat gave the younger woman a cool appraisal. 'I don't think that's a good idea, Lara.'

'Well, I will tell you whether you want to know or not!' Lara practically spat the words at her. 'Remember that night before you were supposed to leave the yacht? Mikhail spent that night with me…that's how little you matter to him!'

The blood drained from Kat's face. Suddenly her skin felt clammy and the palms she had pressed to the handbag on her lap felt damp. For a moment she could not even make sense of what the other woman was saying and only knew that she was being verbally attacked. Just as quickly she was recalling that night that she had spent alone and sleepless and she was also recalling Mikhail's knock on her door. Her tummy lurched in stricken protest.

'Didn't you realise that he slept with me as well?' Lara queried, lifting a scornful brow at such apparent stupidity. 'He always has. I don't make demands on him. I'm *always* available…'

Out of nowhere the strength returned to Kat's rigid body and she leapt upright. She dragged her shattered gaze from the furious blonde and walked out of the door, ignoring the lift and Ark's query to head for the stairs instead. She needed some time on her own to think about the bombshell Lara had delivered and what she would have to do about it. She fled down the fire stairs, flight after flight, heard Ark shout after her and kept on going, not wanting anyone to see or speak to her in the state she was in. Her hurrying feet took her straight out of the building and into the welcome and anonymous crush of the lunchtime crowds on the pavement.

Her heart thudding so fast she was convinced she could hear it actually thumping in her ears, Kat walked at a smart pace with no destination in view. Only the fact that her high-heeled shoes had not been made for that amount of walking finally pierced her miasma of misery. Wincing at the sharp pinches of pain assailing her feet, Kat then headed into a café to get a seat. There she sat hunched over a cup of tea, as dazed as if her head had been struck in an accident. At that point she heard her phone ringing and she pulled it out, saw she had received about six missed calls from Mikhail and switched it off because she didn't want to speak to him, didn't *have* to speak to him, she consoled herself. She sat there a long time struggling to get the turmoil of her thoughts into some kind of rational order.

Lara was an absolutely gorgeous-looking young woman, very glossy and sophisticated and exactly the sort of woman whom Kat had often secretly believed Mikhail *should* have chosen as a girlfriend in place of herself. Why would Lara tell such a lie? In fact, like it or not, the evidence suggested that Lara was telling the truth. Why? For the simple reason that Lara must have been with Mikhail that night to be so certain that he had not been with Kat. Every other night Kat and Mikhail had shared his suite but that one night, which Lara had chosen to mention, Kat had slept alone. Mikhail had had motive and opportunity. Had he taken advantage of it? Had he been carrying on a casual long-term affair with his PA even before he met Kat? She shuddered at the suspicion, sick with pain, jealousy and a growing sense of despair. How could she have been so wrong about the man she loved?

Back at his office in the wake of the drama Kat's sudden exit had caused, Mikhail was also thinking about bad choices and his expression was as hard as granite. In a crisis he was discovering that his strict policy of moderation in his relationship with Kat had a serious basic design flaw. Moderation had kicked him in the teeth when he least expected it: she wouldn't even take a phone call from him. And now she was gone, *lost*, upset, maybe even upset enough to walk out in front of a bus or something stupid like that, he thought with a fear that had a ferociously aggressive edge unfamiliar to his usual self-discipline.

Over her cooling tea, Kat realised that whatever she chose to do she had no choice other than to return first to Danegold Hall. Her passport, important documents, everything she couldn't simply get by without was there. Feeling cold inside and out and fighting distress, Kat headed for the railway station. She might prefer to avoid Mikhail but she had to be practical as well and walking out on her life with him without forethought and planning wasn't possible. In any case, if he had any sense at all, he would be equally keen to avoid the fallout from Lara's revelation—that was assuming Lara admitted what she had done. Ark had heard some of that conversation though, Kat reckoned in mortification, and no doubt Ark would tell his brother, Stas, who would tell Mikhail what they thought he needed to know.

On the train journey, Kat saw nothing of the passing scenery for a constant parade of mental images was playing through her head. Her brain was scouring every glimpse she had ever had of Lara and Mikhail together in the same room in search of some proof of Lara's claim. What amazed Kat then was the reality that she had often been baffled by the way Mikhail treated Lara like a piece of office equipment, seemingly impervious to his PA's stunning beauty and appeal. Kat had not once witnessed the smallest sign of awareness or intimacy between them. Indeed on the face of it Mikhail and Lara hadn't even seemed that friendly. Their working relationship was distant and formal, untouched by banter or even a hint of flirtation.

Could Mikhail be that smooth and effective at deception? That he could treat a lover as though she were nothing more than a barely regarded employee? Kat frowned, for in her experience Mikhail was more naturally blunt and open in nature, so that she could quite easily tell when something annoyed or irritated or worried him. But then, to be fair, he himself had remarked that she was unusually accurate in her ability to read his thoughts. She had almost told him that that was because she loved him and when it came to him love seemed to have given her keener powers of observation. That was how she knew that when he lifted a brow in a certain way he was irritated, that when he moved his hands or stilled them altogether he was usually angry, and that when his mouth compressed it was usually a sign of concern.

On the other hand, men didn't automatically regard the kind of casual sex that Lara had suggested had taken place over a sustained period as a tie worthy of acknowledgement. In that way, sex could be treated as being of no more account than a meal. Was that how Mikhail might have rationalised such behaviour? Had he been amusing himself with Lara on the sidelines while Kat agonised about whether or not she would sleep with him? It was a humiliating, wounding suspicion. Until that moment it had not occurred to her how much she had valued Mikhail's apparent willingness to wait for her to share his bed or her natural assumption that no other woman was satisfying his needs while Kat remained unavailable.

When she got off the train Kat assumed she would have to phone for a taxi and wait because she had not informed anyone what time she was arriving, but she was greeted on the platform by one of Mikhail's drivers and she slid into the waiting Bentley with a sinking heart. Had *he* already guessed that she would soon be back at Danegold Hall? Was she now honour-bound to stage some ghastly sordid confrontation over the head of Lara? Of course, if he was there and she was moving out she would have to give him some sort of explanation. She comforted herself with the awareness that Mikhail would only be home during the day mid-week on the very rarest of occasions and wondered if a brief note would do, in which she would say something meaningless but not unpleasant such as that things were not working out for her.

She ought to hate him, she thought painfully, wondering what the matter with her was. Perhaps she was still too much in shock to be thinking clearly, she reckoned wretchedly, in shock that Mikhail was not the man she had honestly believed he was and that he was a much more lightweight, untrustworthy and dishonest individual than she could ever have guessed from the way he had treated her. Ironically he had treated her very well. So, did he think that sexual infidelity was unimportant? She remembered the clusters of eager young woman who had surrounded him every time he went out in public and accepted that temptation must often have come his way. Yet to have slept with a woman who worked for him, whom Kat knew and accepted, was beyond forgiveness.

Kat mounted the steps to the front door, which was already standing open with Reeves, Mikhail's imperturbable butler, stationed there. With a pained smile in response to his greeting, Kat limped in, acknowledging that if anything her feet were hurting her even more than they had earlier that afternoon. Maybe taking them off on the train had been unwise. Halfway across the hall she came to a halt, slid the beautiful but too-tight shoes off and walked barefoot up the stairs. She headed straight to the bedroom she shared with Mikhail and the dressing room where a miniature trunk held everything from her passport to her birth certificate. She lifted out the papers, slapped them down on the bed and went off to locate a suitcase. She couldn't believe she was leaving the man she loved, couldn't bear even the thought of it, yet knew she had no choice. Lara could only have known that Mikhail had not slept with Kat that night if Lara had spent that same night with him: her brain could not get past that fact.

From drawers she dug out a few basic changes of clothing. She wasn't fool enough to try and pack everything. She would just take what was necessary for a couple of weeks and ask for the rest to be sent on to her. She supposed she would move back to the farmhouse with Emmie and knew her sibling would be glad to have company. What price her fine sensitivity about accepting the house from Mikhail now?

'You're not even giving me a chance to defend myself?'

Kat froze and spun to see Mikhail poised in the doorway, his lean darkly handsome face grim and taut as he asked that question. He had discarded his tie and his jacket and stood there in shirt sleeves, his black diamond eyes hard. He was toughing Lara's confession out, Kat assumed, determined to admit no fault. She turned her head away from him because she felt as if her heart were breaking inside her.

'Kat?' Mikhail prompted.

'Yes, I heard what you said but I don't really know how to respond. Sometimes it's best to say nothing. I don't want to argue with you—what's the point?'

'The point is *us,*' Mikhail growled. 'Isn't what we have worth fighting for?'

Kat dropped the clothing in her hands into the open case and shot him a furious glance of reproach. 'OK. Did you sleep with her?'

'No,' Mikhail framed succinctly, hard dark eyes challenging her.

Kat turned back to her packing. 'Well, of course you're going to say *that*,' she told him, totally unimpressed.

'What the hell was the point of asking me, then?' Mikhail roared back at her. 'You know you've put me through one hell of an afternoon?'

Refusing to be intimidated by that lion's roar, Kat

kept on packing. 'I can't say that I enjoyed my afternoon either—'

'First of all I had to put up with a melodramatic tantrum from an employee, then you went *missing*!' He stressed the word.

Infuriated, Kat whipped back to him. 'I did not go missing!'

'How do you think I felt when you took off after that nonsense Lara spouted to you? I was worried sick about you!' Mikhail bit out furiously. 'I knew you were upset and—'

Kat lifted a russet brow and turned to him again, hating him at that minute, convinced she knew exactly why he was behaving the way he was. 'How could you *know* I was upset? You got a spy hotline to my brain or something? I wasn't upset. Naturally I was surprised, rather disgusted, in fact,' she confided with growing vigour. 'And I needed some time to myself—'

'You needed time to yourself to think about that poison like you needed a hole in the head!' Mikhail shot back at her with lethal derision.

'Don't you *dare* shout at me!' Kat shrieked back at him.

Sudden smouldering silence fell. Mikhail breathed in deep and slow, his broad chest expanding. 'I didn't intend to shout.'

'When you've been accused of infidelity, bellowing like a bull in a china shop is not a good idea,' Kat informed him curtly.

'*Wrongly* accused,' Mikhail fired back at her, his stunning dark eyes scorching hot with annoyance. 'That is the crucial fact.'

'Mikhail…' Kat swallowed hard and collected her churning thoughts, unhappiness bowing her shoulders like a giant weight as she accepted that the scene could not be avoided. 'Lara knew that we didn't spend that last night together before I was supposed to leave *The Hawk*. She must've been with you that night to know that.'

'Wrong!' Mikhail framed grittily. 'She was standing on the deck outside the office below us eavesdropping on our last exchange over dinner that night when you told me you wanted to sleep alone. So, if that's your only piece of evidence against me, you're on a losing streak!'

Kat's lashes fluttered in confusion. 'Are you sure that's how she knew we were sleeping apart?'

'How the hell else could she have known?' Mikhail swore suddenly in Russian and shifted his hands as he moved towards her. 'Kat, you saw me at three in the morning that same night and I was still in my own room,' he reminded her.

'Yes, but—'

Mikhail withdrew a mobile phone from his pocket and pressed several buttons. 'Watch this…' he urged. 'Stas was clever enough to record Lara screaming at me…'

Kat focused on the screen and saw a flurry of blurred movement and heard a noise. The blur became Lara, blonde hair whipping round her enraged face and she was shouting. 'Why didn't you want me? You could have had me! What's wrong with you that you didn't want me? She's old, she's past it! It's an insult. I'm young and beautiful—how could she be the one you move into your home?'

Kat was transfixed. There were another few sentences of distraught ranting from Lara before she suddenly appreciated that a camera was recording her tantrum and she launched herself at Stas in a vitriolic fury, whereupon the recording came to a sudden telling halt.

Mikhail switched it off. 'Do you want to see it again?' he enquired smoothly.

'No...' Kat's admission was small, her face heavily flushed with chagrin. She had listened to a vain and immature hysteric's fantasy and swallowed her ridiculous lies as solid fact. Her legs were wobbly and she sank down on the edge of the bed with *'old, past it!'* still ringing unpleasantly in her ears.

'Ark heard everything she said to you, his attention drawn by the fact that she called you a rude word in Russian,' Mikhail explained. 'He informed me and I confronted her and, as you saw, she went crazy. There was a lot more that Stas didn't manage to record. She was jealous of you and furious that I didn't find her attractive but the situation that developed today was still my fault.'

'How was it your fault?' Kat asked limply, shot from the conviction that he was an unfaithful rat to the conviction that she had misjudged him at such speed that her head was still spinning. She felt dizzy and bewildered and stupid, much as though a huge rock had landed on her from a height.

'Lara came on to me when I first hired her. That's happened to me many times and I didn't consider it sufficient grounds to sack her.'

Kat's eyes were wide with consternation at the news. 'You...*didn't*?'

'I made it clear I wasn't interested and as a rule that is sufficient to bring an end to such behaviour, but Lara is extremely vain about her own attractions and her resentment grew when you came into my life. I suspect she tried to cause trouble between us before in small ways. Luckily she wasn't close enough to me to have the power to do more. I think you can probably blame her for the horrible make-up you wore the first night when you dined with me.'

'And for not telling me when to meet you,' Kat guessed.

'And persuading you to wear red that evening at the club—I hate the colour red, always have,' he confided.

'Such trivial things,' Kat commented seriously. 'I'm grateful she didn't have the ability to cause more trouble.'

'Lara isn't clever enough to appreciate that a man wants a woman for more than her looks…'

Kat wasn't quite sure how to take that statement.

Mikhail laughed out loud, his amusement smashing the strained silence. He snatched up her case and tossed it on the floor and sank down beside her on the bed. 'I find you much more beautiful than Lara.'

'You couldn't possibly. I'm old and past it,' Kat muttered shakily, the tears gathering.

'You knocked me sideways the very first time I saw you. And you had class and strength and you refused to want me back, which shocked me.'

'It did you good to have a woman say no to you for a change,' Kat countered a shade tartly, unwilling to let all her tension go for fear that something bad was still about to happen that would part them.

Mikhail curved a powerful arm round her taut body to draw her close. 'It did, but the fear of losing you that I suffered today almost brought me to my knees,' he admitted gruffly. 'I was so determined to stay in control of our relationship and not give way to my strong feelings for you, and then suddenly I was facing the

prospect of losing you and all that seemed so trivial in
comparison—'

'Strong feelings?' Kat prompted, one small hand
awkwardly engaged in stroking the arm wound round
her.

His fingers curved to her chin to turn her face gently
round to his. His eyes were warmer than she had ever
seen them. 'I love you very much, Kat...so much I can't
contemplate a life without you. But until today I saw
that as a weakness and a fault. I watched my father
slowly drink himself to death after he lost my mother.
He was cruel to her and he was never faithful, but when
she died he went to pieces. He was much more dependent on her than any of us ever realised,' he related
ruefully. 'I was terrified of ever needing a woman that
much. I thought he was an obsessional personality. I
thought I had to protect myself from that because, in
common with my father, I do tend to be rather intense
in personality, and then I met you and right from the
start you had a very potent effect on me...'

The chill still inside Kat was soothed by the tenderness in his gaze and his honesty and she pushed her
face into a broad muscular shoulder, revelling in the
warm familiar scent of him and the new sense of soul-
deep security flooding her. 'I love you too,' she whispered fervently.

'You should have guessed how I felt about you that
morning I prevented you from boarding the helicopter,' Mikhail muttered with a frown. 'I tried to make
myself let you go and I found that I literally *couldn't*
face sending you away. The night before was the longest and worst night of my life. I wanted you. I needed
you: choice didn't come into it. You've owned my heart
ever since.'

'That may be so, but you've been pretty good at hiding it,' Kat voiced, although when she thought back to recent weeks it occurred to her that he had probably shown it every time he looked at her, every time he curled her into his arms and held her tight through the night, only unfortunately she had been too insecure to recognise and interpret what she was seeing.

'I won't be hiding it any more. If you had known I loved you today you might have been more inclined to talk to me and trust my word rather than Lara's. Would you have believed me without having seen that recording?'

'Yes...deep down inside me it was a real struggle to believe that you would behave that way,' Kat acknowledged with quiet certainty.

Mikhail lifted her hand and carefully threaded a ring onto her wedding finger. 'I've had this in my possession since the first day you moved in.'

Kat studied the fabulous diamond solitaire with wide eyes of sheer wonderment. 'But you resisted giving it to me?'

'Yes. I'm a stubborn man, *lubov moya,*' Mikhail groaned. 'That means, "my love" and you are the only woman I've ever loved. You've had the chance to see the worst of me. Will you still marry me? And soon?'

'Oh, absolutely,' Kat carolled, flattening him to the mattress in a sudden marked demonstration of enthusiasm. 'As soon as it can be arranged...when I let you out of bed, which is not going to be any time soon,' she warned him with sparkling eyes from which the last shadow of insecurity had fled.

A wolfish grin of satisfaction slashed his handsome mouth. 'I should have given you the ring the day I bought it.'

'Yes, you're a slow learner as well as stubborn,' his future wife conceded. 'But you did buy the ring weeks ago, which gains you points...not that you need them.'

'I only need you,' Mikhail told her, running his fingers lazily through the spirals of her russet hair. 'And I won't feel secure until I see my wedding ring on your hand.'

His phone buzzed.

'Switch it off,' she said.

A hint of consternation entered his beautiful eyes. 'Have I created a monster?' he murmured with flaring amusement.

Kat ran a rousing hand quite deliberately along a muscular male thigh and he tensed with sensual anticipation. 'I'll switch it off,' he promised instantly. 'Sometimes I'm a very fast learner, *dusha moya.*'

And so was Kat, bending over him to kiss him with a confidence she had never had before while trying to keep a lid on the wild, surging happiness assailing her in glorious waves. He was hers, finally, absolutely hers, her dream come true, and some day he would accept that being obsessionally in love with a woman who loved him every bit as intensely could be wonderful, rather than threatening.

EPILOGUE

THREE YEARS LATER, Kat stood at the foot of the pair of cots in the nursery at Danegold Hall, proudly surveying her twins, Petyr and Olga. They were both tiny and dark-haired with their newborn eyes of blue slowly turning green. Her son, Petyr, was lively, restless and slept very little while Olga was altogether a much more laid-back baby.

As far as their mother was concerned the twins were her personal miracle and, even two months after their birth, she could still hardly believe they were her children. After all, after she and Mikhail had married she hadn't fallen pregnant as she had hoped. It hadn't happened and eventually after fertility tests that proved nothing conclusive she had gone for IVF treatment in a top Russian clinic. She had found the process stressful and hard on the nerves, and the first time they had been very disappointed when conception failed to take place, but the second time she had undergone the process she had conceived. It would have been hard for her to describe the boundless joy she had experienced when she saw the two tiny shapes in her womb on a scan some weeks later. She hadn't even realised that tears were running down her cheeks until Mikhail turned her round to dry her face for her.

The twins' birth had been straightforward, a relief for Mikhail, who had barely let her out of his sight for longer than twelve hours during her entire pregnancy. What had happened to his own mother when she tried to deliver his sibling had still haunted him and had given him the impression that giving birth was the most dangerous thing even a healthy woman could choose to do. Only then had she truly understood why Mikhail had been so careful to tell her that he could be content with her even if they never had children. At the time she had been hurt, worried that he didn't really want a child, but she had been utterly wrong in that fear. Mikhail had been terrified that something might go wrong and had had so many top doctors standing around when she delivered the twins that she ought to have been delivering sextuplets at the very least. Her eyes still stung when she recalled Mikhail pulling her into his arms afterwards, barely acknowledging the existence of his newborn twins to whisper shakily, 'Thank God you are safe. That is all that has concerned me this day, *lyubov' moya*.'

Even after three years, her husband loved her every bit as much as she loved him. Indeed the depth of the bond between them had gone from strength to strength since they married. Once that was achieved, Mikhail's sense of security had enabled him to drop what remained of his reserve. And, as he had promised, he had embraced her sisters as though they were his own so that she was as close to her siblings as she had ever been.

'Gloating again…?' a familiar accented drawl teased.

'Sorry, can't help it, still can't believe they're ours,' Kat confided, her bright head turning to focus on the darkly handsome male poised in the doorway, a flock of butterflies taking flight inside her tummy. Mikhail's effect on her hormones never faded, she thought, her face warming. And how could it have done? He was drop-dead gorgeous.

A faint smile curving his sensual lips, her husband joined her to stare down at their son and daughter. 'They do look cute when they're not squalling,' he conceded with amusement. 'This morning they looked like little red-faced dictators when they woke up.'

'They were hungry,' their mother proclaimed defensively.

Mikhail turned her slowly round. 'So am I, *laskovaya moya*. I am very hungry to have my beautiful wife all to myself for a few days.'

Her sparkling green eyes rounded as she leant up against his lean, powerful body, one hand resting on a broad shoulder. 'Have you actually taken some time off?'

'Even better. I've arranged a holiday for us on a deserted island.'

'Doesn't sound the kind of place you can take babies.'

'They're not coming.' Lean, strong face resolute, Mikhail gazed down at his wife as she parted her generous mouth to object. 'Your sisters are going to look after them for us. Our third wedding anniversary is an important occasion and I want to do something special.'

'But, we *can't* leave them behind—'

A black brow quirked. 'Even with two nannies and your sisters and the entire household staff to look after them?'

Kat's even white teeth worried at her full lower lip in indecision.

'I need you too,' Mikhail husked, lowering his dark head to caress her mouth slowly with his in exactly the way she could never resist, leaving her breathless and quivering. 'And I think you need me in the same way.'

'Well…' Kat hesitated. 'A deserted island?'

'White beach, blue sea, no clothes,' Mikhail outlined.

'So that's the fantasy?' Kat laughed, loving his honesty as much as she loved him and the surprise break he had organised.

'The fantasy I have every intention of turning into fact,' her husband countered with a lethally sexy look in his black diamond eyes. 'More pleasure than you can believe…'

'Oh, I can believe,' she confirmed dizzily, breathless at the smouldering look of desire in his stunning gaze. 'You always deliver.'

'I'm crazy about you,' Mikhail muttered thickly, claiming her mouth in a passionate kiss that sent her every sense singing.

Kat was too happy and too bound up in that kiss to reply. A second honeymoon on a deserted island, Mikhail all to herself. No, she had not a single complaint about that plan of action.

* * * * *

THE BILLIONAIRE'S
BRIDAL BARGAIN

CHAPTER ONE

CESARE SABATINO FLIPPED open the file sent by special delivery and groaned out loud, his darkly handsome features betraying his disbelief.

There were two photos included in the file, one of a nubile blonde teenager called Cristina and the other of her older sister Elisabetta. Was this familial insanity to visit yet another generation? Cesare raked long brown fingers through his luxuriant black hair, frustration pumping through every long lean line of his powerful body. He really didn't have time for such nonsense in the middle of his working day. What was his father, Goffredo, playing at?

'What's up?' Jonathan, his friend and a director of the Sabatino pharmaceutical empire, asked.

In answer, Cesare tossed the file to the other man. 'Look at it and weep at the madness that can afflict even one's seemingly sane relatives,' he urged.

Frowning, Jonathan glanced through the sparse file and studied the photos. 'The blonde's not bad but a bit on the young side. The other one with the woolly hat on looks like a scarecrow. What on earth is the connection between you and some Yorkshire farming family?'

'It's a long story,' Cesare warned him.

Jonathan hitched his well-cut trousers and took a seat. 'Interesting?'

Cesare grimaced. 'Only moderately. In the nineteen thirties my family owned a small island called Lionos in the Aegean Sea. Most of my ancestors on my father's side are buried there. My grandmother, Athene, was born and raised there. But when her father went bust, Lionos was sold to an Italian called Geraldo Luccini.'

Jonathan shrugged. 'Fortunes rise and fall.'

'Matters, however, took a turn for the worse when Athene's brother decided to get the island back into family hands by marrying Luccini's daughter and then chose to jilt her at the altar.'

The other man raised his brows. 'Nice...'

'Her father was so enraged by the slight to his daughter and his family that Lionos was eternally tied up in Geraldo's exceedingly complex will.'

'In what way?'

'The island cannot be sold and the two young women in that file are the current owners of Lionos by inheritance through their mother. The island can only be regained by my family through marriage between a Zirondi and a Luccini descendant and the birth of a child.'

'You're not serious?' Jonathan was amazed.

'A generation back, my father was serious enough to propose marriage to the mother of those two girls, Francesca, although I would point out that he genuinely fell in love with her. Luckily for us all, however, when he proposed she turned him down and married her farmer instead.'

'Why luckily?' Jonathan queried.

'Francesca didn't settle for long with the farmer or with any of the men that followed him. Goffredo had a narrow escape,' Cesare opined, lean, strong face grim, well aware that his laid-back and rather naive father could never have coped with so fickle a wife.

'So, why has your father sent you that file?'

'He's trying to get me interested in the ongoing, "Lionos reclamation project",' Cesare said very drily, the slant of his wide, sensual mouth expressing sardonic amusement as he sketched mocking quotations marks in the air.

'He actually thinks he has a chance of persuading *you* to consider marriage with one of those two women?' Jonathan slowly shook his head for neither female appeared to be a show-stopper and Cesare enjoyed the reputation of being a connoisseur of the female sex. 'Is he crazy?'

'Always an optimist.' Cesare sighed. 'In the same way he never listens when I tell him I haven't the smallest desire to ever get married.'

'As a happily married man and father, I have to tell you that you're missing out.'

Cesare resisted a rude urge to roll his eyes in mockery. He knew that, in spite of the odds, good marriages *did* exist. His father had one, after all, and evidently Jonathan did too. But Cesare had no faith in true love and happy-ever-after stories, particularly not when his own first love had ditched him to waltz down the aisle with an extremely wealthy man, who referred to himself as being seventy-five years young. Serafina had dutifully proclaimed her love of older men all the way to the graveyard gates and was now a very rich widow, who had been chasing Cesare in the hope of a rematch ever since.

Cesare's recollections were tinged with supreme scorn. He would never make a mistake like Serafina again. It had been a boy's mistake, he reminded himself wryly. He was now far less ignorant about the nature of the female sex. He had never yet lavished his wealth on a woman who wasn't more excited by his money than by anything else he offered. A satisfied smile softened the hard line of his wide, expressive mouth when he thought of his current lover, a gorgeous French fashion model who went to great lengths to please him in bed and out of it. And all without the fatal suffocating commitment of rings or nagging or noisy kids attached. What was not to like? It was true that he was an extremely generous lover but what was money for but enjoyment when you had as much as Cesare now had?

Cesare was less amused and indeed he tensed when he strolled into his city penthouse that evening to receive the news from his manservant, Primo, that his father had arrived for an unexpected visit.

Goffredo was out on the roof terrace admiring the panoramic view of London when Cesare joined him.

'To what do I owe the honour?' he mocked.

His father, always an extrovert in the affection stakes, clasped his son in a hug as if he hadn't seen the younger man in months rather than mere weeks. 'I need to talk to you about your grandmother...'

Cesare's smile immediately faded. 'What's wrong?'

Goffredo grimaced. 'Athene needs a coronary bypass. Hopefully it will relieve her angina.'

Cesare had stilled, a frown line etched between his level ebony brows. 'She's seventy-five.'

'The prognosis for her recovery is excellent,' his father told him reassuringly. 'Unfortunately the real problem is my mother's outlook on life. She thinks she's too old for surgery. She thinks she's had her three score years and ten and should be grateful for it.'

'That's ridiculous. If necessary, I'll go and talk some sense into her,' Cesare said impatiently.

'She needs something to look forward to…some motivation to make her believe that the pain and stress of surgery will be worthwhile.'

Cesare released his breath in a slow hiss. 'I hope you're not talking about Lionos. That's nothing but a pipe dream.'

Goffredo studied his only son with compressed lips. 'Since when have you been defeatist about any challenge?'

'I'm too clever to tilt at windmills,' Cesare said drily.

'But surely you have some imagination? Some… what is it you chaps call it now? The ability to think outside the box?' the older man persisted. 'Times have changed, Cesare. The world has moved on and when it comes to the island you have a power that I was never blessed with.'

Cesare heaved a sigh and wished he had worked late at the office where pure calm and self-discipline ruled, the very building blocks of his lifestyle. 'And what power would that be?' he asked reluctantly.

'You are incredibly wealthy and the current owners of the island are dirt-poor.'

'But the will is watertight.'

'Money could be a great persuader,' his father reasoned. 'You don't want a wife and probably neither of Francesca's daughters wants a real husband at such a young age. Why can't you come to some sort of business arrangement with one of them?'

Cesare shook his arrogant dark head. 'You're asking me to try and get round the will?'

'The will has already been minutely appraised by a top inheritance lawyer in Rome. If you can marry one of those girls, you will have the right to visit the island and, what is more important, you will have the right to take your grandmother there,' Goffredo outlined, clearly expecting his son to be impressed by that revelation.

Instead, Cesare suppressed a groan of impatience. 'And what's that worth at the end of the day? It's *not* ownership, it's *not* getting the island back into the family.'

'Even a visit after all the years that have passed would be a source of great joy to your grandmother,' Goffredo pointed out in a tone of reproach.

'I always understood that visiting the island was against the terms of the will.'

'Not if a marriage has first taken place. That is a distinction that it took a lawyer to point out. Certainly, if any of us were to visit without that security, Francesca's daughters would forfeit their inheritance and the island would go to the government by default.'

'Which would please no one but the government,' Cesare conceded wryly. 'Do you really think that a measly visit to the island would mean that much to Nonna?' he pressed.

'The right to pay her respects again at her parents'

graves? To see the house where she was born and where she married and first lived with my father? She has many happy memories of Lionos.'

'But would one short visit satisfy her? It's my belief that she has always dreamt of living out her life there and that's out of the question because a child has to be born to fulfil the full terms of the will and grant us the right to put down roots on the island again.'

'There is a very good chance that clause could be set aside in court as unreasonable. Human rights law has already altered many matters once set in stone,' Goffredo reasoned with enthusiasm.

'It's doubtful,' Cesare argued. 'It would take many years and a great deal of money to take it to court and the government would naturally fight any change we sought. The court option won't work in my lifetime. And what woman is going to marry and have a child with me, to allow me to inherit an uninhabited, un-developed island? Even if I did offer to buy the island from her once we were married.'

It was his father's turn to groan. 'You must know how much of a catch you are, Cesare. *Madre di Dio*, you've been beating the women off with a stick since you were a teenager!'

Cesare dealt him an amused look. 'And you don't think it would be a little immoral to conceive a child for such a purpose?'

'As I've already stated,' Goffredo proclaimed with dignity, 'I am not suggesting you go *that* far.'

'But I couldn't reclaim the island for the family *without* going that far,' Cesare fielded very drily. 'And if I can't buy it or gain anything beyond guaranteeing Nonna the right to visit the wretched place one more time, what is the point of approaching some stranger and trying to bribe her?'

'Is that your last word on the subject?' his father asked stiffly when the silence dragged.

'I'm a practical man,' Cesare murmured wryly. 'If we could regain the island I could see some point of pursuing this.'

The older man halted on his passage towards the door and turned back to face his son with compressed lips. 'You could at least approach Francesca's daughters and see if something could be worked out. You could at least *try*...'

When his father departed in high dudgeon, Cesare swore long and low in frustration. Goffredo was so temperamental and so easily carried away. He was good at getting bright ideas but not so smooth with the follow-up or the fallout. His son, on the other hand, never let emotion or sentiment cloud his judgement and rarely got excited about anything.

Even so, Cesare did break into a sweat when he thought about his grandmother's need for surgery and her lack of interest in having it. In his opinion, Athene was probably bored and convinced that life had no further interesting challenges to offer. She was also probably a little frightened of the surgical procedure as well. His grandmother was such a strong and courageous woman that people frequently failed to recognise that she had her fears and weaknesses just like everyone else.

Cesare's own mother had died on the day he was born and Goffredo's Greek mother, Athene, had come to her widowed son's rescue. While Goffredo had grieved and struggled to build up his first business and establish some security, Athene had taken charge of raising Cesare. Even before he'd started school he had been playing chess, reading and doing advanced maths for enjoyment. His grandmother had been quick to recognise her grandson's prodigious intellectual gifts. Unlike his father, she had not been intimidated by his genius IQ and against a background of loving support Athene had given Cesare every opportunity to flourish and develop at his own pace. He owed his *nonna* a great deal and she was still the only woman in the world whom Cesare had ever truly cared about. But then he had never been an emotional man, had never been able to understand or feel truly comfortable around more demonstrative personalities. He was astute, level-headed and controlled in every field of his life yet he had a soft spot in his heart for his grandmother that he would not have admitted to a living soul.

A business arrangement, Cesare ruminated broodingly, flicking open the file again. There was no prospect of him approaching the teenager but the plain young woman in the woolly hat and old coat? Could he even contemplate such a gross and unsavoury lowering of his high standards? He was conservative in his tastes and not an easy man to please but if the prize was great enough, he was clever enough to compromise and adapt, wasn't he? Aware that very few people were cleverer than he was, Cesare contemplated the startling idea of getting married and grimaced with distaste at the threat of being forced to live in such close contact with another human being.

'You should've sent Hero off to the knackers when I told you to!' Brian Whitaker bit out in disgust. 'Instead you've kept him eating his head off in that stable. How can we afford that with the cost of feed what it is?'

'Chrissie's very fond of Hero. She's coming home from uni next week and I wanted her to have the chance to say goodbye.' Lizzie kept her voice low rather than risk stoking her father's already irascible temper. The older man was standing by the kitchen table, his trembling hands—the most visible symptom of the Parkinson's disease that had ravaged his once strong body—braced on the chair back as he glowered at his daughter, his gaunt, weathered face grim with censure.

'And if you do that, she'll weep and she'll wail and she'll try to talk you out of it again. What's the point of that? You tried to sell him and there were no takers,' he reminded her with biting impatience. 'You're a bloody *useless* farmer, Lizzie!'

'That horse charity across the valley may have a space coming up this week,' Lizzie told him, barely even flinching from her father's scorn because his dissatisfaction was so familiar to her. 'I was hoping for the best.'

'Since when has hoping for the best paid the bills?' Brian demanded with withering contempt. 'Chrissie should be home here helping you, not wasting her time studying!'

Lizzie compressed her lips, wincing at the idea that her kid sister should also sacrifice her education to their daily struggle for survival against an ever-increasing tide of debt. The farm was failing but it had been failing for a long time. Unfortunately her father had never approved of Chrissie's desire to go to university. His world stopped at the borders of the farm and he had very little interest in anything beyond it. Lizzie understood his reasoning because her world had shrunk to the same boundaries once she had left school at sixteen.

At the same time, though, she adored the kid sister she had struggled to protect throughout their dysfunctional childhood and was willing to take a lot of grief from her father if it meant that the younger woman could enjoy the youthful freedom and opportunities that she herself had been denied. In fact Lizzie had been as proud as any mother when Chrissie had won a place to study Literature at Oxford. Although she missed Chrissie, she would not have wished her own life of back-breaking toil and isolation on anyone she loved.

As Lizzie dug her feet back into her muddy boots a small low-slung shaggy dog, whose oddly proportioned body reflected his very mixed ancestry, greeted her at the back door with his feeding bowl in his mouth.

'Oh, I'm so sorry, Archie...I forgot about you,' Lizzie groaned, climbing out of the boots again to trudge back across the kitchen floor and fill the dog bowl. While she mentally listed all the many, many tasks she had yet to accomplish she heard the reassuring roar of a football game playing on the television in the room next door and some of the tension eased from her slight shoulders. Watching some sport and forgetting his aches and pains for a little while would put her father in a better mood.

Her father was a difficult man, but then his life had always been challenging. In his case hard work and commitment to the farm had failed to pay off.

He had taken on the farm tenancy at a young age and had always had to work alone. Her late mother, Francesca, had only lasted a few years as a farmer's wife before running off with a man she deemed to have more favourable prospects. Soured by the divorce that followed, Brian Whitaker had not remarried. When Lizzie was twelve, Francesca had died suddenly and her father had been landed with the responsibility of two daughters who were practically strangers to him. The older man had done his best even though he could never resist an opportunity to remind Lizzie that she would never be the strong capable son he had wanted and needed to help him on the farm. He had barely passed fifty when ill health had handicapped him and prevented him from doing physical work.

Lizzie knew she was a disappointment to the older man but then she was used to falling short of other people's expectations. Her mother had longed for a more outgoing, fun-loving child than shy, socially awkward Lizzie had proved to be. Her father had wanted a son, not a daughter. Even her fiancé had left her for a woman who seemed to be a far more successful farmer's wife than Lizzie could ever have hoped to be. Sadly, Lizzie had become accustomed to not measuring up and had learned to simply get on with the job at hand rather than dwell on her own deficiencies.

She started her day off with the easy task of feeding the hens and gathering the eggs. Then she fed Hero, whose feed she was buying solely from her earnings from working Saturday nights behind the bar of the village pub. She didn't earn a wage at home for her labour. How could she take a wage out of the kitty every week when the rising overdraft at the bank was

a constant worry? Household bills, feed and fuel costs
were necessities that had to come out of that overdraft
and she was dreading the arrival of yet another warning letter from the bank.

She loaded the slurry tank to spray the meadow
field before her father could complain about how
far behind she was with the spring schedule. Archie
leapt into the tractor cab with her and sat panting by
her side. He still wore the old leather collar punched
with his name that he had arrived with. When she
had found him wandering the fields, hungry and bedraggled, Lizzie had reckoned he had been dumped at
the side of the road and, sadly, nobody had ever come
looking for him. She suspected that his formerly expensive collar revealed that he had once been a much-
loved pet, possibly abandoned because his elderly
owner had passed away.

When he'd first arrived, he had hung out with their
aging sheepdog, Shep, and had demonstrated a surprising talent for picking up Shep's skills so that when
Shep had died even Brian Whitaker had acknowledged
that Archie could make himself useful round the farm.
Lizzie, on the other hand, utterly adored Archie. He
curled up at her feet in bed at night and allowed himself to be cuddled whenever she was low.

She was driving back to the yard to refill the slurry
tank when she saw a long, sleek, glossy black car
filtering off the main road into the farm lane. Her
brow furrowed at the sight. She couldn't picture anyone coming in a car that big and expensive to buy the
free-range eggs she sold. Parking the tractor by the
fence, she climbed out with Archie below one arm,
stooping to let her pet down.

That was Cesare's first glimpse of Lizzie. She glanced up as she unbent and the limo slowed to ease past the tractor. He saw that though she might dress like a bag lady she had skin as translucent as the finest porcelain and eyes the colour of prized jade. He breathed in deep and slow.

His driver got out of the car only to come under immediate attack by what was clearly a vicious dog but which more closely resembled a scruffy fur muff on short legs. As the woman captured the dog to restrain it and before his driver could open the door for him Cesare sprang out and instantly the offensive stench of the farm yard assaulted his fastidious nostrils. His intense concentration trained on his quarry, he simply held his breath while lazily wondering if she smelt as well. When his father had said the Whitaker family was dirt-poor he had clearly not been joking. The farmhouse bore no resemblance to a picturesque country cottage with roses round the door. The rain guttering sagged, the windows needed replacing and the paint was peeling off the front door.

'Are you looking for directions?' Lizzie asked as the tall black-haired male emerged in a fluid shift of long limbs from the rear seat.

Cesare straightened and straight away focused on her pouty pink mouth. That was three unexpected pluses in a row, he acknowledged in surprise. Lizzie Whitaker had great skin, beautiful eyes and a mouth that made a man think of sinning, and Cesare had few inhibitions when it came to the sins of sexual pleasure. Indeed, his hot-blooded nature and need for regular sex were the two traits he deemed potential weaknesses, he acknowledged wryly.

'Directions?' he queried, disconcerted by the disruptive drift of his own thoughts, anathema to his self-discipline. In spite of his exasperation, his mind continued to pick up on the fact that Lizzie Whitaker was small, possibly only a few inches over five feet tall, and seemingly slender below the wholly dreadful worn and stained green jacket and baggy workman's overalls she wore beneath. The woolly hat pulled low on her brow made her eyes look enormous as she stared up at him much as if he'd stepped out of a spaceship in front of her.

One glance at the stranger had reduced Lizzie to gaping in an almost spellbound moment out of time. He was simply....*stunning* from his luxuriant black hair to his dark-as-bitter-chocolate deep-set eyes and strong, uncompromisingly masculine jawline. In truth she had never ever seen a more dazzling man and that disconcertingly intimate thought froze her in place like a tongue-tied schoolgirl.

'I assumed you were lost,' Lizzie explained weakly, finding it a challenge to fill her lungs with oxygen while he looked directly at her with eyes that, even lit by the weak spring sunshine, shifted to a glorious shade of bronzed gold. For a split second, she felt as if she were drowning and she shook her head slightly, struggling to think straight and act normally, her colour rising steadily as she fought the unfamiliar lassitude engulfing her.

'No, I'm not lost... This *is* the Whitaker farm?'

'Yes, I'm Lizzie Whitaker...'

Only the British could take a pretty name like Elisabetta and shorten it to something so commonplace, Cesare decided irritably. 'I'm Cesare Sabatino.'

Her jade eyes widened. His foreign-sounding name was meaningless to her ears because she barely recognised a syllable of it. 'Sorry, I didn't catch that...'

His beautifully sensual mouth quirked. 'You don't speak Italian?'

'The odd word, not much. Are you Italian?' Lizzie asked, feeling awkward as soon as she realised that he somehow knew that her mother had been of Italian extraction. Francesca had actually planned to raise her daughters to be bilingual but Brian Whitaker had objected vehemently to the practice as soon as his children began using words he couldn't understand and from that point on English had become the only language in their home.

'*Sì*, I'm Italian,' Cesare confirmed, sliding a lean brown hand into his jacket to withdraw a business card and present it to her. The extraordinary grace of his every physical gesture also ensnared her attention and she had to force her gaze down to the card.

Unfortunately, his name was no more comprehensible to Lizzie when she saw it printed. 'Your name's Caesar,' she pronounced with some satisfaction.

A muscle tugged at the corner of his unsmiling mouth. 'Not Caesar. We're not in ancient Rome. It's Chay-zar-ray,' he sounded out with perfect diction, his exotic accent underlining every syllable with a honeyed mellifluence that spiralled sinuously round her to create the strangest sense of dislocation.

'Chay-zar-ray,' she repeated politely while thinking that it was a heck of a fussy mouthful for a first name and that Caesar would have been much more straightforward. 'And you're here *because*...?'

Cesare stiffened, innate aggression powering him

at that facetious tone. He was not accustomed to being prompted to get to the point faster and as if the dog had a sensor tracking his mood it began growling soft and low. 'May we go indoors to discuss that?'

Bemused by the effect he was having on her and fiercely irritated by his take-charge manner, Lizzie lifted her chin. 'Couldn't we just talk here? This is the middle of my working day,' she told him truthfully.

Cesare gritted his perfect white teeth and shifted almost imperceptibly closer. The dog loosed a warning snarl and clamped his teeth to the corner of his cashmere overcoat, pulling at it. Cesare sent a winging glance down at the offending animal.

'Archie, *no!*' Lizzie intervened. 'I'm afraid he's very protective of me.'

Archie tugged and tugged at the corner of the overcoat and failed to shift Cesare an inch further away from his quarry. To the best of his ability Cesare ignored the entire canine assault.

'Oh, for goodness' sake, Archie!' Lizzie finally exclaimed, crouching down to physically detach the dog's jaw from the expensive cloth, noting in dismay that a small tear had been inflicted and cherishing little hope that the damage would not be noted.

Whoever he was, Cesare Sabatino wore clothing that looked incredibly expensive and fitted too well to be anything other than individually designed for its wearer. He wore a faultlessly tailored black suit below the coat and his highly polished shoes were marred only by the skiff of mud that continually covered the yard at damp times of the year. He looked like a high-powered businessman, tycoon or some such thing. Why on earth was such a man coming to visit the farm?

'Are you from our bank?' Lizzie asked abruptly.

'No. I am a businessman,' Cesare admitted calmly.

'You're here to see my father for some reason?' Lizzie prompted apprehensively.

'No...I'm here to see you,' Cesare framed succinctly as she scrambled upright clutching the still-growling dog to her chest.

'Me?' Lizzie exclaimed in astonishment, her gaze colliding with glittering eyes that gleamed like highly polished gold, enhanced by the thick black velvet fringe of his long lashes. Below her clothes, her nipples pinched almost painfully tight and a flare of sudden heat darted down into her pelvis, making her feel extremely uncomfortable. 'Why on earth would you want to see me? Oh, come indoors, if you must,' she completed wearily. 'But I warn you, it's a mess.'

Trudging to the side of the house, Lizzie kicked off her boots and thrust the door open on the untidy kitchen.

Cesare's nostrils flared as he scanned the cluttered room, taking in the pile of dishes heaped in the sink and the remains of someone's meal still lying on the pine table. Well, he certainly wouldn't be marrying her for her housekeeping skills, he reflected grimly as the dog slunk below the table to continue growling unabated and his reluctant hostess removed her coat and yanked off her woolly hat before hurriedly clearing the table and yanking out a chair for him.

'Coffee...or tea?' Lizzie enquired.

Cesare's entire attention was still locked to the wealth of silver-coloured silky hair that, freed from the woolly hat, now tumbled round her shoulders. It was gorgeous in spite of the odd murky brown tips of colour that damaged the effect. Dip-dying, he thought dimly, vaguely recalling the phrase being used by one of his team who had showed up at the office one day with ludicrously colourful half-blonde, half-pink locks. He blinked, black lashes long as fly swats momentarily concealing his bemused gaze.

'Coffee,' he replied, feeling that he was being very brave and polite in the face of the messy kitchen and standards of hygiene that he suspected might be much lower than he was used to receiving.

In a graceful movement, he doffed his coat and draped it across the back of a chair. Lizzie filled the kettle at the sink and put it on the hotplate on the ancient coal-fired cooking range while taking in the full effect of her visitor's snazzy appearance. He looked like a city slicker who belonged on a glossy magazine cover, the sort of publication that showed how fashion-conscious men should dress. To a woman used to men wearing dirty, often unkempt clothing suitable for outdoor work, he had all the appeal of a fantasy. He really was physically beautiful in every possible way and so unfamiliar was she with that level of male magnetism that she was challenged to drag her eyes from his lean, powerful figure.

Dredging her thoughts from the weird sticking point they had reached, she went to the door of the lounge. A businessman, she reminded herself doggedly. Successful businessmen—and he looked *very* successful—were cold-blooded, calculating individuals, ready to do anything for profit and divorced from sentiment. He certainly emanated that arrogant vibe with his polished image that was so totally inappropriate for a male visiting a working farm. 'Dad? We have a visitor. Do you want tea?'

'A visitor?' Brian Whitaker rose with a frown from his chair and came with shuffling, poorly balanced steps into the kitchen.

Lizzie removed mugs from the cupboard while the two men introduced themselves.

'I'm here about the island that Lizzie and her sister inherited from your late wife,' Cesare explained calmly.

The silence of astonishment engulfed his companions. Lizzie studied him wide-eyed while her father turned his head towards him in a frowning attitude of incredulity.

'It's a rubbish inheritance...nothing but a bad joke!' Lizzie's father contended in a burst of unrestrained bitterness. 'It stands to reason that an inheritance you can't use or sell is worthless... What use is that to anyone? So, that's why you're here? Another fool chasing the pot of gold at the end of the rainbow?'

'Dad!' Lizzie exclaimed in consternation at the older man's blatant scorn.

She wished she had guessed why the Italian had come to visit and scolded herself for not immediately making the association between his nationality and the legacy left to her and Chrissie by their mother. Over the years the island that couldn't be sold had been a source of much bitterness in her family, particularly when money was in such short supply. She lifted the kettle off the range and hastily made the drinks while she wondered what on earth Cesare hoped to achieve by visiting them.

'I'll put your tea in the lounge, Dad,' she said, keen to remove her father from the dialogue, afraid of what he might say in his blunt and challenging way.

Brian Whitaker stole a glance at the Italian's shuttered dark face, not displeased by the effect of having had his say. 'I'll leave you to it, then. After all, the only reason *he* could be here is that he's coming a-courting!' he completed with a derisive laugh that sent a hot tide of colour flaring below Lizzie's pale skin. 'Good luck to you! Lizzie was ditched by the neighbour a couple of years ago and she hasn't been out on a date since then!'

CHAPTER TWO

LIZZIE WANTED THE tiled floor to open up and swallow her where she stood. Being humiliated in front of a stranger felt even more painful than the snide comments and pitying appraisals from the village locals that had followed the ending of her engagement to Andrew Brook two years earlier. A month later, Andrew had married Esther, who had already been pregnant with their son. She stiffened her facial muscles, made the tea and the coffee and even contrived to politely ask if the visitor took sugar.

Wide, sensual mouth set in a grim line, Cesare surveyed Lizzie's rigid back view, noting the narrow cut of her waist and the slender, delicate curves merely hinted at by the overalls. Her father had been cruel taking her down like that in front of an audience. Not a date since, though? He was astonished because, unflattering as her clothing was, Cesare had immediately recognised that she was a beauty. Not perhaps a conventional beauty, he was willing to admit, not the kind of beauty that set the world on fire but certainly the type that should make the average male look more than once. What was wrong with the local men?

'Sorry about Dad,' Lizzie apologised in a brittle

voice, setting the coffee down carefully on the table in front of him, catching the evocative scent of some citrusy cologne as she briefly leant closer and stiffening as a result of the sudden warmth pooling in her pelvis. Never had anyone made her feel more uncomfortable in her own home.

'You don't need to apologise, *cara*,' Cesare parried.

'But I should explain. My parents resented the will—personally, I never think about it. Unfortunately, the island was a sore point in our lives when I was a child because money was tight.'

'Have you ever visited Lionos?'

'No, I've never had the opportunity. Mum went once with one of her boyfriends and stayed for a week. She wasn't too impressed,' Lizzie revealed ruefully while she scanned his lean, strong face, taking in the high cheekbones, straight nose and hard, masculine mouth before involuntarily sliding her gaze upward again to take another sweep of those absolutely devastating dark golden eyes of his. 'I think Mum was expecting luxury but I believe the accommodation was more basic.'

'The will endowed the island with a trust and I understand a caretaker and his family live nearby to maintain the property.'

Lizzie cocked her head to one side, her shattered nerves slowly stabilising at his lack of comment about her father's outburst. Pale, silky hair slid across her cheekbone and Cesare looked up into those wide hazel-green eyes framed with soft honey-brown lashes, and suddenly he was aware of the heavy pulse of heat at his groin and the muscles in his broad shoulders pulled taut as ropes as he resisted that sirens' call of lust with all his might.

'Yes. But the trust only covers maintenance costs, not improvements, and I understand that the house is still firmly stuck in the thirties. Mum also assumed that the caretaker would cook and clean for them but instead the man and his wife told her that they weren't servants and she had to look after herself,' Lizzie volunteered wryly. 'All in all she found it a very expensive jaunt by the time they'd paid someone to take them out to the island and deliver food while they were there.'

'Naturally you want to know what I'm doing here,' Cesare murmured smoothly.

'Well, I don't think you've come a-courting,' Lizzie fielded with a shrug that dismissed her father's gibe but completely failed to hide her discomfiture at that crack.

'Not in the conventional sense,' Cesare agreed, lean fingers flexing round the mug of coffee. It was barely drinkable but he doubted if she expended much concern when it came to the domestic front, which was hardly surprising when it was obvious that she was struggling to keep the farm afloat single-handedly. She was leaning back against the cooking range with defensively folded arms, trying to appear relaxed but visibly as tense as a bow string. 'But I do think we might be able to come to a business arrangement.'

Lizzie frowned, dragging her wandering gaze from his lean, extravagantly handsome features with a slight rise of colour, scolding herself for her lack of concentration, questioning what it was about him that kept her looking back at him again and again, long after curiosity should have been satisfied. 'A business arrangement?'

'I don't think your sister enters this as she's still a teenager. Obviously as co-owner of the island, you would have to confer with her, but I'm willing to offer you a substantial amount of money to go through a marriage ceremony with me.'

Her lashes fluttered in shock because he had knocked her for six. Inexplicably, his cool sophistication and smooth delivery made the fantastic proposition he had just made seem almost workaday and acceptable. 'Seriously? *Just* a marriage ceremony? But what would you get out of that?'

Cesare told her about his grandmother's deep attachment to the island and her approaching surgery. As she listened, Lizzie nodded slowly, strangely touched by the softer tone he couldn't help employing when talking about the old lady. His screened gaze and the faint hint of flush along his spectacular cheekbones encouraged her scrutiny to linger with helpless curiosity. He was not quite as cold and tough as he seemed on the surface, she acknowledged in surprise. But she could see that he was very uncomfortable with showing emotion.

'Isn't circumventing the will against the law?' she prompted in a small voice.

'I wasn't planning to publicise the fact. For the sake of appearances we would have to pretend that the marriage was the real deal for a few months at least.'

'And the "having a child" bit? Where does that come in?' Lizzie could not resist asking.

'Whether it comes into our arrangement or not is up to you. I will pay generously for the right to take my grandmother to the island for a visit and if we were to contrive to meet the *full* terms of the will, you and your sister would stand to collect a couple of million pounds, at the very least, from selling Lionos to me,' he spelt out quietly. 'I am an extremely wealthy man and I will pay a high price to bring the island back into my family.'

Millions? Lizzie's mouth ran dry and she lost colour, eyes dropping to focus on the long, lean brown fingers gracefully coiled round the mug of coffee. For a split second she saw her every hope and dream fulfilled by ill-gotten gains. Her father could give up the farm tenancy, and she and Chrissie could buy him a house in the village where he would be able to go to the pub quizzes he loved and meet up with his cronies. Chrissie would be able to chuck in her two part-time jobs, concentrate on her studies and pay off her student loans. Being freed from the burden of the farm would enable Lizzie to go and train for a job she would enjoy. Archie could get some professional grooming and a new collar and live on the very best pet food…

It became an increasingly stupid dream and she reddened with mortification, hands clenching by her side as she suppressed her wild imaginings in shame at how susceptible she had been when tempted by the equivalent of a lottery win.

'I couldn't have a child with a stranger…or bring a child into the world for such a purpose,' she confided. 'But if it's any consolation, just for a minute there I wished I was the sort of woman who could.'

'Think it over,' Cesare suggested, having registered without surprise that the suggestion of oodles of cash had finally fully engaged her in their discussion. He rose fluidly upright and tapped the business card he had left on the table top. 'My cell number.'

He was very big, possibly a foot taller than she was, with broad shoulders, narrow hips and long, powerful legs.

'Yes, well, there's a lot to think over,' she muttered uneasily.

He reached for his coat and turned back to her, dark eyes bright and shimmering as topaz in sunshine. 'There are two options and either will bring in a profit for you.'

'You definitely talk like a businessman,' she remarked, unimpressed by the statement, ashamed of her temporary dive into a fantasy land where every sheep had a proverbial golden fleece. Could it really be that easy to go from being a decent person to a mercenary one? she was asking herself worriedly.

'I am trying to negotiate a business arrangement,' he pointed out drily.

'Was it *your* father who once asked my mother to marry him?' Lizzie could not stop herself from enquiring. 'Or was that someone from another branch of your family?'

Cesare came to a halt. 'No, that was my father and it wasn't a business proposal. He fell hard for your mother and they were engaged when she came over here on holiday. Having met your father, however, she preferred him,' he advanced without any expression at all.

But Lizzie recognised the unspoken disapproval in the hard bones of his lean, strong face and she flushed because her mother had been decidedly changeable in her affections and there was no denying the fact. Predictably, Francesca had never admitted that she had actually got engaged to their father's predecessor. But then every man that came along had been the love of Francesca's life until either he revealed his true character or someone else seized her interest. Her mother had always moved on without a backward glance, never once pausing to try and work on a relationship or considering the cost of such continual upheaval in the lives of her two young children.

'I'm afraid I'm not a sentimental man,' Cesare imparted. 'I'm innately practical in every way. Why shouldn't you make what you can of your inheritance for your family's benefit?'

'Because it just doesn't seem right,' Lizzie confided uncertainly. 'It's not what my great-grandfather intended either when he drew up that will.'

'No, he wanted revenge because my grandmother's brother jilted his daughter at the altar. My great-uncle was in the wrong but plunging the island into legal limbo simply to keep it out of my family's hands was no more justifiable,' Cesare countered with complete assurance. 'It's been that way for nearly eighty years but I believe that we have the power to change that.'

'The ethics involved aren't something I've ever thought about,' Lizzie admitted, resisting the urge to confess that the island still seemed no more real to her than that fabled pot of gold at the end of the rainbow that her father had mentioned.

Cesare smiled with sudden brilliance, amused by her honesty and her lack of pretence.

His smile almost blinded her, illuminating his lean, darkly handsome face, and she wanted so badly to touch him for a disconcerting moment that she clenched her hands into fists to restrain herself. She was deeply disturbed by the effect he had on her. Indeed, she feared it because she recognised her reaction for the fierce physical attraction that it was. And nobody knew better than Francesca Whitaker's daughter how dangerous giving rein to such mindless responses could be for it had propelled her mother into one disastrous relationship after another.

In the smouldering silence, beautiful, dark golden eyes fringed with velvet black held hers and she trembled, fighting reactions she had never experienced so powerfully before.

'My offer's on the table and I'm willing to negotiate with you. Discuss it with your sister and your father but urge them to keep the matter confidential,' Cesare advised smoothly, staring down into her upturned face, attention lingering on the lush contours of her lips as he wondered what she would *taste* like. 'We could go the full distance on this... I find you appealing.'

And with that deeply unsettling comment, Cesare Sabatino swung on his heel and strode back out to the limousine sitting ready to depart. The driver leapt out to throw open the door for his passenger and Cesare lowered his proud dark head and climbed in.

Appealing? Lizzie pushed her hair back off her brow and caught her surprised reflection in the small age-spotted mirror on the wall. He was really saying that he could go to bed with her and conceive a child with her if she was willing: that was what he meant by the word *appealing*. Her face flamed. She was *not* willing. She also knew the difference between right and wrong. She knew that more money didn't necessarily mean more happiness and that a child was usually better off with a mother *and* a father.

Yet the image of the tiny boy she had glimpsed cradled in her former fiancé's arms after the child's christening in the church had pierced Lizzie with a pain greater than that inflicted by Andrew's infidelity. Lizzie had always wanted a baby and ached at the sight of infants. When Andrew had left her for Esther, she had envied Esther for her son, *not* her husband. What did that say about her? That she was as cold at heart and frigid as Andrew had once accused her of being? Even remembering that hurtful indictment, Lizzie winced and felt less than other women, knowing that she had been tried and found wanting by a young man who had only wanted a warm and loving wife. Lizzie knew that, in choosing Esther, Andrew had made the right decision for them both. Yet Lizzie had loved Andrew too in her way.

Her eyes stung with moisture, her fingers toying with the ends of the brown-tinted hair that Andrew had persuaded her to dye. The dye was growing out, a reminder of how foolish a woman could be when she tried to change herself to please a man...

But where on earth had her strong maternal instinct come from? Certainly not from her volatile mother, who in the grip of her wild infatuations had always focused her energies on the man in her life. Lizzie had not been surprised to learn of the impetuous way Francesca had evidently ditched Cesare's father to marry Lizzie's father instead. Hard Yorkshire winters and life on a shoestring, however, had dimmed Brian Whitaker's appeal for her mother and within weeks of Chrissie's birth Francesca had run off with a man who had turned out to be a drunk. His successor had been more interested in spending Francesca's recent legacy following the death of her Italian parents than in Francesca herself. Her third lover had been repeatedly unfaithful. And the fourth, who married her, had been violent.

Lizzie had always found it very hard to trust men after living through her mother's grim roll call of destructive relationships. She had struggled to protect the sister five years her junior from the constant fall-out of moving home and changing schools, striving to ensure that her sibling could still enjoy her childhood and wasn't forced to grow up as quickly as Lizzie had. Almost all the happy moments in Lizzie's life had occurred when Chrissie was young and Lizzie had the comfort of knowing that her love and care was both wanted and needed by her sibling. When her sister left home to go to university it had opened a vast hole in Lizzie's life. Archie had partially filled that hole, a reality that made her grin and shrug off her deep and troubled thoughts with the acknowledgement that it was time to get back to work and concentrate on what really mattered.

'Marry him and stop making such a production out of it!' Brian Whitaker snapped at his daughter angrily. 'We don't have any other choice. The rent is going up and the bank's on the brink of calling in our loan!'

'It's not that simple, Dad,' Lizzie began to argue again.

But the older man wasn't listening. He hadn't listened to a word his daughter had said since the letter from the bank had delivered its lethal warning. 'Simple would have been you marrying Andrew. He would have taken on the tenancy. I could still have lived here. Everyone would have been happy but could you pull it off?' he derided. '*No*, you had to play fast and loose with him, wanting to *wait* to get married!'

'I wanted to get to know him properly, not rush in. I wanted our marriage to last,' Lizzie protested.

'You might as well have parcelled him up for Esther and handed him over. Andrew was our one chance to keep this place afloat and you threw him away,' he condemned bitterly. 'Now you're mouthing off about all the reasons why you can't marry a man and have a child just to improve *all* our lives!'

'A lot of women wouldn't want to do it!' It was Lizzie's parting shot, tossed over her shoulder as she stomped back into the yard with Archie dancing at her heels. A week had passed since Cesare Sabatino's visit and her father had reasoned and condemned and outright ranted at her every day for her reluctance to accept Cesare's proposal.

Hopefully, Chrissie would not be singing the same tune, Lizzie reflected ruefully as she drove her father's ancient, battered Land Rover Defender down the lane to collect her sister off the train. She had told Chrissie all about Cesare's visit on the phone and her sibling had urged her to follow her conscience and refuse to pay heed to her father's grievances.

That was, however, proving a much more major challenge than she had expected, Lizzie acknowledged heavily. Almost insurmountable problems were forming ahead of her like a string of dangerous obstacles. They could not afford to pay a higher rent when the tenancy came up for renewal and that reality would render them homeless. They could not even afford to live if the bank demanded that the loan be repaid as they were threatening to do. And *where* would they live, if the worst came to the worst? Her father had no savings. Yes, it was all very well following her conscience, Lizzie conceded wretchedly, but right now it was no good at all as a blueprint for economic survival.

Sadly, the stress of the constant arguments and anxiety was taking the edge off Lizzie's usual happy anticipation at the prospect of having her sister home for a couple of days. Chrissie, pale silver hair caught up in a sensible ponytail, blue eyes sparkling with affection, was waiting outside the station, two big cases by her side and a bulging rucksack on her slender shoulders.

'My goodness, you've brought back a lot of luggage... but it's not the end of term,' Lizzie remarked in bewilderment, thinking out loud while Chrissie concentrated on giving her a fierce hug of welcome.

'I've missed you so much,' her sibling confessed. 'And I'm going to ask you all over again—why have you still not had your hair dyed back to normal?'

'I haven't had the time...or the cash,' Lizzie muttered, hoisting a heavy case and propelling it across to the Land Rover.

'No, you're still punishing yourself for not marrying Andrew.'

'They're teaching you psychology now on your English course?' Lizzie teased.

Luggage stowed, Lizzie drove back home. 'I should warn you...Dad's on the warpath.'

'He wants you to marry the Italian and make our fortunes, right?' Chrissie groaned in despair. 'Dear old Dad, what a dinosaur he is. He tried to pressure you into marrying Andrew for the sake of the farm and now he's trying to serve you up on the altar of that stupid island! Well, you don't need to worry, you're not going to come under any pressure from me on that score. We've lived all our lives without the excitement of being rich and what you don't have, you don't miss!'

In spite of her stress level, Lizzie managed to smile. After an unrelieved overdose of her father's reproaches, Chrissie, with her positive outlook, was like a little ray of sunshine. 'You're right,' she agreed even though she knew that her kid sister was not very grounded. Chrissie had always been a dreamer, the creative one with the fluffy romantic and idealistic ideas.

In fact, while she watched Chrissie hurtle across the yard to pet her elderly pony, Hero, and feed him an apple from her pocket, her heart sank from so bald a reminder of her sister's tendency to always look on the bright side even if there wasn't one. Didn't Chrissie appreciate that if they lost their home, Hero would be one of the first sacrifices?

'I've got a surprise for you...' Chrissie told her, almost skipping back to Lizzie's side to help her unload her luggage. 'I'm home for good!'

Lizzie turned incredulous eyes on the younger woman. 'What are you talking about?'

'I'm dropping out of uni...I'm coming home,' Chrissie proffered, her soft mouth set in an unusually firm and purposeful line. 'Even with the two jobs and the student loan, I can hardly afford to eat and my overdraft is *massive*, Lizzie. I'm fed up with it, especially when I know you're slogging away here every hour God gives and still barely scratching a living. I'm going to get a job and help you whenever I can. I'm all grown up now—it's past time I pulled my weight on the home front.'

Shock was reverberating through Lizzie, closely followed by dismay. Much as she missed her sister, the very last thing she wanted was to see Chrissie throw away her education to come home and vegetate. In any case, it was a moot point that they would even have a home to offer her sibling in a few weeks' time. 'I didn't realise that you were having such a struggle.'

'I didn't want you worrying,' Chrissie confided. 'But I've learned a lot. I'd no idea it cost so much just to live. I can't possibly work any more hours, though. I've already had a warning from my tutor about my standard of work slipping... I'm so tired I'm falling asleep in lectures.'

And that was the moment when Lizzie reached her decision. What security her family had was vanishing fast but it was within her power to change everything for the better. How could she stand by and simply do nothing for her family while their lives fell apart? At the very least she should go through with the wedding to enable Cesare to take his grandmother back to the island for a visit. Whatever he paid her for that service would surely settle their outstanding bills and enable her to find a rental property in the village. But how could she go further than that? How could she have a child with him so that he could legally buy Lionos and resolve all her family's financial problems?

The answer came to Lizzie in a blinding flash of

light and she could barely credit that she had not seen the solution sooner. Cesare had said he was very practical and the answer she came up with would not only make the threat of intimacy with a stranger unnecessary but would also be a supremely sensible approach. Suddenly the sensation of weighty responsibility and dread on her shoulders and spine evaporated and she straightened, even cracking a brief smile at the heady prospect of finally being in full control of her life again.

'You're going back to university on Sunday, young lady,' Lizzie told her kid sister firmly. 'You will quit your part-time jobs and concentrate on your studies. I will ensure that you manage.'

'You can't marry the guy, Lizzie!' Chrissie gasped in horror. 'You simply *can't*!'

Lizzie thought fast and breathed in deep before she sat down at the kitchen table. 'Let me be honest with you. I've spent eight years working round the clock on this farm. I've had no time for friends and I've had very little social life. I have no decent clothes or jewellery and I don't even know how to put on make-up properly.'

'But that doesn't mean you have to give way to Dad and make a sacrifice of yourself.'

'Has it occurred to you that maybe I *want* to marry Cesare and have a child? He's a very handsome man and you know how much I've always wanted a baby. I also would like to have enough money not to worry myself sick every time a bill comes through the letter box!' Lizzie declared, her heart-shaped face taut with vehement composure as she watched Chrissie frown and suddenly look unsure of her ground.

'I'm deadly serious,' Lizzie continued with dogged determination. 'I *want* to marry Cesare. It's the best thing for all of us and, believe me, I'm not the sacrificial type.'

'I never thought…I never dreamt…' Bemused and uncertain of such an explanation from the big sister she had always loved and admired, Chrissie shook her head, frowning at her sibling. 'Are you sure, Lizzie? Have you really thought this through?'

No, Lizzie hadn't thought it all through and was determined not to run the risk of doing so before she had tied the official knot. Whatever happened she was going to marry Cesare Sabatino and miraculously sort out her own and her father's *and* Chrissie's problems. No other action now made sense. So, it would be scary and would entail deception—well, she would get braver and she would learn some new skills. My goodness, hadn't she just told a barefaced lie to the sister she loved?

She walked into her bedroom and lifted the business card Cesare had left behind. Before she could take fright, she tapped out the number on her mobile phone and then studied the blank message space.

Will agree to marry you. Talk about the rest when we next meet.

Cesare blinked down at the text and then glanced across the dinner table at Celine, whose sleek blonde perfection had entranced him for longer than most women managed. In his mind's eye, however, he was no longer seeing the French fashion model, he was seeing a slender platinum blonde with luminous green eyes surrounded by soft brown lashes. Surprise was cutting through his satisfaction, perhaps because he had had the weirdest conviction that Lizzie Whitaker would say no to the temptation of the cash he had offered. He wondered why he had thought that, why he had assumed she would be different from any other woman.

Women liked money and he liked women: it was a fair exchange in which neither of them need feel used or abused. Hadn't he learned that a long time ago? Athene would be able to return to her childhood home for a visit at the very least. Was Lizzie Whitaker planning to meet the *full* terms of the will? Raw anticipation of an entirely different kind infiltrated Cesare and he frowned, bewildered by the flood of undisciplined hormones smashing his self-control to pieces. He was thinking about Lizzie Whitaker, *only* thinking about her and he was as aroused as a teenager contemplating sex for the first time.

'You seem distracted,' Celine remarked tentatively.

Cesare studied her without an iota of his usual lust, exasperated by the games his body was playing with his usually very well-disciplined brain. 'A business deal,' he proffered truthfully.

Goffredo would be overjoyed at the news of the upcoming wedding while Cesare was simply stunned at the prospect of getting married, whether it was a business arrangement or not. *Married!* The delicious food on his plate ebbed in appeal. Dense black lashes screened his gaze. It was rare for him to take a night off and somehow Lizzie Whitaker had contrived to kill any notion he had had of relaxing with Celine. What was it about her that unsettled him? After all she was a pretty standard gold-digger, willing to do virtually anything to enrich herself, and how could he criticise her for that reality when he had baited the hook?

CHAPTER THREE

'I DON'T KNOW what the arrangements are likely to be,' Lizzie told her father while she paced the kitchen, a slim figure clad in jeans and a sweater and workman-like boots. 'Look, I've got a few things to check outside. I might as well keep busy until Cesare arrives.'

'What sort of a name is that he has?' Brian Whitaker scoffed.

Lizzie dealt the older man an impatient glance as she put on her jacket because he had no excuse to be needling her or disparaging Cesare. But everything, she told herself in an urgent little pep talk, was *good* in her world. Chrissie had returned to university and soon she and her father would no longer need to worry about rent rises and bank debts they couldn't cover. 'It's an Italian name, just like mine and Chrissie's and Mum's and it's completely normal. Let's not forget that Cesare is about to wave a magic wand over our lives.'

'Even the Garden of Eden had the serpent,' her father countered with a curl of his lip and his usual determination to have the last word.

Lizzie drank in the fresh air with relief and walked to the stone wall bounding the yard to check the sheep in the field. Lambing hadn't started yet but it wouldn't be long before it did. If she had to leave home before then, Andrew would probably take the ewes, she was reasoning in the detached state of mind she had forged to keep herself calm since she had sent that text to Cesare. There were no successes without losses, no gains without costs and consequences. In the middle of that sobering reflection while she watched the lane for a car arriving, she heard a noise in the sky and she flung her head back in the fading light to look up.

A helicopter was coming in over the valley. As she watched it circled the top of the hill and swooped down low to come closer and then noisily hover. For a split second, Lizzie was frozen to the spot, unable to believe that the helicopter was actually planning to land in a field with stock in it. The craft's powerful lights splayed over the flock of fast-scattering sheep, which ran in a total panic down the hill. Lizzie ran for the gate, Archie at her heels, and flew over it like a high jumper while shouting instructions to her dog to retrieve the flock.

Heart pounding, she ran down the hill at breakneck speed but was still not fast enough to prevent the sheep from scrambling in a frantic escape over the wall at the foot and streaming across the next field towards the river. Sick with apprehension, she clambered over the wall and ran even faster while watching as Archie herded the frightened ewes away from the water's edge. The noise from the helicopter unluckily intensified at that point because the pilot was taking off again and the sheep herded close together and then took off terrified again in all directions.

Someone shouted her name and she was relieved to see Andrew Brook racing down the hill to join her. Struggling desperately to catch her breath, while wondering anxiously where Archie had disappeared to, she hurried on towards the riverbank to see if any of the animals had gone into the water. Andrew got there first and she saw him stooping down in the mud over something, whistling for his sheepdog. One of the sheep had got hurt in the commotion, she assumed, hurrying down to join him.

'I'm so sorry, Lizzie. He's hurt. He was too little to handle them in a panic like that,' Andrew told her.

Lizzie looked down in horror at the small prone body lying in the mud: it was Archie and he was whimpering. She knelt in the mud. *'Oh, no...'*

'I think it's only his leg that's broken but there could be internal injuries. He was trodden on,' Andrew, a stocky dark-haired man in his late twenties, reminded her.

'That *crazy* helicopter pilot! Are people insane?' Lizzie gasped, stricken, while Andrew, always resourceful, broke a small branch off a nearby tree, cut it to size with the knife in his pocket and splinted it to Archie's leg, wrapping it in place with twine.

'Nobody should land in a field with animals in it,' Andrew agreed. As Lizzie comforted her pet with a trembling hand he unfurled his mobile phone. 'We'd better get him to the vet. I'll ring ahead to warn Danny.'

Andrew's dog had retrieved the sheep and on the walk back uphill they were returned to the field from which they had fled. Lizzie was in shock and wildly dishevelled by the breakneck pace of her downhill marathon, sweat breaking on her brow, tears trickling down her cheeks as she held Archie's small, shivering body as gently as she could to her chest. Back in the yard, Lizzie went straight to the Land Rover and settled Archie on the front passenger seat.

'I'll come with you,' Andrew announced. 'I know how you feel about that daft dog.'

'Thanks but I can manage,' Lizzie assured him with a warm smile that acknowledged how comfortable she could still feel with her former boyfriend.

'That's the ex-fiancé—Andrew Brook, our neighbour,' Brian Whitaker informed Cesare, who was stationed beside him outside the back door of the cottage. 'They grew up together. I always thought they'd make a match of it but then he met Esther and married her instead.'

Cesare told himself that he had no desire for that information. He was already irritated that Lizzie hadn't been waiting to greet him—didn't she appreciate what a busy man he was? Now watching her smile beguilingly up at her ex-boyfriend, who was an attractive, stalwart six-footer, he was even less impressed. When she looked at the other man like that and squeezed his arm with easy intimacy it made him wonder why they had broken up and that dart of inappropriate curiosity set his even white teeth on edge, sending another wave of annoyance crashing through him.

'Lizzie!' her father called as Andrew strode back home across the couple of fields that separated their properties.

Lizzie turned her head and focused in bewilderment on the tall, darkly handsome male poised by her father's side. Her heartbeat suddenly thudded like a crack of doom in her ears and her throat tightened. Sheathed in an immaculate grey pinstripe business suit worn with a white shirt and scarlet tie, Cesare looked very much at odds with his surroundings but he still contrived to take her breath away and leave her mind briefly as blank as white paper. 'Good grief, when did you arrive? I didn't see a car.'

'I came in a helicopter…'

Lizzie, the Land Rover keys clenched tightly in one hand, froze. She blinked in fleeting bewilderment and then headed towards Cesare in a sudden movement, rage boiling up through the cracks of anxiety and concern for her dog and her flock. '*You're* the bloody idiot who let a helicopter land in a field full of stock?' she raked at him incredulously.

In all his life, nobody had ever addressed Cesare with such insolence. A faint frown line etched between his ebony brows, he stared at her as if he couldn't quite believe his ears. Indeed he was much more concerned with the reality that, in spite of her awareness of his visit, his bride-to-be still looked as though she had strayed in from a hostel for the homeless. A streak of dirt marred one cheekbone and her clothes were caked in mud and displaying damp patches. But when he glanced higher and saw the luminous colour in her cheeks that accentuated her hazel-green eyes and the contrast of that tumbling mane of admittedly messy white-blonde hair, he registered in some astonishment that even had she been wearing a bin liner it would not have dampened her physical appeal on his terms. His usual high standards, it seemed, were slipping.

'What's the problem?' Cesare enquired with perfect cool, reasoning that some sort of cultural misunderstanding could have provoked her sudden aggressive outburst.

'*The problem is...*'

'Don't shout at me,' Cesare sliced in softly. 'I am not hard of hearing.'

'Your pilot landed that helicopter in a field full of sheep...and he should be shot for it!' Lizzie framed rawly. 'They were so terrified they fled. All of them are pregnant, only days off lambing. If any of them miscarry after that crazed stampede, I'll be holding *you* responsible!'

For a fraction of a second, Cesare recalled the pilot striving to persuade him to land a couple of fields away but the prospect of a time-wasting muddy trek to the cottage had exasperated him and he had insisted on being set down as close as possible to his destination. 'The mistake was mine, not the pilot's. I chose the landing spot,' Cesare admitted, startling her with that confession. 'I know nothing about farming or the care of animals. Naturally I will compensate you and your father for any loss of income that results.'

'Well, the man can't say fairer than that,' Brian Whitaker cut in, sending his furious daughter a warning glance. 'Let that be the end of it.'

'Archie was *hurt*!' Lizzie protested fierily, shooting Cesare a seething look that warned him that even admitting his mistake was insufficient to soothe her. 'The flock trampled him at the river. I'm taking him to the vet now for emergency treatment and I haven't got the time...or the patience...to deal with you!'

Cesare watched in disbelief as his future bride unlocked the rusty vehicle several feet away and began to climb in.

'You've done it now. She treats that stupid dog like her firstborn!' Brian Whitaker muttered impatiently and retreated back indoors, bowing out of the situation.

With the split-second timing that matched Cesare's lightning-fast intellect, he strode forward and opened the passenger door of the Land Rover to take the only step left open to him. 'I'll accompany you to the vet's,' he informed her flatly.

Very much disconcerted by that announcement, Lizzie flicked him a frowning appraisal. 'You'll have to hold Archie.'

Cesare, so far out of his comfort zone that he already felt as if he were trapped in something of a nightmare, finally noticed that it was a two-seat vehicle and that the scruffy dog lay comatose on the only seat available for his own use.

Lizzie leapt back out of the car. 'I'll move him and *then* you can get in,' she told him, racing round the back of the vehicle to scoop up Archie in trembling hands and usher him in.

'I could drive,' Cesare pointed out drily.

'You don't know where you're going and I know where the potholes are,' Lizzie told him incomprehensibly as she very gently rested Archie down on Cesare's lap. 'Please make sure he doesn't fall.'

Tears were choking Lizzie's throat. Archie was so quiet and he had never been a quiet dog. Right at that very minute, he could be *dying*, his brave little life and loving spirit ebbing away, and that was why she wasn't going to waste time arguing with Cesare Sabatino about anything.

'Is he still breathing?' Lizzie demanded, turning out onto the road.

'I can feel his heart beating,' Cesare proffered quietly, blocking out his uneasy awareness that the vehicle stank of animals and was far from clean. He stroked the still body for want of anything else to do and was startled when the dog twisted his head to lick at his hand.

'He trusts you,' Lizzie informed him.

'He doesn't have much choice in the matter,' Cesare fielded, reckoning that he had been sent to Yorkshire solely to suffer. In his opinion she drove like a maniac. He had spent the day travelling and his day had started at six in the morning in Geneva. Now it was eight in the evening and, not only had he not eaten for hours, but he was also convinced that many more hours would pass before he could even hope for the opportunity. He knew she had no idea that he had planned to take her out to dinner and, since he didn't have a woolly fleece and cloven hooves, it would never occur to Lizzie to feed him.

Unaware of her unwelcome passenger's thoughts, Lizzie rammed the Land Rover to an abrupt jolting halt in a small car park. Carefully carrying Archie, Lizzie stalked into the surgery, leaving Cesare, a male who was unaccustomed to being ignored, to follow her. An older man greeted them and carried the dog off to be X-rayed, leaving Lizzie and Cesare in the small, dull waiting room.

In consternation, Cesare watched Lizzie fighting off tears again. Driven by a desperate masculine urge to shift her thoughts to what he viewed as more positive issues, he murmured, 'So, we're getting married?'

Lizzie marvelled at his lack of compassion and understanding. Did he really think she was in any frame of mind to discuss that while she was waiting to hear whether Archie would live or die? 'Yes, but it won't really be a marriage,' she parried, striving not to look at him because he really had the most stunning dark golden eyes and every time she looked she ended up staring and she didn't want him to notice her behaving like a silly schoolgirl.

'We're not going for gold, then,' Cesare assumed, referring to the requirement for a child in the will while surveying her down-bent head with a sense of deep dissatisfaction that took him aback. Why was he feeling that way? Common sense suggested that he should settle for taking Athene for a visit to Lionos and think himself lucky to have gained that much from the exchange.

A tangle of silvery hair brushed the delicate cheekbones of Lizzie's heart-shaped face and she glanced up through the silken veil of her lashes, green eyes clear and direct. 'Well, yes, we are. I've thought of a way round that.'

'There's no way round it,' Cesare informed her impatiently, marvelling at the luminous quality of those tear-drenched eyes.

'AI,' she declared quietly.

His straight ebony brows lifted. 'AI?'

'Artificial insemination. We use it with the stock and we can do it that way too,' Lizzie muttered in an undertone, trying not to succumb to discomfiture because he was *really* staring at her now as if he had never heard of such a process. 'I mean, that way there's no need at all for us to get up close and personal. We can both conserve our dignity.'

Cesare was staggered by the suggestion. 'Dignity?'

he queried thinly, his first reaction being one of male offence until his clever brain examined the suggestion. For him, it would be a win-win situation, he acknowledged grudgingly. He would not have to sacrifice his freedom in any field because the marriage would be a detached charade from start to finish. That *was* the civilised sensible approach because there would always be the risk that sexual involvement could muddy the waters of their arrangement. But while his intellect reinforced that rational outlook, he discovered that he was curiously reluctant to embrace the concept of a child fathered in a lab rather than in the normal way and equally reluctant to accept that Lizzie Whitaker would never share his bed.

'Well, obviously neither one of us would want to be put in the position where we would have to have sex with a stranger.'

Without warning, unholy amusement burnished Cesare's lean, darkly handsome features. 'I don't think you know much about the average male.'

Colour flared like a banner in Lizzie's cheeks. 'And if that's the sort of man you are, I don't think you should be boasting about it!' she snapped pointedly.

Cesare breathed in slow and deep and resisted the urge to ask her if she ever lightened up. It was something of a shock for him to discover that there was a woman alive utterly impervious to his looks and charisma. He didn't believe in false modesty and had been well aware since the teen years that he could attract women in droves, a success rating that had only been enhanced by his gradual rise to billionaire status. Lizzie, however, put out no encouraging vibes and was not remotely flirtatious.

Watching the cool forbidding expression spread across his lean bronzed face, Lizzie took fright and said, 'I'm sorry...I'm too worried about Archie to mind what I say. I didn't intend to be rude but you must understand that two people with as little in common as we have really do need a get-out clause when it comes to having a baby,' she framed with a shy upward glance. 'And if I agree to that, there would be additional safeguards I would require.'

'Such as?'

Lizzie breathed in deep. 'You would have to agree to take on the role of acting as a father to the child until it grew up. Obviously we'll marry and then divorce... whenever.' Lizzie shifted an uncertain hand. 'But a child has specific needs from a parent and those needs must be met with love and security from *both* of us. That would be quite a responsibility for you to take on for the next twenty years and I need to be sure that you're willing to accept that.'

A very faint darkening of colour across Cesare's spectacular cheekbones highlighted his discomfiture. He had assumed that Lizzie was planning to discuss the financial rewards for her willingness to fulfil the terms of the will and her true, infinitely more responsible and caring angle of interest had pierced him with a rare sense of guilt. 'Why are you so willing to take on that responsibility?' he prompted.

'I've always wanted a child of my own,' Lizzie responded, quite comfortable and secure in making that admission. 'But I don't really want a man to go *with* the child, so the arrangement you suggested would probably suit me best of all. At the same time I don't want to raise a fatherless child, so an occasional father such as you would be is even more acceptable.'

Cesare was quietly stunned by those statements. The women he socialised with were never so frank about a desire to conceive either now or in the future. He wondered if she was still in love with her ex or simply some sort of man-hater because it was unusual for so young a woman to decide that she wanted to live her life alone. And then in dawning dismay he heard himself say, 'Are you gay?'

Lizzie turned bright pink but recognised why he had interpreted her words in that light. 'No, that's not the problem,' she responded stiffly, determined to keep her reasons for her solitary choice of lifestyle strictly private. There was no requirement whatsoever for her to explain herself to him and she was grateful for the fact.

'If we had a child together, I would hope to meet all your expectations of a father,' Cesare informed her with quiet conviction. 'As it happens, I have a very good father of my own and appreciate the importance of the role he plays.'

Lizzie nodded. 'That was my only real concern… Oh.' She hesitated but there was no way of avoiding the most pressing requirement. 'If we're to proceed with this I'm afraid I'll need some money from you upfront. I have to be honest—we are all stony broke. My sister needs some cash to stay on at university and I'll have to rent a property in the village for my dad because when I leave, he'll be relinquishing the tenancy of the farm.'

Absorbing the fluctuating expressions of embarrassment and apprehension skimming her heart-shaped face, Cesare sent her a soothing smile. 'Naturally it's not a problem. I expected something of the sort.'

'You knew how we were fixed...*before* you visited?' Lizzie queried in surprise.

'I never enter a situation blind,' Cesare countered unapologetically.

Danny the vet appeared in the doorway. 'Archie will be out in a minute. My nurse is just finishing up with him. His leg's broken and he's had a blow to the skull, which means he's a little woozy, but other than that he seems fine.'

After the vet had explained his treatment and proffered medication for the coming days, Archie emerged in the nurse's arms, a cast attached to one small leg and a balloon collar round his neck to prevent him from nibbling at it. Lizzie gathered him close, tears tripping from her eyes again as she huskily thanked the older man while Cesare insisted on taking care of the bill.

'I'm very attached to Archie,' Lizzie explained, dashing tears of relief from her eyes with her elbow. 'You can drive back if you want. The keys are in my pocket.'

Cesare fished out the keys and unlocked the car. 'I was hoping you would fly back to London with me tonight.'

'*Tonight?*' Lizzie exclaimed in disbelief. 'That's impossible!'

'We have a tight time schedule. I have everything arranged. Is it really impossible?' Cesare prompted drily. 'You appear to have no presentable clothes and can't need to pack much.'

'But I have to sort out somewhere for Dad to live and move him out of the cottage.'

'I have staff who will hire professionals to deal with those tasks for you,' Cesare told her with complete cool. 'You've had your say. I have agreed to your terms and now I need you to come to London.'

It was bite-the-bullet time, Lizzie registered, angrily colliding with brilliant dark eyes as hard as jet. He was being unreasonable. Surely there was no excuse for such haste? But what choice did she have? The arrangement having been agreed, he was now in charge of events. 'I'll have to call in with my neighbour to ask him to look after the flock.'

'Andrew Brook?'

Lizzie stiffened. 'Yes.'

'Why did you break up?'

'That's private,' Lizzie told him waspishly.

Cesare gritted his teeth. 'We'll go and see him now, so that you can make your preparations.'

Lizzie left Archie asleep in the Land Rover. Esther opened the door and her look of dismay mortified Lizzie, although she had always been aware that Andrew's last-minute exchange of would-be wives had caused Esther almost as much heartache and humiliation as it had caused Lizzie. People had condemned Esther for sleeping with a man who was engaged to another woman. They had judged her even harder for falling pregnant and thereby forcing the affair into the open and some locals had ignored Esther ever since.

Andrew sprang up from the kitchen table while Lizzie carried out introductions whereupon Cesare startled her by taking charge. 'Lizzie and I are leaving for London tonight—we're getting married,' he explained. 'Lizzie wants to know if you'll take her sheep.'

Lizzie saw the surprise and relief darting across Esther's face and looked away again, her own colour high. Esther would be glad to see her leave the neighbourhood and she didn't feel she could really blame the other woman for that, not after the way people had treated her.

'This is a surprise and it calls for a celebration,' Andrew pronounced with genuine pleasure. 'I didn't even know you were seeing anyone, Lizzie.'

Home-made peach wine was produced. Cesare found it sickly sweet but he appreciated the sentiment while he watched and read his companions and made certain interesting deductions. Andrew Brook appeared fond of Lizzie but no more than that. Indeed his every look of warmth was for his wife, who was a rather plain, plump young woman who couldn't hold a candle to Lizzie in the looks department. Lizzie, on the other hand, Cesare could not read at all. She chatted but was clearly eager to leave as soon as was polite.

'Are you planning to enlighten me yet?' Cesare drawled when they returned to the Land Rover, his Italian accent licking round the edges of every syllable in the sexiest way imaginable.

Lizzie was bitterly amused by that stray thought when she didn't do sex or even know what sexy was. That had lain at the heart of her disastrous relationship with Andrew when she had learned that she was simply one of those women who did not like to be touched. She had assumed—*wrongly*—when she agreed to marry him that her own response would naturally change as time went on and they became closer. But that hadn't happened and her feelings hadn't changed.

'Andrew had an affair with Esther while we were engaged and she got pregnant. We broke up six weeks before our wedding day and he married her the following month. They're very happy together,' Lizzie explained flatly. 'That means I've got an unused wedding gown in my wardrobe, so I'll bring that down to London.'

'No!' Cesare sliced in with innate distaste. 'I will buy you another dress.'

'But that's silly and wasteful when there's no need for it!' Lizzie reasoned in bafflement.

'If we are trying to persuade my family that this is a genuine marriage, you will need a designer gown with all the usual trimmings.'

'But how could anyone possibly believe it was genuine? We're chalk and cheese and we only just met.'

'You'll be enjoying a full makeover in London and only my father knows when we first met. By the time I'm finished with you, they *will* believe, *cara*,' Cesare insisted.

'And what if I don't want a makeover?'

'If you want to be convincing in the role you're being paid to take, you don't have a choice,' Cesare told her softly. Of course she wanted a makeover, he thought grimly, unconvinced by her show of reluctance. She was willing to do just about anything for money. Hadn't she already demonstrated the fact? She was prepared to become a mother simply to sell the island to him. But then to be fair, he acknowledged, he was willing to become a father to buy Lionos although, in his case, he had additional and far more presentable motives.

What was the use of working so hard when he had

no heir to follow him? What easier way could he acquire a child to inherit his empire? He had seen too many marriages explode into the bitterness and division of divorce, heard too many stories about children traumatised by their parents splitting up. The will had given him a chance to avoid that kind of fallout *and* the imprisonment of taking 'for ever after' vows with one woman. A marriage that was a marriage only on paper and a child born prior to a low-key civilised divorce would suit Cesare's needs very nicely indeed.

Out of Cesare's response, only one phrase assailed Lizzie: *you're being paid*. It was an unwelcome but timely reminder and she chewed at her full lower lip, restraining a tart response. Hopefully within a couple of months he would have no further use for her and she would get her life back and, even more hopefully, a life that would stretch to include the sheer joy of becoming a mother for the first time. When that time came, maybe she would be able to find some sort of work training course and accommodation near Chrissie. Or maybe that was a bad idea, she reflected uneasily, suspecting that her sibling had the right to her independence without a big sister hovering protectively somewhere nearby.

'A moment before we go inside...' Cesare breathed, striding round the bonnet of the rusty farm vehicle.

A frown drew Lizzie's brows together as she hovered by the back door. When he reached out and tugged her close, Lizzie was so taken aback that she simply froze. His hands came up to frame her cheekbones and she gazed up into glittering golden eyes that reflected the lights shining out from the farmhouse windows, her nostrils flaring on the faint fresh scent of his cologne and the underlying hint of clean, fresh man.

At that point while she was mulling over why he smelled so good to her, Cesare lowered his proud dark head and kissed her. Lizzie stopped breathing in shock, electrified by the sensation and taste of his firm sensual mouth on hers with her heart hammering and her pulse racing as if she were riding a Big Dipper at an amusement park. He nibbled her lower lip and thunder crashed in her ears, the earth literally moving when he swiped his tongue along her full lower lip in an erotic flick that made her quiver like a jelly.

Forbidden warmth burst into being inside her, swelling her breasts, tightening her nipples, spearing down between her legs in a twin assault on her senses. A hard urgency now laced the passionate pressure of his mouth on hers and her head fell back, lips parting by instinct to welcome the deeply sensual dart of his tongue. He pulled her closer, welding her to every powerful line of his lean, powerfully masculine body with a big hand splayed across her hips to hold her in place and in spite of their clothing she felt his arousal, the hard, unmistakeable ridge between them. With almost superhuman force of will because she was on the edge of panic, Lizzie pressed her hand against his shoulder to push him back from her and, to be fair to him, he freed her immediately.

'That's enough,' she framed unevenly, her breath rasping in her tight throat as an ache of what she knew could only be dissatisfaction spread at the heart of her. 'Why the heck did you do that?'

'If we intend to fool people into crediting that we are a genuine couple, we have to be able to behave like a couple…at least, occasionally,' Cesare delivered with an audibly ragged hitch in his breathing.

'I don't like being touched,' Lizzie told him in a small flat voice.

You could've fooled me, Cesare thought in disbelief, still tasting the sweetness of her soft, lush lips and struggling to suppress the rush of hungry excitement that had lit him up like a burning torch.

She was out of bounds, he reminded himself stubbornly. He was not planning to bed her. She didn't want it and *he* didn't want it either. Regrettably his body was out of step with his brain, though, and somehow she exuded all the allure of a juicy hamburger to a very reluctant vegetarian. But, Cesare reminded himself stubbornly, he could get sex anywhere. He had Celine for uncommitted sexual satisfaction. He wasn't about to risk screwing up his marital arrangement with Lizzie by flirting with that kind of intimacy. It would blur the boundaries and she might start behaving like a real wife and even start thinking that she could attach strings to him.

'So, it was just a sort of test?' Lizzie gathered in relief, assuming that it was an approach that was unlikely to be repeated very often.

'You won the gold medal for excellence, *bella mia*,' Cesare quipped, striving to will his libido back down to a manageable level but that was a challenge while all he could think about, all he could see in his head, was Lizzie spread across a bed, stark naked and not only willing but also wild. The imagery didn't help, nor did it help that he knew he, who prided himself on his detachment in business situations, was indulging in a deeply improbable but very male fantasy.

Two hours later, Lizzie was seated in a limousine with Cesare in silence. Her case was stowed, Archie was asleep on her knee and Cesare was working on his laptop. She was still thinking about that kiss, wondering what magic spark Cesare had that Andrew had so conspicuously lacked. Was it truly just a case of physical chemistry?

Frustration filled Lizzie to overflowing. There had been very few men in her life, very few kisses and she was still a virgin. Andrew had repulsed her, yet he was a young, attractive man and she had loved him. Naturally, she had assumed that she simply wasn't a very sexual woman. But within seconds of Cesare kissing her, fireworks had gone off inside her in a rush of excitement unlike anything she had ever felt. And now, for the very first time in her life, she was studying a powerful masculine thigh and the distinctive bulge at the crotch and wondering what a man looked like naked. Colour washed in a veil to her hairline and she studied Archie instead, fondling a shaggy ear as the dog slept.

It was sexual curiosity, that was all. Silly, immature, she labelled with growing embarrassment, but nothing to really worry about. After all, nothing was going to happen with Cesare. And as for that moment of panic in his arms? One kiss and she imagined she was about to tumble into an adolescent infatuation as easily as her mother had once done? No, she was much too sensible for that, she told herself soothingly. Cesare was gorgeous and well-off and arrogant and he probably slept around as such men reputedly did. He was not her type at all...

Absolutely *not* his type, Cesare was reflecting with

satisfaction. One dynamite kiss didn't alter the fact that she dressed like a bag lady, had poor manners and barely a feminine bone in her body. Or that she treated him rather like a lost umbrella someone had left behind on a train seat...

CHAPTER FOUR

THE MAKEOVER, ALONG with the shopping and the ultra-grooming at a very fancy beauty salon, shook Lizzie to her very depths.

She was transformed and she knew it and was surprised by how very much better it made her feel to see herself polished to glossiness, with that awful brown dye gone from the last few inches of her pale silvery hair. Every time she had seen that dye in the mirror it had reminded her of Andrew and the bad times, so it was a relief to be finally rid of it and stop wondering if he ironically had tried to change *her* into Esther, who had mud-brown hair of no great distinction. She regarded her long, glittery nails with positive girlish delight because she had never known such beauty tweaking could transform her work-roughened hands. The calluses were gone as well, her entire skin surface buffed and moisturised to perfection. There was no doubt about it: it made her feel like a new woman, a woman of greater assurance than she had been when she first slunk through the doors of the salon, feeling like a crime against femininity in her untouched, unpolished state.

How would Cesare view her now?

Her cheeks flushed at the thought. Why should that matter to her? What was his opinion worth? Presumably without the polishing he wouldn't have wanted to be seen out with her in public and that was a lowering reflection, she acknowledged ruefully. She had been transformed and she appreciated it, best not to think too deeply beyond that, she decided wryly. And now all dressed up to the nines she felt more armoured to cope with the hen party ahead even if it was without the support of her sister.

Sadly, Chrissie had an exam the next day and there was absolutely no way she could join Lizzie and Cesare's sisters. Lizzie was disappointed. She liked Cesare's friendly siblings very much but they were still strangers and somewhat more uncomfortably, strangers she had to keep a front up with. They thought it was a normal wedding with a bride and groom in love and happy. Unfortunately, living up to that false expectation was a strain even on a shopping and beauty trip.

'You mean, you really *aren't* pregnant?' Sofia, Cesare's youngest half-sister, gasped as she watched Lizzie down a vodka cocktail with every sign of enjoyment. 'Cesare told us you weren't but we didn't believe him.'

'This conversation is not happening,' Paola groaned in apology, the eldest of the trio of sisters, a teacher and married woman and rather more circumspect than her single, fun-loving sisters in what she chose to say. 'I'm so sorry, Lizzie.'

Lizzie smiled, masking her loneliness and chagrin. 'It's all right. I'm not offended. I know you're surprised that your brother's getting married in such a hurry—'

'When we never thought he'd get married at all,' his third half-sister Maurizia slotted in frankly.

'Obviously he's nuts about you!' Sofia giggled. 'That's the only explanation that makes sense. When I sent him that photo of you all dressed up to go out tonight, he wasted no time telling me that he wanted you to stay at home and that he saw no reason for you to have a hen night.'

Of course Cesare didn't see any reason, Lizzie reflected ruefully, glugging her drink because she didn't know what to say to his very accepting and loveable sisters or indeed to his pleasant stepmother, Ottavia, none of whom had a clue that the wedding wasn't the real thing. She had guessed, however, that his father, Goffredo, was simply playing along with their pretence but she found that same pretence stressful and knew it was why she was drinking so much and living on her nerves. Luckily Cesare had not been required to put on much of an act, she conceded resentfully, as he had taken refuge in his city apartment, after marooning her in his unbelievably luxurious town house with his family, before flying off to New York on urgent business.

Apparently it was the norm for Cesare to move out of his flashy and huge town house into his exclusive city apartment when his family arrived for a visit. Lizzie had found that strange but his family did not, joking that Cesare had always liked his own space and avoided anything that might take his main focus off business, which evidently involved socialising with his family as well. Lizzie thought that was sad but had kept her opinion tactfully to herself.

He was *so* rich: in spite of the limo and the driver and the helicopter, she had had no idea *how* rich her future fake husband was. Lizzie was still in shock from travelling in a private jet and walking into a house the size of a palace with over ten en-suite bedrooms and innumerable staff. She had then done what she should have done a week earlier and had checked him out on the Internet, learning that he was the head of a business mega-empire and more in the billionaire than the multimillionaire category.

Indeed the house, followed by the experience of being literally engulfed by his gregarious family, had only been the first of the culture shocks rattling Lizzie's security on its axis. Two solid days of clothes shopping followed by a physical head-to-toe makeover had left its mark. For that reason it was hardly surprising that she should be at last enjoying the chance to relax and have a few drinks in good company for the first time in more years than she cared to count.

Seated on his jet, furiously checking his watch to calculate the landing time, Cesare enlarged the photograph on his tablet and scrutinised it with lingering disbelief.

Don't you dare take Lizzie out dressed like that to a club! he had texted his half-sister Maurizia, with a confusing mix of anger, frustration and concern assailing him in a dark flood of reactions that made him uncomfortable to the extreme.

He still couldn't take his eyes off the photograph: Lizzie smiling as he had never seen her and sheathed in an emerald-green, 'barely there', strappy short dress with perilous high heels on her shapely legs. It was an amazing transformation. A magic wand had been waved over the bag lady. She looked fantastic and would outshine every woman around her now that her natural beauty had been polished up and brought to the fore. Her glorious mane of hair had been restored as he'd instructed, *not* cut. It gleamed in a silken tumble of silver strands round her delicately pointed face, green eyes huge, pouty mouth lush and pink. Cesare swore under his breath, outraged by his sisters' interference and the hen-party nonsense. Lizzie was no more fit to be let loose in a London nightclub than a toddler and now he would have to go and retrieve her!

'You're not supposed to be here... This is *her* night!' one of his sisters carolled accusingly as soon as he arrived at the women's table.

'Where is she?' Cesare ground out, unamused, while he scanned the dance floor.

Looking daggers at her big brother, Sofia shifted a reluctant hand to show him. 'Don't spoil her night. She's having a whale of a time!'

Cesare centred his incredulous dark gaze on the sight of his bride-to-be, a pink hen-night sash diagonally dissecting her slender, shapely body as she danced, arms raised, silvery hair flying, feet moving in time to the fast beat. What infuriated him was the sight of the two men trying to attract her attention because she appeared to be dancing in a world of her own. Suddenly Lizzie teetered to a stop, clearly dizzy as she swayed on her very high heels. With a suppressed snarl of annoyance, Cesare, ignoring his siblings' wide-eyed disbelief at his behaviour, stalked across the floor to hastily settle steadying hands on Lizzie's slim shoulders.

'Cesare…' Lizzie proclaimed with a wide, sunny smile because it only took one lingering glance to remind her how tall, dark and sleekly gorgeous he was. He towered over her, lean bronzed face shadowed and hollowed by the flickering lights that enhanced his spectacular bone structure, stunning dark golden eyes intent on her. She was really, *really* pleased to see him, a familiar reassuring image in a new world that was unnervingly different and unsettling. In fact for a split second she almost succumbed to a deeply embarrassing urge to hug him. Then, luckily remembering that hugging wasn't part of their deal, she restrained herself.

'You're drunk,' his perfectly shaped mouth framed, destroying the effect of his reassuring presence.

'Of course I'm not drunk!' Lizzie slurred, throwing up her hands in emphasis only to brace them on his broad chest while she wondered why her legs wanted to splay like a newborn calf's trying to walk for the first time.

'You are,' Cesare repeated flatly.

'I'm *not*,' Lizzie insisted, holding onto his forearms to stay upright, her shoe soles still displaying a worrying urge to slide across the floor of their own volition.

'I'm taking you home,' Cesare mouthed as the deafening music crashed all around them.

'I'm not ready to go home yet!' she shouted at him.

Lizzie couldn't work out what Cesare said in answer to that declaration. His deep-set eyes glittered like banked-down fires in his lean, strong face and he had bent down and lifted her up into his arms before she could even begin to guess his intention.

'Think we're going home,' Lizzie informed his sisters forlornly from the vantage point of his arms as he paused by their table.

'You *didn't* look after her!' Cesare growled at one of his sisters, in answer to whatever comment had been made.

'What am I? A dog or a child?' Lizzie demanded, staring up at him, noticing that he needed a shave because a heavy five o'clock shadow outlined his lower jawline, making it seem even harder and more aggressive than usual. It framed his wide, sensual mouth though, drawing attention to the perfectly sculpted line of his lips. He kissed like a dream, she recalled abstractedly, wondering when he'd do it again.

'Think we should kiss so that your sisters believe we're a *real* couple?' Lizzie asked him winningly.

'If we were real, I'd strangle you, *cara*,' Cesare countered without hesitation. 'I leave you alone for three days and I come back and you're going crazy on the dance floor and getting blind drunk.'

'*Not* drunk,' Lizzie proclaimed stubbornly.

Cesare rolled his eyes and with scant ceremony stuffed her in the back of the waiting limousine. 'Lie down before you fall over.'

'You're so smug,' Lizzie condemned and closed her eyes because the interior of the limousine was telescoping around her in the most peculiar way.

Cesare consoled himself with the hope that such behaviour was not a warning sign of things to come. How could he blame her for wanting some fun? He had a very good idea of what life must have been like for her on that farm with her misery of a father, always there at her elbow, keen to remind her of every mistake and failure. For the very first time in his life he realised just how lucky he had been with Goffredo, who saw everything through rose-tinted, forgiving spectacles. In comparison, Brian Whitaker's view of life was seriously depressing.

Lizzie opened her eyes. 'Do you want to kiss me?' she enquired.

Cesare skimmed his disconcerted gaze to her animated features, taking in the playful grin she wore. 'Do you *want* me to kiss you?'

Lizzie flushed and shifted on the seat. 'You're not supposed to ask that.'

'You expect me to act like a caveman?'

Lizzie thought about that. She had rather enjoyed being carried out of the club. Was that weird? She scolded herself for that enjoyment while mustering up a dim memory of her mother giggling and tossing her hair, eyes sparkling at the latest man in her life. Inwardly she cringed a little from the comparison she saw.

'Only when you're sober and you know what you're doing,' Cesare extended infuriatingly.

'You believe I could only want to kiss you when I'm drunk?'

Cesare suppressed a groan and studied her. If truth be told, it would take very little encouragement for him to flatten her along the back seat and take inexcusable advantage of her delightfully feminine body. 'We have a business arrangement,' he reminded her doggedly, cursing the hot swell of the erection disturbing his poise because just the thought of doing anything to her turned him on hard and fast.

Her honey-brown lashes flickered. 'I'm open to negotiation.'

'*No*, you're not,' Cesare informed her grimly, lean bronzed face set in forbidding lines, mobile mouth compressed. 'There will be absolutely no negotiation on that score tonight.'

Was it so wrong, Lizzie asked herself, that she should want to experience just once what other women commonly experienced? She had always wanted to be normal, to *feel* normal. Was that wrong? Indecent? Her cheeks burned. Naturally she had picked him. *That* kiss... Somehow he had become her forbidden object of desire. How had that happened? Treacherous heat curling in her pelvis, Lizzie breathed in slow and deep.

Cesare watched her feathery lashes dip and the sound of her breathing slow as she slid into a doze. Well, he wouldn't be letting her loose around alcohol again. Sex, drink and business arrangements did not make for a rational or successful combination. And he was a *very* rational guy, wasn't he? Here he was being a saint and protecting her from doing something she would regret. Or would she? he wondered with inbred cynicism. She was a gold-digger, after all, and sure to be on a high after the orgy of spending that had centred on her in recent days.

He was acting against his own nature, he acknowledged grudgingly. In reality, he wanted to fall on her like a sex-starved sailor on shore leave and keep her awake all night. Instead he was likely to spend half the night in a cold shower. He should have made more of an effort to see Celine. Clearly, it was the lack of regular sex that was playing merry hell with his hormones.

Lizzie awakened as Cesare half walked, half carried her into the town house only to stop dead as Goffredo and his stepmother, Ottavia, appeared in the doorway of the drawing room.

'Your daughters are still partying,' Cesare announced. 'Lizzie was falling asleep, so I brought her home early.'

'Cesare is a party pooper,' Lizzie framed with difficulty.

Goffredo grinned and Ottavia chuckled and the older couple vanished back into the drawing room.

At the foot of the stairs, Cesare abandoned the pretence that Lizzie could walk unaided and swept her up into his arms.

'I like it when you do this,' Lizzie told him. 'It's so...so...masculine.'

'We are lucky you don't weigh more,' Cesare quipped, barely out of breath as they reached the top of the stairs.

A sudden lurch in the stomach region made Lizzie tense and she crammed a stricken hand to her mouth, mumbling, 'Cesare...'

To give him his due, Cesare was not slow on the uptake and he strode through the nearest door at speed and deposited her in a bathroom.

Lizzie was ingloriously ill. He pushed her hair out of the way, gave her a cloth, extended a toothbrush, which he unwrapped, and politely ignored her repetitive apologies for her behaviour. When she couldn't stand up again, he removed her shoes for her and supported her over to the sink.

'I don't make a habit of this,' she declared, rinsing her mouth several times over while hanging onto the vanity unit.

'I should hope not, *bellezza mia.*'

'What does that mean? The Italian bit?'

And he told her that it meant 'my beauty'.

'But that's a downright lie,' she protested, studying her bleary-eyed reflection in dismay. The make-up girl's artistry and the hairdresser's skill were no longer apparent in the flushed face, smudged eyeliner and tousled hair she now saw in the mirror.

'You need to lie down,' Cesare asserted, lifting her again so that the bathroom spun and then the bedroom that followed.

Lizzie lay flat and dead still on the bed, afraid to move lest her surroundings began revolving again. 'Where's Archie? I want Archie.'

'Archie stays downstairs.' Cesare reminded her of the household rule, announced by Primo, his imperturbable manservant, on the day she moved in.

'But that's just mean... He always sleeps with me,' she mumbled.

Cesare almost groaned out loud. She lay splayed across his bed, clearly trusting him when he didn't trust himself because she was displaying a wanton amount of bare slender thigh.

'If I can't have Archie for company, I'll have you,' Lizzie muttered. 'Lie down.'

Cesare snatched up the phone and issued a terse instruction. Within the space of a minute, Primo arrived at the door with Archie. Cesare clasped Archie and carried him over to the bed, whereupon the dog curled up obediently at Lizzie's feet with his head resting across her ankles.

'You should get into bed…you can't sleep in your clothes,' Cesare told her.

'Why not?'

Cesare released his breath in an exasperated hiss and came down on the bed beside her to run her zip down.

'What are you doing?' she whispered curiously as he smoothed the straps of the dress down off her slim shoulders.

'Making you more comfortable.' Business arrangement, *business* arrangement, bloody business arrangement, Cesare was dutifully repeating inside his head as he eased her out of the dress to expose a filmy and provocative bra and panties set in turquoise lace. He wasn't looking, he wasn't reacting, he told himself doggedly while his dark golden gaze clung of its own volition to the surprisingly full, plump curves swelling the lace cups, revealing pale pink nipples that made his mouth water and the shadowy vee at her crotch. He yanked the sheet over Lizzie's prone length so fast that she rolled and, having been disturbed and crammed in below the sheet without warning, Archie also loosed a whimper of complaint.

Lizzie stretched out a searching hand, her eyes closed. The room was going round and round and round behind her lowered eyelids and she felt lost and nauseous. 'Where you going?'

Weary after a day spent travelling and his last-minute sprint to deal with Lizzie, Cesare surrendered to the obvious. If he left her alone, might she wander off? Sleep on the floor? Have an accident? Stumble into the wrong bedroom? And what if she was sick again? 'I'm not going anywhere.' He stripped down to his boxers and lay down on the other side of the bed. A small, callused hand closed over the thumb of his right hand and held on tight. He wasn't used to sharing a bed and he liked his own space.

Lizzie settled up against a warm solid shape while Archie tunnelled below the sheet to settle down by a less restive set of feet.

Lizzie wakened with a desperate thirst at some timeless hour of the night while it was still dark. She slid her feet off the side of the bed, her soles finding the floor, and slowly straightened. A wave of dizziness immediately engulfed her and she compressed her lips hard, sober enough now to be furious with herself. Despite having hardly eaten all day she had foolishly downed all that alcohol and got carried away by the party atmosphere. Suppressing a groan of frustration, she fumbled for the switch on the bedside light and then stared in bewilderment round the unfamiliar room before focusing on the male sharing the wide bed with her.

Cesare was half naked and lying on top of the sheet she had been lying beneath. He was beautifully built with a broad bronzed torso and corded abdomen that rippled with lean muscle. One long, powerful, hair-roughened thigh was partially raised, the other flat. Unshaven, he exuded a rough, edgy masculinity that made her breath hitch in her throat as she peered down at him in the lamplight. His lashes were like black silk fans and almost long enough to touch his amazing cheekbones.

She remembered asking him if he wanted to kiss

her, absolutely angling for his attention, and she almost screamed out loud at that demeaning memory. She headed for the bathroom with hot cheeks and a frustrated sense of self-loathing and shame that she could have been so silly. Had she asked him to stay with her as well? For goodness' sake, it was obviously his bedroom and he had only brought her there the night before because it was the nearest option when she felt sick. Now he had seen her in her underwear and she was mortified, although not as mortified as she would have been had he removed that as well. Her head throbbing, she drank about a gallon of cold water and freshened up as best she could without her own toiletries. She crept out of the bathroom in search of something to wear so that she could return to her own room.

Tiptoeing like a cat burglar, she opened the door into a massive wardrobe and eased back a sliding door to yank a man's white shirt off a hanger. The bra was digging into her midriff and she released the catch and removed it and the panties, wondering if she dared go for a shower. Donning the shirt, she rolled up the sleeves and buttoned it.

Being around Cesare made her feel out of control but was that so surprising? She hadn't dated since Andrew, hadn't seen the point, and before him there had only been a handful of unremarkable men. In recent times, she had had no social outlets and had only occasionally left the farm. It cost money to socialise and there had been none to spare. Being with Cesare's light-hearted sisters had been so much fun that she had forgotten to monitor how much she was drinking. One glimpse of Cesare when she was in that weakened condition had had the same effect on her as a hit man shooting her directly between the eyes. He was a very good-looking male, that was all. Noticing the fact simply meant she was female and alive and not that she wanted to pursue anything with him.

Hovering by the bed, Lizzie tried to work out how to get Archie out from below the sheet without either hurting him or waking Cesare.

'What are you doing?' Cesare husked as she yanked at the sheet to try and reach her dog. Blinking up at her with frowning dark eyes, he lifted a muscular arm to check the gold watch he still wore. '*Inferno!* It's three in the morning.'

'I should go back to my own room.'

'Don't wake up the whole household. Stay and go back to sleep,' Cesare advised her drily, flipping onto his side in a display of indifference that made her grit her teeth.

Would she wake anyone up? Stifling a sound of frustration, Lizzie doused the light and snaked back below the sheet.

Early morning was sending pale light through the blinds when she next surfaced, feeling considerably healthier than she had earlier but decidedly overheated. An arm was draped round her ribcage and she was locked intimately close to a very male body, a very *aroused* male body. A surge of heat that had nothing to do with his higher temperature pooled in Lizzie's pelvis. She eased over onto her back and looked up unwarily into heavily fringed eyes the colour of melted bronze. Her throat ran dry, her breathing ruptured.

'You're a very restless sleeper, *cara mia*,' Cesare

censured softly, his breath fanning her cheek. 'I had to clamp you in one place to get peace.'

'Oh…' Lizzie framed dry-mouthed, entranced by her view of his lean, darkly handsome features in the golden dawn light, even her hearing beguiled by his melodic accent.

'Archie, on the other hand, sleeps like the dead and doesn't move at all,' Cesare quipped. 'I've never had a dog in my bed before.'

'There's a first time for everything.'

'First and *last*,' he stressed. 'Unfortunately you wouldn't settle without him last night.'

'I'm sorry I drank too much.' Colour slowly rose to drench her porcelain skin as he stared down at her. 'Was I really awful?'

Long fingers stroked her taut ribcage, making her violently aware of the breasts swelling mere inches above. 'No, you were bright and breezy until the alcohol took its toll.'

Her breathing pattern fractured as she felt her nipples pinch tight while a hot, achy sensation hollowed between her legs. 'I'm not used to drinking like that,' she muttered jaggedly.

His golden eyes smouldered down at her and a wicked grin slanted his shapely lips, ensuring that the rate of her heartbeat accelerated. 'Don't make a habit of it.'

'Of course, I won't,' she began with a frown, tightening every muscle in an urgent, almost panic-stricken attempt to smother the sexual responses trickling through her and awakening every skin cell.

Cesare, who planned everything in Machiavellian detail, had not planned to kiss Lizzie. Having decided

not to touch her, he fully expected to abide by that pro-
hibition because he virtually never gave way to im-
pulses. Unhappily for him, the burning desire to pin
Lizzie to the bed and have wild, sweaty sex with her
had no rational base: it was driven by pure instinct.
And when she shifted her hips below the shirt that had
most definitely ridden up to ensure that bare skin met
bare skin, Cesare was lost.

One minute, Lizzie was drowning in dark golden
eyes framed by lashes longer than her own and downright jealous of the fact, and the next Cesare brought
his mouth crashing down on hers with the kind of raw,
driving passion that she was defenceless against. It
was glorious and the taste of his tongue delving deep
into the moist interior of her mouth was unsurpass-
able and an intoxication in its own right.

He traced the pointed bud of a straining nipple
and her spine undulated of its own accord, sensation
piercing straight to her pelvis. Her breasts had suddenly become achingly sensitive to the palms cupping
them and the fingers tugging gently on the prominent tips. That felt amazingly good. A stifled gasp
was wrenched from low in her throat and her spine
arched, her body rising up to cradle his in an involuntary move of welcome as old as time. He skated
his fingers along a slender thigh to discover the hot
wet core of her, sliding between the delicate folds to
moisturise the tiny bud of thrumming nerve endings
above with a skilled fingertip.

Lizzie tore her lips from his to cry out, hungry beyond bearing for that sensual touch and plunging her
fingers into his tousled black hair to hold him to her.
She was no more capable of thinking about what she

was doing than she was of stopping breathing on command. Her heart was thumping, her ragged gasping breaths audible, her entire body was tingling madly with seething heat and need. With his free hand, he ripped at the buttons of the shirt. The shirt fell partially open, exposing the rounded fullness of a breast crowned by a pale pink nipple. He closed his mouth there, teasing the distended bud with the flick of his tongue and the graze of his teeth while his fingers stoked an erotic blaze at her feminine core. She shuddered, talon claws of fierce need biting into her, shock assailing her that anything physical could feel so intense that she could neither fight it nor control it.

'I love the way you respond to me, *mi piace*,' Cesare growled with satisfaction while switching his attention between her pouting breasts and sending fantastic ripples of ravishing sensation right down to her unbearably hot core.

Lizzie couldn't find her voice, her breath or a single functioning brain cell. Her entire being was welded to his every caress, wanting, needing more. And kissing an erotic path down over her flat, quivering stomach, Cesare gave her much more and she didn't have the strength of will to deny him.

With ruthless cool he zeroed in on the tender heart of her with every weapon in his erotic mastery, stroking delicate flesh with his tongue and his mouth and his expert fingers. Lizzie careened into shock at the intimacy and then moaned below the onslaught of wicked, delirious excitement. Intense pleasure followed, sweeping her up into a wild, yearning climb towards a peak that she felt she would never reach. But that climb was unstoppable. Suddenly her body wasn't her own any more and she was flying like a comet into the sun in a climax so powerful it brought shaken tears of reaction to her eyes.

Still ragingly aroused, Cesare sprang out of bed, his fists angrily clenched. What the hell had he been thinking of? No matter how great the temptation, he should *never* have touched her. They had a business agreement and a planned marriage of convenience ahead of them. They were not lovers, not friends with benefits. He did not want to muddy the waters with the kind of physical intimacy that women often assumed meant more than it did. If he wasn't careful, he might find himself more married than he had ever wanted to be, he acknowledged grimly.

Paralysed by a crazy sense of peace in the aftermath of orgasm, Lizzie closed her eyes, her body still trembling from the sweet aftermath of agonising pleasure. The mattress gave but she didn't open her eyes again until a phone rang, shattering her dream state. The phone fell silent in answer to a man's voice speaking Italian. Her lashes lifted then and she stared at Cesare while he paced the floor, mobile phone clamped to his ear. He still wore his boxers and his state of arousal was blindingly obvious. An almost painful tide of colour burned her face.

He tossed the phone down by the bed. 'Do you want the shower first?'

That prosaic question made Lizzie frantically pull the edges of the shirt she wore closed and she sat up in an agony of discomfiture. 'I'll go back to my own room.'

As she scrambled out of bed and reached for Archie, Cesare murmured without any expression at all, 'We made a mistake and we won't repeat it.'

Clutching Archie in an awkward hold, Lizzie attempted to pick up her discarded clothing one-handed. 'Is that all you've got to say?' she prompted shakily.

'It was just sex...nothing worth fussing over,' Cesare opined in a tone that was as cold as a winter shower on her overheated skin. 'Look, I'll see you downstairs in an hour. I have some papers you have to sign before I leave.'

'You're going away again?' she asked in surprise, fighting the roar of temper rising from a secret place deep down inside her.

'We have forty-eight hours to go before the wedding and I intend to use it,' he advanced calmly, deepset dark eyes hooded, wide, sensual mouth clenched hard.

Just sex...nothing worth fussing over? Lizzie mulled that putdown over while she showered. She wasn't hurt by his dismissal, of course she wasn't. *A mistake that would not be repeated.* Didn't she feel the same way as he did? What had happened shouldn't have happened. It was much more sensible if they stayed uninvolved and detached. So, if he had left her feeling a little crushed and foolish, it was her own fault for acting like an idiot and inviting such a denouement. If she couldn't quite shake off the sense of intimacy he had imbued her with, it was only because she had been more intimate with him than she had ever been with anyone else but that was a secret not for sharing...

CHAPTER FIVE

LIZZIE FASTENED THE cropped trousers and straightened the lilac cashmere sweater she wore with it. Her feet shod in flat ballerina pumps, her face lightly made up, she bore not the smallest resemblance to the woman she had been a mere week earlier.

Of course she was now in possession of a vast wardrobe and owned a choice of outfits for every conceivable occasion. Most probably many of the garments would never be worn because she could not imagine Cesare taking her sailing or out to dinner or indeed to the kind of dressy venue where she would require a full-length gown. The wardrobe was totally wasteful in its size and probable expense but she had already learned that once Cesare had instructed his underlings that she was to be dressed from head to toe in designer fashion, his orders were carried out without question.

A pity she was a little more rebellious in that line, Lizzie acknowledged wryly. A lifetime of counting the pennies meant that extravagance made her feel guilty. Breakfast in bed made her feel even guiltier although, to be honest, any excuse to escape the ghastly prospect of having to breakfast alone with Cesare had been extremely welcome.

After all, she had made a huge fool of herself the night before, hadn't she?

Lizzie inwardly cringed, colour marking her cheeks afresh. It would be a very long time, if ever, before she contrived to forget how she had writhed in ecstasy in Cesare's bed. But mercifully, they hadn't actually got as far as having full sex, she reminded herself bracingly, and she assumed that that reality would make it a little easier for her to reinstate normal boundaries between them. She was no natural wanton, never had been, had simply let alcohol, curiosity and temptation steer her briefly in the wrong direction. She wasn't like her mother either because she was not prone to sudden blinding infatuations. For years, there had been no other man for her but Andrew, a reality that had made the slow death of their relationship all the more painful to endure because it had started out with such high hopes.

It offended her sense of decency, however, that the intimacy she had shrunk from exploring with Andrew, whom she had loved, could be so very tempting when offered by a male like Cesare Sabatino, who had no respect for her at all. Cesare didn't give two hoots what happened to her or how she felt about any issue. Cesare merely wanted to *use* her to regain the island of Lionos and he thought that paying her richly for the privilege should take care of any doubts she might have.

'Mr Sabatino is in the office at the end of the corridor,' Primo informed her as she reached the foot of the grand staircase.

Almost sick with self-consciousness, Lizzie found the door ajar and walked in without knocking. Cesare's arrogant dark head flew up from his laptop, subdued fire flaring in his dark, glittering eyes at the interruption until he realised who his visitor was. A wellbred smile lightened his darkly handsome features and curved his hard mouth as he leapt upright, his attention automatically pinning to the lissom curves revealed by the casually elegant outfit she wore. In startling comparison a pink and white X-rated image of Lizzie splayed across his bed erupted at the back of Cesare's mind and he ground his teeth together as his body leapt in response to the provocation. Not for the first time he regretted the interruption that had left him burning with sexual frustration.

When he had last called Celine, he had grasped that he had a problem he had not foreseen. Aware that he was getting married, his French lover no longer wished to be seen in his company. Celine guarded her reputation because the clients who paid her a small fortune to advertise their exclusive perfume were conservative and Cesare had perfectly understood her determination to put her career first. It was, nonetheless, a challenge for him to work out how he was to cope for the next few months being married and *not* married at the same time.

He had not gone without sex for more than a couple of weeks since he was a teenager. Was he now supposed to sneak around seeking a discreet outlet? Without a doubt, he would have to avoid being seen consorting with any woman other than his wife or their marriage would appear dubious and, after going to such lengths to bring about the marriage, that was not a risk he was prepared to take. Whether he liked it or not and whether anything came of it or not, Lizzie was his only option for the foreseeable future, he acknowledged grudgingly.

'You look terrific, *cara*,' Cesare told Lizzie truthfully, politely tugging out a chair for her to use. The jasmine scent of her perfume flared his nostrils and before he could suppress the memory he recalled the wild, hot sweetness of her response. No man could easily forget that kind of passion, he reasoned, exasperated by his stubborn libido and the effect those turbulent hormones had on his usually cool intellect.

'Thanks but it's all fancy packaging, not really me,' Lizzie parried uncomfortably, because he was towering over her and close enough that she could smell the citrusy cologne that overlaid the erotic undertones of clean, warm male. Her colour fluctuating, she sat very straight-backed in her seat.

'Learn how to accept a compliment gracefully,' Cesare advised softly. 'You have a great figure, gorgeous hair and a beautiful face. Clothes merely provide an effective frame for the looks that nature gave you.'

Lizzie dealt him a pained half-smile. Unlike her, he was a master of the ready word and the right thing to say and had probably never been stuck for a quote in his entire gilded life. She evaded his shrewd gaze because she felt vulnerable, almost naked in his presence, stripped as she was of her usual working clothing and countryside assurance because his privileged world was so foreign to hers. She loved the way good clothes that fitted perfectly made her feel, but she wondered if he would still want her without that superficial gloss, a thought that made her feel inadequate and a little pathetic. In short, the spectacular luxury of his home, the costly garments and the preponderance of staff made Lizzie feel out of her depth and drowning. All she had required to crown her discomfiture was that ill-judged sexual episode that morning. 'I want you to sign these documents.' Evidently impervious to the unease afflicting Lizzie, Cesare extended a slim sheaf of papers. 'I need your permission to make alterations to the villa on Lionos.'

Her brow furrowed in surprise. 'Alterations? But you haven't even *seen* the house yet.'

'Because we won't be married until Friday,' Cesare pointed out drily. 'While we're on our honeymoon in Italy, my grandmother will be having her surgery and recuperating. As soon as she is strong enough we will fly out to Lionos and stay in the villa with her.'

'I didn't realise we were having a honeymoon.'

'It will only be a honeymoon in the eyes of the outside world,' Cesare qualified wryly.

'And your grandmother falls into that category too?' Lizzie checked.

'I've already explained that,' Cesare reminded her. 'For all that Athene's strong, she's an old lady. I don't want her to guess that our marriage is a fake. If she knew the truth she'd feel responsible and unhappy.'

'I can understand that.' Lizzie studied him uneasily. He emanated sleek, expensive elegance in a black business suit that outlined his broad shoulders, narrow hips and long, powerful legs to perfection but, unfortunately for Lizzie, she was still seeing him in his form-fitting boxers, an energising image of him half-naked and rampant with masculine potency. She chewed hard at the soft underside of her lower lip, fighting her awareness and her disobedient and thoroughly embarrassing thoughts.

'Before we can stay at the villa, however, some improvements must be made to the accommodation and for that I require your permission as the property belongs to you and your sister.'

'What sort of improvements?' Lizzie prompted with a frown.

'I want to send Primo out to the island immediately with a team of kitchen and bathroom specialists. The house needs to be brought up to date before we can live there and I want to ensure that Athene enjoys her stay.'

'But won't she be sentimental about changes being made to the house where she grew up?' Lizzie asked in surprise.

'That's a fair point but times have changed since she was a girl and I believe she'll recognise that. She's a practical woman and she likes her comforts.'

'From what my mother said, most of the soft furnishings will need to be replaced as well,' Lizzie told him in wry warning. 'Drapes, beds, sofas. I don't think it's possible to achieve so much within such a short time frame and if you don't watch out…once you start removing fitments, the villa will quickly become uninhabitable.'

His supreme assurance untouched, Cesare dealt her an amused smile. 'Believe me, if I'm prepared to throw enough money at the problem, someone will accept the challenge, *cara*.'

Lizzie shrugged because it was immaterial to her what he chose to have done to a house that she had never seen and would only briefly visit. But it was a painful reminder that Cesare only wanted her because she owned the island and could sell it to him if he married her and nobody, but nobody, could make a relationship out of that, she told herself wretchedly. None of her anxious feelings showing on her face, she dutifully scribbled her signature in the indicated places and provided her sister's address for the documents to be couriered to her.

A wholehearted smile softened her taut mouth when Archie poked his head round the door and trotted across the polished wooden floor to greet his mistress.

Cesare watched the dog receive a warm welcome and decided it was educational. Archie looked pathetic with only three working legs and the fourth in a cast and the dog played his advantage for all he was worth, rolling his tummy up in the air to be petted and then struggling pitifully to get up off the floor again. Cesare bent down to lift the terrier and help him upright again. In reaction to his sudden proximity, Lizzie rammed her chair back out of the way, her nervous response setting Cesare's teeth on edge as he straightened again.

Lizzie collided with stunning dark golden eyes fringed with black velvet lashes and forgot how to breathe, feverish tension snaking through her every muscle as she rose hurriedly from her chair again and moved towards the door, keen to be gone.

'Your father and your sister will be attending the wedding?' Cesare sought confirmation.

'Yes…' Lizzie coughed to clear her convulsed throat. 'And I'll ring Chrissie now to explain about the papers she has to sign.'

'I doubt if I'll see you again before we meet at the church on Friday,' Cesare imparted softly. 'Somehow try to practise not leaping away when I come close. It's a dead giveaway that our relationship is a sham.'

Lizzie flushed with mortification. 'Then practise keeping your distance,' she advised.

Well, that was telling him, Cesare conceded grimly. She was angry with him. He had been less than diplomatic after that phone call that interrupted them earlier that day. He ground his even white teeth together. He had only told the truth. Did women always punish men for telling the truth? If their arrangement was to work, however, he would need to make more of an effort to sustain their relationship, he acknowledged grudgingly. Women were emotional creatures. Her anxious, uneasy attitude towards him had just underlined that unwelcome reality.

Furthermore, Lizzie might be a gold-digger who had chosen money over ethics when given the choice, but how could he blame her for that when she had lived in poverty for so many years? It was not a crime for her to seek to better herself. And how could he fault her avaricious streak when, without it, she would have sent him and his proposition packing? It was unjust of him to view her in the same unforgiving light as the many mercenary women who had shared his bed, he conceded wryly. Serafina, after all, had made a straight-up choice to ditch Cesare and marry a man who had been much wealthier, even though he was also much older. He had to be less judgemental and more generous to Lizzie. In any case, as his wife and potentially the future mother of his child, Lizzie was also the equivalent of a long-term project. Somehow he would have to make her happy and *keep* her happy, because if he didn't all his plans could still come to nothing.

* * *

'You look totally amazing!' Chrissie exclaimed as Lizzie spun to show off her wedding gown, slender shoulders and arms sheathed in the finest see-through lace, her tiny waist accentuated by the fullness of her skirt.

'My brother's a closet romantic. He's going to love that dress,' Maurizia forecast as a knock sounded on the door and she and Sofia went to answer it.

'I'm having so much fun. I wish I hadn't put that exam ahead of attending your hen do,' Chrissie lamented, a slight willowy figure in the topaz-coloured bridesmaid dress that she and Cesare's sisters all wore.

Lizzie gazed fondly at her sister, thinking that she was the real beauty in the family with her perfect features and superior height.

'A pressie for you from Cesare,' Sofia announced, placing a jewel case in Lizzie's hands.

A gloriously delicate diamond necklace and drop earrings met Lizzie's stunned appraisal and a chorus of admiration rose from her companions. Of course, Cesare was playing to the gallery, assuming the role of besotted bridegroom for his siblings' benefit, Lizzie guessed. She put on the necklace and the earrings and realised that she was rather pathetically wishing that her wedding were the genuine article. She loved Cesare's family and would have given just about anything for them to be her family as well. Instead she had to live with the unlovely truth that she was deceiving them and would soon be deceiving Cesare's grandmother as well.

'You're really sure about doing this?' Chrissie whispered in the church porch as she made an unnecessary adjustment to Lizzie's gown while their father hovered, looking irritable. 'Because it's not too late to change your mind. All I have to do is call a taxi and we're out of here.'

'Are you trying to cause trouble? Of course, she's not going to change her mind!' Brian Whitaker declared in exasperation. 'That Sabatino fellow has to be the best thing that ever happened to her! At least he has an ounce of sense between his ears.'

'*We* certainly think so,' Paola piped up without hesitation. 'But sometimes the bride does get cold feet.'

'Not this one,' Lizzie countered steadily, smoothing over the awkwardness that had settled over the bridal party with her father's tactless words.

Cesare turned to look at Lizzie only when she reached the altar. Eyes the colour of melted bronze assailed her and she stopped breathing, gripped by the ferocious force of will in that appraisal. He had no doubts, she interpreted. He knew exactly what he was doing, had come to terms with the drawbacks and was concentrating on the end game. She had to do the same, she told herself urgently. She had to stop trying to personalise their relationship and stop wondering whether or not he would kiss her after they had been pronounced man and wife. Such treacherous thoughts were far removed from businesslike behaviour and utterly inappropriate, she scolded herself in exasperation.

'You look fantastic,' Cesare murmured softly while he threaded the wedding band onto her finger and she followed suit, copying his manoeuvre with less cool and more nerves.

Indeed, Cesare was taken aback by just how fabulous she looked. The effect she had on him was ever so slightly unnerving. It was his libido, he told himself impatiently. As long as he stuck to his rules of never getting tangled in anything that smacked of an emotional connection, he would be fine and perfectly happy.

And then the deed was done and they were married and there was no kiss, nor indeed any instruction to kiss the bride. Her hand trembling on Cesare's arm, she walked down the aisle, seeing a sea of smiling faces on every side of her. It was not her idea of a small wedding because the big church was crammed with guests. Out on the steps, Cesare escorted a tiny woman with vibrant brown eyes set in a round wrinkled face to meet her.

'Athene…meet Elisabetta, known as Lizzie,' he murmured quietly. 'Lizzie, this is my grandmother.'

The two women stood chatting about nothing in particular for several minutes beneath Cesare's watchful eye. Athene grinned at Lizzie. There was an astonishing amount of mischief in that unexpected grin and she squeezed Lizzie's hand. 'We'll talk later,' she promised cheerfully.

Later became much later once the bridal merry-go-round took over. The bride and groom greeted their guests at the country house hotel chosen to stage the reception, dined in splendour while being entertained by a famous singer, listened to the speeches and danced the first dance with Lizzie stumbling over her own feet. In the circle of Cesare's powerful arms and surrounded by so many well-wishers, Lizzie had to struggle to remember that their wedding was a fake.

In fact when Cesare lowered his darkly handsome

head and kissed her, Lizzie was so unprepared for the move and so taken back by it she fell into it like a child falling down a bottomless well. His mouth moved on hers and his tongue darted across the roof of her mouth and excitement leapt so high inside her she felt dizzy and intoxicated, her head tilting back, her hands tightening round his neck, fingertips flirting with the silky strands of his black hair. It was heavenly and devastating; heavenly to glory in her womanhood and appreciate that she had now discovered her sensual side and devastating to register that the wrong man was punching her buttons, simply to impress their audience.

In passionate rejection of that belittling image, Lizzie jerked her head back and pressed him back from her. 'Enough...' she muttered unsteadily.

'*Dio mio*, not half enough for me, *bellezza mia*,' Cesare rasped in a driven undertone. 'I want you.'

Lizzie had become as stiff as a board. 'We talked about that and decided that it wasn't sensible.'

'To hell with being sensible!' Cesare shot back at her with smouldering dark golden eyes framed by black velvet lashes, so breathtakingly handsome in that moment that he took her breath away. 'Passion isn't sensible...don't you know that yet?'

No, but he was teaching her what she had never wanted to know. Experimentation was acceptable to Lizzie as long as she remained in control. She didn't want to be out of control, didn't want to risk getting hurt or making a fool of herself again. Suddenly all her worst fears were coalescing in the shape of Cesare Sabatino and she had only gone and married the guy!

Sofia approached her. 'Athene wants you to come

and sit with her for a while. I expect she wants to get to know you... Cesare is by far her favourite grandchild.'

Lizzie rolled her eyes in sympathy. 'He's the only boy.'

'She practically raised him—that's why they're so close,' Sofia explained. 'Cesare was only four when our mother married his father and although he was supposed to come and live with our parents straight away, he and Athene kept on putting it off and Papa didn't like to interfere too much. Cesare's never been easy—he and Papa are so different.'

'Goffredo is a pet,' Lizzie said warmly. 'You're so lucky.'

'Cesare's too clever for his own good,' his sister opined. 'Papa was in awe of his brain and he was such an argumentative little boy.'

A smile of amusement tilted Lizzie's mouth. 'I can imagine. He likes everything his own way.'

Athene patted the comfortable armchair beside her own. 'Tell me about yourself. I'm a typical nosy old lady,' she confided. 'You talk and I ask the questions.'

Naturally there were questions about Lizzie's mother, whom Athene had met while Goffredo was dating her.

'My son could not have made her happy.' Cesare's grandmother sighed with regret. 'Francesca was always dissatisfied and she was disappointed that Goffredo already had a son. I wasn't that surprised when she broke off the engagement.'

'She wasn't happy with anyone for very long,' Lizzie admitted quietly.

'That must have been very difficult for you and your sister when you were growing up. The things that happen when you're young leave scars,' Athene remarked wryly. 'I believe that's why it's taken so long for Cesare to put Serafina behind him where she belongs…'

'Serafina?' Lizzie queried tentatively, wondering worriedly if this was some family story that she should have been acquainted with and if her ignorance would strike the older woman as suspicious.

'I didn't think he would've mentioned her to you,' Athene told her with a wry smile. 'Cesare hides his vulnerabilities very effectively.'

Lizzie resisted the temptation to admit that she hadn't believed he had any.

'Cesare fell in love with Serafina when he was a student. He wanted to marry her but she said she was too young,' Athene related, her wise old eyes resting on Lizzie's absorbed expression. 'In her first job, she met a very rich man in his seventies and within weeks they were wed.'

Lizzie froze in consternation. 'That must've been devastating for him,' she muttered ruefully, thinking that she had unkindly misjudged Cesare when she had assumed he simply had no heart and no room in his life for anything but business and profit.

'But today I know that he has finally put Serafina back where she belongs in the past,' his grandmother proclaimed with satisfaction and patted Lizzie's hand. 'Today I am joyful that Cesare has married you and changed the whole course of his life for the better.'

Lizzie suppressed a groan of disagreement. She was discovering where Goffredo's optimistic outlook came from—he had inherited it from his mother. It was a source of wonder to her that Cesare had grown up surrounded by people with such sunny natures and yet contrived to retain his cold, unemotional attitude to life. Yet he was also careful to maintain a certain distance from his loving family, she conceded reflectively, wondering if he secretly feared that his family loving softness might dull his own ruthless cutting edge.

A couple of hours after that, Lizzie boarded Cesare's private jet. Her feet, shod in spindly high heels, were killing her. Even the short walk through the airport had been too much and she collapsed into her leather upholstered seat and kicked off her shoes with intense relief.

'You did very well today,' Cesare pronounced, disconcerting her as he took his own seat opposite. 'I don't think anyone suspected the truth.'

'Your father knows,' she reminded him uncomfortably.

'He'll believe the truth for all of ten minutes. Give him a few weeks and he'll persuade himself that we fell madly in love within hours of getting married,' Cesare forecast with sardonic bite. 'That's the way Goffredo functions.'

'You have a lovely family,' Lizzie countered, colour springing into her cheeks. 'Don't be so critical. They love you very much and they aren't afraid to show it.'

Cesare stiffened until he recalled his father-in-law's behaviour throughout the day. Brian Whitaker had turned down the opportunity to make a speech, had kept to his own company in the midst of the crowd and had steadfastly managed not to smile even for the photographs. 'Your father's…different,' he conceded quietly. 'Not the demonstrative type.'

'When my mother left him, it soured him on life,' she muttered ruefully. 'And life has been tough for him ever since. He'll be more content living in the house he's hoping to rent in the village. I think it will be a relief for him not to be looking out of windows at the farm and fretting about the jobs I'm not getting done.'

'Isn't it a relief for you as well?' Cesare prompted, thinking of the long and gruelling hours of work she must have endured while she endeavoured to keep the farm going without help.

Lizzie compressed her lips and frowned reflectively. 'From dawn to dusk I worried about everything and anything and I'm not sorry to be free of that stress. The bank threatening to withdraw the loan was our biggest fear but then the rent was raised...and, that was a body blow, totally the last straw,' she confided honestly. 'That was followed by Chrissie announcing that she was going to drop out of uni and come home because we were having such a struggle. I couldn't let that happen. She *needed* to get her education.'

Cesare was listening intently. 'So that's why you suddenly changed your mind and agreed to marry me?' he breathed in a tone of disconcertion. 'I had no idea that you were under that much financial and emotional pressure.'

'But you said you *knew* our situation,' she reminded him in surprise. 'I assumed you'd used a private investigator to check us out before you came to visit.'

Level dark eyes gazed back at her, a frown line pleating his ebony brows. 'No, I didn't. I didn't know about the bank loan, the rent rise or your sister's plans to drop out. I only knew about your father's ill health and that you were trying to keep the farm afloat on your own.'

'Well, you know the whole story now,' Lizzie commented mildly. 'I was ready to sell my soul for thirty pieces of silver.'

'No,' Cesare contradicted, his sibilant Italian accent vibrating in the silence to send a current of awareness travelling down her slender spine. 'You were desperate to protect your family, regardless of what it might cost you personally. That's loyalty and I admire that trait.'

As the silence stretched, Cesare went back to work at his laptop. Driven by something stronger than he was, he found himself glancing up to watch Lizzie leaf through a glossy fashion magazine, pulling faces whenever she came on a picture of any garment she considered too extreme while absently fondling Archie's ear beneath his balloon collar. She was so very natural. What you saw was what you got from Lizzie Whitaker and he had totally misunderstood her. It was a sobering discovery for a male who prided himself on his ability to read others. He had made all too many assumptions about Lizzie, not least that she was a gold-digger, and now that he had discovered that she had been driven more by desperation than greed his innate curiosity about her was finally set free.

'Why did you dye your hair brown?' he asked her abruptly.

Lizzie twined a shining silver strand round a self-conscious finger and winced in evident embarrassment. 'Andrew didn't like my hair. He thought it attracted too much attention and that it looked white and made people think I was an old lady at first glance,' she told him uncomfortably. 'I could see his point.'

'Did you really want to please him that much?' Cesare pressed. 'Your hair's beautiful, unusual but undeniably beautiful, *cara*.'

Lizzie shrugged but her face glowed at the compliment. His lean, darkly handsome features held her intent gaze and she switched her attention back to the magazine, a pool of liquid heat gathering in her pelvis that made her squirm with chagrin. He was so very, *very* good-looking, it was natural for her to stare a little, she told herself ruefully, but she had to keep her feet on the ground and learn to distinguish between what was real and what was more probably fake.

The limousine that collected them from the airport in Italy wended its way along winding roads and through some spectacular scenery. It was late spring and the fields were green with fava beans and wheat dotted with yellow broom. Medieval villages in picturesque hilltop locations were ringed by vineyards and olive groves while the rolling hills were covered with groves of cypresses and umbrella pines. Lizzie was enchanted and plied Cesare with questions.

'You still haven't told me where we're going,' she complained.

'We're almost there.'

Lizzie stared out at the rustic stone farmhouse on the ridge of the hill and blinked because it was not what she expected. Cesare was so sophisticated that she had been convinced that they were heading for some exclusive spa. 'It just doesn't look like your style,' she breathed helplessly.

'I love old buildings. When I first saw it I was a

student out hiking with friends. The roof had fallen in, the first floor had gone and the end wall had collapsed. We took shelter in the barn during a thunderstorm,' Cesare explained as the driver turned down a dirt track that steadily climbed the hill. 'I watched the sun go down over the valley and swore I'd buy it with my first million.'

'Your first...*million*?' she exclaimed.

'It was a money pit,' Cesare told her cheerfully, his dark eyes gleaming with rueful amusement. 'I learnt that the hard way.'

The car drew up in a paved courtyard ornamented with urns full of tumbling flowers. As they climbed out, a rotund little woman in an apron hurried out to greet them. Her name was Maria and she was the housekeeper and, seemingly, Cesare's biggest fan. Ushered into a great vaulted hall, Lizzie looked around herself with keen interest, glancing through to a gracious drawing room rejoicing in a vast pale stone fireplace and an array of vibrant turquoise sofas. The outside might be antique and rustic but the inside was all contemporary elegance.

Maria led her upstairs and into a glorious light-filled bedroom with a window overlooking the valley below. Lizzie fingered the fine white linen bedding and admired the beautifully draped bed while wondering where Cesare was planning to sleep. The driver brought their cases up, closely followed by Cesare, lean and lithe in khaki chinos and an open-necked shirt that screamed Italian designer style.

'Where's your room?' Lizzie asked quietly.

'We *share*,' Cesare told her without skipping a beat.

'I'm not sharing a bed with you!' Lizzie gasped in consternation.

'We're supposed to be married. Let's stay in role,' Cesare fielded. 'Having gone this far, it would be stupid to take risks by using separate bedrooms.'

Lizzie kicked off her shoes and mulled over that argument. 'Maria's not going to talk.'

'She's not the only member of staff with access to the upper floor,' he shot back drily.

'OK…' Lizzie stood at the foot of the bed, prepared to admit that it was huge, but she was still doubtful that she could lose him in it. 'But you have to stay on *your* side of the bed.'

'Are we five years old now?' Cesare quipped, studying her with incredulity. 'You're making a fuss about nothing.'

Lizzie settled glinting witch-green eyes on him. 'I'm not used to sharing a bed. It's not nothing to me.'

'We'll discuss it over dinner,' Cesare decreed.

Lizzie threw her arms wide in emphasis, her temper mounting. 'I don't want to discuss it…I just don't want to do it!'

'Only forty-eight hours ago, you *did*,' Cesare countered, lean, strong face hard, dark golden eyes smouldering with recollection and unforgotten hunger.

Lizzie reddened. 'I was wondering how long it would take you to throw that back in my face. I was drunk, for goodness' sake,' she protested.

'At least you know what you want when you're drunk,' he riposted.

Lizzie slammed shut the door lest they be overheard arguing. 'That's a horrible thing to say!'

'Whether you like it or not, it's the truth. You want

me every bit as much as I want you. You just won't admit it.'

Lizzie was so enraged by that arrogant statement that she walked into the bathroom and closed the door behind her to escape him. The fixtures took her breath away. An antique tub took up prime position by the window while rustic stone walls and a pale marble floor provided an effective frame.

'And hiding in the bathroom isn't going to persuade me otherwise!' Cesare completed loudly outside the door.

Lizzie threw open the door again and marched out with compressed lips to drag one of the cases across the beautiful oak floor. 'I was *not* hiding.'

Cesare snatched up the case and planted it on the bed, helpfully springing the locks for her.

Lizzie hovered, her colour high, her eyes veiled.

Cesare stalked closer like a predator about to spring and she tensed from head to toe. 'Look at me, *bellezza mia*,' he urged.

Almost involuntarily, Lizzie lifted her head, platinum hair flying back from her heart-shaped face. 'Why?' she said flatly.

Lean brown hands lifted to frame her cheekbones and turn her face up. A muscle pulled taut at the corner of his wide, sensual mouth. 'I want to make a baby with you the normal way. I don't want to use artificial insemination. If we're going to become parents, let's try the natural approach first.'

He had taken her entirely by surprise. Her entire face flamed and even worse the heat darted downward to engulf her whole body. 'But that's not what we agreed.'

'We didn't agree anything. You made a suggestion. I didn't like it but I wasn't prepared to argue about it at that point and turn you off the whole idea of marrying me,' Cesare admitted without hesitation.

His sheer honesty bemused her and then touched her deep. *I want to make a baby with you.* The very words made Lizzie melt and she tried to squash her reaction and deny it. It would not be safe or sensible to have actual sex with Cesare Sabatino because it would smash the barriers she had carefully erected. But the prospect of undergoing some cold scientific procedure in a fertility clinic was, she suddenly appreciated, even less attractive to her.

'I'll think about it,' Lizzie mumbled half under her breath. 'Now, if you don't mind, I'd like to get changed into something more comfortable.'

'I'll go for a shower,' Cesare told her, peeling off his shirt without an ounce of inhibition.

Her heart hammering, Lizzie averted her gaze but the enthralling image of his bronzed, muscular torso was still seared across her vision. She pulled an outfit out of the case, nothing fancy for she had had her fill of fancy outfits that day. She caught an accidental glimpse of Cesare striding naked as the day he was born into the en suite and she almost groaned out loud. They were so different, so ill matched. He had seen it all, done it all, while she had only dreamt of the seeing and the doing. If she slept with him, she would develop feelings for him and she would get hurt because he wouldn't respond. Or maybe she would discover that she was the kind of woman who could have sex without getting more deeply involved, she reasoned abstractedly. She might not get attached to him at all, might be grateful to wave goodbye to him after a few months. How could she know how she would react?

When the shower was free, she made use of it and removed most of the heavy make-up she had worn for her big day. Applying only a dash of lipstick and blusher, she pulled on a stretchy maxi skirt and a sleeveless silk top, thrusting her feet into flat sandals. When she reappeared, a maid was in the bedroom hanging their clothes in the built-in closet and Lizzie went straight downstairs.

Cesare strode out to the marble-floored hall. 'Let me show you around before dinner,' he suggested.

'Where's Archie?' she asked.

Cesare held a finger to his handsome mouth in silencing mode and pointed into the drawing room. Archie was stretched out on a shaggy rug, his contented snores audible.

As dusk was folding in fast, Cesare showed her the outside of the house first. Lizzie stood on the covered stone terrace where Maria was fussing over a table covered in a snowy white cloth and admired the stunning view of the valley, which was overlooked by a superlative infinity pool. 'The views are out of this world. I'm not surprised you fell for this place,' she admitted, the tension of the day slowly seeping out of her.

Without warning, Cesare reached for her hand. 'This marriage can be as real as we want it to be, *bellezza mia*,' he pointed out quietly.

Her fingers flexed within the firm hold of his and her colour heightened. Real didn't mean for ever, did it? But then how many marriages truly lasted for ever? They were together now and would stay together until a child was born. The child she longed for, she reminded herself ruefully. Surely the closer she and Cesare became, the easier it would be to share their child both now and in the future?

Her lips parted almost without her volition, green eyes wide and anxious as if she was stunned by her own daring. 'I'll give it a go,' she told him softly. 'But I can't make any promises.'

Cesare smiled. It was a brilliant smile that illuminated his darkly beautiful features and enhanced his stubborn, passionate mouth. 'I'll try to make sure you don't regret it, *cara*.'

CHAPTER SIX

'MARIA IS WHIPPING out her entire repertoire for this one meal,' Cesare commented in amusement as the lazy meal wound through course after necessarily dainty course of appetising dishes.

Already unable to credit that she had agreed to try being married for *real*, Lizzie was too stressed to eat much of anything. A bite here and there was the best she could do and she proffered fervent apologies to the plump little cook when she came out to the terrace bearing her *pièce de résistance*, a fabulous layered chocolate cake.

They were about to embark on their marriage as if they were a normal married couple. And this was their *wedding night*. All of a sudden something Lizzie hadn't even had to consider in the run-up to the wedding was looming like a concealed tripwire in front of her. If she admitted that she was still a virgin he was sure to think she was a freak. After all, he knew she had been engaged. It would be better to keep quiet, she decided, and hope he didn't notice that there was anything different about her.

'You've barely touched alcohol today,' Cesare commented, wondering why she had fallen so quiet.

Not that she was ever a chatterbox, he acknowledged wryly. In fact there was always a stillness about her, a sense of tranquillity at the heart of her that was disconcertingly attractive.

'In the light of our…er…plans,' Lizzie muttered awkwardly, 'I thought it was better to abstain.'

'You're referring to the alcohol and pregnancy safety debate?'

Kill me now, Lizzie thought melodramatically. 'Yes. The argument about what might be a safe level goes back and forth, so it seems wiser just to avoid it altogether.'

'Is that why you made the most of your hen night?' Cesare asked, strong jawline tensing as he remembered her on the dance floor, full of vital energy and playfulness as she cast off her usual restraint.

'No. That wasn't planned. I missed Chrissie,' she admitted, colouring, 'and it had just been a very long time since I had been out like that and I overindulged.'

'Don't beat yourself up about it,' Cesare urged, stunning dark golden eyes shimmering in the candlelight against his bronzed skin.

He was so…hot, he was literally on fire, Lizzie reflected dizzily. And she was married to him, about to share a bed with him…and she was fretting, shrinking, *sighing* over the fact? What was wrong with her? That chemistry he had mentioned was in overdrive, lighting her up from the inside out with a prickling, tingling energy that her body could no longer contain. In an abrupt movement, she rose from the table and walked to the edge of the terrace to study the lights of the fortified village on the other side of the valley.

Her heart was as locked up tight as that village, hidden behind high defensive walls, she reminded herself bracingly. Having sex with Cesare didn't mean she was about to get silly ideas about him and start pining when he was no longer available. She had watched her mother careen blindly from one man to the next, hooked on love, her drug of choice. Lizzie had loved once and learned her lesson. If she couldn't even make it work with Andrew, there was little chance of it working with anyone else. She would have a baby to love though, she told herself in consolation.

'You're very tense, *cara*.' Cesare sighed, stilling behind her and gently resting his hands on her taut shoulders. Her delicate frame was dwarfed by his. 'You don't have to do anything you don't want to do...'

That he could read her nervous tension that accurately mortified Lizzie. In truth the problem was that she wanted him too much and feared the strength of that yearning. He turned her slowly round into the circle of his arms and she looked up at him and her knees went weak and her heart leapt in helpless response.

'I know that,' she asserted valiantly, wondering why he found the sudden change in their relationship so much easier. Were men just built that way? Was he more adaptable than she was? Or more relaxed at the concept of a marriage in which the only glue keeping them together would be sex and the hope of parenthood? *Just sex, nothing worth fussing over*, he had said after he got out of a bed where he had literally rocked her world. It was true that the only pleasure had been hers but his cold-blooded, practical take on what had happened between them had still knocked her for six. Yet she still couldn't drag her gaze from his beautifully shaped, passionate mouth.

Cesare studied her with veiled eyes, black lashes rimming the glint of smouldering gold. Desire was lancing through him with lightning-force potency, sending tiny ripples of tension through his big, powerful frame. He couldn't take his eyes off her lush mouth and the pouting crowns of her small breasts, which stirred softly below the fine silk of her top every time she shifted position.

It was years since Cesare had been so aware of a woman and he loathed the edgy bite of frustrated hunger that made him tense. He wanted to have sex with her and persuade his libido and his brain that, after all, she was just like any other woman he had bedded. He hadn't been with anyone since the day he had first met her and that bothered him. He hadn't wanted Celine when he'd had the opportunity and no other woman had since attracted his attention. Of course the problem was doubtless that his affair with Celine had run its natural course and left him bored. Lizzie was new and different, which had obvious appeal. There was even something strangely, weirdly sexy about the idea of getting her pregnant. He wasn't sure what it was but he knew that just the thought of it made him hard and ready. Given even the smallest encouragement, he would've ditched Maria's wedding banquet of a meal and headed straight for the bedroom.

Shaking off that foolish thought, Cesare gazed down at his bride with the sudden piquant recognition that she was his wife. *His* legal wife, *his* to have and to hold, *his* to protect. Without further ado, he pulled her close and kissed her, a husky growl sounding in the back of his throat when her firm little breasts brushed against his chest. She liked being carried; he remembered that and smiled. He hoisted her up into his arms and Archie scrambled up from his position of repose by the sun-warmed wall and barked in consternation at the sight of them.

'Keep quiet, Archie,' Cesare groaned. 'You can't come between a man and his wife…and I warn you, Lizzie, he's not sleeping with us tonight or any other night.'

Lizzie was challenged enough to think of sleeping with Cesare and her mouth was still tingling from the hungry pressure of his mouth. As he carried her upstairs she decided that she was turning into a shameless hussy. A gasp escaped her lips when she saw the bedroom, which had been transformed into a bower of candlelight and flowers while they had been dining. Candles flickered light from metal lanterns set round the room and lush vases of pristine white flowers completed the magical effect.

'Did you organise this?' Lizzie asked in wonderment when he settled her down at the foot of the bed.

Cesare laughed. 'No. Maria has waited a long time for me to find a wife and I think she's celebrating.'

Sudden shyness reclaimed Lizzie as he gazed down at her, the lights picking out the hollows below his high cheekbones, lending him an enigmatic quality. In that lambent light, he was truly beautiful, sleek and dark, exotic and compellingly male. With sure hands he pushed her hair back from her face, letting the long, silky strands flow down her back. He tipped up her face and claimed another kiss, feeding from the sweetness of her mouth with hungry fervour, crushing her soft full lips below his while her fingers clung to his shoulders.

'I've been thinking about this from the first moment I saw you,' Cesare growled against her reddened mouth, his dark deep voice vibrating down her spinal cord, the very essence of masculinity.

'You do talk nonsense sometimes and please don't tell me that's a compliment that I should gratefully receive. The first time you saw me I was in my dungarees and looked a complete mess!' Lizzie protested on the back of a rueful laugh.

'There's no accounting for taste or the male libido,' Cesare quipped, impervious to her disagreement. 'I saw your face, your skin, your eyes…it was enough, *delizia mia*.'

'I like it when you talk Italian,' Lizzie confided breathlessly. 'You could be reciting the multiplication tables but it wouldn't matter. It's your accent, your voice, the pitch you use.'

Surprised by that unexpected burst of loquaciousness, Cesare grinned, a slanting wicked grin that utterly transformed his lean, darkly handsome face, wiping away the cool vigilance and control that was usually etched there. 'What I like most about you is that you surprise me all the time.'

'Right now I'm surprising me,' Lizzie told him truthfully, uncertainty darkening her hazel eyes as it crossed her mind that she was behaving impulsively, not something she made a habit of after growing up with an impetuous mother. But then she was *not* her mother, she reminded herself squarely, and at the age of twenty-four was surely old enough to make her own decisions.

He took her mouth in a long, intoxicating kiss and sober thought became too much of a challenge. A tension of a very different kind began to lace her body. She became ridiculously conscious of the silk rubbing against her swollen nipples and the dampness at her feminine core. Her body was responding to the chemistry between her and Cesare with a life of its own, blossoming like a flower suddenly brought into bloom by the sunshine. Only chemistry, *just* sex, she reflected in an abbreviated fashion as she warded off her insecurities. There was nothing to fear, nothing to be ashamed of, nothing she need avoid to protect herself. Dimly she was registering at some level of her brain that her mother's disastrous affairs had made her far too reluctant to take a risk on a man.

Her silk top fell in a colourful splash of silk to the wooden floor and, with a ragged sigh of appreciation, Cesare closed his hands to the pert swell of her breasts, his thumbs expertly capturing and massaging the protruding pink peaks until they were taut and throbbing and the very breath was catching in her tightening throat. Her hips dug into the mattress beneath her, seeking to sate the hollow ache tugging at her pelvis.

One-handed, he wrenched at his shirt. 'You see how I forget what I'm doing when I'm with you, *delizia mia*?' he rasped.

Lizzie only needed that invitation and she tugged at his shirt, delicate fingers stroking over his taut, muscular shoulders, adoring the heat and strength of him. He put his mouth to her neck and skimmed the tip of his tongue along her delicate collarbone and then, gently lowering her flat on the bed, he roamed down over her ribcage, sending delicious little jolts of desire through her each time he captured the tender peaks of her breasts.

Passion had claimed Lizzie. Her temperature was rocketing higher and higher, a sheen of perspiration on her brow, and her heart was hammering so fast it felt as if it were at the foot of her throat. Her hand delving into his luxuriant black hair, she pulled him up to her and kissed him with all the urgent hunger racing through her. He pushed her skirt up above her knees and trailed his fingers slowly up her inner thighs. Every inch of her felt stretched taut with the extreme wanting that had taken her over and she gritted her teeth as he anchored his fingers to her knickers and trailed them off. She wanted his touch so bad it hurt and she squirmed in a fever of need.

'I'm trying to go slow,' Cesare bit out raggedly, 'but I feel like an express train.'

'Talking too much,' she told him, her teeth chattering together at the unwelcome pause.

With an almighty effort, Cesare stepped back from the source of temptation. Haste wasn't cool, especially not the first time. He didn't think a woman had ever responded with that much passion to him and it was setting him on fire with overriding need. He told her that in Italian and she gave him a blissful smile, evidently glorying in the sound of his language or his voice or whatever it was that she liked. He stripped off the shirt, unzipped his chinos, pushed off everything in one urgent forceful assault on his clothing. Naked, he came back to her, revelling in the way her eyes locked to him and the sudden blush that warmed her porcelain complexion. He couldn't recall when he had last been with a woman who blushed. And in the bedroom? Never.

Lizzie was transfixed. There he was in all his

glory, her every piece of curiosity answered in one fell swoop. He scooped her up in his arms, pulled off the skirt that was her only remaining garment and settled her down, equally naked, in the centre of the turned-back bed.

Lizzie froze. 'I think we need to put out the candles!' she exclaimed, her entire body burning with embarrassment as she grasped in desperation for the sheet, which was out of reach.

In the very act of surveying her pale slender curves with rapt attention Cesare raised stunning golden eyes to study her in growing wonderment. 'I've already seen you naked,' he reminded her gently.

'That's different...I was too hung-over to be shy!' Lizzie pointed out loudly.

Cesare grinned and with a stretch of a long brown arm flipped up the sheet. 'This is not likely to hold me back,' he warned her.

As the cool cotton settled over her quivering length Lizzie lost some of her tension. Resting on one arm, she found Cesare gazing down at her with slumberous dark golden eyes. He rubbed a slightly stubbled jaw against her cheek in a sensual gesture on his path to her ready mouth.

One kiss melted into the next but as his hands roved skilfully over her, lingering on pulse points and teasing erogenous zones, lying still beneath his ministrations became tougher and tougher. Her nipples throbbed from his attentions, sending arrows of fire down to the tender, pulsing heart of her.

He stroked her and her spine arched. 'You're so wet, so ready for me,' Cesare husked.

A tiny shiver racked her slight frame, all the heat

coalescing in the swollen, delicate tissue between her thighs. She squeezed her eyes tight shut, striving to stay in control and not betray how new it all was to her. But with every ravishing caress, he seduced her away from control. Soft gasps parted her lips, her neck extending, tendons clenching as the stimulation became almost too much to bear.

'You know this will be a first for me, *cara*,' Cesare confided, running the tip of his tongue across a turgid rose-pink nipple.

Lizzie could hardly find her voice. 'What will?'

'Sex without a condom...I've never done that before and it excites me,' he admitted huskily, shifting against her thigh, letting her feel the smooth, hard length of his erection.

Lizzie was trying not to think about the size of him in that department. She was a modern woman, well acquainted with averages and gossip and popular report. Being a virgin didn't mean she was entirely ignorant, she told herself in consolation, striving not to stress as her excitement built and built. Hands biting into his strong shoulders, she lifted her hips upward, succumbing to an almost uncontrollable urge to get closer to him. He toyed with her lush, damp opening, honeyed quivers of sensations rippling through her womb, and circled the tiny bud of her arousal until almost without warning a wild, seething force of irresistible sensation engulfed her like a flood. Her eyes flew wide and she bucked and jerked and sobbed in the grip of rush after rush of intense and enthralling pleasure.

He tipped her up, hooking her legs over his shoulders in a move that unnerved her. He plunged into her tight channel and for a moment she was preoccupied with the sense of fullness, the certain knowledge that this was exactly what her body had craved throughout his teasing foreplay. In fact everything was wonderful until the hot glide of his flesh within hers sank deeper and a sudden sharp, tearing pain made her stiffen and cry out in dismay.

Cesare froze as though a fire alarm had gone off and stared down at her, dark golden eyes like hungry golden flames in his lean bronzed face. 'You *can't* be...'

Enraged by her own bodily weakness and chagrin, Lizzie dealt him a look that would have dropped a grizzly bear at ten paces. 'Well, don't stop now.'

'You're a *virgin*?' Cesare emphasised, his incredulity unconcealed as he held himself at an angle above her, muscles straining in his bulging forearms.

'How's that your business?' Lizzie slung back argumentatively.

Cesare swore long and low in his own language and cursed her stubbornness. He burned for her but he was fighting his hunger with all his might. It struck him as unjust that the hot, tight hold of her body on his gave him pure pleasure while she had only experienced pure pain.

'It's my business,' he told her grimly. 'I think this is my cue to back off.'

'No... No!' Lizzie exclaimed in consternation. 'You don't get to go that far and then *stop*... I want to know what it's like...'

In receipt of that plaintive plea, Cesare groaned out loud, belatedly recognising that marriage was proving a much bigger challenge than he had expected.

She was experimenting with him, he thought in all-male horror.

'Please...' Lizzie added, tugging him down to her, pale fingers framing his cheekbones as she reached without success for his beautiful, passionate mouth.

In the mood to be easily encouraged, Cesare shifted his hips, his entire attention nailed to her flushed and expressive face so that he could register the smallest wince she might make. Instead Lizzie smiled up at him with a look of wonderment that was uniquely soothing to his momentarily threatened male ego.

Lizzie closed her eyes again, mortified at the fuss she had made, the lengths she had had to go to to persuade him to continue. She had always believed that a man found it hard to stop in the middle of sex, so the fact that he had offered to withdraw altogether did not strike her as a compliment. But she had wanted to know, had wanted so badly to know what all the fuss was about.

He moved against her and tingling, driving sensation awakened in her pelvis again. She relaxed a little. The slow, almost provocative thrusts became enticing and she relaxed completely, indeed began to arch up to greet him with an enthusiasm she had never expected to feel. His skilled acceleration delivered sensation like nothing she had ever experienced and her excitement soared to delirious heights that climbed and climbed until she reached a peak and soared effortlessly over it and then down and down into the cocoon of lethargy and satiation, exhaustion pulling at her every sense.

Cesare settled her back down on the pillows and smoothed her tangled hair off her damp brow. His hand trembled a little because he was struggling to do two opposing things: firstly treat Lizzie like the bride she was and, secondly, suppress the anger tearing at him. 'Why didn't you tell me I'd be your first lover?' he demanded in a roughened undertone.

His tone, his exasperation, cut through Lizzie in her sensitive state like the sudden painful slice of a knife and she sat up abruptly, clutching the sheet to her chest. 'I didn't see that it was anything to do with you.'

'In other words, you chose to deliberately conceal it,' he condemned, leaping out of bed in one lithe, powerful movement. 'How the hell could you still be a virgin when you were once engaged?'

'Don't you dare raise your voice to me, Cesare Sabatino!' Lizzie yelled back at him furiously, but she was trembling with an innate fear she could not have expressed at that moment. 'As for why I was still a virgin, that's private.'

'You're married to me now, *cara*. I don't think it's unreasonable of me to expect an answer to something so basic.'

'When you have the right to ask me private questions, I'll let you know,' Lizzie slung back flatly, snaking out of the far side of the bed to avoid him and yanking the sheet free of the mattress with a violent jerk to wrap it round her body. 'Now, I'm going for a bath.'

'*Lizzie...*' Cesare ground out in frustration to her rigid back as she reached for the door of the en suite.

'I'm not feeling nice, *wifely* or the slightest bit chatty right now, so please excuse me,' Lizzie breathed icily and stepped into the bathroom, shutting and locking the door behind her within seconds.

Lizzie filled the glorious antique bath to the brim, filled it with bubbles and lowered her body into the warm water. Angry, Cesare could be incredibly intimidating, towering over her, dark eyes glowing with hostility in his lean dark face. She couldn't help that her first reaction to an angry man was to run to the nearest place of safety. Her mother's violent second husband had taught her to get herself and Chrissie out of harm's way fast.

But Lizzie refused to *be* intimidated by Cesare, whom she sensed would never be violent. What did he have to be so angry about? Hadn't their lovemaking been good for him? It had certainly been good for her, apart from the hiccup as such in the middle when she had discovered that her first experience of intimacy could actually be painful. Ironically she was more hurt by Cesare's withdrawal and grim mood in the aftermath, which had made her feel—all over again—inadequate. Why couldn't he have simply let the subject go? Had he no sensitivity? Couldn't he see that she didn't want to talk about it?

Cesare paced the bedroom in fierce frustration. Why hadn't she warned him? Had she been embarrassed about being untouched? He recalled the blushing and gritted his teeth, acknowledging that he was totally unfit to deal with sexual innocence when he had failed to recognise it even though it was right there in front of him. He had screwed up, screwed up even worse when he sprang an immediate interrogation on her.

This was not how he had pictured their marriage kicking off. She was all emotional now, very probably weeping in the bath and regretting their new agreement while wishing she had never laid eyes on him. And yet the sex had been amazing…so amazing he couldn't wait to repeat it. Galvanised into motion by that shameless motivation, Cesare threw on a disreputable pair of jeans and padded downstairs, pondering possibilities to redeem himself in his offended bride's eyes. Before he even got that far he heard the distant howls of Archie marooned in an outside kennel and he grinned at the sound. He was a very clever man and he would turn the wedding-night breakdown back into a honeymoon regardless of what sacrifices it demanded of him!

Archie broke off his cries mid-howl and pranced towards him on three little legs. Archie was not particularly attached to Cesare but he recognised him as a potential lead to his mistress…

CHAPTER SEVEN

ARCHIE WHIMPERED OUTSIDE the bathroom door.

'You know you can do better than that,' Cesare told him, tossing him a fragment of chicken from one of the plates on the table by the bed.

For a three-legged dog, Archie could move fast and he caught the scrap in mid-air.

'Now…you have a mission,' Cesare reminded the scruffy little animal. 'You get her out of the bathroom.'

Archie hovered by the door, tried to push it but the balloon collar round his neck got in the way. Sitting back on his haunches, Archie loosed a sad howl that would not have shamed a banshee. Cesare threw him another piece of succulent chicken in reward. Archie gave a grand performance.

Lizzie woke up feeling cold, water sloshing noisily around her as she sat up wide-eyed. Archie was howling at the door…or had that just been a dream? Clambering hastily out of the bath, she snatched up a fleecy towel and wrapped herself in it, just as Archie howled again. Glancing at the watch on the vanity to see how long she had slept, she was taken aback to realise that a couple of hours had passed and that it was now almost one in the morning. Depressing the lock, she opened the door in haste.

'Oh, pet, I forgot about you! Have you been lonely?' Lizzie asked, squatting down to the little dog's level.

'Want some supper?' Cesare asked lazily from the bed on which he reclined.

Small bosom swelling at that insouciant tone, Lizzie was about to tell him in no short order what he could do with supper and then her tummy growled and she registered in surprise that she was actually very hungry. Of course, she hadn't eaten very much at dinner...

Straightening, she looped her damp hair back behind her ear and focused on Cesare's lean, darkly devastating face, clashing with the banked-down glitter of his stunning eyes. 'You still want answers, don't you?'

'I'd be a liar if I said otherwise,' he admitted, sprawling back with his hands linked behind his head, a position which only threw into prominence the muscular torso and flat ribbed stomach beneath his black T-shirt.

Lizzie breathed in slowly, belatedly registering the table of snacks by the bed and the candles that must have been relit while she slept. A surprising sense of calm after the storm enclosed her. The worst had already happened, hadn't it? What did she have to fear now? Not marriage, not sex, she decided, her chin coming up. Cesare had...*briefly*...scared her but that wasn't his fault. No, that fault could be laid at the door of her late mother's misjudgement of men and a stepfather who had given Lizzie nightmares long after he had passed out of her life.

'You know, when you got so angry, you scared me,' she told him baldly. 'My mother was married to a man who beat her up when he got angry.'

Cesare sprang off the bed, a frown pleating his ebony brows. 'I would never hurt you.'

'I think I know that already,' Lizzie said quietly. 'But running is still a reflex for me when men get angry. I can't help it. The two years Mum was married to that man were terrifying for Chrissie and me.'

'Did he hit you as well?' Cesare growled in disgust, appalled that he could have, however unwittingly, frightened her.

'He tried to a couple of times but he was drunk and clumsy and we were fast on our feet,' Lizzie confided. 'Let's not talk about it. It's in the past. But I should make one thing clear…' She hesitated. 'I'm only willing to talk about Andrew if you're willing to talk about Serafina.'

'And exactly who has been talking to you?' Cesare demanded, a muscle pulling taut at the corner of his stern, handsome mouth.

'Your grandmother mentioned her…and I'm curious too,' Lizzie confessed while she walked into the dressing room in search of a nightdress. Shedding the towel behind the door, she slipped it on, catching a glimpse of herself in a tall mirror. What remained of her fake glamour had evaporated in the long bath she had taken. The moist atmosphere had added frizz to her formerly smooth tresses and she suppressed a sigh. Cesare was getting the *real* Lizzie Whitaker on this particular night.

Emerging from the dressing room with Archie at her heels, she tried not to visibly shrink from Cesare's acute appraisal. The silk nightie was long and, to her, the very antithesis of sexy because it revealed neither leg nor cleavage. Her face coloured as she stilled for a split second, disturbingly aware of the intensity of that assessment from his smouldering dark golden eyes. A wave of heat shimmied over her, settling at the tips of her breasts and between her thighs in a tingling, throbbing awareness that mortified her. She knew he was thinking about sex. She also knew that he was making *her* think about sex. And she didn't know how he did it. Hormonal awareness was like an invisible electric current lacing the atmosphere.

Cesare watched the candlelight throw Lizzie's slender legs into view behind the thin silk and his mouth ran dry while the rest of him ran hot and heavy. Her pert breasts shimmying below the material in the most stimulating way, she curled up at the foot of the bed and reached for a plate of snacks. 'So, who goes first?'

'I will,' Cesare surprised himself by saying. Although he had initially been disconcerted by her demand he was now more amused that she should want to travel that far back into his past. It simply irritated him, though, that his grandmother was willing to credit that a youthful love affair gone wrong could still have any influence over him.

'Serafina…it's a beautiful name,' Lizzie remarked thoughtfully.

'She is very beautiful,' Cesare admitted, quietly contemplative as he sprawled back indolently against the headboard of the bed. 'We were students together. I was doing business, she was doing business law. It was first love, all very intense stuff.'

Lizzie watched him grimace at that admission. 'My first love was a poster of a boy-band member on the wall,' she confided in some embarrassment.

'A poster would've been a safer option for me. I fell hard and fast and I wanted to marry Serafina. She said we were too young and she was right,' he conceded wryly. 'She was always ambitious and I assumed that I'd have to start at the bottom of the business ladder. But then I made a stock-market killing and took over my first company and my prospects improved. Serafina started work at an upmarket legal practice with some very rich…and influential clients…'

'And at that point, you were still together?' Lizzie prompted when the silence dragged, his delivery becoming noticeably less smooth.

'Very much so. We were living together. Second week in her new job, Serafina met Matteo Ruffini and he invited her out to dinner with a view to offering her the opportunity to work on his substantial account.' His beautiful mouth took on a sardonic slant. 'Suddenly she became unavailable to me, working late in the evening, too busy to join me for lunch.'

His tension was unhidden. Lizzie registered that Serafina had hurt him and hurt him deep because he still couldn't talk about the woman with indifference. 'She was seeing Matteo?'

'*Sì*…and the moment *Prince* Matteo proposed, I was history. He had everything she had ever wanted. Social position, a title and immense wealth. The only flaw in his perfection was that she was twenty-five and he was seventy-five.'

'Good grief! That's a huge age gap!' Lizzie exclaimed. 'Did she tell you she'd fallen in love with him?'

'No. Possibly that would have been easier to accept, if not believe. No, she told me that he was just too good a catch to turn down and that if she contrived to give him a son and heir, she'd be rich and blessed for the rest of her life,' Cesare breathed with derision. 'I realised I'd never really known her. It crushed my faith in women.'

'Of course it did,' Lizzie agreed, the nails of one hand biting into her palm while odd disconnected emotions flailed her, particularly when she found herself thinking aggressive thoughts about the woman who had broken Cesare's heart. She had read him *so* wrong when they first met. He had been prepared to leap into the commitment and responsibility of marriage at a very young age. Clearly, he had genuinely loved Serafina and yet she had betrayed him in the worst possible way when she chose a life of rich privilege over love.

'Andrew?' Cesare pressed in turn.

'He was my best friend growing up. We had so much in common we should've been a perfect match and we stayed great friends although he never actually asked me out until I was in my twenties. I was already in love with him…at least I *thought* it was love,' she said ruefully. 'Everybody assumed we would be great together and when he asked me to marry him, Dad was ecstatic. I said yes but I wanted us to just date for a while.' Her face paling, she studied her tightly clasped hands. 'It was in private that Andrew and I didn't work out.'

'Obviously you didn't sleep with him,' Cesare murmured softly, watching the fragile bones of her face tighten, the vulnerable curve of her mouth tense, feeling his own chest tighten in response.

'No, I just didn't want to sleep with him,' she admitted in an awkward rush. 'I froze every time he got close and he said I was frigid but I didn't find him attractive that way. I thought I had a real problem with being touched. That's why I wouldn't date anyone after him and why I never blamed him for turning to Esther.'

'You don't have *any* kind of a problem,' Cesare asserted with quiet confidence. 'You were inexperienced; maybe he was as well—'

'No,' Lizzie broke in, running back through her memories while remembered feelings of inadequacy and regret engulfed her.

Yet even before she had fallen asleep in the bath she had realised that her enjoyment of Cesare's attentions had shed a comforting light on the past, which had always troubled her. Her only *real* problem with Andrew had been that he had always felt like the brother she had never had. She could see things as they had been now, not as she might have wished them to be: sadly, there had been zero sexual attraction on her side. She had sincerely cared for Andrew but he had always felt more like a good friend than a potential lover. When she compared how she had reacted from the first moment with Cesare, she could clearly see the difference and finally understand that what had happened with Andrew was not her fault.

'I liked and appreciated him but I never wanted him that way,' Lizzie admitted with regret. 'I still feel guilty about it because I was too inexperienced to realise that he was just the wrong man for me…and my rejections hurt him.'

'He seems happy enough now.' Cesare toyed with another piece of chicken.

Encouraged to think that further treats were in the pipeline, Archie got up on his haunches and begged.

'Oh, my goodness, look what he's doing!' Lizzie exclaimed, sitting forward with wide eyes to watch her pet. 'He can beg…I didn't even know he could *do* that.'

Cesare rewarded Archie with the chicken because he had made his mistress smile and laugh.

'Of course, I've never fed him like that. If he'd come to me for food when I was eating my father would have called that bad behaviour and he would have blamed Archie. I kept Archie outside most of the time.'

'I suspect Archie would've been clever enough to keep a low profile around your dad,' Cesare surmised.

'Did you ever have a pet?'

'I would have liked one when I was a kid,' Cesare confided. 'But I was constantly moving between my grandmother's home and Goffredo's apartment and a pet wasn't viable.'

'Did you organise all this food?' she asked, smothering a yawn.

'The staff are in bed. I don't expect service here late at night,' he told her quietly. 'I emptied the refrigerator.'

'And let Archie up to lure me out of the bathroom,' Lizzie guessed, settling their discarded plates on the low table and clambering in the far side of the bed to say apologetically, 'I'm tired.'

'Brides aren't supposed to get tired, particularly not when they've been lazing in the bath for hours,' Cesare informed her, amusement dancing in his dark golden eyes.

He could still steal her breath away at one glance, she acknowledged wearily as she closed her eyes. It was, as he had termed it, 'just sex' and she had to learn to see that side of their relationship in the same casual light. She wondered if that would be a chal-lenge because she was already drifting dangerously close to liking him.

'Archie can sleep under the bed,' Cesare decreed. 'He's not sharing it with us.'

'We can't do anything, you know,' she muttered in a sudden embarrassed surge, her cheeks colouring. 'I'm...I'm sore...'

'It's not a problem.'

Relieved, she smiled and closed her eyes. As he stripped by the side of the bed Cesare studied her re-laxed features and thought, *Mission accomplished, honeymoon back on track*. It was the same way he handled problems at work, mentally ticking off items on a to-do list while always seeking the most success-ful conclusion. But as he slid into bed beside Lizzie he reached for her and it wasn't a pre-programmed task. He reasoned that she was a very restless sleeper and if he left her free to move around she would annoy him.

Strangely enough, he acknowledged, in spite of the bathroom shenanigans, she hadn't annoyed him once. But then she wasn't the greedy, grasping type of woman he had deemed her to be. Why had he been so biased? After all, he had a stepmother, a grand-mother and three sisters, none of whom were rich *or* avaricious. Had he deliberately sought out lovers who only cared about his wealth? And if he was guilty of that, had it been because he genuinely only needed carefree sex with a woman? Or because he preferred to avoid the possibility of anything more serious developing? Almost ten years had passed since Serafina had waltzed down the aisle to her prince. He refused to think that she had burned him so badly that he had declined to risk getting deeply involved with anyone else. Yet he hadn't even got an engagement or a live-in relationship under his belt during those ten long years.

In the darkness, Cesare's wide, sensual mouth framed a silent but vehemently felt swear word. He did not appreciate the oddity of having such thoughts about the sort of thing he had never ever felt the need to think about before. It was that ring on his wedding finger that was getting to him, he brooded impatiently. It was feeling married and possibly just a tiny bit trapped...with Archie snoring beside the bed and Lizzie nestled up against him like a second skin.

Just like him, she was in this marriage for the end game and the prize, he reminded himself squarely. It wasn't a normal marriage but, if they planned to conceive a child, the marriage had to work on a daily basis and why should physical intimacy always lead to a closer involvement than he wanted? The answer was that sex didn't need to lead to anything more complex, he reminded himself stubbornly, certainly nothing that would break his rules of never getting more closely involved with a woman. And it was no wonder that he was feeling unsettled when he was in such unfamiliar territory. He hadn't tried to please a woman since Serafina and he wasn't going to make a fool of himself trying to please Lizzie, was he?

Archie's snores filtered up in direct disagreement.

CHAPTER EIGHT

CESARE GLANCED AT his wife and then at the party of men watching her every move in a pantomime version of dropped jaws as she alighted from his Ferrari. She was a lissom figure in a turquoise sundress, her gorgeous silvery mane blowing back from her delicately flushed face in the breeze, her shapely legs tapering down to impossibly delicate ankles and high-heeled sandals. He pushed up his sunglasses and gave the men a warning look before closing his hand round Lizzie's in a display of all-Italian male possessiveness that he could not resist.

Lizzie sank down at the table in the *piazza* and the waiter was at their side within seconds, doubtless drawn by one glimpse of Cesare's sleek sophistication. He had an air of hauteur and command that got them fast service everywhere they went and it was so inbred in him to expect immediate attention that he rarely even noticed the fact, although she was very sure he would notice if he didn't receive it.

Now she feasted her attention on his lean bronzed face. She was magnetised by his stunning dark golden eyes as they rested on her and wondered what he was thinking. She was *always* wondering what he was thinking, had to bite her tongue not to ask, but it was hardly surprising that she was living in a state of constant befuddlement because their business-based marriage of convenience had become something else entirely...at least for *her*...

They had now been in Italy for a solid month. Cesare had made several business trips. He had flown his family *and* Chrissie in to visit for one weekend and the two days had passed in a whirlwind of chattering liveliness and warmth. Lizzie had never been so happy before and it scared her because she knew she was nourishing hopes that would ultimately lead to disappointment and the stark biting pain of rejection. *What? Only possibly?* jibed her more truthful self. Lizzie's emotions had got involved the very first night they'd slept together and she'd wakened in the morning to find herself secure in Cesare's arms.

For four whole weeks she had been living an idyllic life with an attentive husband, who was also a passionate lover, by her side. He had taken her out sightseeing, shopping, out to dinner in sun-baked *piazzas*, fashionable squares, and to wander through old churches lit by candles and the sunlight piercing the stained-glass windows. Today they had walked the seventeenth-century ramparts of Lucca. Her fingers toyed momentarily with the slender gold watch encircling her wrist, her most recent gift. If he went on a trip or even noticed that she lacked something he considered essential, he bought it for her. He was incredibly generous in bed and out of it. He was curious about her, knew everything there was to know about her childhood. His interest was intoxicating because she had never seen herself as being particularly interesting.

In fact, being the focus of attention of a very handsome, entertaining male had made her see herself in a kinder, warmer light.

In truth, when Cesare Sabatino was faking being a husband, he faked with the skill and panache of a professional, she conceded ruefully. He hadn't asked her to fall in love with him. It wouldn't occur to him that bringing an ordinary woman out to beautiful Tuscany and treating her like a much appreciated, highly desirable wife while keeping her in luxury might turn her head. But Lizzie knew her head had been thoroughly turned. She found him fascinating. He was a spellbinding mix of rapier-sharp intellect and disconcerting emotional depth and, of course, she had fallen head over heels for him. Archie now rejoiced in a collar with his name picked out in diamonds and a four-poster bed of his own. How could she *not* love the man who had given her adored pet those quite unnecessary, ridiculously expensive but deeply touching things?

And the result was that now she was terrified of falling pregnant, fearing that that announcement would ensure that their marriage cooled back down to a businesslike arrangement in which Cesare would expect her to be terribly civilised and behave as if she didn't give a damn about him. Within days of the wedding she had had the proof that she had not yet conceived and Cesare had just laughed and said that they had all the time in the world, as if it truly didn't matter to him if it took months to reach that goal.

'What if there's something wrong with one of us and it doesn't happen?' she had asked him anxiously.

He had shrugged and suggested that they give it a year before seeking medical advice. If for some reason having a child turned out not to be possible, they would deal with it when it happened, Cesare had told her fatalistically while urging her not to stress about getting pregnant.

'I hope you've got something special lined up to wear tonight,' Cesare mused over their wine. 'It's a real fashion parade.'

'I thought it was a charity do.'

'In Italy such events are always fashion parades.'

'I have at least four long dresses to choose from,' Lizzie reminded him. 'I won't let you down. Don't worry about it.'

'*Ma no*…certainly not,' Cesare cut in, stroking a long forefinger soothingly over her hand where it curled on the table top. 'You always look fantastic, *gioia mia*. Why would I be worried about you letting me down?'

'I'm not part of your world and I never will be. It's a challenge for me to put on fancy clothes and pretend I'm something I'm not,' Lizzie admitted in an undertone.

'You only need to be yourself. You have two, no, three…' he adjusted reflectively, amusement gleaming in his gilded gaze '…advantages.'

'Which are?'

'Beauty and class and my ring on your finger,' Cesare completed with cynical cool. 'I'm a powerful man. You will be treated with respect and courtesy.'

An involuntary grin lit up Lizzie's face and she laughed, biting back foolish words of love. What an embarrassment it would be if she were to lose control of her tongue around him now! After all, he was playing a very sophisticated game with her, utilising his charm and a whole host of other extraordinary gifts to make their marriage work as if it were a real marriage. If she were to suddenly confess how she felt about him, he would be embarrassed and appalled to learn that she didn't know how to play the same game.

'We should head back soon,' she commented unevenly.

'Would that leave us time for an hour or so in bed?' Cesare sprang upright, dropping a large-denomination note down on top of the bill, smouldering dark eyes flashing over her with a sexual intensity that never failed to thrill.

'Again?' There was a slight gasp in her low-pitched response because she had yet to adapt to Cesare's high-voltage libido. He seemed to want her all the time, no matter where she was, no matter what she was wearing or what she was doing. She thought he was possibly a little oversexed but she didn't complain because she always wanted him too and, in any case, the whole point of their marriage was for her to conceive a child.

A light hand resting in the shallow indentation of her spine, Cesare urged her back to the Ferrari. As she clambered in beside him he turned his head and closed a hard hand into the tumble of her hair to hold her fast while he kissed her. His mouth was hungry and hot and erotic on hers and every sense was on overdrive by the time he freed her again and started up the car.

The air conditioning cooled her overheated skin but the ache throbbing between her thighs was far less controllable. Cesare skimmed up her skirt to bare her thighs. 'I like looking at your legs, especially when I know I'm about to part them,' he husked soft and low, laughing when her cheeks flamed.

Early evening, Lizzie inspected her reflection in a black shimmering dress that delineated her slender figure with a spare elegance that appealed to her. She was learning what she liked and didn't like in her wardrobe and she didn't like fussy trims or frills or neon-bright colours that seemed to swallow her alive.

Warmth speckled her cheeks as she thought about the intimacy of the late-afternoon hours. She moved slowly in her heels, a touch of tenderness at the heart of her reminding her of Cesare's passionate energy between the sheets. In bed, sensual excitement ruled her entirely and she was enjoying every moment of exploring that brave new world.

Even so the image that lingered longest was of Cesare, lithe and bronzed and breathtakingly beautiful, relaxing back against the tumbled pillows and finally admitting how very relieved he was that Athene was now well on the road to recovery, having initially suffered a setback in the aftermath of her cardiac surgery. For days, he had tried to pretend he wasn't worried sick even though Lizzie had watched him freeze at every phone call, fearful of receiving bad news. That he had finally abandoned that macho pretence of unconcern to share his true feelings with Lizzie had meant a lot to her. She valued the little signs that revealed that Cesare was behaving more and more like one half of a couple rather than an independent, entirely separate entity. They had visited his grandmother in her convalescent clinic in Rome several times and Athene's sparkling personality even in a hospital bed and her strong affection for Cesare had touched Lizzie's heart.

In the morning they were flying out to Lionos and

one day after that Athene was coming out to join them. Cesare had married Lizzie purely to gain that right to bring his grandmother out for a stay on the island and Lizzie regularly reminded herself of that unflattering reality. But she was looking forward almost as much as Athene was to seeing Lionos, which the older woman had described in such charmed terms. She only hoped that the enhancements engineered by the imperturbable Primo lived up to Cesare's expectations.

A limousine ferried Cesare and Lizzie to the venue for the charity benefit in Florence. It was being held in a vast mansion with every window lit and crowds of paparazzi waiting on the pavement to take photographs of the guests arriving. Lizzie froze in surprise when they were targeted, belatedly appreciating that she was married to a male who, when in his homeland, received the attention worthy of a celebrity for his looks and spectacular business accomplishments.

'Did you enjoy having your photo taken?' Cesare asked.

'No, not at all. I didn't feel glossy enough for the occasion,' she confided.

'But you spent ages getting ready,' Cesare countered with all the incomprehension of a male who had merely showered and shaved before donning a dinner jacket.

Her hazel gaze roving swiftly over the level of extreme grooming clearly practised by the other female guests, Lizzie suppressed a rueful sigh. She didn't look perfect and she knew it, reckoned she should have foreseen that the attentions of a hairstylist and a make-up artist would be necessary. But then how important was her image to Cesare? Did he really care?

Or would he soon be comparing her, to her detriment, to the women who had preceded her in his bed? Lizzie had done her homework on the Internet and she was uneasily aware that in recent years Cesare had spent a lot of time in the company of fashion and beauty models, invariably the very image of feminine perfection. Possibly she needed to make more of an effort, she conceded, uncomfortable with the comparisons she was making.

As they were surrounded by the leading lights in the charity committee of which Cesare was a director, the crowd parted and an exquisite brunette, wearing a very fitted pink dress overlaid with a see-through chiffon layer that simply accentuated her stupendous curves, approached them. Cesare performed the introduction. 'Our hostess, Princess Serafina Ruffini... Serafina, my wife, Lizzie.'

'Welcome to my home, Lizzie.' Serafina air kissed her on both cheeks and gave her a wide, seemingly sincere smile.

Shock winged through Lizzie and she was furious that Cesare hadn't warned her that the benefit was being held at his former girlfriend's home. Impervious to her mood and the manner in which her hand clenched tensely on his arm, Cesare talked about cancer research to an older man who seemed to be a doctor while Lizzie made awkward conversation with his wife, who spoke very little English. Italian lessons were going to be a must in the near future, Lizzie promised herself. Her attention crept back to Serafina, holding court on the other side of the room with a lively group who frequently broke into laughter.

Cesare had described his ex as *very* beautiful and

he had not been kidding. Serafina had almond-shaped dark eyes, skin like clotted cream, a wealth of dark tumbling curls and one of those enviable cupid's-bow scarlet mouths that men always seemed to go mad for. And, more worryingly, Serafina appeared to move in the same social milieu as Cesare, possibly to the extent that Cesare had not even felt it necessary to mention that Lizzie would be meeting her that very evening. For goodness' sake, he broke up with her almost ten years ago, Lizzie reminded herself impatiently. How likely was it that he was still hankering after what he had lost?

In conversation with one of the organisers, who spoke great English, Lizzie learned how indebted the charity felt to Serafina, not only for her recent decision to become their patroness but also for allowing her magnificent home to be used for a fundraising benefit. La Principessa, she learned, was worth a small fortune to the charity in terms of the PR and publicity she would bring their cause, which was raising sufficient funds to open a new hospice for terminally ill children.

It was very warm in the crowded room and perspiration began to bead on Lizzie's brow. She glanced longingly across the room to where several sets of doors stood open onto an outside terrace. As she stood there, a glass of water clasped in one hand, a sick sensation composed of both dizziness and nausea washed over her, leaving her pale.

'Excuse me, I'm warm and I think I'll step outside for a few minutes,' she told her companion and turned away, wondering if she should be taking refuge in the cloakroom instead, but praying that the cooler night air would revive her.

The terrace was furnished with tables and chairs, and lights and candles held the darkness at bay. Lizzie took a seat, gratefully feeling the clamminess of her skin and the faint sickness recede again and breathing the fresh air in deep while she wondered if she was simply tired or if, indeed, she could be in the very earliest stage of a pregnancy. Wonder at that faint suspicion curved her mouth into a ready smile but delight at the prospect was swiftly tempered by fear of what such a development might mean to her relationship with Cesare. Would he back off from their current intimacy? Would he stop treating her like a real wife?

'I saw you come outside,' a female voice said lightly. 'I thought we should get acquainted. I've known Cesare for so many years,' Serafina Ruffini told her with apparent warmth. 'You haven't been married long, have you?'

'No, only for a month,' Lizzie admitted, struggling to maintain her relaxed attitude in the face of Serafina's shrewdly assessing gaze.

'My husband, Matteo, passed away last year. I'm fortunate to have my seven-year-old son to comfort me,' Serafina confided.

'I'm sorry for your loss,' Lizzie murmured, guiltily dismayed at the news that the brunette was a widow. 'It must be hard for you and your son.'

'We're getting used to being a twosome.' Serafina signalled a waiter hovering by the door with an imperious gesture wholly in keeping with her rather royal air of command. 'Champagne?'

'No, thanks.' Lizzie smoothed a fingertip round the

rim of her glass of water while smiling valiantly as the brunette continued to watch her closely.

The champagne was served with a flourish. Serafina leant back in her upholstered seat. 'Of course, you'll know about my history with Cesare...'

Lizzie stiffened. 'Yes.'

'How honest can I be with you?'

'As honest as you like but I don't think Cesare would like us talking about him behind his back,' Lizzie opined quietly.

'He's an Italian male with a healthy ego.' Serafina laughed. 'Being wanted and appreciated by women is the bread of life for him.'

'Is that why you didn't marry him?' Lizzie heard herself ask helplessly. 'You believed he would be a womaniser?'

'No, not at all. I married for security. I didn't grow up like Cesare in a comfortable middle-class home,' Serafina confided, startling Lizzie with her frankness. 'I came from a poor background and worked very hard for everything I got and I had a great fear of being poor again. Matteo was a proven success while Cesare was only starting out in the business world. I loved Cesare but I'm afraid that the security which Matteo offered me was irresistible.'

Thoroughly disconcerted by that unembarrassed explanation, Lizzie murmured without expression, 'You made the right decision for you.'

Serafina saluted her with her glass in gratitude. 'I believe that I did but once I saw how well Cesare was doing in business, I naturally wished I had had more faith in him.'

'I expect you did,' Lizzie conceded tautly. 'But you

had a husband and a child by then and everything had changed.'

'But I still never stopped loving Cesare and, I warn you now, I intend to get him back.'

'You expect me to listen to this?' Lizzie asked, beginning to rise from her seat, having heard enough of Serafina's self-absorbed excuses.

'No, don't go,' Serafina urged impatiently. 'I'm sorry if I shocked you but I want you to understand that, right now, Cesare is set on punishing me for what I did to him almost ten years ago.'

Involuntarily, Lizzie settled back in her seat. '*Punishing* you?'

'What else could he have been doing when he married you? He married you to *hurt* me. Here I am, finally free and available and he marries you. What sense does that make?'

'Has it occurred to you that maybe he's over you and doesn't want you back?' Lizzie asked helplessly, provoked by the brunette's conviction that she would always be Cesare's most desirable option and reminding herself that she was supposed to be Cesare's real wife and should be reacting accordingly to Serafina's little spiel. 'Your affair ended a long time ago.'

'You *never* forget your first love,' Serafina argued with ringing conviction. 'He's even living in the house we planned together.'

'What house?'

'The farmhouse. We first saw it as students. It was a wet night and we made love in the barn,' Serafina admitted, a rapt look in her bright eyes as Lizzie hastily dropped her lashes to conceal her expression.

Too much information, Lizzie was thinking anxiously, an odd pain clenching her down deep inside. She could not bear to think of Cesare making love with Serafina and could have happily tossed Serafina's champagne into her sensually abstracted face. Serafina had married her older man for security and wealth while still loving and wanting Cesare. Lizzie did not think the brunette had any right to expect to turn the clock back or indeed any excuse to risk upsetting Cesare's new wife with intimate and threatening images from the past she had once shared with him.

'Even though I was already married to Matteo, Cesare still bought the farmhouse as soon as it came on the market,' Serafina told her smugly. 'Look across the valley in the evening from the pool terrace and you will see the Ruffini *palazzo* blazing with lights on the hillside. He wants me back, Lizzie, he's simply too proud to admit it yet.'

'I don't think he would've married me if that was his intention,' Lizzie commented in a deflated tone.

'Oh, I guessed that he married you to get that stupid island back into the family,' Serafina retorted with a wry little laugh and she shrugged. 'I don't care about that. Your marriage is temporary and I'll be waiting when he decides to forgive me.'

'Whatever,' Lizzie mumbled, thrusting her chair back and rising. 'You can hardly expect me to wish you luck with my husband and I really don't understand why you wanted to talk to me in the first place.'

'Because you can make things a lot easier for all three of us by quietly stepping back the minute Cesare admits that he wants his freedom back,' the princess pointed out smoothly. 'If it's a question of money.'

'No, I don't *need* money and I can't be bribed!'

Lizzie parried grittily, her cheeks reddening. 'I wish I could say it was nice meeting you…but it would be a lie.'

'You're a farmer's daughter with no education. Surely you don't believe you have what it takes to hold a man like Cesare's interest?' Serafina fired back with a raised brow. 'Cesare and I belong together.'

CHAPTER NINE

LIZZIE COMPRESSED HER LIPS, said nothing and walked back indoors.

A pounding headache had developed at the base of her skull. How she got through what remained of the evening, she had no idea, but she smiled so much her mouth felt numb and she made polite conversation until she wanted to scream. She was angry with Cesare for ever loving a woman as selfish and grasping as Serafina. Serafina only wanted Cesare now because he had built up an empire worth billions. Nevertheless a few of her remarks stayed with Lizzie like a bruise that refused to heal.

'You never forget your first love. He married you to hurt me. Cesare and I belong together.'

And who was she to assume that that wasn't true? Cesare had never dreamt of regaining the island of Lionos in the way his father and grandmother had. Never having seen it, he had never learned to care for it and could probably well afford to buy his own island should that have been his wish. Was it possible that Cesare had been willing to go through with marrying Lizzie because he had a stronger motive? A desire to punish Serafina for her betrayal all those years ago? *Revenge?* Certainly that was how the princess had interpreted his behaviour of getting married just at the point when she was finally free again. Exasperated by the pointless thoughts going round and round in her sore head, Lizzie tried to blank them out by acknowledging that she knew no more about what Cesare felt for Serafina than she knew about what he felt for herself.

'You've scarcely spoken since we left the benefit,' Cesare commented as the limo drew up outside the farmhouse. He had noticed that she had seemed unusually animated throughout the evening. That had proved a surprise when he had assumed she might feel the need to cling to him in such exclusive and high-powered company. When she failed to demonstrate any desire to cling, instead of being relieved he had felt strangely irked and could not explain why. He had always felt stifled by women who clung to him. He had always valued independence and spirit in a woman more than feminine weakness and soft words of flattery.

Yet when the spirited and independent woman whom he had once loved had approached him at the benefit for a private word, he had been totally turned off by the experience, he acknowledged grimly.

'I'm very tired,' Lizzie said stiffly.

Cesare followed her into the bedroom, unzipping her dress without being asked. Lizzie let the dress glide down to her feet, stepped out of it and, regal as a queen in her underwear, walked into the bathroom without turning her head even to look at him.

He knew when he was getting the silent treatment. She was sulking and that was childish. He had never had any patience for sulks. He pulled a pair of jeans out of a drawer and stripped off his suit. Casually clad, he noted the beady little eyes watching him from below the canopy of the four-poster pet bed and surrendered. 'Come on, Archie...time for something to eat...'

Archie limped across the floor. The cast had been removed from his broken leg only the day before but Archie still thought he was a three-legged dog and had yet to trust the fourth leg to take his weight again. Cesare scooped the little dog up at the top of the stairs and carried him down to the kitchen where he maintained a one-way dialogue with Archie while feeding them both as he raided the fridge.

Teeth gritted, Lizzie emerged from the bathroom to a frustratingly empty bedroom. She had decided that it was beyond cowardly not to ask Cesare why he hadn't warned her that the benefit was being staged at his ex-girlfriend's home. She had not been prepared for that confrontation and was convinced she would have made a more serious effort to look her very best had she known she would be meeting the gorgeous brunette. The problem was that she was jealous, she acknowledged ruefully, green and raw and hurting with ferocious jealousy. She looked out of the landing window at the dark silhouette of the old stone barn and her heart clenched as if it had been squeezed dry. Cesare had made love to Serafina there, love, *not sex*. He had loved Serafina, cared about her, *wanted* to marry her. Yet Serafina had turned her back on his love in favour of wealth and social status. Having achieved those staples, she now wanted Cesare back.

Pulling a silky wrap on over a nightdress, Lizzie

headed downstairs. Cesare was sprawled on a sofa in the airy living room. In worn jeans and an unbuttoned blue shirt, he was a long sleek bronzed figure and heartbreakingly beautiful. Her heart hammered out a responsive and nervous tattoo as she paused in the doorway.

'Why didn't you tell me?' she asked abruptly.

Cesare always avoided dramatic scenes with women and walking out on the risk of one came as naturally as breathing to him. One glance at Lizzie's set, angry face and the eyes gleaming like green witch fire in her flushed face was sufficient to warn him of what was coming. Springing lithely upright, he strolled out past her and swiped the car keys off the cabinet in the hall. 'I'm going for a drive...don't wait up for me. I'll be late,' he spelled out flatly.

Taken aback, Lizzie moved fast to place herself in his path to the front door. 'Are you serious?'

'Perfectly. I don't want to argue with you, *cara*. I'm not in the mood. We're flying to Lionos tomorrow and Athene will be joining us. That is enough of a challenge for the present.'

It was a shock for Lizzie to register how cold the smooth, perfect planes of his lean dark face could look. His spectacular eyes were veiled by his thick lashes, his superb bone structure taut, his shapely mouth, defined by a dark shadow of stubble, a hard line of restraint. Alarm bells sounded in her head. 'You could've warned me that we were going to Serafina's house and that she would be our hostess.'

'I am not going to argue with you about Serafina,' Cesare asserted, his jawline clenching hard as granite.

'I'm *not* arguing with you,' Lizzie reasoned curtly. 'And why won't you discuss her with me?'

Velvet black lashes flew up on scorching golden eyes. 'She's none of your business, nothing to do with you.'

Lizzie flinched and leant back against the door to stay upright. She felt like someone trying to walk a tightrope in the dark and she was terrified of falling. 'She spent ten minutes talking to me outside on the terrace and made me feel very much as if she was my business.'

Feverish colour laced his incredible cheekbones. '*You*...discussed me with...*her*?' he framed wrathfully.

Lizzie found it interesting that, instead of being flattered as Serafina had suggested, Cesare was absolutely outraged by the idea. 'What do you think?' She hesitated, hovering between him and the door. 'I only wanted to know why you didn't mention that she would be entertaining us.'

Cesare ground his perfect white teeth together because he *had* thought of mentioning it, only to run aground on the recollection that theirs was not a normal marriage. They were not in a relationship where he was bound to make such personal explanations, were they? He focused on Lizzie's pale face on which colour stood out only on her cheeks. She looked hurt. He saw that hurt and instinctively recoiled from it, frustration rippling through him. He didn't want to share what had happened earlier that evening with Lizzie, not only because it would rouse her suspicions, but also because it was tacky and he *refused* to bring that tacky element into what had proved to be a glorious honeymoon.

'Serafina is very much part of the local scenery. Many of my friends are also hers. I have no reason to avoid her. Seeing her is no big deal,' he delineated stiffly, reluctantly, willing to throw that log on the fire if it satisfied her and closed the subject.

'I don't believe you,' Lizzie whispered unhappily. 'If it had been no big deal, you would've mentioned it.'

'You know me so well?' he derided.

Lizzie paled even more. 'I thought I did.'

Cesare closed his hands firmly to her ribcage and lifted her bodily away from the door.

'If you walk out, I'm not going to Lionos with you!' Lizzie flung the worst threat she could think to make in an effort to stop him in his tracks.

'In what fantasy world are you living that you think you can threaten me?' Cesare breathed, freezing with the door ajar so that cooler night air filtered in to cool her now clammy skin.

'I only wanted you to explain.'

'I have nothing to explain,' Cesare parried drily. 'But you will definitely be telling me at some point what Serafina said to you.'

'Honesty has to be a two-way thing to work. We've been living like a married couple.'

'Because we *are* married.'

'You know what I mean…' Lizzie hesitated, reluctant to probe deeper but driven by turbulent emotional forces she could not suppress. 'You've been treating me as though I'm really your wife.'

There it was—the truth Cesare had hoped to evade

because he didn't know *how* that had happened, didn't know what to say to her, didn't even know how he felt about that development. Why did women always have to drag unmentionable issues out into the open and do them to death at a time of their choosing? How the hell had he got himself into such an untenable situation? He had started out fine, he acknowledged broodingly, laying down the rules, seeing what made sense, knowing what he should not do lest it lead to exactly this situation. And somehow it had all gone to hell in a hand basket in spite of *all* that careful pre-planning, *all* that practical knowhow and knowledge of the female sex. And here he was trapped as he had never wanted to be trapped...

'I want to know what Serafina said to you.'

'That she wants you back, that you married me to punish her, that I wasn't educated enough to hold you... Oh, yes,' Lizzie recounted and then, with a ghastly attempt at an amused smile, added, 'and that this was your mutual dream house, planned by you both on the wet night you made love in the barn...'

Cesare's eyes flashed flaming gold, his outrage unconcealed. He closed a hard hand to the edge of the door as if to emphasise the fact that he was still leaving. '*Madonna diavolo!* She shouldn't have involved you in this.'

At those words, at that suggestion that there was an involvement that she was unaware of, Lizzie swore her heart cracked right down the middle. 'No,' she agreed woodenly, because it was true.

Cesare steeled himself. He knew he had to speak, could not comprehend why ESP was suddenly warning him to shut up and say nothing. 'We don't have a genuine marriage. We are not a couple in the true sense of the word. We both know that...'

He paused as if he was hoping she would leap in and say something but Lizzie couldn't have found her voice had her life depended on it. At that moment she felt as if her life's blood were draining away in a pool on the floor and that dramatic image made her feel dizzy.

'I'm going to bed,' she mumbled, knowing that she was lying, knowing that sleep had never been further from her mind, but it seemed so incredibly important in that silence to act as if she were still able to function normally even if it was a complete lie to try and save face.

'This is all my fault,' Cesare breathed in a roughened undertone. 'Don't think I'm not aware of that. I shouldn't have brought something as volatile as sex into the equation.'

'And you were still doing it...only a few hours ago,' she framed unevenly.

Unusually indecisive, Cesare hovered in the rushing silence. Archie was looking at him from across the hall as if he had two heads, which absolutely had to be his imagination playing tricks on him, he reasoned wildly. He felt sick, he felt bad, he felt... No, he was being dangerously emotional and he knew what emotion did to him: it made him irrational and reckless and he wasn't going to go there again...*ever*! He was taking the right approach in correcting a serious mistake before it did any more damage. Aside of that aspect, they were both consenting adults.

'So, it's back to the business arrangement,' Lizzie assumed in a tight little voice.

'I think that would be wiser, don't you?'

Not recognising that cold, detached intonation, Lizzie finally dared to look at him again. He was poised by the door, devastatingly handsome, a long slice of bare brown torso showing between the parted edges of his shirt, tight jeans defining long, powerful thighs and lean hips. Slowly she raised her gaze, determined to be brave, determined to hold on to her pride even though he had rejected her in the worst possible and most hurtfully humiliating way. He had made it clear where he stood and she supposed that brutal honesty was for the best.

'Goodnight,' Lizzie said quietly and she turned on her heel.

In a split second the front door closed and he was gone. The Ferrari engine growled to life and she literally ran out to the terrace above the pool, frantically determined to see if she could pick out the Ruffini *palazzo* on the hillside. And there it was, a big white classical building lit up like a fairground. She had noticed it before but had never thought to ask about it. Now she watched the lights of Cesare's car heading down into the valley and she stood and she stood, arms wrapped defensively round herself while she waited to see if her very worst suspicions were correct.

At such a distance, she could not have been a hundred per cent certain but she was convinced that it was the Ferrari that she saw heading up the long, winding, steep drive to the *palazzo*. Cesare was going straight to see Serafina. Lizzie was in shock. Perhaps he had been seeing the other woman all along; Lizzie hadn't been keeping tabs on him everywhere he went. It seemed pretty obvious to her that Cesare had a dark

side and more secrets than she had ever had cause
to suspect and she had been ignorant and irresponsible and very naive not to smell a rat sooner...but it
wasn't much good or any comfort to feel wise *after*
the event, was it?

CHAPTER TEN

THE FOLLOWING MORNING, with her heart beating very fast, Lizzie studied a test wand, relieved that she had taken the opportunity to discreetly buy a pregnancy kit some weeks earlier.

And there it was straight away, the result she had both feared and craved: she was pregnant. It changed everything, she acknowledged in shock, and she walked out to the bedroom and unlocked the door she had locked the night before. Cesare would need access to his clothes but had she cared about that last night when her dream world had collapsed about her ears? No, she had not.

But now that she knew for sure that she was carrying Cesare's baby, she had to look to the future and beyond the business agreement they had originally made. She could not afford to be at odds with her child's father. That would only foster resentment between them and their child would suffer in that scenario. Unfortunately that meant that she had to be a bigger person than she felt like being just at that moment. She had to rise above what had happened, bury the personal aspect and stick to the rules from here on in.

He'd broken her heart. Well, she'd recovered from

Andrew; she would eventually recover from Cesare. Of course, she had never loved Andrew the way she loved Cesare; consequently getting over Cesare would be more of a challenge. Andrew had hurt her self-esteem and damaged her trust but Cesare had torn her heart out. To think of living even one day without Cesare somewhere nearby tore her apart, teaching her how weak and vulnerable her emotions had made her.

Yes, Lizzie acknowledged, tidying her hair, adding more concealer to hide the redness of her eyes, she had a long, long way to go in the recovery process. But now that she knew about the baby, it would have to start right now. She would have to put on the act of the century. She couldn't afford to show the smallest interest in what was going on between Serafina and him. He had made it clear that she had no right to ask such questions and she would have to respect that.

Had Cesare behaved badly? She thought he had. Scrapping the business-agreement-based marriage had been *his* idea, not hers. But honesty forced her to acknowledge that he had suggested at the time that they would have to see how well their marriage worked. In short, their marriage as such had been on a trial basis. And obviously, while it had worked incredibly well for Lizzie, it had not worked at all for Cesare. That hurt; that hurt her very much. It was a complete rejection of everything they had shared in and out of bed over the past month and it made her feel such an idiot for being so deliriously happy with him while failing utterly to notice that he did not feel the same way.

Lizzie went downstairs for breakfast, Archie at her heels. The instant the dog saw Cesare, who spoiled him shamelessly and taught him bad manners by feeding him titbits during meals, Archie hurried over to greet him. Cesare vaulted upright the minute she appeared. Unshaven, noticeably lacking his usual immaculate grooming, he still wore the same jeans and shirt. He raked a long-fingered brown hand through his tousled hair, looking effortlessly gorgeous but possibly less poised than he usually was.

'I won't lock the bedroom door again,' Lizzie promised, her heart-shaped face as still as a woodland pool. 'I'm sorry, I didn't think about what I was doing but the room's free now.'

'I'll get a shower before we leave for the airfield,' Cesare countered, his dark golden gaze scanning her expressionless face as if in search of something. 'Lizzie, we need to talk.'

Already having foreseen that he might feel that that was a necessity, Lizzie rushed to disabuse him of that dangerous notion. The very last thing she needed in her current shaky state of mind was a re-hash of the breakdown of their relationship the night before. It wouldn't smooth over anything, wouldn't make her feel any better. How could it? Essentially he was dumping her and nothing he could say would ease that pain.

'That's the very last thing we need,' Lizzie told him briskly. 'All that needed to be said was said last night and we don't need to go over it again.'

'But—'

'What you said made sense to me when I thought it over,' Lizzie cut in, desperate to shut him up. 'This is business, nothing else. Let's stick to that from now on and I'll keep to my side of the bargain while your grandmother is staying with us on the island. I see no reason why we shouldn't bring this…er…project to a successful conclusion.'

Cesare blinked, disconcerted by the sound of such prosaic language falling from her lips. He was relieved that she was calm and grateful that she now intended to accompany him to Lionos for Athene's sake but he didn't agree with a single word she was saying. While, uniquely for him, he hesitated in a frantic inner search for the right approach to take with her, Lizzie took the wind out of his sails altogether.

'And that successful conclusion I mentioned?' Lizzie continued, a forced brightness of tone accompanying her wide fake smile. 'We're almost there because I'm pregnant.'

'Pregnant?' Cesare exclaimed in almost comical disbelief, springing back out of his seat again and yanking out the chair beside his own for her use. *'Madre di Dio…*sit down.'

Taken aback by his astonished reaction to her news, Lizzie sank down on the chair. 'It's not earth-shaking, Cesare. Women get pregnant every day.'

'You're my wife… It's a little more personal than that for me,' Cesare parried thickly, stepping behind her to rest his hands down on her slim, taut shoulders.

Alarmingly conscious of that physical contact, Lizzie froze in dismay. 'Could I ask you not to do that?'

'Do what?'

'Touch me,' she extended in an apologetic tone. 'I'll understand if you're forced to do it when your grandmother's around to make us look like a convincing couple but we're alone here and there's no need for it.'

Off-balanced by that blunt response, Cesare released her shoulders and backed away. He was thinking about the baby and he was fighting off an extraordinarily strong urge to touch her stomach, which he knew was weird, not to mention an urge destined to go unfulfilled.

'Forgive me,' he breathed abruptly. 'My immediate response was to touch you because I am full of joy about the baby.'

He had never looked *less* full of joy to Lizzie. In fact he looked a little pale and a lot tense, eyes shielded by his ridiculously long lashes, wide, sensual mouth compressed. She wanted to slap him so badly that her hands twitched on her lap. Like a magician pulling a white rabbit out of a hat, she had made her unexpected announcement, depending on it to wipe away the awkwardness lingering after their confrontation the night before. She had just let him know that he would never have a reason to touch her again *because* she had conceived. He should have been thrilled to be let off the hook when he didn't deserve it. Instead, however, a tense silence stretched like a rubber band threatening to snap.

'I didn't think it would happen so...*fast*,' Cesare admitted half under his breath.

'Well, it saves us a lot of hassle that it has,' Lizzie pronounced with as much positive emphasis as she could load into a single sentence. Hovering on the tip of her tongue was the highly inappropriate reminder that, after the amount of unprotected sex they had had, she thought it was more of a surprise that they hadn't hit the jackpot the first week.

'Hassle?'

'If we'd had to go for the artificial insemination, it

might have been a bit...*icky*,' she mumbled, momentarily losing her grip on her relentless falsely cheerful front.

Icky, Cesare repeated inwardly. It was a pretty good description of how he was feeling. *Icky.* He had suffered a Damascene moment of revelation while he was with Serafina the previous night. A blinding light that even he could not ignore or sensibly explain away had shone over the events and emotions of the past month and he had finally understood how everything had gone so very wrong. Unfortunately for him, since Lizzie had joined him for breakfast, he had realised that 'wrong' was an understatement. He had dug a great big hole for himself and she was showing every intention of being perfectly happy to bury him alive in it.

Cesare went upstairs, ostensibly for a shower but he wanted privacy to make a phone call. In all his life he had never ever turned to Goffredo for advice but his father was the only touchy-feely male relative he had, who could be trusted to keep a confidence. His sisters were too young and out of the question. Each would discuss it with the other and then they would approach Lizzie to tell all because she was one of the sisterhood now and closer to his siblings than he was. Goffredo had one word of advice and it was an unpalatable one. Heaving a sigh, he then suggested his son imagine his life without her and take it from there. That mental exercise only exacerbated Cesare's dark mood.

Lizzie wore a floaty white cotton sundress to travel out to the island and took great pains with her hair and make-up. She knew that in the greater scheme of things her appearance was unimportant but was convinced that no woman confronted by a beauty like Serafina could remain indifferent to the possibility of unkind comparisons.

Close to running late for their flight, Cesare strode down the steps, a cool and sophisticated figure in beige chinos and an ivory cotton sweater that truly enhanced his bronzed skin tone and stunning dark eyes. Climbing into the car, he barely glanced at Lizzie and she knew all her fussing had been a pathetic waste of time.

Archie sat right in the middle of the back seat, halfway between them like a dog trying to work out how he could split himself into two parts. To Lizzie's intense annoyance, her pet ended up nudged up against a hard masculine thigh because Cesare was absently massaging Archie's ear, which reduced her dog to a pushover.

By the time they reached the airfield and boarded the helicopter, Lizzie was becoming increasingly frustrated. Cesare's brooding silence was getting to her and she wanted to know what was behind it. How could he simply switch off everything they had seemed to have together? It hadn't ever just been sex between them. There had been laughter and lots of talking and an intense sense of rightness as well. At least on *her* side, she conceded wretchedly.

His long, powerful thigh stretched as he shifted position and a heated ache blossomed between her thighs. That surge of hormonal chemistry mortified her. She reminded herself that that side of their marriage was over, she reminded herself that she was pregnant and she *still* ended up glancing back at that masculine thigh. Suddenly she was remembering that only the day before she would have stretched out a hand and stroked that hard male flesh, taking the initiative in a way that always surprised and pleased him. How had they seemed to be so attuned to each other when they so patently could not have been? Had she deceived herself? Had she dreamt up a whole fairy tale and tried to live it by putting Cesare in a starring role? Was this mess all her own wretched fault?

With such ideas torturing her and with a companion, who was almost as silent, it was little wonder that Lizzie had been airborne for over an hour when she was jolted by Cesare simply and suddenly turning round from the front passenger seat of the helicopter and urging her to look down at what he called *'her'* island.

'And Chrissie's,' she said unheard above the engine noise, stretching to peer over his broad shoulder as the craft dipped. She saw a long teardrop-shaped piece of land covered with lush green trees. *'That's* Lionos?' She gasped in astonishment for it was much bigger than she had expected. In her head she had cherished a not very inviting image of a rocky piece of land stuck in the middle of nowhere, for her mother had not made it sound an attractive place. At the same time their inheritance had never seemed very real to either her or her sister when they could not afford even to visit it.

Within minutes the helicopter was descending steeply to land in a clearing in the trees and for the first time in twenty-four hours a feeling of excited anticipation gripped Lizzie. Ignoring Cesare's extended hand, she jumped down onto the ground and stared up at the white weatherboard house standing at the top of a slope. Like the island, it was bigger than she had expected.

'Athene told me that her father built it in the nineteen twenties and she had five siblings, so it had to be spacious,' Cesare supplied as he released Archie and the dog went scampering off to do what dogs did when they'd been confined for a long time. 'Primo says it really needs to be knocked down and rebuilt but he's done his best within the time frame he's had.'

'He's frighteningly efficient,' Lizzie remarked, mounting the slope, striving to ignore and avoid the supportive hand Cesare had planted to the base of her spine and a little breathless in her haste.

'Take it easy. It's hot and you're pregnant,' Cesare intoned.

'For goodness' sake!' Lizzie snapped. 'I'm only a tiny bit pregnant!'

In silence, Cesare rolled his eyes at that impossibility. He had all the consolation of knowing that he was reaping what he had sowed. Lizzie was not naturally either moody or short-tempered. In fact, in spite of her troubled childhood she had a remarkably cheerful nature, he conceded grimly. At least she had had a remarkably cheerful nature until he had contrived to destroy everything in what had to be an own goal of even more remarkable efficacy.

Primo greeted them at the front door and spread it wide. 'Workmen are still finishing off the utility area,' he admitted. 'But I believe the house is now presentable.'

Wide-eyed, Lizzie drifted through the tiled hall, which had been painted white, and moved on into a spacious reception room furnished with pieces that were an elegant mix of the traditional and the more contemporary. French windows draped with floral curtains opened out onto a terrace overlooking a secluded sandy cove. The view down the slope of a path through the trees to the beach was incredibly picturesque and unspoilt.

She walked through the house and as she peered into rooms some of her tension began to evaporate. In the wake of her mother's unappreciative descriptions, she was surprised to discover that it was actually a very attractive house and full of character. A room with a bathroom had been prepared for Athene's use on the ground floor. Lizzie mounted the stairs, which had wrought-iron ornamental balusters and a polished brass handrail. A bedroom had been sacrificed to provide en-suite bathrooms. Everywhere had been freshly decorated and kitted out, fabrics stirring softly in the breeze through open windows.

'What do you think?' Cesare asked from his stance on the landing.

'It's magical. I can understand why your grandmother never forgot this island. It must've been a wonderful house for kids,' she confided.

'Soon our child will follow that same tradition,' Cesare said gruffly.

'Well, possibly when he or she is visiting you. I won't be here as well,' Lizzie pointed out, quick to puncture that fantasy.

Cesare hovered in the strangest way, moving a step forward and then a step back, lashes suddenly lifting on strained dark golden eyes. 'And what if I wanted you to be here as well?'

'But you *wouldn't* want that,' Lizzie countered with

unwelcome practicality. 'You will either have remarried or you'll have a girlfriend in tow.'

'What if I don't want that? What if I want you?' Cesare shot at her without warning, unnerved by that veiled reference to the divorce that would be required for his remarriage.

Lizzie lost colour, wondering what he was playing at, wondering if this was some new game on his terms. 'But you *don't*…want me, that is. You made that quite clear last night.'

'I *do* want you. I want to stay married,' Cesare bit out almost aggressively. 'Last night, you took me by surprise and I was confused. I made a mistake.'

Lizzie shook her pale head slowly and studied him in angry wonderment, temper stirring from the depths of the emotional turmoil she had been enduring since he had blown all her hopes and dreams to dust. 'I can't believe I'm hearing this. First you ask me for a business-based marriage, *then* you ask me to give our marriage a try and then you tell me we don't have a *real* marriage. As I see it, that's pretty comprehensive and not open to any other interpretation!'

She swivelled on her heel and deliberately walked past him to enter the room on the other side of the landing.

'I'm trying to say I'm sorry and you're not even listening!' Cesare growled from behind her.

'You can't apologise for what you feel…neither of us can,' Lizzie parried curtly as she lodged by a window, hoping to look as though she were entranced by the view when in actuality all she could think about was escaping this agonising going-nowhere conversation with Cesare, who seemed not to have the first clue about how she might be feeling. 'I'm going to get changed and go off and explore.'

'Alone?' Cesare exclaimed.

'Yes. I like my own company. I had to—I worked alone for years,' she reminded him doggedly, walking past him on the landing, relieved when she saw the cases being carried upstairs into the master bedroom. 'I realise once Athene arrives tomorrow it'll be "game on" or whatever you want to call it...but could we... please not share a bedroom tonight?'

'Why are you not listening to anything I'm saying?' Cesare demanded in apparent disbelief. 'You won't even look at me!'

Lizzie had only felt free to look at him when he was *hers*. Now that he wasn't any more, she didn't want to fall victim to his essential gorgeousness all over again. Not looking was a form of self-defence, she reasoned wildly.

'Lizzie...' he breathed in a driven undertone.

Lizzie stiffened, tears prickling behind her wide eyes. 'I can't afford to listen to you. You upset me a lot last night and I really don't want to talk about that kind of stuff. It's pointless. I'm not really your wife. I may be living with you—'

'Expecting *my* child!' Cesare slotted in with greater force than seemed necessary.

'But you didn't choose to marry me because you cared about me, therefore it's not a proper marriage,' Lizzie replied as she reluctantly turned back to face him. 'And in your own immortal words everything else we've shared can be written off as "just sex".'

Cesare flinched at that reminder, his pallor below

his bronzed skin palpable. 'I care about you *now*. I want to *keep* you.'

'I'm not a pet, Cesare...' Lizzie stared at him and frowned. 'Are you feeling all right? You know, you're acting very oddly.'

Goffredo's one-word piece of advice returned to haunt Cesare. 'I'm fine,' he said brusquely, lying through his teeth.

All of a quiver after that pointless exchange, her nerves jangling, Lizzie vanished into the bedroom, closed the door and opened her case to extract a sun top and shorts. She needed to blow the cobwebs off with a good walk. Cesare was nowhere to be seen when she went downstairs again and she went into the kitchen where Primo reigned supreme and eventually emerged with Primo's luxury version of a picnic meal and a bottle of water. With a little luck she could stay out until dark, then dive into bed and wake up to a new day and the big show for his poor grandmother's benefit.

Cesare was furious when he discovered that Lizzie had left the house. He strode down to the beach but there was no sign of her and not even a footprint on the pristine strand to suggest that she had come that way.

Several hours later, sunburned, foot weary and very tired after her jaunt across Lionos, Lizzie returned to discover that Cesare had gone out. Thankful, she settled down to supper as only Primo could make it. Sliding into her comfortable bed, she slept like a log.

Athene arrived mid-afternoon the next day. Cesare decided to be grateful for that because it brought Lizzie out of hiding. It had not once crossed his mind that she could be so intractable that she wouldn't even give him a hearing and then he thought of all the years she had slaved for her unappreciative and critical father and realised that she would have needed a strong, stubborn backbone.

Relaxed and colourful in a red sundress, Lizzie ushered Athene into her former childhood home. Tears shone in the old lady's eyes as she stood in the hall, gazing down the slope at the beautiful view. 'I thought it would all be overgrown and unrecognisable.'

'You showed me a photo once. I had the trees cut back,' Cesare told his grandmother softly. 'Shall I show you around?'

'Yes, this is your home and Lizzie's now,' Athene said a little tearfully and fumbled for a tissue. 'I have so many memories of my brothers and sisters here and now that they're all gone...'

Lizzie watched Cesare mop up his grandmother's tears with a deft touch and the right words and, minutes later, Athene was laughing as she recounted a childhood adventure with her brothers. She accompanied them on the official tour and Primo served afternoon tea out on the terrace, apparently an old tradition that Athene loved.

'Primo is an absolute treasure,' Athene told Lizzie as Cesare murmured an apology and withdrew to answer his phone before walking back into the house.

'And even better he *cooks*, which I'm not very good at,' Lizzie admitted, topping up the older woman's tea.

'Have you and Cesare had a row?' her companion asked without warning. 'I'm not an interfering old woman but I can feel that something's wrong.'

Lizzie felt that even an award-winning actress would have been challenged to carry off a smile at that point. 'A hiccup,' she downplayed studiously, her cheeks burning tomato-red as if the lie might be emblazoned on her forehead.

'My grandson has a remarkable brain, which serves him well in business. He's not quite so good at relationships,' Athene remarked wryly, gentle amusement in her warm brown eyes. 'There's bound to be hiccups as you call them. He's set in his ways and you'll challenge him. That's good for him. After all, anyone with eyes can see how deeply attached you are to each other.'

Lizzie's opinion of Athene's shrewdness nosedived at that pronouncement but the awkward moment passed over and she managed to relax again. The old lady eventually nodded off in the shade and Lizzie went back indoors.

'I need to warn you,' Lizzie almost whispered round the corner of the door of the room Cesare had set up as an office. 'Athene thinks we've had a row but that that's normal, so not really anything to worry about...but we'll need to make a real effort to impress.'

'Wouldn't it be easier simply to talk to me?' Cesare suggested, rising from behind his desk, all sleek Italian designer style in his tailored oatmeal-coloured casuals.

Lizzie continued to hover defensively in the doorway. 'I just don't think we have anything to talk about.'

'Do you know what time I went to bed last night?'

Lizzie blinked in confusion. 'How would I?'

'I was out tramping round the island looking for *you*. Primo couldn't raise a signal on my cell phone until midnight and I only found out then that you had returned to the house hours earlier!'

Lizzie dealt him an astonished look. 'But why were you looking for me in the first place? I wasn't lost.'

Cesare studied her as if she were irretrievably dim. 'There are all kinds of hazards out there. Fast currents in the sea, steep drops, dangerous rocks...'

Definitely behaving oddly, Lizzie labelled as she breathed in deep. 'Cesare, I'm not some little fluffy woman who can't look after herself. I'm an outdoors woman, used to working in all weathers and accustomed to constantly considering safety aspects on the farm.'

'But I was *worried* about you!' Cesare shot back at her in furious frustration.

Lizzie tossed her head, platinum-blonde hair shimmering across her slight shoulders in the sunlight, green eyes wide and wary. 'Well, you didn't need to be. I should've thought you would've been more worried about how Serafina is managing while we're together here when you belong with her.'

'I do not *belong* with Serafina!' Cesare raked at her so loudly, she jumped.

'No?'

'Do I strike you as being an idiot? I was a boy when I fell in love with her and full of romantic idealism but I'm all grown-up now,' he completed grimly.

'Well, you went rushing over to that *palazzo* fast enough the other night,' Lizzie argued in a less aggressive prompt. 'That *was* where you went, wasn't it?'

His stunning gaze widened to smouldering gold eyes of challenge. 'You think I went over there to *be* with her?'

'What else was I supposed to think?' Lizzie asked tightly. 'You left me in anger...'

'I wasn't angry with you, I was angry with *her*!' Cesare exclaimed in full-volume contradiction and Lizzie hastily backed to the door to close it firmly shut. 'How dare she have the insolence to approach my wife with the tacky details of an affair that happened a decade ago? I'd never heard such rubbish in my life and I was determined to finally have it out with her.'

Tacky details scarcely dovetailed with Serafina's suggestion that the barn episode had been a very precious memory for them both. Furthermore Lizzie was transfixed by the idea that he had rushed out of the house in a rage because Serafina had dared to approach his wife. Lizzie went pink over her misreading of the situation. 'And did you have it out with her?'

'*Sì*...I said a lot that she will not forget in a hurry. If she wasn't so vain, she would have accepted a long time ago that I would sooner chew off my own arm than have anything to do with her again. How could you think *that* of me?' Cesare raked at her in apparent wonderment. 'A woman who walked out on me because I wasn't rich enough? A disloyal, deceitful woman with the morals of a whore... She first offered herself back to me three years after she married Matteo and she did it again last night, which outraged me.'

Lizzie was so astonished by what she was finding out that she was rooted to the floor where she stood. Not only did he no longer care about Serafina, he evidently despised her and her eagerness to get him back. There was nothing fake about the driving derision he exuded. 'And of course you said no?'

'I never thought about her again after that first incident,' Cesare admitted flatly. 'By that stage I was grateful that, by marrying her, Matteo had saved me from making a serious mistake. No sane man would want a treacherous woman but, unfortunately for him, Matteo was besotted with her.'

Lizzie nodded slowly.

'Serafina won't be bothering either of us again, I assure you,' Cesare spelled out. 'She told me that she's bored with the countryside and will be moving back to her home in Florence.'

Lizzie was thinking about him having spent hours searching for her the night before because he was concerned that she might have met with an accident. Even though she was a seasoned outdoorswoman, she could not help but be touched by his naive assumption that she required his protection. She had made so many silly assumptions about Serafina and suddenly it was obvious that she had been listening to an extremely vain and spoilt woman spouting her belief that she was both irresistible and unforgettable. Cesare, on the other hand, had recovered from Serafina's betrayal by appreciating what a narrow escape he had had. That, she recognised, was absolutely in line with his character while rushing off to be with Serafina while he was married would not have been.

'I'm glad she's moving…I didn't like her,' Lizzie confided in a case of severe understatement. A light-headed sensation engulfed her and she gripped the back of a chair. 'Sorry, I get a bit dizzy now and again.'

'Is that like being only a tiny bit pregnant?' Cesare enquired, scooping her up as she swayed and planting her carefully down into the armchair. 'You need to be taking more rest and eating more food.'

'And what would you know about it?' Lizzie mumbled, momentarily giving way to the heaviness of her body and slumping into the depths of the chair like a sagging cushion.

'Possibly as much as you,' Cesare dared. 'I contacted an obstetrician for advice.'

Her lower lip dropped. 'You did...what?'

'It's my baby too,' he countered defensively. 'I had no idea how to look after you properly. It made sense to consult someone with the relevant knowledge.'

Her eyes stung again. Against all the odds, he was making such an effort to put across the point that, although he didn't want a real marriage with her, he did care about her welfare and their child's. Her throat convulsed. The tears she had been holding back were gaining on her, no matter how hard she tried to hold them back.

As Cesare stared across the barrier of his desk he saw two tears rolling down Lizzie's cheeks and his last defences fell to basement level. *He* had caused this fiasco. *He* had made her unhappy.

'I'm sorry...I'm *so* sorry,' Cesare told her gruffly.

Lizzie opened her wet eyes to find Cesare on his knees at her feet, stunning dark golden eyes stricken. 'Sorry? What about?'

'I'm sorry I hurt you. For years I had this set of rules with women,' he breathed raggedly, grabbing both her hands and crushing them between his. 'I never got involved. I never got involved with anyone after Serafina. And then I met you and I...I thought it would be the same with you and I tried to stick to the same rules but you were too much for me, only I didn't see it...'

'Slow down...' Lizzie begged, struggling to work

out what he was telling her in such a rush. 'What are you saying?'

'That I'm mad about you, that I love you and I never want to lose you,' Cesare told her, crushing the life out of her poor fingers, his physical intensity as great as the emotional intensity now clear in his eyes.

Her lashes fluttered in bemusement. 'But you *said*—'

'Forget what I said. I was still trying to stick to my rules but it was idiocy,' he told her with a fierce fervour that was in itself impressive. 'I drove to Serafina's in a rage because she'd dared to try and upset you and I was driving back, thinking about what a vicious witch she is and thinking about you too…and that's when I realised.'

'That you love me?' Lizzie probed numbly, unsure what to believe, her thoughts spinning.

'I think I was scared to deal with what I was feeling for you, so I avoided thinking about it altogether…' Cesare hesitated. 'You know, I'm not much like Goffredo. I don't spend much time thinking about feelings and stuff.'

Lizzie was pleasantly surprised to learn that he had spent *any* time thinking about feelings but she couldn't smile when she was in shock. For the first time ever outside the bedroom she was seeing Cesare without the cool front he wore to the world and he wasn't half as smooth with words in the emotional category as he was with other things. Yet there was something hugely endearing about that inept surge of sentiment and confession because every syllable of it rang with raw honesty.

'So, you think you love me?' she pressed a little

shakily, scared to hope, scared to dream, scared he didn't yet know his own heart.

'I *know* I love you. I only had to think of how warm and happy everything has seemed since we got married. I only have to think of being without you to know that what I feel for you is so much more than I ever felt for Serafina,' he confessed huskily.

A huge smile suddenly lit up Lizzie's face as she finally dared to really look at him again, scanning the superb bone structure, the straight nose and the perfect mouth. This time around, she revelled unashamedly in his essential gorgeousness because for the first time ever he felt like *hers*.

'I didn't want to fall for you either. Mum made so many mistakes and she was never really happy. I was afraid of falling for you,' Lizzie admitted, freeing a hand to brush his thick black hair off his brow in a gesture that came very close to an adoring caress. 'I really did think we were going to go the business route and then…my goodness, I couldn't stop thinking about you, couldn't take my eyes off you, couldn't keep my hands off you. You're sort of addictive but I didn't want to get hurt.'

'I hope I will never hurt you again.'

'Why are you still on your knees?' Lizzie whispered, genuinely bewildered.

'I rang my father for advice. I didn't give him *details*,' Cesare stressed when she looked at him in dismay. 'I just admitted that I'd said some very stupid things and he had only one word of advice…'

Lizzie viewed him expectantly.

Cesare bit the bullet and confided, *'Grovel.'*

'Seriously?' Lizzie giggled, tickled pink.

'I'm only going to do it once because I'm never ever likely to screw up as badly with you again, *amata mia*,' Cesare delivered, springing back upright without any loss of presence to open the door before striding back to scoop his wife up out of her chair. 'I've learned a lot from this experience.'

'Have you?' Lizzie asked curiously, resting back against his broad chest, sublimely happy just to be in his arms again, breathing in the delicious scent of him and free to think about all the wicked bedroom skills he was undoubtedly about to unleash on her.

'For a whole month I took you for granted. I'll never make that mistake again. I love you. My family loves you.'

'Even my father said that you were a sensible man,' Lizzie inputted with amusement.

'Very sensible. You're a wonderful woman, *cara mia*.' Cesare lowered her the whole formidable length of his lean, hard body to the landing floor and kissed her with hungry, driving passion.

Lizzie was more than ready to drown now in his potent fervour to reconnect with her. Excitement laced her happiness with a heady sense of joy and quiet security. She simply knew that she had a glorious life ahead of her with her husband and her child.

On the ground floor, Athene was in a self-congratulating mood.

'I do hope I've sorted them out. Cesare's stubborn but his wife is soft. As if I would simply fall asleep in the middle of a conversation!' Athene chuckled as she took over Primo's kitchen to make her grandson's favourite cake. 'I think we'll have a rather late dinner tonight, Primo…'

* * *

Three years later, Lizzie relaxed on the front veranda of the house on Lionos while she awaited Cesare's return from a business trip. Her children were with her. Max was two, a toddler with the unusual combination of his mother's pale hair and his father's dark eyes. He was industriously racing toy cars on the boards beneath her feet and making very noisy vroom-vroom sounds. In a travel cot in the shade a dark-haired six-month-old baby girl slumbered, sucking her thumb, while Archie dozed on the front doormat.

Gianna had not been planned, Lizzie reflected, her eyes tender as she bent down to try and extract her daughter's thumb from her rosebud mouth. She managed it but even in sleep within minutes the thumb crept back. She gave up when she heard the distant beat of the helicopter's approach, sliding upright to get a better view over the bay.

Max abandoned his cars and joined her. 'Papa... Papa!' he exclaimed, well aware of what that sound presaged in his secure little world.

Lizzie stroked her son's silky head and smiled dreamily. She always enjoyed the sunshine and the peace on Lionos but it would soon be disrupted by Cesare's forceful, exciting presence and she couldn't wait; she really couldn't wait. Three years had not dimmed the chemistry between them.

Athene spent spring to summer on the island, preferring her Rome apartment and its greater convenience in the winter. Lizzie had grown to love her husband's grandmother as much as she loved the rest of his family. He had been so blessed by all that love and warmth and to give him his due becoming a parent had made Cesare more sensitive towards his own relatives. He was much more relaxed with his large and convivial family than he had once been and his father and his sisters were frequent visitors to their homes in London, Tuscany and Lionos. Lizzie often teased her husband that she had stayed married to him because she couldn't bear the thought of losing his family.

Sadly, since her marriage she had seen much less of her own father and sister. Brian Whitaker came on occasional visits but he didn't like flying or foreign food or even people talking their own language in his vicinity. Lizzie had purchased a compact home for the older man in the village where he had grown up and he seemed as happy there as he would be anywhere. She had taken him to see a consultant for his Parkinson's disease and he was on a new drug regimen and showing considerable improvement.

Disconcertingly, although Chrissie regularly hitched a flight home with Cesare when he was in London on business, she had become fiercely independent and now had secrets she was reluctant to share. Lizzie had watched anxiously from the sidelines of her sister's life as things went badly wrong for the sibling she adored and troubled times rolled in. Cesare had advised her to let Chrissie stand on her own feet and not to interfere when Lizzie would more happily have rushed in and tried to wave a magic wand over Chrissie's difficulties to make them vanish. She had had to accept that Chrissie was an adult with the right to make her own decisions…and her own mistakes. That said, however, she was still very close to her sister and very protective of her.

The helicopter finally appeared in the bright blue

cloudless sky and descended out of sight behind the trees. Max was jumping up and down by that stage and clapping his hands. In a flash he was gone and running down the slope to greet his father with Archie chasing at his heels, shaggy ears flying, tongue hanging out.

'Go ahead,' a voice said softly from behind Lizzie. 'I'll sit with Gianna.'

Lizzie flashed a grateful smile at Athene and raced down the slope after her son like a teenager. Cesare took one look at his wife, pale hair flying, cheeks flushed below brilliant green eyes full of warmth and welcome, and set Max down again to open his arms.

'I really missed you!' Lizzie complained into his shoulder. 'You're far too missable.'

'I'll work on it,' Cesare promised, smoothing her hair back from her brow, wondering whether or not he should admit that he had worked night and day to get back to her within a week. He missed his family more every time he left them behind and planned complex travel schedules that minimised his absences.

'I shouldn't be whingeing,' Lizzie muttered guiltily, drinking in the familiar musky scent of his skin, her body quickening with the piercingly sweet pleasure-pain of desire that made her slim body quiver against his long, lean length.

'It's not whingeing. You missed me…I missed you, *amata mia*,' Cesare said huskily. 'We are so lucky to have found each other.'

They walked slowly back up the slope, Max swiftly overtaking them, Archie lagging behind. Cesare stilled to turn Lizzie round and curve loving hands to her cheeks to gaze down at the face he never tired of studying. 'I'm crazy about you, Signora Sabatino.'

'And me…about you.' Beaming in the sunshine, Lizzie linked her arms round his neck and tilted her head back invitingly.

She slid into that kiss like melting ice cream, honeyed languor assailing her in the safe circle of his arms. Cesare was home and a rainbow burst of happiness made her feel positively buoyant.

* * * * *

LET'S TALK
Romance

For exclusive extracts, competitions
and special offers, find us online:

f facebook.com/millsandboon

◎ @millsandboonuk

𝕏 @millsandboon

Or get in touch on 0844 844 1351*

For all the latest titles coming soon, visit
millsandboon.co.uk/nextmonth

*Calls cost 7p per minute plus your phone company's price per minute access charge